TOMBSTONE
TALES

Stories from The Town
Too Tough To Die…
and Beyond

By Gary Ledoux

Illustrations by
Joyce Aros

Goose Flats Publishing ~ Tombstone, Arizona

Tombstone Tales

Stories from The Town Too Tough to Die… and Beyond

Copyright © 2010 by Gary Ledoux
ISBN 978-0-9825963-1-9

Published and printed in the U.S.A.

Library of Congress Control Number: 2010929913

First Edition

Published by Goose Flats Publishing
P.O. Box 813
Tombstone, Arizona 85638
www.gooseflats.com

Illustrations by Joyce Aros
Tombstone, Arizona

Cover design by Keith Davis ~ Goose Flats Graphics
Tombstone, Arizona

Back cover photograph courtesy of Rachel Ledoux
Whitewater, California

Edited by Rachel Ledoux
Whitewater, California

Disclaimer

Tombstone Tales

Dedication

This book is dedicated to early Tombstone authors Frederick Bechdolt, Alfred Henry Lewis, Walter Noble Burns, William Breckenridge, and Stuart Lake - men who brought a small, Arizona mining camp to life with their own "Tombstone Tales."

TABLE OF CONTENTS

Forward

"I am a merchant, Mr. Schieffelin. You might call me a dream merchant. I help make people's dreams come true. And I happen to know that there will be a lot of people who will want their dreams to come true – right out here in the Arizona desert!"

Ezra T. Thornton August 23, 1877

"There are two ways out of here. The red door leads to... well... oblivion. The front door leads to your future. Which will it be, Mr. Earp?"

Ezra T. Thornton October 26, 1881

"I watched the whole thing from here. A shot to the chest with a .45 slug at about 15 feet... Wyatt was dead before he hit the ground. There was nothing you could do after that. Nothing! Nothing anyone could do!"

Ezra T. Thornton April 15, 1994

"I sell a number of products, sir. But mostly I make dreams come true and occasionally... I dispense justice."

Ezra T. Thornton March 15, 1981

"I know who knows the truth – and they can tell you – and you can tell the world. But are you ready to do that? Are you ready to stand up for the truth? Are you the lawyer, the seeker of the truth you think you are?"

Ezra T. Thornton October 11, 2003

Table of Contents

"What I need from everyone here, and as many people as you can muster together, is the most important thing of all – the strong belief that Tombstone is truly the town too tough to die. If you believe in that mantra, we can make this happen. Together we can save Tombstone!"
Ezra T. Thornton October 27, 2029

Tombstone Tales

Forward

For years, millions of words and gallons of ink have been spent telling the stories surrounding Tombstone and the Tombstone characters. Thanks to a veritable army of writers, the names Wyatt Earp, Doc Holliday, Johnny Ringo, Curly Bill, Ike Clanton and many others have become well-known to followers of the genre.

But who were these authors - the seminal writers that started it all? Who first brought Tombstone and the Tombstone stories to the public and started the legend?

In 1914, it looked like things couldn't get any worse for Tombstone. The mines were flooded, most of the residents had fled, and business in general was at a low ebb. But things did get worse. State prohibition in 1914 forced the closure of all Tombstone's saloons, the town's only draw for the meager cadre of soldiers that ventured the 18 miles from Fort Huachuca for a cool drink. Some saloon owners turned their places into full fledged restaurants, others became movie theaters and others simply shuttered their windows and doors and left. Tombstone continued to limp along as best it could. It was perhaps Tombstone's lowest point.

But things were about to improve! Tourists were about to discover Tombstone!

The summer of 1919 saw journalist Frederick Bechdolt in southern Arizona, covering miners' labor disputes and gathering historical data for a series of stories he wanted to write. At the time, Bechdolt had the unique opportunity to talk with old-timers, people who had come to Tombstone and the surrounding areas in the 1880's and had lived through the Earp era, had seen the Bird Cage during its glory days, and sat side by side with the Clanton's and McLaury's at the Crystal Palace Saloon. He even interviewed "Texas" John Slaughter, long-time rancher and one-time Cochise County Sheriff. It was the only interview Slaughter ever gave.

Under the title, *Stories of the Old West*, Bechdolt's series of stories began running in the *Saturday Evening Post* in November, 1919. He described Tombstone as a "roaring town" that "had a man for breakfast every morning" – words that have been used by writers ever since.

The legend, as it is known today, had begun.

Gradually, Bechdolt's stories garnered interest in Tombstone and with the advent of the automobile and improved highways, people began journeying to Tombstone to see the places they had only read about.

In 1922, Bechdolt cobbled his stories together in book-form and released, *When The West Was Young.* The book went on sale in Tombstone and was an instant hit! With a stroke of the journalists' pen, the world was introduced to a series of characters that might have been forgotten, but today have become practically household words.

Other writers and books would soon follow.

It was about this time that mass-produced magazines, like the *Saturday Evening Post,* were looking for editorial content. A cottage industry of writers emerged providing a cadre of fictional stories. Among the most prolific of these writers was Alfred Henry Lewis. He, and other writers like him created a series of fictional tales loosely based on stories that they had garnered from other old-west writers or from talking to "old timers" who had lived through the "old west." Typically, the characters and locales would be thinly-veiled images of real people and real places. Lewis based his stories in "Wolfville"... his term for the city of Tombstone and his stories were called "Wolfville Tales." Those, and similar stories became so popular, that the entire sub-genre became known as "Wolfville Tales."

One of the earliest non-fiction works, and still popular today, was writer Walter Noble Burns' *Tombstone – An Iliad of the Southwest* released in 1927. Much of the material was sourced from the pages of *The Tombstone Epitaph* newspaper, piles of which could then be pawed-through at the Arizona Pioneers Historical Society.

Old copies of *The Epitaph* also served as the primary source for Douglas Martin's *Tombstone's Epitaph* released in 1951.

Helldorado, a tell-all book written by former Cochise County Deputy Sheriff Billy Breckenridge was released in 1928. The book slammed the Earps and is one of the few ever published that does not treat the Earps kindly, or at least on even-footing with other contemporaries. Breckenridge along with his boss, Sheriff Johnny Behan were on opposite ends of the social and political stick facing the Earps and Doc Holliday in 1881.

In October, 1931, Stuart Lake's *Frontier Marshal,* an early effort covering the life of Wyatt Earp was released and became an instant success starting what could be considered the first wave of Earp-mania.

Early writers had nowhere to go to source material other than contemporary newspaper accounts and interviews with old timers. Sometimes newspapers were biased, sometimes old-timers had failing memories. It all went into the mix that ground-out story after story.

Over time, many other writers, sometimes due to carelessness, sloppiness, time constraints, political pressures, or just plain maliciousness began to get their facts wrong. Other writers, using the same bad material as a source also got the facts wrong, and the mis-information and bad information, no matter its impetus, was perpetuated.

Gradually, the information and poor writing was debunked by more careful research and emerging facts. Each writer subsequently wanted to be known as the provider of the "truth" about Wyatt Earp, Tombstone, and the OK Corral shootout. Each proclaimed to reveal what "really happened" in Tombstone in 1881.

Today, thankfully, for fans of Tombstone history, the writing... and legend continues.

I hope you enjoy reading this book as much as I did writing it. In it, I provide a fanciful interpretation of what might have happened in Tombstone, and to people who are associated with Tombstone. And then, I provide the true story based on the most current information from some of the finest researchers and historians in the country. You, the reader, can then decide which is more fascinating, the fanciful story, or the truth. Or... perhaps the *real story* is somewhere in between.

While reading, pay close attention to the dates and times because, as mercantilist Ezra T. Thornton was known to say, "In Tombstone, time is all relative."

Gary Ledoux

"I'm Ezra Templeton Thornton – at your service. Welcome to Goose Flats, Mr. Schieffelin. I'm here to help you – and the many people who will come here. I'm here to make your dreams come true...."

Ezra T. Thornton – Mercantilist   August 23, 1877

Chapter 1: THE PROSPECTOR

"I am a merchant, Mr. Schieffelin. You might call me a dream merchant. I help make people's dreams come true. And I happen to know that there will be a lot of people who will want their dreams to come true – right out here in the Arizona desert!"

Ezra T. Thornton August 23, 1877

Wednesday, August 20, 1877 3:00ᴾᴹ   Goose Flats, Arizona Territory

Ezra T. Thornton's enclosed circus-style wagon moved slowly over the desert floor; the four, large yellow wheels creaking and groaning with each turn over the uneven ground. Despite a team of six hardy mules, the wagon lumbered slowly along. With its short stairway leading up the back to a small, glass-paned door, and its overall bright red color, the wagon looked more like the caboose of a train rather than a mule-drawn conveyance. The bright red color seemed very fitting as red is the color usually associated with hell and the devil; and the day's heat made Ezra feel he must be getting closer to hell than the paradise he sought.

Fancy lettering splashed boldly across the length of the wagon's sides in yellow, gold leaf, and blue as if it were an advertising poster for the Barnum and Bailey circus, announced to the world how Ezra made his living - "E.T. Thornton – Mercantile".

And what a mercantile it was. Ezra carried a wide variety of items with him, and was proud of his ability, through his contacts "all over the Union", to get practically anything his customers wanted. The sound of his approach could likely be heard for quite a distance as his wares verily banged together as the wagon moved. Pots against pans, shovels against an iron stove, loose tools in an open tool box, and every so often, the sound of a small music box could be heard when the wagon was jarred enough to start it playing.

On the outside of the wagon were strapped large lengths of rope, large pick-axes and other tools and implements and two large barrels of water from the San Pedro River... enough to last for what Ezra hoped would be several days.

Despite the heat and choking dust, Ezra Templeton Thornton was dressed as he was always dressed, as a man of station; a man of distinction. His tall, black, top hat sat on top of long, white hair, which reached almost to his shoulders and swayed back and forth with each move of the wagon. His closely cropped beard matched the white of his hair and greatly contrasted the ruddy darkness of his exposed skin, tanned by several weeks of travel out in the open. His face, somewhat gaunt with long days of travel was set off with gold-rimmed spectacles.

The intense heat prevented him from wearing his usual black frock coat. But he still maintained his cravat-style tie, a vivid maroon on this particular day, set off by his white, high-collared shirt, and signature red brocade vest. His black and white striped pants were held up with brown, leather suspenders. Tall boots, rather than his usual lace-style shoes, completed his ensemble. Except for the rifle set across his lap, Ezra certainly looked like a man on his way to conduct a medicine show in a major town rather someone looking for his future in a desolate area of southeastern Arizona Territory.

Tall and ancient, several saguaro cactus trees stood vigil alongside lowly, squatting creosote bushes along the otherwise barren landscape. Off in the distance, seemingly shrouded in purple glow stood the Whetstone Mountains. Looking in the opposite direction, the Dragoon Mountains loomed on the horizon. Not far away was the San Pedro River, a source of water for the area's indigenous inhabitants, Apache Indians.

Ezra had followed the San Pedro River allowing his team to drink frequently due to the heat. But now, he was away from the river, away from the coolness of the river's tree-lined banks and clumps of cottonwoods. Now, he was out in the open desert – a barren, arid, snake infested, dust-washed area that seemed the most inhospitable place on earth.

There were no trails, no roads; seemingly no points of interest whatsoever in this area. Only the mountains on either side of him, and the movement across the sky of a scorching Arizona sun gave any reference as to where a person was. There seemed no reason for anyone to be where Ezra was. Camp Huachuca, a US Army base was about twenty miles due west. The next closest bit of civilization was Tucson, some 50 miles northwest of him. Indeed, to any person who knew this area, there seemed no earthly reason for anyone to be here. No reason. None!

Suddenly, as if approaching a Stop sign, Ezra pulled his wagon to a standstill. Reaching into his vest pocket he pulled out a small map, unfolded it across his lap, and studied it intently for a moment. A smile came across his face as he stood up.

"Ladies and gentlemen!" Ezra announced, seemingly to a crowd of people but heard only by the jackrabbits, snakes, and buzzards inhabiting the immediate area, "This is the place. I'm home!"

Saturday, August 23, 1877 6:00AM - Brunckow's Cabin, Arizona Territory

Ed rose, as he always did, when the first rays of sun shone through the small window of his adobe hut. It wasn't much of a place, four walls of thick mud, a door, a window facing east, table, two chairs and two cots. But it served his needs. A prospector has few needs – a good pick, shovel, canteen, some knowledge of geology, and a desire to persevere, to continue to look for that elusive mother-lode no matter how long it takes.

Ed dressed, stepped outside, started a small fire and got a pot of coffee going. Just outside the cabin was a small corral, bigger than what he needed for his two horses. But the soldiers of nearby Camp Huachuca had built the corral. They would frequently use his cabin as a base of operations when they were out scouting for marauding Apaches.

Once his chores were complete he poured a cup of coffee and stepped inside the cabin. From a sack full of personal belongings he pulled a small book, his daily journal. Ed sat down at the table and began to make his entry for the day. "No luck again yesterday, but I have only been here less than a month. Perhaps today I will hit the mother lode. Also expect to see soldiers today as Capt. Rohde said they would return today on another scouting party. Ed Schieffelin August 23, 1877"

Ed hurried down two biscuits he had baked the prior day and gulped down the last of his coffee. Going outside he saddled one horse and outfitted the other with two canteens of water, some food, his pick and shovel, rifle and gun belt. Having completed these same preparations so many times, Ed was ready to go in practically no time.

Ed wore his usual red, flannel shirt., black corduroy pants, tall, black boots and a floppy, wide-brimmed beaver hat. His ensemble made him look like the quintessential "man of the desert", a wanderer, an adventurer, a man who was ready for any danger. Or any fortune he may find. As he mounted his chestnut mare, and grabbed the lead-rope for his pack-horse, Ed leaned forward and directed his speech to his horse's ears, as if sharing an intimate thought. "Which way today girl? Due east? OK!"

Ed headed east, crossed the San Pedro River, and continued on into open country. Riding into the rising sun caused Ed to squint and made seeing difficult. "In another hour" he thought, "the sun will be high enough that it won't bother me. There isn't much to see around here anyways. I've already been out this far several times with no luck. I need to go a mile or so farther before I can start looking for ore."

Ed rode along with his head down allowing the wide brim of his hat to shield his eyes from the sun's rays. Every few moments he would lookup and scout the horizon for Apaches. He didn't want to meet the same fate other miners and emigrants had met – killed and scalped and left for buzzard dinner. Ed was looking down when his horses began to act skittish. It wasn't like them to act nervous for no reason. Was it a snake? Or Indians? Or bandits? Ed's heart raced as he looked up, wishing that his pistol were on his hip rather than on his pack-horse.

Ed was relieved, as his head came up and he faced the sun, that he did not see any Indians, or snakes, or bandits. But what he saw, he could not believe. Off in the distance, distorted through the heat already rising from the desert floor, appeared to be a full, two-story building. Not a house, not a military-looking installation. But what looked like a mercantile building! Out here, in the middle of the desert – a mercantile building!

"It is too early in the day for the heat to be affecting me!" Ed thought. "It has to be real. It has to be what it looks like. But - why? There is no reason for that building to be out here! None!" Ed stopped and dismounted. After retrieving his gun belt from his pack horse and strapping it on, Ed remounted and moved forward toward the building.

As he got closer, Ed could make out more details. It was a mercantile style front all right – about 30 feet wide and what appeared to be about 60 feet deep. It appeared to be whitewashed adobe with wood planks showing on the second floor level. Two large windows flanked a door in the center of the building. The second floor of the building had several windows and a door, which opened out, onto a balcony. The balcony was about six feet wide, the same width as the boardwalk at ground level. To one side of the building was a small corral holding six mules. On the other side of the building was a huge, red, completely enclosed wagon with its back facing out.

When he was about 100 yards away Ed could make out a sign hung just under the balcony overhang, which read, "E.T. Thornton – Mercantile". He could also make out a man, well dressed in city-clothes complete with a frock coat, tie, vest, and top-hat, dozing in a rocking chair with a rifle across his lap. A second rocking chair sat unoccupied next to the dozing man. Ed put his hand on his pistol as he slowed his approach.

Finally, Ed and his two horses were standing right in front of the dozing man. Ed thought, "Was he dozing or was he dead? He appeared to be breathing. But he wasn't saying anything. Surely he must have heard me come up on him. Is this an apparition? What in blazes is this man and this building doing here in the middle of Apache country?"

Finally, without looking up, Ezra spoke in a cheery voice. "Good morning Mr. Schieffelin. I've been expecting you!" When he finished talking, Ezra finally looked up at Ed, with a broad, warm, smile.

More expecting to get shot, or for this seeming apparition to disappear as if waking from a dream, Ed was somewhat relieved that at least this ghost seemed friendly. "How do you know my name? Do I know you? Have we met? And what in blazes are you doing out here in the middle of the Territory, in Apache country? Mister, you've got me real confused!"

Ezra rose from his chair, leaned his rifle against the building behind his rocking chair, stuffed his hands into his vest pockets, and walked toward Ed, stepping down the two steps from the boardwalk to the desert floor. Ed still had his right hand on his revolver. Ezra spoke again, "I'm Ezra Templeton Thornton – at your service. Welcome to an area of the Territory known as Goose Flats, Mr.

Schieffelin. I'm here to help you – and the many people who will come here. I'm here to make your dreams come true. Step down, Edward Lawrence Schieffelin. I'm going to make you a very rich man. That is what you want isn't it – riches?"

"Everyone wants to be rich; don't they?" replied Ed, still sitting in his saddle.

"Don't they?" replied Ezra. "Come on down. Let's talk about it." Extending his arm, the two men shook hands, and Ed dismounted.

"Would you like a cold drink?" Ezra asked as the two men walked onto the boardwalk and headed for the two rocking chairs.

Ed hesitated. His new friend was not holding a canteen, or anything else that held a cold drink. This meant that he would likely go into the store. Would this bearded merchant emerge from the store with a bullet for him rather than cool refreshment? Ed thought for a second. "Sure – that would be good!" Ezra seemed harmless. And besides, Ed didn't have anything the merchant could want. This dapper desert businessman already had guns, and mules, and a whole store full of things. This realized, Ed felt a little safer.

Ezra disappeared into the darkness of the store and emerged a moment later with two dark-brown bottles and handed one to Ed. "Sarsaparilla my good man - the finest around. Bottle it myself right here on the premises... and ice cold."

Ed uncorked the bottle and took a deep draught of the frosty liquid. "It is ice cold? How do you manage that out here? I don't understand?"

The two men sat in the rocking chairs and moved them around to almost face each other. Ezra smiled broadly. "Ice-cold is a good thing. Sometimes you just don't need to question good things that happen to you. And there will be many things about me that you won't understand. Just accept it!"

Ed sat up straight to emphasize his next statement, "I certainly don't understand how you happen to have a mercantile out here in the middle of Apache country. This is a real mercantile...isn't it?"

Ezra smiled, "It is as real as you and me. I own it... 30 feet wide by 60 feet deep. I own the building and the dirt it sits on and the minerals underneath it. I also own about 20 acres just north of here... on what will become known as Route 80. But enough about me... let's talk about you!"

Ed's head was spinning as he tried to make sense of the term, "Route 80." Ezra paused for a long moment, and then began in his rather deep, assuring voice. "Edward Lawrence Schieffelin, born in Tioga County, Pennsylvania 30 years ago. You grew up hearing about the riches made in the California gold fields of 1849 and have been prospecting, hoping to strike it rich ever since... looking for another Sutter's Mill. You've been all over Idaho, Nevada, almost burned to death in Death Valley when you ran out of water that one time. Then you went on to Colorado... then New Mexico. And now, here you are in Arizona Territory. Still looking for riches. Still looking for that pot of gold at the end of your rainbow. But, I must ask you again sir... is riches what you really seek?"

"Everyone wants to be rich...of course I want to strike it rich. It's the easy life I'm looking for." retorted Ed. "You seem to know a lot about me. I'm not sure how you know all that. But... what about you? What are you doing out here?"

Ezra smiled again seemingly taking amusement in Ed's befuddlement, but not in a malicious way. It seemed to Ed that Ezra was looking upon him more as a father would look upon a son. Ezra took another swig of sarsaparilla, swallowed, and began to speak again. "I am a merchant, Mr. Schieffelin. You might call me a dream merchant. I help make people's dreams come true. And I happen to know that there will be a lot of people who will want their dreams to come true – right out here in the Arizona desert!"

Ed sat back in his chair and laughed heartily. "You're kidding... right? Who, besides a few prospectors and few soldiers would want to come out to this God-forsaken hunk of nothing? Especially since it is infested with Apaches!"

Ezra chuckled. "You laugh Mr. Schieffelin. But destiny will bring thousands of people out here. In fact, I began wiring the most prominent of them yesterday, inviting them here. And I will be ready for them – and so will you."

"You're quite a story teller, Mr. Thornton. Very amusing." Ed smiled at his new friend. "Maybe in a hundred years people will come here. Once the Indian problem has been taken care of and somebody figures out how to conveniently get water from the San Pedro out this far – maybe."

"Perhaps." replied Ezra. "But now let's get back to you and what you want – right now... riches."

Ed looked decidedly more serious. "Well Mr. Thornton, do you have anything in your store that's going to make me rich?"

"Not exactly." Ezra rose from his chair and motioned for Ed to join him as he walked off the boardwalk and over towards the horses. Ed picked up his bottle of sarsaparilla and followed. Ezra pointed out to one side of the building. "You see that outcropping of rock about 100 yards up on the rise? Take your pick, go up there, break off a piece of the rock and bring it back here."

Ed looked at where Ezra was pointing, then looked back at Ezra with a puzzled look.

"Go ahead." Ezra urged. "Break off a chunk and then tell me what you find."

Without saying a word, Ed grabbed his pick from the back of his pack horse and headed up to the rock. In a few moments, Ed was in front of the outcropping, set his sarsaparilla bottle down to one side, and got ready to swing his pick.

Before sinking the sharp point of his huge pick into the rock he thought about what he was about to do. Would this black rock that stood before him make him rich? The rock looked promising. Without even breaking off the top piece, it looked like silver ore. It was fairly soft. But how did this old man, Ezra, know that about this rock. And if he knew about it, why didn't he break off his own chunk and make the claim for himself. Why didn't Ezra want all the riches that this rock could provide?

Ed swung the pick over his head and brought it down hard against the rock. Several pieces broke off. Ed examined them thinking that they looked pretty good. Good indeed! Ed picked up as much as he could carry and headed back to Ezra's store. As he got closer he concentrated his gaze on Ezra's building thinking that Ezra had just told him about wiring a notice to some of what would become the area's most prominent people. Ed could not help but notice that there was no wire coming from Ezra's building. "Obviously, this man is liar." thought Ed. "There is no way he could have sent any messages from here!"

While waiting, Ezra had gone back to the cool shade of the storefront overhang where he sat slowly rocking in his chair. Ed walked up to the front of the store, all the while looking at his rocks. His attention was broken when Ezra spoke. "Stay right there in the sunshine a moment!"

Ed stopped just short of walking up onto the boardwalk. Ezra rose from his chair. "How does that ore look, Mr. Schieffelin?"

Ed dropped his pick where he stood, using his now-free hand to shade his eyes as he looked up at Ezra. He held up the rock in his other hand for Ezra to see. "Looks mighty fine. Best I've seen in a long time!"

Ezra smiled. "Even from here, I would estimate its value at $2,000 per ton. Maybe more!"

Ed smiled back. "Sure, it looked good." He thought. "But how could this old man assay ore from ten feet away. Probably the same way he could send out a wire message from a building with no wires!"

Ezra looked off in the distance behind Ed. Raising his hand to shade his eyes and squinting, Ezra looked intently at the horizon. Lowering his hand, he looked directly at Ed. "Soldiers are coming. They will be in sight in the next few minutes. Stay right where you are. Don't move. You're in exactly the right position. In a few moments, you'll have the most important conversation of your life. Ed Schieffelin – are you certain that riches is what you want?"

Ed stood in amazement. "I'm in the right position? What do you mean I'm in the right position? You're talking crazy! And how do you know what this ore is worth? And how can you send a wire when you don't have the means to send one? Who are you!"

Ezra looked back at Ed, raised his right hand and pointed to the hills behind Ed. "Watch for the soldiers. They'll be here any moment. If riches are what you want, greet the soldiers. If peace and solitude is what you want, join me here on the boardwalk."

"I'm not sure what you're up to, old man." said Ed. "But riches is what I've looked for the last 10 years and riches is what I want."

With that, Ed turned around and looked off in the distance. A plume of dust could be seen not far off and was rapidly approaching. Within minutes, Ed watched as a column of mounted soldiers from Camp Huachuca appeared from over a small rise. In the lead was a man he knew, Captain Rohde.

Ed took one look over his shoulder at Ezra who continued to rock in his chair. Their eyes met and Ezra winked at Ed. Ed turned back to greet the soldiers.

Captain Rohde spoke first, "Good morning Ed!"

"Good morning Captain!"

"Another fine day here in the Territory isn't it?"

"Indeed it is, Captain!"

Ed thought it odd that the Captain did not address Ezra. Yet he thought it might be impolite to call this indiscretion and slighting to the attention of an officer of the US Army in front of his command; especially since Captain Rohde was a personal friend of his. Ed looked over his shoulder once more and again, Ezra smiled and winked at him.

The Captain spoke again, "What are you holding there, Ed?"

"Rocks, Captain." came Ed's reply. "I'm looking for rocks, preferably those containing silver ore. And I think I may have found some!"

The Captain looked down at Ed, smiled and adjusted himself in his saddle. "Ed, you know this area is infested with savages. The only thing you'll find out here is your tombstone."

The two men smiled at each other. The Captain thought Ed was a fool-hardy dreamer who would soon make his permanent home six feet under the parched desert surface, courtesy of Geronimo and his followers. Ed liked his friend, Captain Rohde, but smiled thinking that the Captain would spend the rest of life riding across desolate lands and would have nothing to show for it but saddle sores.

Captain Rohde raised his right hand motioning forward and the column of 10 soldiers moved past Ed, which seemed odd to Ed since Ezra's store was directly behind him. Ed spun around to find Ezra, his mercantile, his large, red wagon, small corral, and his team of mules had vanished. The column of men moved directly through the space that had been occupied by Ezra's store a few moments before.

Ed looked down at the rocks in his hand. They had not vanished. And his mount and pack horse were still with him. Ed walked over to his mount, grabbed the canteen, and took several deep swallows. He then turned, leaned his head down and poured some of the still-cool water over his head. "I've been out in the sun too long!" Ed thought. "I must be imagining things. Ezra – his mercantile – his wagon. It was all a mirage. Must have been a mirage. But these rocks certainly aren't!"

Ed carefully stuffed the rocks into his saddlebags and mounted his horse. Leaning forward, Ed talked to his horse like it was an old friend; "The closest assay office is in Tucson, about a two, maybe three day ride. We'll have these rocks assayed and if they pan out like I think they will - well, we'll be back to pull the money out of the ground! And we'll forget all about Ezra T. Thornton – or whoever that was!"

Ed grabbed the lead rope from his pack-horse. Ed thought to himself, "Well...maybe I'll look around a little more. Where there was one good outcropping, perhaps there will be more. Maybe my luck will hold for a while."

Before going in search of more ore, Ed headed one more time over to the rock outcropping and prepared to mark it to show his ownership of his first mining claim in Arizona Territory. He looked down to see where he had broken off the piece. Yes, it looked promising all right. And there, just to the right of where he had stood only a few moments ago was a bottle – an open bottle of sarsaparilla - condensation caused by it's cool contents still clinging to the bottle's sides.

September 3, 1877 Pima County Court House, Tucson, A.T.

Still dressed in his dirty prospecting clothes, but now sporting a broad smile, Ed Schieffelin stepped out of the hot, mid-day Tucson sun and into the cool darkness of the large, brick building that housed the Pima County Court and attendant offices. Ed had good reason to smile. The rocks he had brought all the way from Goose Flats were as he suspected, and what Ezra had declared – full of silver ore – assayed at $2,000 to $2,500 per ton at current prices.

Ed stepped briskly into the County Clerk's Office and up to the clerk's desk. "What can I do for you?"

"I want to file a mining claim!" Ed smiled broadly and spoke with a sense of conviction yet could not help put a hint of glee in his voice. He had been waiting over 10 years to say those words.

"Certainly." The clerk reached in his desk drawer and pulled out a form and began to write.

"Name?"

"Edward Lawrence Schieffelin."

Place of residence?"

"Camp Huachuca – I'm a scout for the US Army."

"Location of the claim?"

Goose Flats mesa – about 18 miles almost due east of Camp Huachuca."

"Assay value?"

"I have the assay statement right here. I just came from the assay office. He says it's $2,000 to $2,500 per ton!"

The clerk looked up at Ed. "Well sir... if this is a vein, you could be very rich!"

"Yessir – I surely know that!"

"And what would you like to call this claim of yours? How would you like it to be known?"

Ed thought for a moment. He couldn't help but think of his exchange with Captain Rohde, and how Ezra had told him that it was going to be the most important conversation of his life. But could Ezra have known? How could he? Was Ezra real, or a figment of his imagination, or a mirage or...? The last several days seemed surreal, like maybe it wasn't really happening. Yet, here he was; standing in front of the Pima County Clerk recording his first claim. Was it because of Ezra... or was he just lucky? Ed decided he would get back to Goose Flats as soon as possible, and if the outcropping was still there... if the bottle of sarsaparilla was there, he would know that the claim was real.

The clerk broke Ed's concentration. "Mr. Schieffelin... what would you like to call this claim of yours?"

Finally, Ed looked straight at the clerk and with all the sincerity and conviction he could muster he said, "Call it Tombstone...!"

*****

It didn't take long for the word to spread about Ed's find. A silver or gold strike in those times brought people from all walks or life – all looking to strike it rich. Miners mined ore from the ground, and others mined the money from the miners. It became a microcosm of society with some hard working, God-fearing citizens, Godless killers and scammers, and everything in between. At first, Tombstone was just a collection of tents and crude shanties. This eventually became the Village of Tombstone and in 1881, the City of Tombstone in the newly formed Cochise County.

Tuesday, May 5, 1894 8:00AM Grand Hotel, Tombstone, A.T.

Seventeen years later, Ed was back in the city he helped create. When Ed had arrived in Tombstone the previous evening he was too tired to do anything but have a meal at the Grand Hotel, and go to bed. The stagecoach had carried him the 23 miles from Benson to Tombstone at a fairly good pace, the road being much improved since he was here in the city he helped to found some seventeen years before. Going from the stagecoach to the front door of the hotel gave him very little time to see what had become of this silver camp of some notoriety, he couldn't help but notice, even in those brief glimpses of an almost-set sun, that it was not the booming metropolis that he had left in December of 1880.

Ed rose, and dressed in a decidedly better manner than the city's residents had previously seen him. A white shirt with high, starched collar, black tie, dark brown sack coat and vest with matching pants, topped with a smart, black derby completed his outfit. Ed looked at himself in the room's full-length mirror and remembered the Ed Schieffelin who had left Tombstone. The Ed Schieffelin of 1877 who had two changes of clothes to his name, one pair of boots, one pair of shoes, two horses, two canteens, a pick, a shovel, and a whole lot of determination. The determination that had made him rich, given him a whole lot of obligations, and made his life quite complicated more complicated than he had ever wanted it.

Ed went down to the hotel's restaurant for breakfast. He could not help but notice there were very few people in the hotel. A look through the restaurant window revealed very few people on the streets. Ed had heard about water filling the mines and the difficulty that companies had encountered getting water and silver out of the ground. With the recent drop in silver prices, it was almost not worth the effort any more.

Ed finished his breakfast, walked out onto Allen Street, the town's main thoroughfare, and, for no apparent reason, headed east. He walked the half-block to Fifth Street, crossed it, and continued on the next block between Fifth and Sixth. Ed could not help but notice the many changes in this once-booming town. Tombstone had once been described by a visiting reporter from San Francisco as, "A town of fast women and faster men. A town of streets lined with dens of debauchery!"

It was painfully apparent that many of the so-called "dens of debauchery" had closed and were now boarded up. This was especially true along Sixth Street, the famed red-light district of Tombstone where women with names like "Squirrel Tooth Alice", "Soap Suds Sal" and "Gold Dollar Gertie" plied their trade.

But for as many windows and doorways that were boarded up, one thing remained the same – the sidewalk. While many cities, even some mining camps now had concrete sidewalks, Tombstone still had it's original, heavy, wooden board walk. There was nothing like the sound of boot heels on heavy timbers, a clumping sound that brought back so many memories of a time when Tombstone ran at full-blast!

Ed walked, undisturbed by the few residents that passed him on the sidewalk. Nobody recognized him. Why should they? Fourteen years, a clean-shaven face, short hair, a new set of clothes, and a million dollars certainly have a way of changing a person! At first, it seemed a bit odd that, despite his different physical appearance, that nobody would recognize him. But, on second thought, perhaps there was nobody here that was around in Tombstone's early days. Maybe, they were all gone!

Finally, Ed reached the corner of Allen and Sixth Street and he stood, staring at what was once described as the wildest place east of San Francisco, the Bird Cage Theatre. The Bird Cage had been built after Ed left, but he remembered hearing stories about it –reading about it in the newspapers. How a single card game had gone on for months with various players coming and going, how the place ran 24 hours a day, 7 days a week for many years. Owners Billy Hutchinson and then Joe Bignon had made fortunes in the place. But now, here it stood, vacant and boarded up, just a specter of it's former self.

Ed's concentration was broken when he heard someone call his name, "Mr. Schieffelin! Mr. Schieffelin! Good morning to you!"

Ed turned around to see a well-dressed man with a white beard, flowing, white hair, gold-rimmed spectacles, and a top hat calling to him from across Allen Street. He thought the man looked familiar. Even the building looked familiar – could it be – could it be the building he had seen out in the desert back in '77? Ed's eyes moved from the man wildly waving at him to a sign hanging under the boardwalk overhang, "E.T. Thornton – Mercantile."

Ed headed across Allen Street and approached the waving man who caught Ed just before he stepped onto the boardwalk. "Stop. Stay right where you are. Don't move. You're in exactly the right position. "

Without thinking, Ed stopped in his tracks and looked incredulously at Ezra. It seemed to Ed that he had had this conversation before. "Exactly the right position for what?"

Ezra leaned back and laughed. "My good man; you are in exactly the same spot as you were standing on the morning of August 23,

1877 when I told you were about to have the most important conversation of your life. And now, you are in precisely the right spot for me to tell you that you have come full circle; standing at the precise spot where you started this strange odyssey of life as a wealthy person. So tell me – how has it been? Is being rich all that you thought it was going to be?"

Ed could not believe he was again talking to someone he had summarily dismissed all these years as an apparition – a day too long in the sun or some bad water he had consumed the day he first met Ezra. Had he returned to a mirage? Was Ezra flesh and blood now – was he flesh and blood back then?

As he tried to figure out how to answer Ezra, or even if he should answer at all, first one, then two people passed on the street behind. Both exchanged greetings with Ezra and he returned their hails. Obviously, Ed could see the people on the street, the people could see Ezra and it appeared that he was talking to a real, live person.

Ezra continued, "Ah, where are my manners? Come. Sit on the bench up here on the boardwalk."

The two men walked up onto the boardwalk. Ed, still stunned and unsure what to say sat on the bench in front of Ezra's store.

Ezra smiled and said, "Wait here. I'll be right with you." and disappeared into the darkness of his store.

A moment later, Ezra walked through the swinging screen door of his store with a dark brown bottle in each hand, dripping wet from sitting in a barrel of ice water. "I refilled the bottle for you, Mr. Schieffelin. You do still like sarsaparilla don't you?"

Ed looked up in disbelief, "My God... it *is* you!"

Ezra continued. "Quite so, Ed. Quite so. Well...it's been quite an interesting seventeen years hasn't it, Mr. Schieffelin? You've traveled all over the country, seen Europe, stayed at the finest hotels, eaten in the best of restaurants and lived in a number of places in the best of luxury. And now you are married to a fine and lovely woman. Was it for love? Or was it for money? There are many things I know about you Ed Schieffelin, but many things only you know about yourself and your life... things you know in your heart."

Finally, Ed collected himself, and began to speak. "It has been quite a life. And yes, money has bought me many things. There are many things that I enjoy about being rich... and many things I detest about it. But I am getting older now. I'm not 30 years old anymore. And I have decided to go and find those things that my money didn't buy me."

"And where would you find those things, Mr. Schieffelin?" asked Ezra. "Many people are headed out to a new silver and turquoise find about twenty miles from here. Already the settlement has a name –

Pearce. Is that where you will go?"

Ed took a long swing from his bottle of sarsaparilla. "What I am looking for is not in another boomtown. In fact, it's not even in the Territory. I only wanted to come back here one last time before I leave the desert forever. I'll soon be meeting my wife in Oregon."

Ezra who had been leaning forward on the bench and listening intently to Ed now sat back to an eased position, as if he knew what Ed was going to say and was only waiting for Ed to say it. "And what is in Oregon, Mr. Schieffelin?"

"Solitude, Mr. Thornton. Solitude. There are places in Oregon that are still untouched by white men. I want to get back into prospecting; just me, my horses, and a pick and a shovel. Solitude is something I've not seen for a long time and it is something that money can't buy."

The two men sat, just looking at each other for several minutes. Then Ed rose from his seat and prepared to leave. "I am sure that if it weren't for you, I never would have found that outcropping. I may never have found any riches at all. I never would have known both the good, and the bad side of wealth. For whatever you did – thank you."

Ezra looked up at Ed. "Have a safe trip to Oregon... and enjoy the rest of your life."

The two men shook hands, an affirmation Ed thought; that Ezra Thornton was a real person. But he couldn't help but think what had actually happened, on apparently that exact spot, so many years ago. Ed turned, and walked back down Allen Street, passed the boarded-up windows and doorways, and back into the Grand Hotel.

May 12, 1897, a forested area along Day's Creek, Oregon

In Oregon, three years later, there was less than an hour's daylight left. Clell Jackson had been out prospecting all day and was tired. He needed to find shelter soon or spend another night outside in the elements. Although it was May and the days were warm, the nights were still quite cool in the Oregon woods. He remembered passing a cabin in this general area and hoped that it's inhabitant, if it was inhabited, would share their roof with him for a night.

Just as the sun began to peek below the highest mountain, Clell spotted the cabin and hurried to it. Located among the pines on a hill, only a few yards above a cold, mountain stream, the place looked quite inviting. And it also looked quite empty. There appeared to be nobody around and with the coming darkness, if there had been a fire in the fireplace, he would have been able to see the light through the windows.

Clell approached the cabin slowly and called out, "Hello the camp!

Is anyone about?"

There was no answer. And the place looked deserted. But Clell had an eerie feeling and drew his pistol just in case someone who didn't like visitors inhabited it. Clell approached the cabin's only door and knocked on it. No answer. Clell pushed gently on the door, which was unlatched. Slowly, the door opened about two thirds of the way, then stopped. Something on the inside was preventing the door from being opened fully. Taking a deep breath, Clell raised his pistol, and burst through the door directing his attention and his aim directly behind the door.

What he was suspecting was a hermit, or some crazed person ready to shoot him for trespassing. What he saw, was a man, lying sprawled on the floor, a booted foot preventing the door from fully opening. Clell looked around quickly. A small fireplace dominated one wall, on the other was a single bed and on the third wall was a table with one chair neatly pushed against it, the other overturned. Clell surmised that the man on the floor had been sitting at the table when he suffered from some traumatic malady.

Clell placed his pistol in his pocket and bent over the man to check him. He was quite dead. And judging from the flies surrounding him apparently had been dead for at least a day. But the hapless man's cause of death could not immediately be determined. There were no apparent bullet holes, no stab wounds, no mauling marks from a bear or bite marks that could have been inflicted by other wild animals.

Clell looked around the small, one-room cabin for any hint of who this person was; any way to identify the poor soul sprawled on the cold, damp floor. On the table sat a small, open book, pen, and inkbottle.

Clell opened the book to the first page. It read: Journal of Edward Lawrence Schieffelin. Each page was dated. Clell turned to the last entry, apparently made the day before. It read: "Found it at last. Richer than Tombstone ever hoped to be!"

Sunday May 23, 1897 11:45PM Tombstone, A.T.

Ed Schieffelin suddenly became conscious that he was standing up... standing in the middle of Allen Street near the intersection of Allen and Sixth Street in Tombstone, dressed as had been the first time he had stood in that same spot, in rough miner's clothes.

But Tombstone didn't look anything like it did the last time he wore those clothes in town. The new, rough lumber of just-built buildings had long-since been painted over; many times! Many store fronts were boarded up and the entire street was in dilapidated condition.

The Prospector

A warm breeze rustled a crumpled newspaper as it tumbled down Allen Street. A few people hurried along the boardwalks. Ed looked at them, but no one seemed to notice him standing there – in the middle of Allen Street – in clothes that were 20 years behind the times.

Ed's concentration was broken when he heard someone call his name, "Mr. Schieffelin! Mr. Schieffelin! Good evening to you!"

Ed turned around to see a well-dressed man with a white beard, flowing, white hair, gold-rimmed spectacles, and a top hat calling to him from across Allen Street. He thought the man looked familiar – and the building looked familiar. He read the sign hanging in front of the building, "E.T. Thornton – Mercantile." The man waved wildly, excited to see him.

Ed's head was reeling! The last thing he remembered was sitting at a table in his cabin in Oregon. He remembered scrawling an entry in his journal – something about a rich mining claim. And now... here he was back in Tombstone – experiencing a strange feeling – like he had lived this moment in time before!

Ed headed across Allen Street and approached the waving man who caught Ed just before he stepped onto the boardwalk. "Stop. Stay right where you are. Don't move. You're in exactly the right position. "

Without thinking, Ed stopped in his tracks and looked incredulously at Ezra as he experienced another wave of deja' vu. It seemed that he had had this conversation before – maybe more than once or twice. He wasn't sure. Ed blurted out, "Exactly the right position for what?"

Ezra leaned back and laughed. "My good man; you are in exactly the same spot as you were standing on the morning of August 23, 1877 when I told you were about to have the most important conversation of your life. Then, we had another conversation – about your life – three years ago. You found riches in Arizona, in Oregon you re-discovered solitude, and here you are again! Did life give you everything you wanted?"

Ed could not believe he was again talking to Ezra Thornton – and that he was back in Tombstone, although he could not figure out how he had returned to his town of good fortune.

As he tried to figure out how to answer Ezra, or even if he should answer at all, first one, then two people walked up to Ezra, said hello and he returned the gesture, but they did not acknowledge Ed, and Ezra did not bother to introduce him.

"Surely" Ed thought, "Ezra being the well-mannered man that he is, he would certainly introduce me - especially seeing that I am the man responsible for the founding of this place!"

Ezra continued, "Ah, where are my manners? Come. Sit on the bench up here on the boardwalk."

The two men walked up onto the boardwalk. Ed, still stunned and unsure what to say sat on the bench in front of Ezra's store.

Ezra smiled and said, "Wait here. I'll be right with you." and disappeared into the darkness of his store.

A moment later, Ezra walked through the swinging screen door of his store with a dark brown bottle in each hand, dripping wet from sitting in a barrel of ice water. "You still like sarsaparilla I trust, Mr. Schieffelin?"

Without saying a word, Ed took the bottle, and drew a long swig of the cool, refreshing brew. Ezra took a swig from his own bottle, and continued, "The first time we met, I told you we were going to have the most important conversation of your life – and that is exactly what you did. Tonight, you will have the most important conversation of your death."

Ed looked straight at Ezra, his eyes fairly bulging out of his head. Ezra continued, "I know you thought ill of me a few moments ago when I didn't introduce you to those two people that stopped to say hello to me. Well, there's a good reason for that. You see, they can't see you. Oh, they saw your casket when your body was laid to rest at your monument at the far end of Allen Street earlier in the day. But as a dead person, they just can't see you – you no longer exist in the corporeal world.

Ed suddenly jumped to his feet exclaiming, "You mean I'm... I'm... dead? And if I'm dead, how is it that you can see me? What does that make you? Are you dead too? I'm so confused"

Ezra smiled, "Dead? Well, in a sense, I guess that's what you could call your new state of being. I like to think of it as leaving one reality, and entering into another! As for me – well – you might recall that I told you I was a dream merchant; and as a dream merchant, well, I exist between multiple realms. But that's enough about me. Tonight is about you! There are people waiting for you – expecting you. Some you will know, some I will be happy to introduce to you!"

It was all too much for Ed Schieffelin to absorb. He looked across the dark street to the Bird Cage Theatre as dark shadows eerily danced across the boarded facade of the once-proud place of merriment. Ed turned to Ezra who remained calm and collected, sipping his sarsaparilla while sitting on his bench, "So where are these people I should meet?"

Very matter-of-factly, Ezra replied, "At the Bird Cage!"

Ed looked the Bird Cage, boarded-up and abandoned years prior, devoid of any sign of life. Again, he turned back to Ezra, "You're joking... aren't you?"

Ezra rose, straightened his black top-hat and pulled his vest down to straighten it so he would look "fully presentable", and replied "Follow me!"

Not knowing what else to do, and hoping to find some answers, Ed Schieffelin followed Ezra across Allen Street to the Bird Cage and to a side door that oddly, was not boarded-up!

Inside, Ed found himself back-stage, the area dimly lit from an unknown and unseen source. The place was quiet – very quiet – "as quiet as death" Ed thought to himself as a sudden chill came over him.

Ezra smiled and looked directly at Ed asking, "Are you ready?"

"Ready?" came the incredulous reply, "Ready for what?"

Ezra smiled again, put his hand on Ed's shoulder, eased him to the front of the stage, and pulled back the curtain. Suddenly bright light and applause filled the room. Ezra announced in a loud voice that could be heard over the din, Ladies and Gentlemen, may I introduce Mr. Edward Lawrence Schieffelin – founder of Tombstone!"

Ed stood on the stage, stunned at all the people in the theatre, a theatre that otherwise looked closed from the outside; it's main doors boarded-up and sealed. And then he noticed something else – obviously, everyone could see him!

In a moment, the applause died-down, band music began, and everyone began dancing.

Ezra led Ed down the stage stairs onto the dance floor. They continued to the front of the theatre where a beautiful mahogany bar stood alongside one wall, where several men were drinking beer and whisky. The front doors which Ed had seen moments ago all boarded-up were now open onto Allen Street and a soft summer breeze blew off the street mixing cigar smoke with the smell of whisky and dust.

Ed and Ezra walked up to one young man of about 30 standing at the bar. Ezra turned to Ed, "Ed, I'm sure you remember Marshal Fred White. He was cut down right on this very spot by Curly Bill Brocious in 1880!"

Ed looked at Marshal White, remembering him but not knowing what to say.

Ezra then called Ed's attention to another corner of the room, "And look, there's Mary Clum, Mayor Clum's wife. Troubles with childbirth caused her death in December of 1880. And there's Charlie Storms, died in '81. Oh... and there's..."

Ed cut Ezra off in mid-sentence, "Mr. Thornton... tell me... is this heaven... or hell?"

Ezra smiled his all-knowing smile, "Heaven? Hell? It depends on your perspective, Mr. Schieffelin. The only thing that's certain is... this is where the spirit, the very essence of Tombstone is kept alive!

And you play a key role. Others will be along later to keep you company... and help you. Wyatt Earp will be along in 1929, John Clum in '32. In the mean time, enjoy yourself. There is a party here every night – mid-night to dawn! And you will always be the guest of honor. Enjoy eternity, Mr. Schieffelin!"

The Real Story Behind "The Prospector"

Edward Lawrence Schieffelin, a 30 year-old scout and prospector came to southeastern Arizona Territory in the summer of 1877. Born in Tioga County, Pennsylvania, he had been prospecting for over 10 years starting in Idaho, moving on to Nevada, Death Valley, Colorado, New Mexico but had never found the riches he sought.

A large, powerful man, Ed had long, brown hair, a full beard and a face bronzed from the sun which gave him the appearance of being much older. Despite the modern-day depiction of an old and wizened prospector trudging through the desert with his trusty mule, Ed, and others like him, were the quintessential miners of the latter half of the 19th century – strong, fairly young, and ready for any hardship or danger. Many miners fell prey to Indians, wild animals, and the elements. Ed Schieffelin and a handful of others found great prosperity.

Ed chose as his base of operations, a small place known as Brunckow's cabin, about 3 miles west of Tombstone. Each day he would leave the cabin, search for his elusive dream of gold or silver riches, and return each night. The soldiers at nearby Camp Huachuca (presently known as Fort Huachuca and still an active US Army base) would watch over Ed, and other settlers in the area.

At one point, one of the soldiers asked Ed why he continued to go out into the desert. "To find rocks!" was the answer Ed gave. Ed was known as being "close-mouthed" meaning that if he was even close to finding any gold or silver ore out in the desert, he wasn't about to tell anyone about it. To Ed's terse reply, the soldier supposedly said, "If you keep fooling around out there, the only thing you'll find is your tombstone!"

The word tombstone stuck in Ed's mind and in September, 1877, Ed Schieffelin traveled to Tucson to record his first silver strike, the "Tombstone", located on a mesa known then as "Goose Flats."

Ed knew he needed money and supplies to carry on a sustained mining operation so he sought out his brother, Al. Eventually Al, and another man named Richard Gird formed a 3-way, equal partnership and they headed to Goose Flats to begin mining operations. Since the area was Apache country, the men were in constant fear of attacks. One always stood watch while others dug.

The "Tombstone" mine played out in a very short time. But soon other outcroppings were found. One such find was named the "Lucky Cuss" mine as this is what Ed was called by his two partners after making the find. The Lucky Cuss and Graveyard mines were established in February, 1878.

It wasn't long before other prospectors came into the area. Henry Williams and Oliver Boyer made a discovery on land claimed by Gird as part of his mining claim. The two parties argued. But anyone who could legally end the dispute was over 50 miles away in Tucson. As more prospectors began to filter into the area, both sides felt that if they left the area to settle their claim in Tucson, they would both lose out. Claim jumping was fairly common and sometimes, this type of dispute was settled at the end of a gun.

The two parties chose to split the claim. Williams and Boyer called their end of the claim, the "Grand Central" while Gird and the Schieffelin brothers called theirs "The Contention" mine. Ironically, these two turned out to be the richest in the area. Altogether, the Tombstone mines turned out over $85,000,000 worth of silver.

By December 1878, town lots were being surveyed and a city was forming. Early in 1879, town lots on Allen Street sold for $5 apiece. The town boasted forty cabins and a population of 100. By that summer, the now-famed Alhambra Saloon had opened as well as the Cosmopolitan Hotel and by the end of the summer; Tombstone's population had grown to over 1,000!

As with any boomtown of that era, people of all sorts began to pour in. Those who wished to make money digging in the hard dirt and rock of the desert, and those who wished to take the money away from them – legally or otherwise. By December 1880, 5,000 people occupied a 4 square-mile piece of desert. A 30X60 foot lot on Allen Street sold for $6,000 and a shanty rented for $50 a month. Many miners lived in boarding houses because they could not afford to rent a house nor had the time or money to build one.

By December, 1880, Ed and his brother Al had had their fill of the dirty, backbreaking work of mining. Al sought an easier lifestyle while Ed longed for the solitary lifestyle he had become accustomed to in all those years of prospecting throughout the country. Al sold his mining interest for $625,000. Ed sold his for $1.4 million and the two men left Tombstone. Ironically, in that same month, construction began on a large meeting hall on Fremont Street near Fourth. It would be called Schieffelin Hall in honor of Ed. The building still exists and is in use today by Tombstone's residents.

In 1883, Ed Schieffelin sailed to Alaska in search of even more riches. Slightly ahead of his time (gold was discovered in Canada's Klondike area in the summer of 1896) he soon returned empty-handed.

In 1883, Ed married M.E. Brown and continued to move around the west. The couple turned up in Colorado, Salt Lake City and California. Eventually, Ed and his wife settled on a ranch in Oregon.

On May 12, 1897, a man named Jackson found Ed in a little prospector's cabin above Day's Creek, dead of an apparent heart attack. He was only 49 years old and in apparently good health. Was it really a heart attack – or did someone kill him over another rich mineral find. Reports exist that say the last entry in his journal reads, "Found it at last. Richer than Tombstone ever hoped to be!

Ed Schieffelin was buried near his cabin but he didn't stay there long. Once his personal effects were reviewed, it was found that his final wish was to be buried near Tombstone, dressed in the garb of a miner, with his pick, shovel, and canteen. As a grave marker, he requested a monument of the type miners build with rocks to mark a mining claim.

On Sunday, May 23, 1897, Ed Schieffelin was re-interred on top of a granite hill, about three miles west of Tombstone. As per his wishes, a monument of large proportion (sixteen foot base and a height of twenty-five feet) was erected in his honor. An inscription near the base reads, "Ed Schieffelin, died May 12, 1897, aged 49 years, 8 months. A dutiful son, a faithful husband, a kind brother, and a true friend." Businesses closed as the entire town turned out to pay their respects to the man that help found a town, and begin a legend that lasts to this day.

Just as the soldier had prophesied, Ed Schieffelin found his Tombstone on the mesa known as Goose Flats.

Chapter 2: THE GUNFIGHTER

*"There are two ways out of here. The red door leads to...
well... oblivion. The front door leads to your future. Which will
it be, Mr. Earp?"*

Ezra T. Thornton October 26, 1881

Tuesday September 6, 1955, 9:05PM

"Bobby, is your program finished?"

"Yes mom!"

"Then come upstairs and get ready for bed!"

"Aw mom!"

"Bobby...remember... that was our agreement. You could stay up
and watch your program if you went right to bed afterwards!"

"Oh alright!"

The TV room in the basement of his parent's Derry, New
Hampshire home was a great place to watch television thought
Bobby. They could only pick up three or four channels, maybe five
on a good day, but that was ok with him. The soft light and knotty
pine wood paneling combined with the warmth given off by the oil-
fired furnace in an adjoining room made everything feel cozy. The
furniture was old and sort of lumpy but he hardly ever sat on it
anyway. The braided rug on the floor was new and felt good. He was
usually on the floor; lying on his stomach, with his head in his hands
watching television.

Television was getting better and better he thought. His
"program", the one his mother let him stay up late to see, far too late
for a seven year old, was a western. But it wasn't just any western.
Bobby was crazy about anything to do with the old west. He wasn't
sure why... he just was. And this program really piqued his interest –
"The Life and Times of Wyatt Earp!"   Thoughts of Wyatt's wide
brimmed hat, his fancy vest, and that Buntline Special pistol were
still swirling around in Bobby's mind. More than anything, Bobby

wanted to be a gunfighter.

He thought back to Christmas a year ago when his parents bought him a "bucking bronco", a plastic horse suspended on four springs set into a stand. He "rode" that horse hard, practically every day for a month after Christmas! He could rock it back and forth hard enough to get the stand to travel across the hardwood floor in his bedroom. He would hit the wall, turn the horse around, and start back across to the other side of "The Territory." Some days he was the Pony Express rider, the next day he was performing trick riding stunts in Buffalo Bill's Wild West Show. It was all the same to Bobby.

Of course, this Christmas, he was older. Bobby was hoping for a Daisy air rifle this Christmas. The one that made the loud bang with a ricochet sound at the end of each bang! His pistols and gun belt were ok. He enjoyed them. But that Daisy air rifle would be the envy of every kid on his block. When he played cowboys and Indians in the woods down by the park, he would be sure to shoot more Indians because he had the best rifle. The best!

"Bobby – are you coming upstairs sometime tonight?"

"Yes mom!"

Bobby stood up, turned off the TV and headed up to his room stopping to say goodnight to his mother and father, and headed off to his bedroom. As Bobby got into bed he looked at his toy gun-belt and cowboy hat hung on the post at the foot of his bed. The gun belt was a beauty – a double-holster rig with lots of fancy metal-work - what his dad called "conchos." It was real leather! Not the cheap plastic some of the other kids had. He wore it real low – like he had heard the gunslingers wore their belts so as to "get the drop" on the bad guys.

And the pistols – oh those pistols. They had a bright finish. A little door on the side of the pistol could be opened for loading it. His father called it a gate" which would allow plastic bullets to be loaded, just like the real thing! When he fired the pistols, the cylinder would revolve and the hammer would move back and forth – just as if it was a real Colt. It was fascinating just to watch the action as the trigger was pulled. Other kids had cap guns that made a lot of noise. But Bobby preferred the working action to the noise anyway. It was more "true to life."

Something else occurred to him as he thought about "The Life and Times Of Wyatt Earp". Arizona, and Tombstone were in the desert. He wasn't quite certain where "the desert" was but he was sure he hadn't seen any desert, or cactus trees in New Hampshire. It seemed like it was always hot in the desert too. That sure wasn't the case in New Hampshire.

"Well, I'll just have to wait until next week to see what happens in Tombstone" he thought. Bobby crawled down to the foot of his bed, grabbed his cowboy hat, and lay back down again pulling his cowboy hat over his face. He pretended he was "on the trail" and lying by a campfire waiting for sleep to come. He wasn't sure what trail he was on, where he was going, or where he was coming from. He didn't even know why he was "on the trail". It didn't matter. He was lying by the campfire waiting to fall asleep.

As sleep approached, Bobby's mind wandered. "I wonder what it's like to be a gunfighter" he thought. "You have be fast as lightening – no – faster than lightening. You have to let the other guy draw first; that way, it was legal. That's what dad always told me. The other guy had to make the first move. I'll have to watch for that the next time Wyatt gets into a gunfight. But then... if you were the Marshal, then whoever you shot it was ok.. right? Because you were the Marshal, the law was on your side anyway... so you didn't have to wait for the other guy to draw first. Right?"

Oh it was too confusing.

Friday morning, July, 1960

It was a typical summer morning in Derry, New Hampshire with bright sunshine. The air was heavy and muggy. Bobby, and two of his friends were busy trying, sometimes in vain it seemed, to get a basketball into a net-less hoop that was nailed over the garage door. Their blue jeans were heavy with sweat and their white tee shirts fairly soaked. A red steel pitcher of ice water sat on a white wooden table on the nearby porch with three matching glasses that the boys would sip from every few minutes. All agreed it was tough work to put the ball in the basket. But they would be going into junior high school in the fall where they would have to take physical education class and didn't want to look like losers not being able to sink a few baskets!

But try as he might, Bobby couldn't get his mind on basketball, or any other sport for that matter. He could care less! He liked westerns – western movies – western TV shows – anything to do with the old west in general and Tombstone in particular was OK with Bobby. It was a good time to like westerns too. It seemed everyone else liked them as well. Over the past two or three seasons TV programs like "Gunsmoke", "Have Gun Will Travel", "Wagon Train", "The Rifleman", "Tombstone Territory", and "Wanted: Dead Or Alive" were all very popular. But his favorite remained, "The Life and Legend Of Wyatt Earp".

The mailman approached the house to deliver the day's mail. Seeing the boys in the driveway, the mailman walked right up to them. He had known the family for as long as they had lived there on Pembroke Street. He handed a small bundle of envelopes and the usual ad flyers directly to Bobby.

"I'm not one for lookin' at people's mail" he said "But there's a letter in this pile all the way from Arizona! From some attorney I think! It's addressed to your mom!" Looking down at the envelope he reassured himself, "Yep – Mrs. Elaine Dumas". Just then, Bobby's mother appeared on the porch.

"Good morning Mrs. Dumas!"

"Good morning Ed. What's this about a letter from Arizona?"

"Now I'm not one for snooping you understand. But this looks real official and it comes from some lawyer!"

With a wry look on her face, Bobby's mother took the envelope, opened it and began to read. At first, she looked saddened, and then strangely relieved.

"What is it mom?"

All ball-playing stopped and the boys gathered around to hear the news. Derry was a small town, and most folks lived their life very close to home so getting something direct from Arizona was cause for some attention. Even Ed, the mailman gave an interested ear.

"My sister died." Bobby's mother looked right at him and continued. "Your Aunt Hazel was one heck of smoker – I'll bet that's what did it. She was only two years older than me. And I am mentioned in her will. My goodness, we haven't even talked for years!"

"What is it?" queried Bobby smiling. "Did she leave us a million dollars?"

Bobby's friends sort of snickered at the joke; but had the presence of mind not to do so too emphatically. After all, someone had died.

"No. But we did inherit her car – and it's only a year old. All we have to do is get it from Phoenix to Derry. It looks like we'll be seeing Arizona rather than the lake for our vacation next month!"

That evening Bobby sat on the floor of the basement television room watching a rerun of "The Life and Legend Of Wyatt Earp" as his parents sat and discussed the upcoming trip. He could hear his parents talking and the sound coming from the television but it was all background noise to him as his mind wandered. What was Tombstone like today he wondered? Was the town still there? Did they even remember Wyatt Earp? Were the streets still dirt? How close was Tombstone to Phoenix?

Bobby watched the TV screen but his mind wandered to a point where it felt like he was right there on Tombstone's famed Allen Street with Wyatt Earp himself. He pictured himself wearing a fancy brocade vest with a watch-chain dangling from the left pocket. He wore a wide-brimmed black sombrero, just like Wyatt wore. And he carried a Buntline special, in .45 caliber – just like Wyatt did. In fact, the more he thought about it, the more he thought how great it would have been had he been born 100 years ago. He could have been right there – in Tombstone – in 1881! He could have witnessed the OK Corral gunfight. He could have played pool at Hatch's Saloon, just like Wyatt and his brother Morgan did the night Morgan was shot. He could have read *The Tombstone Epitaph* every morning. He could have had is picture taken by the famed Tombstone photographer, C.S. Fly. He could have seen a show at the Bird Cage Theatre. He could have....

"...Bobby!" his mother said emphatically. Bobby snapped out of his mind's meanderings and all of a sudden the noise of the television and his parent's talking became painfully loud. He turned around and looked at his father who was leaning forward in his chair to get Bobby's attention.

"Phoenix isn't that far from Tombstone, son. What do you say we take a little side trip on our way home from Arizona?"

Saturday morning, August, 1960

The airplane ride from Boston to Phoenix seemed to Bobby like it took forever. If it weren't for the several favorite copies of *True West* magazine he had brought with him to read, the ride would have been unbearable. But reading about the exploits of Doc Holliday and the Earps made the ride tolerable.

But now here he was – out in Arizona – seeing things that Wyatt and Doc saw – and probably feeling the same heat! Boy... it was hot! In New Hampshire, when you had all the car windows rolled down, you were cooled from the breeze. Here, the breeze through the windows was so hot it was hard to breathe! He had only been in Arizona for a short time and already his lips were dry and starting to crack! Bobby wished now that he had worn his shorts and sneakers. He estimated that his blue jeans, soaked with sweat, now weighed about 40 pounds! His feet were sweating too – a lot. But tucked into his new cowboy boots, they could do little else. And his long-sleeved western-style shirt didn't make it any cooler either!

The wind whistled through the four open windows of the shiny, black 1959 Chevrolet as the car sped along a two-lane blacktop road just outside of Phoenix. The buildings of the city gradually gave way to a few houses here and there and then it was just desert; hot, dry, desert which seemed to stretch out forever – as far as the eye could see. The wide expanse was punctuated with the occasional cactus, or Burma-Shave sign.

Bobby's father turned from his position in the driver's seat. "Is Arizona what you thought it was going to be, son?"

"There's a lot of nothing here dad! I guess on television, the camera doesn't really show you how much nothing there really is out here. This is boring!"

His parents both laughed out loud.

"Relax, we'll be in Tombstone in a couple hours. That's what you really came to see isn't it?"

"Why don't we play a game" his mother suggested. "See how many New Hampshire license plates you can see on the other cars on the highway."

Bobby didn't answer. It was a stupid game he thought, left over from his "childhood" days. Besides, he was busy thinking about how Tombstone would look. What he would see and where they would go in town. Maybe they would meet some celebrities. Maybe they were filming a new western down there. Maybe that's where they filmed "The Life and Legend Of Wyatt Earp"! Maybe he would meet some movie or TV stars or, then again, maybe not. That was probably filmed in some Hollywood studio. The car continued down the highway, the hot wind blowing in the open windows.

A few hours, and what seemed like an eternity of nothing-desert later, the big Chevy approached a sign that read, "Tombstone 2 miles". Bobby was sitting on the edge of the back seat with his arms folded on top of the front seat-back with his head resting on his hands. His father turned and smiled at him as only a father can when both father and son share a common bond. Bobby's father loved the old-west too. He guessed that it kind of ran in his family. *True West* magazine had been floating around the house for as long as he could remember. His father had every issue that was ever produced secured in a cabinet in the basement. Since he was old enough to read, Bobby had pored over those magazines, some several times!

Two miles later, the big Chevy zoomed past "Boot Hill", the most famous graveyard in the west, and swung onto Tombstone's Allen Street! As the car slowed, the breeze stopped. Hot as it was, the breeze at least provided moving air. Now, it was just plain hot. But it didn't seem to matter much to Bobby, or his father. They were in Tombstone - Tombstone!

The town was choked with tourists, their cars lining both sides of the street. People walked up and down the wooden sidewalks covered with an overhanging roof on both sides of the street.

The big Chevy moved slowly down Allen Street. "Look Mom, Dad – there it is! The OK Corral. Wow!" Bobby's head hung out the open window as they moved slowly past one of the "most hallowed places" in the west. "We have to go there Dad! We have to see it! Maybe they have cowboys there that act it out – you know – the actual gunfight! Can we go? Please?"

"I'm sure both you boys want to see that!" his mother replied. They all laughed as the car continued to move slowly down the street, Bobby hanging out the window and his father wearing a wide grin.

"Look dad – the Crystal Palace! I wonder if they still sell beer there? I read somewhere where whisky was twelve and half cents a shot. What's a shot of whisky?" Bobby looked in amazement as two "cowboys" lounged in front of the Crystal Palace; similar to the classic picture of the Palace he had seen in several books. They're probably the guys that do the OK Corral shootout he thought.

One block later, they had reached the end of the historic section of Allen Street – the corner of Sixth and Allen. As the Chevy swung left onto Sixth, Bobby slid across the wide, red upholstery to the right side of the car to get a better view of what had been billed as the "bawdiest showplace in the west", the Bird Cage Theatre. "Look at that dad – mom! Do you think they still have shows there? Let's go see it! Lets go there first!"

The Chevy eased to the right curb of Sixth Street and stopped. As they stepped out of the car, the intense heat reflecting off the asphalt in the mid-day sun caught them all by surprise. The three of them stood outside the car for just a moment getting used to the heat, and stretching muscles, unexercised for several hours during the trip from Phoenix.

"Check out that wagon, son! Why, it looks almost brand new!" Bobby's father moved across Sixth Street peering intently at a wagon, backed into an ally-way behind a building that faced Allen Street. "It looks like it might have been a drummer's wagon!"

"Drummer?" queried Bobby.

"Yes – that was the word used to describe a traveling salesman in the old west. People that went from town to town selling everything from medicines, to clothing to stoves and practically anything you can imagine." his father replied.

The fully-enclosed wagon was red - fire engine red – with huge, bright-yellow wheels – heavy wheels - capable of cross-country travel. Bobby and his father walked over to the wagon noting its enormous size. "Yep, this was definitely built to go long distances." His father noted as he looked underneath the wagon observing the heavy axels.

As they moved to the back of the wagon Bobby laughed, "Look at the stairs leading down the back of the wagon. This looks like it must have been the world's first tourist travel trailer!"

Bobby and his father moved around the back of the wagon and

along the opposite side returning to Bobby's mother standing on the sidewalk. Bobby and his father finally diverted their attention from the undercarriage of the wagon to observe the fancy lettering spread boldly across the length of the wagon's sides in yellow, gold leaf, and blue as if it were an advertising poster for the Barnum and Bailey circus, "E.T. Thornton – Mercantile".

"It sure is a drummer's wagon, Dad!"

"Probably just used for parades and such I suppose, son. But very nicely done. How about a trip to the Bird Cage Theatre?"

"Let's go!"

For the next 30 minutes, the New England family marveled at the trappings of old Tombstone preserved within the walls of what had been one of the focal points of a booming mining community. Satiated with Bird Cage history, they stepped back out onto the boardwalk and headed west on Allen Street toward the OK Corral. Bobby marveled at the sound of his boot-heels on the heavy boards imagining himself walking out of the Bird Cage, in 1882, after a rowdy evening of entertainment, and headed to the Crystal Palace to "slake" his powerful thirst. But it was daytime – and boy, it was hot! The three continued west on the boardwalk stopping occasionally to peer into store windows and ponder a trinket or two to take home as a reminder of their stop in Tombstone.

A few minutes, and few blocks later they arrived at a place Bobby had wanted to see his whole life. He had read about it, seen movies about it at the theater, and watched TV shows about it. And now – here it was – right in front of him – the OK Corral! The OK Corral!

"The next show begins in just 5 minutes folks. And there's still a few good seats left. Step right on up!" Bobby looked at the smiling "cowboy" standing on the boardwalk in front of the OK Corral ticket office. He was wearing the same type of wide-brimmed sombrero-styled hat Wyatt Earp wore in his favorite television show and carried a shiny six-shooter in a dark leather holster speckled with silver studs and conchos.

Bobby's father bought tickets and the three of them stepped inside, finding a place a few rows up into the bleacher seats. Bobby looked at the painted back-drop against which the gunfighters would act out the gunfight thinking it looked quite out of place. "The gunfight was actually held within these walls. So why would anyone try to make it look like a street" he thought. There was a bank, a Crystal Palace Saloon, Bird Cage Theatre and of course, an office-front of The Tombstone Epitaph newspaper.

Moments later, music started, and a narrator stepped onto the stage area to tell the audience what they were about to see. He gave a brief history of the events leading up to the gunfight – about the

two opposing political entities operating in Tombstone at the time –
the Cow-boys and the Earp-Holliday faction, and about how Johnny
Behan was tied to the Cow-boys. "Yeah I know all that stuff" thought
Bobby. "Just get to the action!"

The music intensified, then stopped. Four cow-boys appeared at
one end of the stage and the *'Earps'* and *'Holliday'* appeared at the
other end.

"Throw up your hands. We're here to disarm you!" growled *'Virgil'*,
'Holliday's' cane held in his left hand.

"You boys have been looking for a fight. Well now you can have
it!" *'Wyatt's'* voice was loud and clear.

Bobby knew what was coming yet he couldn't help but be excited.
His heart raced. His eyes were the size of saucers. He tried to look at
both sets of actors at the same time trying to discern who would be
the first to pull their pistol, and who would be the first to fire. Who
shot who first was a debate that had been going on since that fateful
day in 1881.

'Virgil' had the next line as he held Holliday's cane high in the air,
"Wait! That's not what I want!"

A half-second passed – the first two shots were fired. Bobby
looked intently at both sides watching the gun smoke wafting across
the stage area, trying to figure out who had fired. And then, as Wyatt
Earp had testified at Judge Spicer's hearing, "the fighting became
general."

Just as it happened in 1881, *'Ike Clanton'* ran up to *'Wyatt'*
pleading, "Don't shoot me Wyatt. I'm not heeled" to which *'Wyatt'*
replied, "The fight's commenced. Get to fighting or get away!"

Just like the original gunfight, it was all over in 30 seconds.
"Wow – look at all the gun smoke!" Bobby exclaimed! Bobby turned
and laughed at his mother who had shoved her fingers into her ears
to drown out the loud noise.

The narrator re-appeared through the clearing smoke to explain
the outcome of the fight. "...and despite the enormous amount of
flying lead from the big-bore guns, Wyatt Earp walked away without a
scratch. *This* is where the legend began!"

The shadows on the boardwalk had begun to lengthen with the
waning day as Bobby and his parents emerged from the OK Corral
and headed east, down the north side of Allen Street heading back to
their car. Bobby kept re-living the demonstration he had just seen
over and over in his mind. It seemed that Wyatt Earp was super-
human – invincible – or incredibly lucky. All those bullets, and never
hit. What were the chances that would ever happen again – ever.

"Still thinking about that gunfight, son?"

"Gee dad; it sure would be great to be Wyatt Earp. He was in a lot of gunfights - including the most famous gunfight of all – and walking away from all of them - without getting hit. Wow!"

Before long, they had walked the length of Allen Street and were again approaching Sixth Street and their car. A fire-engine red sign hanging overhead from the ceiling of the sidewalk covering read, "E.T. Thornton – Mercantile" written in the same yellow- gold, and blue lettering as the drummer-wagon they had inspected when they first arrived in Tombstone. A small sign posted in the window said "cold drinks."

E.T. Thornton's store-front had an "original" look to it, as if it was 1879 and the store had just been built- eerily similar to the way his wagon, parked behind the store, had looked. The Crystal Palace Saloon had an "old" look to it, but it had obviously been renovated, perhaps many times. The Bird Cage Theatre had an "old" look to it that was truly old. Modern-day hands had done nothing to scrub-away or paint-over the many years of sunrises and sunsets on the Grand Old Lady. The Bird Cage showed every one of her 78 years.

A neat, screen door, set into a nearly-new looking wooden casing marked the entrance to E.T. Thornton's store. The window casings were covered in the same fire-engine red paint that was used on his wagon. Gold trim around the window and door casings gave the place a very ornate and rich look. The darkness inside the building, except for a single lamp hanging in the center of the store, prevented anyone seeing inside.

"Anyone up for a cold drink?" Bobby's father realized *that* question was not needed as he turned to his wife and son; sweat dripping from their noses.

Stepping into the relative darkness of the store was, as his exterior store-front intimated, like stepping back in time. Nineteenth-century-style, curved-glass display cases lined both sides of the store positioned a few feet out from the walls allowing customer traffic only down the center of the store. Shelves full of all sorts of goods, from pots and pans, to blankets, to canned foods including several rows of beans, extending to the 12-foot ceilings lay against each side-wall allowing barely enough room for a person to walk between the shelves and the display cases. The floor was made of wide-pine boards running from front to back, well-worn in the middle from constant customer traffic, but the edges, the few inches directly in front of the display cases looked practically new.

Mid-way between the front and back of the store was a large, wooden barrel filled with ice and label-less brown bottles. The bottles were not capped in a way the family was used to, metal caps crimped over a lip requiring a bottle opener. These bottles were sealed with what appeared to be a stopper held in place with a tensioned heavy-wire retainer. "I've seen this type of bottle in antique stores." Bobby's father noted. "Isn't it interesting how this guy was able to get a company in the 1960's to produce bottles the way they were produced almost 100 years ago!"

At the far end of the store was a small, pot bellied stove, it's metal chimney running directly into the ceiling and behind it, a single, windowless door painted with the same fire-engine red paint.

A voice came from the deeper shadows of the back of the store. "Welcome to my humble mercantile. Ezra Templeton Thornton, at your service!"

Bobby looked to the back of the store but could see nothing. Between the relative darkness of the store's interior, and coming in from the bright Arizona sunshine, his eyes, and the eyes of his mother and father was greatly impaired. It seemed like the voice was completely devoid of a body.

Bobby's father turned his attention from the gold pocket-watches displayed in one of the cases to stare intently toward the voice. "My family would like some cold drinks. What have you got?"

Ezra stepped from the shadows and at last, the voice had a body. While going in and out of the various Tombstone stores for the past several hours, Bobby – and his parents, had both noted that none of the people who worked in the stores were dressed in "period" clothing – to make it look and feel like it was still 1881. But Ezra T. Thornton was different – very different – very 1881! He stood just under six feet tall. His build was not slight but not overly large. Despite his apparent age of about 60, he appeared to be strong and vibrant. His long, white hair was swept back and tucked behind his ears. His closely cropped beard matched the color of his hair. He wore black shoes that laced up, similar to construction-worker boots Bobby thought. His gray and black striped pants, like his white shirt was neatly wrinkle-free and the pant-legs were crease-less. Ezra's shirt was buttoned to his neck topped by a black and white striped cravat-style tie. But the one piece of clothing that really set him off from the other Tombstone merchants, was his bright-red brocade vest set in a paisley design.

"We have but one cold drink here at E. T. Thornton's – sarsaparilla. But it's the best sarsaparilla in town – bottle it myself!" Ezra pointed proudly to the barrel in the middle of the floor. "And it's still the same price as it was in 1881 – five cents a bottle."

"What a bargain! Make it three!" Bobby's father reached into his pocket for some change.

They all stood near the barrel as Ezra reached into it to retrieve the bottles, his long, snow-white hair, which had been pushed back behind his ears, now fell across his shoulders and his gold wire rimmed glasses fell down a little further on his nose. With a broad, warm smile, he collected the change from Bobby's father and handed over the three bottles, the cold water dripping from them onto the dark wooden floor. Ezra then tuned his attention to Bobby. "And who is this fine looking young man? With those boots, he looks like he's ready to ride the range – or walk down the dusty streets of Tombstone!"

Bobby took a swig from his bottle. "I'm Bobby Dumas – from Derry, New Hampshire! And I can't believe I'm in Tombstone. I've wanted to come here all my life. I've read about this place – and seen it on TV. And now, well... I still can't believe it!" Bobby's incredulity brought a laugh from the adults.

"I can't believe I'm here either!' chuckled Ezra. "I've been here a very long time. And will probably be here for – well – a long time more! But... as places go... it's not a bad place to be – especially if you like the old west that is!"

Bobby's father turned his attention to the six-shooters in one of the display cases. Bobby's mother took another sip of her sarsaparilla, trying to be as lady-like as she could swilling a drink from a bottle; something she was not used to. She looked at Ezra. "We could not help but notice your wagon outside in the back. It looks like it's fairly new! Is it a reproduction wagon – I mean – did you build it? It can't be original. It's in too good a shape."

"It is all original ma'am!" Ezra replied with a hint of stateliness to his demeanor. "It was built by the Studebaker Wagon Company in 1870 as a freighting wagon. I adapted it for my own use adding the enclosure and rear steps and the bright red paint. I.. err.. the original owner drove it out here from Albany, New York using a team of mules. They arrived here in Arizona just about the time Ed Schieffelin made his silver strike! I work very hard to keep my wagon in tip-top shape!"

Bobby's father turned to Ezra. "You certainly know a lot about that wagon! Do you know who the original owner was?

"I do indeed sir!"

Ezra's reply came quick and sharp. Bobby's father was looking for some additional elaboration on the family that drove the wagon to Arizona. It seemed that a man who was that self-assured about the history of the wagon would surely know something about the original owners and would be willing to share what would certainly be a fascinating tale about their cross-country trek.

Just then the door to Ezra's store swung wide open. A young boy of about seven or eight stumbled in. Dressed in bib-type overalls, out of breath, and with his longish blonde hair scattered about on his head, the youngster looked at Ezra, "Hey Mister, you got any candy in this store?"

"We carry rock candy" came the reply. "It's in the small open bin to your right. Would you like to buy some?"

Almost before Ezra could finish his sentence, the boy turned, stuffed several pieces in his mouth and was in the process of filling his pockets with the sweet, crystalline confection.

"Buddy...! Buddy Philpot! Where are you? Come back here this minute!" A woman, obviously Buddy's mother, burst into the store. Frazzled, with her hair a mess and full skirt trailing behind her in the breeze created by her quick movements, the woman grabbed Buddy by the arm.

"Didn't I tell you not to run off! I don't want you getting lost here! Buddy... are you listening to me? You can't just run off and do whatever you want to do whenever you want to do it! That's being naughty! Do you hear me? You're a very naughty boy! You're... you're ... incorrigible! I can't imagine what you're going to be when you grow up!" his mother screamed.

"But mom... I wanted some candy. This place is boring. All I wanted was some candy! Can I keep what I got in my pockets... please!"

Buddy's mother looked apologetically at Ezra, "What do we owe you for the candy?"

Ezra thought for just a moment. "Buddy, do you get an allowance at home?"

"Yes sir..." came the apologetic reply. "I get ten cents a week to spend on whatever I want."

"Well..." said Ezra in his most judicious manner looking at Buddy's mother, "... how about if I forego pressing charges against young Buddy; you pay me ten cents for the candy, and take it out of his next allowance."

Buddy just looked down at his toes knowing that he not only got caught doing something he wasn't supposed to do. But now he was going to lose next week's allowance too. Ezra took that moment to slyly wink at Buddy's mother.

"Yes Mr....ahhh....?"

"Thornton is the name."

"Yes Mr. Thornton. That will do just fine. Buddy has to learn... somehow... that he can't just run around doing whatever he wants to do whenever he wants to do it. Here is your...I mean...Buddy's money."

Buddy's mother reached in her purse, pulled out a dime, and

handed it to Ezra. Then, looking at the Dumas family like she was seeing them for the first time said, "Sorry to bother you folks. We'll be on our way now."

As the mother and son turned to leave, Ezra spoke up, "Enjoy your candy son!"

Bobby's father took another swig from his bottle. "Well family – it's a long ways to Derry, New Hampshire. What do you say we mosey along!"

Taking their bottles with them, the three New Englanders turned to leave. Ezra looked at Bobby.

"Good-bye folks. Good-bye Bobby Dumas from Derry New Hampshire." Ezra said, half mocking Bobby's words just a few moments earlier.

Bobby stopped and turned around on his way out through the screen door. "Good-bye Mr. Thornton. I sure hope I get to come to Tombstone again. This was fun but I sure would like to spend more time here. Maybe I'll get to see you again sometime."

Ezra smiled back. "I'm sure of it my good boy – I'm sure if it."

The Dumas' walked around the corner and stepped into the black Chevrolet, which by this time was excruciatingly hot inside. Bobby's father swung the car around, and headed west down Allen Street, one last time. Slowly, as before, they moved past the Bird Cage, the site of the Oriental Saloon, the Crystal Palace, the OK Corral, and headed out of town. Bobby turned around placing his knees on the back seat and stared out the broad curved-glass back window. The car turned north onto State Road 80. The car sped up and in a few seconds passed Boot Hill.

"We never got to see Boot Hill!" Bobby exclaimed. "Doggonit! We missed Boot Hill!"

Bobby' s mother turned around. "I'm sure you'll be back here again, Bobby. For as much as you like the old west and Tombstone, I'm sure you're going to come back. Lord knows Tombstone isn't going anywhere! It will all be here for you when you want to visit it again!"

His parents both chuckled. Bobby was a little disappointed. There was more he wanted to see but there wasn't a lot of time on this trip; maybe next time. "But will I get back here again?" he thought. Bobby looked at the brochure he had picked up in one of the stores advertising Boot Hill. On the inside cover was a picture of the tombstone of Lester Moore which read, "Here lies Lester Moore – Four slugs for a .44 – No Les, No More." Bobby stared out the back window as the city of Tombstone gave way to endless desert, cactus, and hot black top. "Lester Moore..." Bobby mumbled. "I wonder who

Lester Moore was...?"

Five days later...

The black Chevy swung into the Dumas' driveway and stopped in front of the garage. They were back – to green trees, green lawns, green bushes – quite different than the brown desert of Arizona.

Although it had only been a few days since he had walked the streets of Tombstone, it seemed to Bobby that it was already so distant and yet, the memories, especially of seeing the OK Corral gunfight remained vivid in his mind. Bobby and his parents walked back and forth from the car to the house unloading the suitcases – and debris from the long trip. Bobby reached under the front seat to retrieve his brown sarsaparilla bottle and stood outside the car just staring at it – and thinking about the strange-looking man who had handed it to him.

"I can't believe you saved that bottle, son!"

"It's kinda neat. I've never seen one like this before, dad. I thought I would save it to remember my trip to Tombstone."

"But it doesn't even say Tombstone on it – or anything for that matter! A year from now, you'll look at it and wonder where the heck it came from!"

Just then, Bobby turned to see his best friend, Ray walking up the driveway. They exchanged their usually greetings.

"Hey"

"Hey"

"Wanna shoot some baskets?"

"Just as soon as we finish unloading all this junk."

"Watcha got there?"

"Just a bottle. We had sarsaparilla in Tombstone and I saved the bottle because it was so neat lookin'"

"Tombstone? You went to Tombstone?"

"Yeah!" Bobby's eyes lit up and he became decidedly more animated as he shrugged off the long ride home and began to tell his tale of the OK Corral gunfight, seeing the Bird Cage Theatre, and meeting the man who had given him the bottle.

Ray didn't seem impressed. "Aw that's kid stuff. Cowboys n' Indians are for little kids. I want to be an astronaut. I'm going into space. I'm going forward in time – not backwards. C'mon, lets shoot some baskets!"

Bobby was crushed. But... Ray was his best friend so... well... he guessed it was alright. Maybe it was little-kid stuff. But then why did his father enjoy *True West* magazine so much? He even had a few copies of *The Tombstone Epitaph* lying around. Surely that stuff wasn't just for kids. In fact, he didn't know any other kids who read it – other than himself.

"I'll go get my basketball; be right back." Bobby took his sarsaparilla bottle and went into the house, up the stairs to his bedroom, placing it carefully, almost lovingly, on the top of his dresser.

Sunday afternoon, December 26, 1993

It had been a hard move for Bobby Dumas and his wife, Kate. After spending an entire lifetime in New Hampshire and now, in their mid-forties, having to move to Riverside, California, with their 10 year old son, Greg in tow, was a real challenge. Bobby's new position with his company, the reason they had moved, was going well. They had only been in their new house for about a month but they were already getting used to the lack of trees – and the abundance of traffic in and around the Southern California area.

Needing a break from the move, the Christmas holiday, and the challenge of his new job, Bobby, his wife and son decided to take in a movie. As they sat in the back row of the theater munching popcorn, the room darkened and the light from the black and white images playing against the huge screen began to flicker as if they were sitting in a turn-of-the century movie house. The high-pitched tinkling of an upright piano could be heard just below the narrator's voice.

1879. The Civil War is over and the resulting economic explosion spurs the great migration west. Farmers, ranchers, prospectors, killers and thieves seek their fortune. Cattle drovers turn cow towns into armed camps with murder rates higher than that of modern day New York or Los Angeles. Out of this chaos comes legendary lawman Wyatt Earp retiring his badge and gun to start a peaceful life with his family. Earp's friend John "Doc" Holliday, a southern gentleman turned gunfighter and gambler also travels west hoping the dry climate will relieve his tuberculosis. Silver is discovered in Arizona and Tombstone becomes a boom-town where the latest Paris fashions are sold from the backs of wagons. Attracted to this atmosphere are over 100 exiled Texas outlaws who band together to form the ruthless gang known by the red sashes they wear. They emerge as one of the earliest forms of organized crime in America. They call themselves, The Cowboys.

Suddenly, the picture turned from black and white to color. The word "TOMBSTONE" flashed across the screen. Kate looked at Bobby, smiled, and leaned over and whispered in Bobby's ear. "So now I get to find out what that little brown bottle sitting on the fireplace mantle is all about!"

Bobby just looked at his wife and grinned from ear to ear. The little brown sarsaparilla bottle he had picked up on his visit to Tombstone as a kid had survived all this time. As a kid, it had a place of distinction perched on his dresser for many years. When he went away to college, the bottle found its way into a box in the garage of the white clapboard home in Derry, New Hampshire. When he and Kate got married and moved into their first house he had looked for the bottle but it remained buried in boxes in the attic. Now, with the move to a larger house in Riverside, California, the box was fully unpacked and the bottle had again found a prominent place in Bobby's home. Now living in California – the West – and having rediscovered his sarsaparilla bottle had renewed Bobby's interest in the old west.

Two hours, and a large bucket of popcorn later, as actors Kurt Russell and Dana Delaney as Wyatt Earp and Josephine Marcus danced across the screen in a Denver snowstorm, Bobby's interest in Tombstone was totally transformed from semi-latent to "virulent!"

As they strolled out into the waning light of the late afternoon Bobby turned to his wife. "I've got to get back there, Kate! I want to see how Tombstone looks today. Hopefully it hasn't changed. I wonder if the Bird Cage is still there and the Crystal Palace. It must still be there. I wonder if Mr. E.T. Thornton is still there. He can't be. He'd be about 90 years old by now! Let's take a look at a map when we get home. Heck – from here, Tombstone can't be that far – just a hop, skip and a jump down the 10 freeway!"

Embroiled in his own conversation, and with Kate listening intently, neither one saw the man standing on the sidewalk that they both unceremoniously walked into. Bobby stopped for a moment, collected himself and gave a meek, "Excuse me – sorry". Then he stopped in his tracks. The man looked like he had just walked off the screen from the movie he had just seen. He wore broad-brimmed, sombrero-style hat, just like the Earps wore in the movie, except it was brown. Under the long, brown frock coat the man wore a tan corduroy vest and matching pants, which were tucked into knee-height, stovepipe boots with Cuban heels set off by silver spurs with jingle-bobs. His white shirt was barely visible as his bright green cravat with the gold tie-tac in the form of a six shooter hid all but a small portion of it. The only thing that looked out of place was the man's obviously modern-day eyeglass. For a brief second, Bobby flashed back to the first time, and only time, he had met Ezra T.

Thornton.

The man flashed a warm grin at Bobby and Kate. "Want to go to Tombstone huh? You sound like my kinda man. The kinda person we need!"

"Need? Need for what?" Bobby replied.

The man continued to smile. "My name is Harold. But I'm better known as Virgil Earp – at least that's the alias I like to use. I own a store here in Riverside called the Old West Mercantile. We sell old west clothing, boots, hats, that sort of stuff. And we also sponsor a rather large reenactor group called The Gunfighters. We do gunfight shows at places like county fairs, parties, and other events where people want old-west themed entertainment. I thought this might be a good opportunity to recruit some new members for our group. If you like the old west, if you like to socialize, if you like to get dressed up in period clothing, I'm the man to see!"

Bobby couldn't help but think that Harold came across not unlike the Johnny Behan character in the movie in the scene where Behan greets the Earp brothers when they arrive in Tombstone. Bobby smiled. "Sure... you run the club, recruit people... sell them the clothes and boots and everything that goes with an outfit... and make a bunch of money! And oh... by the way... my name is Bobby and this is my wife Kate and son Greg."

"I do indeed make a few dollars sir! And have a lot of fun doing it. And so does everyone that belongs to the group." Harold then turned his attention to Kate. "Why we even have outfits for the ladies too. In no time at all we can have you both looking 'Very Cosmopolitan.'"

"Very cosmopolitan..." Bobby thought to himself. Harold had obviously just seen the movie himself.

Harold chuckled at his use of the partial line from the movie and continued. "We have a big event coming up this spring. In April, The Gunfighters are going to perform the OK Corral gunfight, and a few other skits, at the Best Of The West old west event here in Riverside. There will be live-round competitive shooting, which is something a few of our members get involved in, plus a lot of vendors, lots of food and a whole lot of fun. And... the guy that plays our Wyatt Earp in the skit just left the group. We need another Wyatt.. whadda ya say?"

Bobby stuffed his hands into his pockets. "Gee, I dunno. I'm not really an actor. I've never acted before! Not in high school, or college, or anything like that."

"C'mon Bobby!" Harold now had is head cocked downward and was looking at Bobby over the top of his eyeglasses. "How many times have you read the story of the OK Corral shootout? How many times have you seen it portrayed in the movies? Heck... how many times will you go back and watch *Tombstone*? You know you only have one line in the whole thing! Just walk out there and do what I bet you've done a hundred times in the mirror!" They all laughed at Harold's "mirror" reference.

Kate turned to Bobby. "Here's your chance. You told me you always wanted to be a gunslinger like Wyatt Earp. You won't get any closer than this!"

Bobby thought for a moment, and then grinned widely at Kate, then at Harold, and quickly ripped another line from the movie, "I'm your huckleberry! That's *just* my game!"

Saturday afternoon, April 15, 1994   Riverside, California

Bobby and Kate drove into the dirt parking lot on a ridge overlooking the event-grounds, parked, and walked through the gate into what looked like 1879. It was like magic! A 150 acre county park that was usually inhabited on weekends by exercise walkers, picnickers, and kids on bicycles looking for whatever adventure they could conjure up on the winding dirt trails and occasional clumps of trees, had been transformed into what closely resembled a burgeoning western town. As they approached the main event area, Bobby and Kate could see tents. Lots and lots of tents of all sizes and descriptions! Vendors selling all sorts of old-west related item including clothing, hats, boots, saddlebags, holsters as well as lady's pantaloons and polonaise dresses had lined up their tents forming a "Main Street" through the center of the area. At one end of the "Main Street" was what resembled Boot Hill with cardboard headstones. At the other end of "Main Street" was a stage with a painted backdrop made to resemble an old west town complete with a saloon, bank, and, of course, a store with a sign over the door that said "Old West Mercantile."

Civil War era soldiers were "bivouacked" on the "outskirts" of town, Union soldiers in one camp, Confederate in another. Their rifles were stacked in a standing position, "Civil War style" next to the now-cold campfires from the night before. The area was just teeming with people. Many were dressed in old west or Civil War period clothing. Many members of the public were dressed in shorts and tank-tops. "Except for the shorts, tank-tops and sneakers, it was very much like a burgeoning mining camp probably looked." Bobby thought to himself.

A reproduction Wells Fargo stage coach pulled by four horses wound its way around the perimeter of the park generating a tremendous cloud of dust. It was filled with "civilians", members of the general public who had come to experience a little piece of the old west – if only for a day. The stage-driver held the "ribbons" securely and paid close attention to what his team was doing. Just like stage-drivers have always had to do – no matter what year it was. The man riding shot-gun was Harold, hat in hand and waving wildly at people as they drove past.

Bobby and Kate approached "Boot Hill" just as the stage reached the same point. In a swirl of choking dust, Harold yelled down as he passed. "Howdy Wyatt! The rest of the Gunfighters are already here. Meet us in 5 minutes behind the saloon!"

Bobby was ready for his part as Wyatt Earp in the OK Corral shootout skit. Like the first time he met Harold, Bobby looked like he had just stepped out of the movie *Tombstone*. He wore the traditional "black and whites" -   black Cuban-heeled boots with spurs, black pants, vest and wide-brimmed sombrero style hat, starched white shirt and a black string tie. To complete the look, he had earlier visited a local costume shop where he picked up a long, sweeping, Hollywood-prop moustache. Kate looked equally "period" in her, brown, high-laced shoes, dark green polonaise dress with a matching hat topped with a red feather, worn stylishly cocked to one side.

They made their way down the "Main Street" stopping a few times to greet friends and acquaintances. "How odd" Kate thought, "to shake hands with a man dressed in a Confederate uniform one minute, a person in a baseball cap and shorts the next, and an Indian in full war paint a moment later!

As they approached the saloon, Bobby could see the other Gunfighters standing around, talking about the upcoming performance. Other members of the group were starting to clear people off the Main Street to create an open area where the shootout would soon take place. Kate pulled a small camera from the carpet-bag she carried. "I'll see you after the show, Bob. I'll try to find a good spot to shoot some pictures. These pictures will be famous some day... your first acting job!" They both laughed as Bobby waved good-bye to Kate, and then approached the Gunfighter group.

Harold had just stepped off the stagecoach. As the skit director, he started looking around at the group and began to pull things together. "Ok... it looks like we have everyone here... we have a "Doc", a "Wyatt", a "Morgan"... and yours truly, Virgil W. Earp! How about the cow-boys? Sills, are you playing Ike Clanton today? Please remember not to wear your pager on stage!"

Henry Sills was a Riverside County paramedic, historian, and 19th century railroad aficionado. Although he was off-duty on this day he was always on-call. On one prior occasion he had forgotten to remove his pager prior to starting a re-enactment. The pager had gone-off in the middle of a gunfight much to Harold's chagrin and Henry's embarrassment. "Yes Harold... yes I'm playing Ike and yes I put my pager on vibrate mode in my shirt pocket!" was the sardonic reply.

Harold continued, "Ok... we have Ike, Billy Clanton, Tom McLaury... and ... hey... where's our Frank McLaury? Has anyone seen Frank?"

Everyone just stared at Harold. Then "Doc" spoke up. "I think he said he would be finishing up his last set about this time. He's shooting in the live-round competition today."

Bill Salter, one of the founding members of the group always played the part of Frank McLaury. But Bill would play any part, as long as he could shoot his pistol and "play cowboy." If it had anything to do with the old west, Bill was into it – and with both feet! In fact, he got so involved with so many things, sometime he would forget what part he was playing; right in the middle of a skit!

Harold cupped his hands around his mouth in an effort to amplify his voice. "Frank McLaury! Where are you! Hey Bill!"

A voice could be heard coming from the opposite side of a large earthen berm where the live-round shooting competition had been taking place since early morning. "Here I am! Don't start the shooting without me!"

Harold looked rather disgusted having to again wait for Bill, "Hurry up – we're on in a minute... and clear your weapon. Make sure you're not carrying any live ammo!"

"Yah yah...you know me. Safety first!" came the reply.

"Yah yah...I *do* know you! Make damn sure you take out those live rounds and replace them with these." Harold handed Bill several plastic blank rounds.

"Ok boys...this is it!" announced Harold. I'm going out front to make the announcement to the crowd. Cow-boys, get into position in the "corral" area. Earps, get ready to do the walk-down on my cue! Let's do it like it was 1881!"

Harold walked out into the open area, which would serve as Tombstone's Fremont Street and began addressing the crowd giving some background on what they were about to see. The sweat trickled down Bobby's back and began to soak through the sweat band on his black hat as he tried to remember his lines, where he was going to stand, how he had to shoot. "It sure is difficult being a reenactor gunfighter." he thought.

Harold completed his monolog to the crowd and returned to the other "Earps and Holliday" behind the saloon. They waited, what seemed to Bobby to be an eternity for the Cow-boys to deliver their lines. Then, the cue was given and the "Earps and Holliday" walked onto the set in front of what seemed to Bobby to be thousands of spectators. It was a few hundred at best, but still quite intimidating to an inexperienced reenactor. As he walked, he remembered, as a kid, how he had seen this same skit performed in the actual OK Corral and how that, more than anything else, made him want to be a "gunfighter." And now, here he was, living his dream. Never mind that it was a mock gunfight with mock bullets being dressed in reproduction clothes. This is as close as he was ever going to come to his dream here in the 20th century.

Bobby delivered the first Earp line as Wyatt, "You boys have been looking for a fight. Well now you can have it!"

Harold then spoke as Virgil, "Throw up your hands. We're here to disarm you!"

Just as they had rehearsed, the next few moments were tense as both sides eyed each other with their hands on their pistols. The click of a .45 being cocked could be distinctly heard as the crowd stood deafeningly quiet. Finally Harold, acting as Virgil, and holding Doc's walking stick in his left hand, held the stick high over his head and spoke those famous final words before the shooting started, "Wait…that's not what I want!"

That was the cue. Some people in the crowd stuck their fingers in their ears as the loud gun-blasts filled the air with acrid smoke. Some smaller children got scared and began crying, some mothers looked horrified, some men were smiling being so close to something they had only read about or seen on TV and in movies.

Bobby began firing his pistol, pulling back on the hammer and then pulling the trigger, one-handed as he thought Wyatt would have done. He tried to "aim" at his "assailants", but also tried to aim down and to one side of the opposing man as he was trained to do for a re-enactment.

Suddenly, Bobby felt a sharp pain in his chest, like he had been stabbed with a hot knife, and he was blown back on his heels, falling to the ground flat on his back. At first he wondered if he had taken a direct hit. "But even a direct hit with a blank should not feel like this!" he thought. "Beside, those other guys were at least 15 feet away, just as they should be for a re-enactment shooting! What the heck…?"

Bobby felt something wet on his chest. His free left hand went instinctively to his burning chest. He felt something wet and sticky. Blood…and then, everything went black.

The action continued for the prescribed 30 seconds, then stopped, and the crowd began to applaud and cheer. "Ike Clanton" had run off, just as he was supposed to. "Frank" and "Tom McLaury" and "Billy Clanton" lay dead, just exactly the way the script read. "Doc Holliday" slightly "wounded" but ambulatory was helping "Morgan" who had been "wounded" to his feet.

In all the excitement of the moment, Harold had not noticed that Bobby had "gone down" during the fight. Harold approached Bobby and thought, "Bobby's rehearsed this skit many times before! He knows Wyatt doesn't go down in this skit. What's he doing...trying to re-write history!"

As Harold approached he could see the blood stain continuing to spread on Bobby's white shirt. He knelt down in disbelief to take a closer look. Yes, it was blood! Real blood! Horrified, Harold sprang to his feet and yelled, "Is there a doctor about! We need a doctor! This man's been shot!"

Thinking it was all part of a continuing skit, several in the crowd began to chuckle and some applauded again.

Tears began to stream down Harold's face. "This is not a joke. This is not part of the show. This man's been shot. We need help..now...is there a doctor...?"

Everyone stood motionless for just a moment as time seemed to stand still. The crowd went quiet, the reenactors stood motionless, their facial expressions blank. This was not supposed to happen...not to Wyatt.. not to Bobby Dumas... not to a reenactor! This was not supposed to happen!

In that moment of indecision when everyone was trying to evaluate the situation and understand what was going on, Harold's mind went back to a few moments just before they walked out on stage.

"Bill!" Harold yelled out angrily, "Bill Salter...lemme see your damn gun!" Turning his attention back to Bobby, Harold yelled, "Where's Sill's?? Somebody find Sills! Tell him to get his medical kit!"

By this time Bill, playing Frank McLaury, had risen to his feet and placed his pistol back into its holster. As he heard Harold demand to see his pistol a cold chill went down his spine. Had he replaced all of his live ammo with the plastic blanks? There could be no other explanation...

Bill approached Harold and handed over the blue-steel .45. It was a replica of the 1873 model Colt that was carried by many a cowboy and lawman in the days when everyone carried a gun. By this time Henry Sills had emerged from the crowd with his medical kit and he began to look over Bobby's wound. "It doesn't look good for Bobby!" came the initial prognosis.

Harold took Bill's gun by the grip, moved a few steps to where they were now standing at Bobby's feet. Harold opened the loading gate on the side of the pistol and began to push on the ejector rod to expel the spent cartridges. First one then two, then three, four and five spent plastic cartridges fell to the ground. Harold looked at Bill in a tense moment. Harold spun the cylinder one last time and pushed the ejector rod as Bill's horrors were realized. A spent brass shell, one that a moment before had held a lead bullet, the lead bullet which was now buried in Bobby's chest, fell to the ground and came to rest beside the heel on Bobby's boot.

Henry Sills, kneeling beside Bobby turned his head and looked up at Harold. In a low and somber, barely audible voice he declared, "Legally, I can't declare a death, but, my medical training tells me, this man is dead."

By this time, Kate and their son Greg realized something had gone horribly wrong and arrived at Bobby's side. Instantly, Kate could tell from the look everyone gave her that her husband was gone and she began to weep uncontrollably. Greg, being only 10 years old could not fully grasp the gravity of what had happened, and stared at his slain father. Greg remained motionless, staring blankly as the life drained from his father's chest.

Wednesday, October 26   1:30PM

Bobby opened his eyes. He was standing upright; which was rather strange he thought as his last memory was of lying on the ground after the OK Corral gunfight and feeling very woozey... and cold.

Bobby looked around. He was on a street corner in what looked to him like it might have been a Hollywood movie set – for an old-west movie. He looked at the sign post at the corner of the street. It indicated that he was standing on Allen Street, and the cross street was 6th. "Tombstone?" he thought? But it couldn't be.

"If it was a movie set, it was a darned good one!" he thought. "Everyone is in costume – all the ladies, all the men, all the kids. The street is dirt. Wait a minute – how am I dressed?"

Bobby looked at his reflection in the plate-glass store-front to reveal that he was dressed in his "black and whites", his Wyatt Earp outfit complete with the long black coat made famous by actor Kurt Russell in the movie *Tombstone*. He was thankful that he was wearing the coat because a sudden breeze made him chilly, and caused small swirls of dust to come off the street and dance around his boots as he stood on the sidewalk. He also noticed his moustache – the one he had purchased at the movie props store. It looked – real. Bobby tugged at it to pull it off and felt that unmistakable twinge when hair follicles abruptly leave one's upper lip. The moustache *was* real!

He also noticed something else. His shirt was white – not blood stained. He touched his chest with his right hand as he had remembered that was one of the last things he had done before everything went black. His shirt was dry – no blood – no stabbing pain in his chest.

As he stared incredulously into the plate-glass window he noticed something else. The reflection showed what was – or more precisely put – what was not there. The Bird Cage was not there! The Bird Cage Theatre, long a symbol of Tombstone was not on the corner of 6th and Allen. But there was something under construction on that spot. "Could it be that I am seeing the Bird Cage under construction?" Bobby thought. "Where the hell am I? Where's Kate? Where's Greg? Where's Harold and the other guys? What's happening to me?"

A sudden terror gripped Bobby as he turned around and looked out onto the street again. "This must be a dream" he thought. "What other explanation can there be? It can't be a Hollywood set. There are no cameras, no lights, no director. I don't see anyone running around with sound mikes. This looks... REAL!"

A voice behind him brought Bobby out of his daydream. "Good afternoon Mr. Earp! Thirsty?"

Bobby turned around to see a man standing in the now-open doorway of the store whose pane-glass window he had been staring into. It seemed that he had seen the man before but could not place him. He was also dressed in "period" clothing, very dapper looking, Bobby thought, and despite his apparent age of about 60, he seemed healthy and strong. His long, white hair was swept back and tucked behind his ears. His white beard was closely cropped. He wore black shoes that laced up around his ankles. His gray and black striped pants, like his white shirt was neatly wrinkle-free and the pant-legs were crease-less. The man's shirt was buttoned to his neck topped by a black and white striped cravat-style tie. In one hand he held a small, brown bottle with water dripping from it the residue of having pulled it from an icy repository. His other hand was firmly placed in the pocket of his bright-red brocade vest.

Bobby looked at the man who was now smiling at him. "You can't be talking to me mister. Oh I know I probably look like Wyatt Earp but I'm... err..."

As Bobby tried to figure out who or what he was, the man interrupted him and gently waved the little brown bottle he held in his hand. "Sarsaparilla is your favorite isn't it, Mr. Earp. Come on inside. Let's talk."

Bobby thought for a moment. What did he have to lose by talking to this man? Nothing. And since he was so confused and this man seemed to know what was going on...and knew who he was... or who he was supposed to be, Bobby figured he would go inside to talk.

Beside, the guy looked familiar. Bobby figured if he talked to the man, he would soon figure out who it was, and how he knew him.

Just as he was about to step inside, Bobby noticed for the first time the lettering on the window he had been staring into. He had been so intent on looking at himself in the window, and trying to figure out what was going on, he had completely missed the letters painted on the window as big as life – "E.T. Thornton – Mercantile".

Bobby's jaw dropped. "That's why you look familiar! You're Mr. Thornton! I know you! I met you when I was a kid – in Tombstone. Does that mean – I mean – is this Tombstone? Where - ?"

Ezra interrupted him again, "Thirsty Mr. Earp? Step inside. It's my treat on the sarsaparilla."

Bobby followed Ezra into the store. It was rather dark inside, especially after stepping in from the brighter light of outdoors. But today was a rather cloudy, overcast day – unseasonably cool and rather damp. Suddenly it occurred to Bobby that that was exactly how the weather was on the day of the OK Corral shootout.

The store was exactly as Bobby remembered it. Shelves against the walls stacked to the ceiling with all sorts of products – from canned goods to blankets to soap and a vast array or elixirs and other medicines. The curved-glass display cases were filled with all sorts of products, including some blue-steel 1873 model Colts which looked new. A pot-bellied stove stood at the far end of the store, with a fire apparently burning inside to ward off the air's chill.

Bobby placed his black hat on one of the glass cases, and took a sip from the brown bottle. "Now I remember. You're Mr. Thornton, the drummer. And I'm..."

"You are Wyatt Earp!" announced Ezra.

"No... I'm Bobby Dumas from..." came the sharp reply.

"Derry, New Hampshire?" said Ezra in a rather inquisitive tone and a smile.

Bobby came back with, "I was going to say Riverside, California. And besides that, I have a wife and a new job and whole bunch of new friends. And I'd like to see them now if you don't mind. This is a very elaborate trick – all very cute. Now the trick is over."

Ezra grabbed a bottle of sarsaparilla from the barrel in the middle of the floor, the same barrel Bobby had remembered was there when he visited Tombstone as a kid. Ezra opened the bottle, took a drink, and began to explain. "Well, what you say is partially correct. You have a new job, as a lawman here in Tombstone. And you have a lot of new friends, and several enemies. And, sometime soon, you will have a new wife. Her name is Josephine, but you will call her Sadie."

Bobby, who had been facing Ezra and the back of the store now turned, looked out the store's front window and the building of the Bird Cage Theatre, then turned again and looked intensely at Ezra. "Lawman... what do you mean lawman! I'm Bobby..."

Ezra interrupted him again, "Mr. Earp; Wyatt; Bobby Dumas died a very tragic death in a county park in Riverside, California while performing a re-enactment of the OK Corral shootout. And now you have a choice. You see that bright red door at the back end of the store?"

"Yes." came the reply. Bobby began to tremble.

Ezra smiled, "There are two ways out of here. The red door leads to... well... oblivion. The front door leads to your future. Which will it be, Mr. Earp?"

"My future? Bobby was more confused than ever. "What kind of future is this! What kind of town is this, anyway? Where the hell am I?"

Ezra smiled again. "You're in Tombstone. And if you don't believe me, here is yesterday's Epitaph newspaper. Check the date."

Ezra handed Bobby a newspaper. Bobby looked at the date – October 25, 1881. "No! This can't be! Today is October 26 – the day of the famous gun battle? This has been a lot of fun but..."

Ezra again interrupted, "Check your watch. What time is it?"

Bobby reached into his vest pocket. The pocket-watch that he normally carried for reenactments, a Norwich which he had purchased at an antique show and had a fine patina to it looked brand new and shiny. "It's 1:45."

Ezra now looked at Bobby over the top of his glasses, similar to the way Harold used to look at him. "One forty-five you say. You'd better hurry. You don't want to be late for your appointment with destiny."

"My appointment with destiny?" Bobby looked quizzically at Ezra and for the first time, almost felt like he understood what was going on.

Just then, a voice could be heard calling into the store from outside, "Hey Wyatt – you in there?"

Bobby turned and looked at the door to see a rather large man with a wide brimmed, "Tombstone –style" hat peering through the glass in the door. Then, he turned back to Ezra. "You mean I'm..."

Ezra took Bobby's hat from the countertop and handed it to him. "You're brother, Virgil, is calling you. Go see what he wants."

Bobby set his bottle on the counter and took his hat from Ezra placing it firmly on his head. He reached down to his side. Yes – his six-shooter was in his right coat pocket. Bobby stepped over to the door, looked back at Ezra one last time. He wasn't too keen on walking through Ezra's back door and into "oblivion" – whatever that was - even if he *was* dead. And if his future, whatever that was, could be accessed through the front door, he figured that's where he should go. By this time, he wasn't sure if he was Bobby Dumas or Wyatt Earp... but whoever he was, it seemed there was only one thing he could do. He stepped outside through Ezra's front door and came face-to-face with a man he had only seen pictures of – Virgil Earp.

Virgil started in immediately, "Wyatt, where have you been? We've been looking all over for you. The Clantons and McLaury's and few other Cow-boys are starting to collect in the vacant lot next to Fly's studio. One person after the other has come to me and Morg saying that Ike is going to kill us on sight. Now here's what I figure we'll do. We have to disarm those cow-boys and..."

The Real Story Behind "The Gunfighter"

On Wednesday, October 26, 1881, an unusually cool and overcast day, at approximately 2:30 in the afternoon, Wyatt, Morgan, and Virgil Earp along with their friend Doc Holliday faced down Frank and Tom McLaury, and Billy Clanton in what has become the most famous 30 seconds in old west history. The fight, mostly over political differences, and a love triangle between Wyatt Earp, Cochise County Sheriff Johnny Behan (who sided with the cow-boy gang) and the lovely Josephine Marcus actually took place in an empty lot behind the OK Corral, between the photography studio of C.S. Fly and Harwood's Boarding House where Doc Holliday was residing at the time. At the time, the affair was called a street fight. It wasn't until years later that it became known as the Shootout or Gunfight at the OK Corral.

On October 26, 1881, the Bird Cage Theatre did not yet exist. It opened for business in late December 1881.

Wyatt Earp actually died in 1929, in a small bungalow in Los Angeles, California, about 90 miles from Riverside, California, at the ripe old age of 80. His last words were, 'Suppose... suppose..."

And as for Bobby Dumas, he could have been any one of millions of kids who grew up in the late 1950's and early 1960's watching TV and movie westerns, and wishing they were Wyatt Earp.

Chapter 3: THE MAN WHO SAVED WYATT EARP

"I watched the whole thing from here. A shot to the chest with a .45 slug at about 15 feet... Wyatt was dead before he hit the ground. There was nothing you could do after that. Nothing! Nothing anyone could do!"

Ezra T. Thornton April 15, 1994

Friday November 18, 1881 Noon Tombstone, Arizona Territory

The whistle on the Vizina hoisting works let off a shrill howl signaling mid-day in Tombstone. Miners filed out into the sunshine. Many shops and stores closed their doors for a mid-day break, and the Cochise County Superior Court took a recess – giving the hapless defense attorneys, Tom Fitch, Webster Street, James Howard, and T.J. Drum a short respite in their court battle.

In the wake of a street fight behind the OK Corral on October 26, 1881 between the Earp brothers and Doc Holliday and the Clanton and McLaury brothers, a coroners' inquest was being conducted in the courtroom of Judge Wells Spicer – and things didn't look good for the Earp faction. The cow-boys wanted them tried for the murder of Frank and Tom McLaury and Billy Clanton. The Earps maintained that they, along with their friend, Doc Holliday, were doing their duty as sworn police officers.

Ezra T. Thornton strode into the Can-Can Restaurant for a brief lunch - just behind defense lawyers Tom Fitch and Webster Street. Noticing Ezra, Fitch and Street invited the mercantilist to join them at their table.

Pulling out his chair to be seated, Ezra could tell from the looks on the faces of his friends that things were not going well. The deep-furrowed brow on one, and sweat on the forehead of the other, despite the rather cool autumn breeze, denoted severe anxiety.

51

Ezra seated himself, looked at both men for just a moment, and they at him. Nothing need be said. Things looked and felt grim for the Earp brothers and Doc Holliday.

"This isn't right" said Fitch. "The Earps are good men... good men doing their duty as police officers. Those lying SOB's... Ike Clanton and his cronies! They deserve what they get... if we can just find the right words to bring justice to that courtroom and give it to them!"

Ezra turned to Street, "Things going poorly for you as well?"

Street rubbed his hand over his mouth and chin as if to wipe away some of his angst, "Ezra, I've fought a lot of court battles, but this one is tough – real tough. And it's not even a bona-fide trial... just an inquest. Ike Clanton and his cowboy friends swear to tell the truth on the stand but it would appear they have their own version of the truth!"

The men ordered their noon-day lunch, then Tom Fitch piped in, "That street –fight seemed to be a defining moment, Ezra. The Earps and Holliday have gone from being entrepreneurs, lawmen and gamblers to denizens of the town. Everyone blames the Earps and Holliday for the carnage behind the OK Corral – not the Clantons or McLaurys. They are now seen as bad men... and bad public sentiment is difficult to defend against. Think about it! The Earps and Holliday are actually being tried in the street, not Judge Spicer's courtroom!"

Ezra finished a mouthful of sandwich and took a sip of coffee. "What about Addie Bourland's testimony yesterday? You told me it seemed to help your cause. After all, her dress shop is right across the street from the alley where all the fighting occurred. She was in a position to see quite a bit!"

"It did" replied Fitch. "Putting her on the stand was the smartest thing we've done so far. It's about the only testimony that was unbiased – and Judge Spicer seemed to like what he heard."

"Yes" replied Street, "But that damned William McLaury from Texas – he's relentless, and one hell of a showman. He's not here just as a defense attorney for his brothers. He's here to bury the Earps and Holliday in the Yuma Territorial Prison for the rest of their lives. He's here to execute a vendetta against our boys."

The three men looked at each other for just a moment in silence. Then Fitch spoke, "Ezra, we are trying our best – but it may not be good enough. We may need a miracle here. Having two dead brothers is certainly a strong driving force for Will McLaury."

Ezra smiled and broke the tension, "Miracles are my specialty. I'll see what I can do."

Neither attorney was amused, and thought the less of Ezra for making light of a serious situation. But they also knew that Ezra had always been friendly with the Earps and Doc Holliday. Doc was known for being irascible and cantankerous and a man who had few friends yet, Ezra was always kind to him. Despite their troubles and the fact that Ezra may have been disingenuous, the two attorneys looked at each other and could not help but think that maybe Ezra did have a trick up his sleeve.

Ezra paid for his lunch and stood, securing his top-hat on his head covering most but not all of long white locks, "Meet me here tomorrow for lunch – same time." He then turned, and without saying good-bye, walked out into the sunshine and the throngs of people in the street.

Turning west, Ezra moved down the boardwalk to the OK Corral where he walked through the gate and into the open yard. A young boy of about 15 greeted him, "Good day Mr. Thornton. What can I do for you?"

Ezra reached in his pocket and pulled out a few coins, tossing them to the youngster, "Hello Toby. Please hitch up my team if you would. I have a long trip to take!"

Saturday afternoon, April 15, 1994 Riverside, California

Bobby and Kate Dumas with son Greg drove into a dirt parking lot on a ridge overlooking a wide field filled with people, tents, temporary buildings and vendor's carts. If one imagined the area minus the modern vendor carts, it almost looked like a boom-town of the late 1870's. The 150-acres county park had been transformed, almost transported to another time and place.

Bobby imagined that this was what Tombstone looked like in its early days. Kate and Bobby smiled at each as they exited their car. Kate looked at her son, dressed in period clothing, then looked at her husband, resplendent in his "black and whites" the "uniform" of the Earps, "You look like a kid in a candy store!"

Greg didn't get the joke. "Whadda ya mean? He looks like he's supposed to look. He looks like Wyatt Earp!" They all laughed. To Greg, the whole thing about getting dressed in old-west clothing seemed a little absurd. "Imagine... a grown man playing cowboy" he thought.

Bobby was ready for his part as Wyatt Earp in the OK Corral shootout skit at the area's premier old-west event. Bobby and Kate made a striking couple in their period clothes.

Kate had purchased a green polonaise dress from the Old West Mercantile, a store carrying a wide array of reenactor clothing and supplies owned by Harold, the leader of their gunfighter reenactment group. In an antique store she had found some genuine period shoes, still in good shape which she wore – they were brown, with a short heel and laced up over the ankle. From a catalog she had ordered a very fashionable lady's hat with a sweeping brim, topped by a rakish red feather.

Bobby wore the traditional sombrero style hat with a wide flat brim – the same style worn by the Earp actors in the movie *Tombstone*. His "boiled" white shirt was topped off with a black cravat-style tie covered with a black vest. His black duck pants were neatly stuffed into the tops of his black Cuban-heeled boots to which hung a pair of silver spurs. His look was complete with a long, sweeping Hollywood-prop moustache.

Greg was less stylish than his parents, but "period-correct' in his brown, drover shirt and brown wool pants held up by a pair of black suspenders. On his feet was a pair of 1880's style reproduction brown shoes, laced up over his ankle. A black hat of non-descript form topped off his outfit.

Greg was quite surprised, as they walked down the small ridge and "into the town" of tents and false-fronted buildings. Hundreds of people milled about, people of all ages, including kids – dressed in similar period clothing.

The tents and vendor booths were lined up to form a "Main Street" where everyone congregated. Vendors selling all sorts of old-west related item including clothing, hats, boots, saddlebags, holsters as well as lady's pantaloons and polonaise dresses had lined up and were doing a "land office" business. Bobby smiled as he thought of the line from the *Tombstone* movie narrative, "Silver is discovered in Arizona and Tombstone becomes a boom-town where the latest Paris fashions are sold from the backs of wagons."

"Yep" he thought. "This is great fun!"

As the family walked down "Main Street", Bobby tipped his hat to all the ladies as he would have been done in 1879. Kate laughed at him and slapped his arm. "You're silly."

"I have a date with destiny!" Bobby said to no one in particular. Kate looked at him and smiled with, "Mr. Destiny huh? You are sooo silly!"

They passed a small group of Civil War Confederate soldiers – many more were bivouacked on the "outskirts of town." They were slightly out of time with the Tombstone motif, the Civil War ending more than 10 years before Tombstone was founded, but it was good fun nonetheless. And the Civil war reenactors took great pride in their dress and accoutrements and looked positively real.

The general public, dressed in shorts, sneakers, tank-tops and base-ball caps looked weirdly out of place. Especially when they were outnumbered by reenactors, and people that came dressed for the occasion in period clothing.

A reproduction Wells Fargo stagecoach pulled by six horses wound its way around the perimeter of the park generating a tremendous cloud of dust. The "civilians" inside, some in period costume, others in normal street clothes thrilled to a ride in the meticulously recreated conveyance. The driver skillfully held his "ribbons" steering the horses around rocks, and people who had wandered onto the trail.

As the stage drew closer, Kate and Bobby could see Harold, the head of their reenactor group sitting "on the box" alongside the driver – riding "shotgun" – yelling and waving his hat as the stage passed friends and fellow reenactors.

Bobby, Kate and Greg approached "Boot Hill", a small "cemetery" with cardboard tombstones made to look like the Tombstone iconic burial grounds, just as the stage reached the same point. In a swirl of choking dust, Harold yelled down as he passed. "Howdy Wyatt! The rest of the Gunfighters are already here. Meet us in 5 minutes behind the saloon!"

Bobby felt the excitement build as he beamed a wide grin at his wife and son. "I'm going to follow in some great footsteps" he said to no one in particular. "Not only will I get to portray Wyatt Earp, a great man and one of my heroes, I'll get to follow in the footsteps of all the great actors and who have played this part."

Kate laughed, "Come on Mr. Movie Star - the rest of the cast are waiting for you!" The two laughed as they hurried on to the saloon, passing a small "tribe" of Apaches in full "war paint."

As they approached the saloon, they could see the other members of their reenactor group, "The Gunfighters," getting ready for the OK Corral re-enactment. Kate and Greg got ready to leave Bobby as Kate pulled a camera from her period carpetbag. "I'll see you after the show, Bob. I'll try to find a good spot to shoot some pictures. These pictures will be famous some day... your first acting job!" They both laughed as Bobby waved goodbye to his wife and son.

The stagecoach had just pulled up to the back of the saloon where Harold stepped down from the lofty seat next to the driver. Usually quite jovial, Harold now looked quite serious as he pulled his thoughts together. As the skit director, it was his job to make sure everything went as planned.

He began to address the reenactors assembled there. "Ok... it looks like we have everyone here... we have a "Doc", a "Wyatt", a "Morgan"... and yours truly, Virgil W. Earp! How about the cow-boys...we have Ike Clanton, Billy Clanton, Tom McLaury... and ... hey... where's our Frank McLaury? Has anyone seen Frank?"

Everyone just stared at Harold. Then "Doc" spoke up. "I think he said he would be finishing up his last set about this time. He's shooting in the live-round competition today."

Bill Salter, one of the founding members of The Gunfighters always played the part of Frank McLaury. Bill loved to shoot his guns. It didn't matter if he was shooting blanks for a skit or shooting live rounds for a competitive-shooting match. It didn't matter if he was shooting his pistols, of which he had many, or his beloved "coach -gun" – a short-barreled shotgun. If it had anything to do with the old west, Bill was involved in it.

Harold cupped his hands around his mouth in an effort to amplify his voice and yelled in the direction of where the live-shooting competition had recently ended. "Frank McLaury! Where are you! Hey Bill!"

A voice could be heard coming from opposite side of a large earthen berm, the site of the morning's live-round competition. "Here I am! Don't start the shooting without me!"

Harold looked rather disgusted having to again wait for Bill, "Hurry up – we're on in a minute... and clear your weapon. Make sure you're not carrying any live ammo!"

"Yah yah...you know me. Safety first!" came the reply.

"Yah yah...I *do* know you!" Harold sounded miffed. "Make damn sure you take out those live rounds and replace them with these." Harold handed Bill several plastic blank rounds.

"Ok boys...this is it!" announced Harold. I'm going out front to make the announcement to the crowd. Cow-boys, get into position in the "corral" area. Earps, get ready to do the walk-down on my cue! Let's do it like it was 1881!"

Other members of The Gunfighters had previously been clearing the public off the "Main Street" and roping off an area where the gunfight would take place. Harold stepped into the middle of the cleared area and began addressing the crowd, giving them some background information on what they were about to witness, admonishing everyone to stay outside the ropes for safety's sake. He explained that the rounds they were about to use were "fake" – blank "bullets" like the type used in Hollywood movies and that nobody would be in any danger..

The sweat trickled down Bobby's back. He took off his hat and mopped his brow with a handkerchief, the sweat beginning to soak through the sweatband on his black hat. He tried to remember his lines. He didn't have to say much, but he had to say it correctly. He tried to remember where to stand, how to move, how to make it all look real. "It sure is difficult being a reenactor gunfighter." he thought.

Harold completed his monolog to the crowd and returned to the other "Earps and Holliday" behind the saloon. Harold looked at the others and smiled, "Here we go, boys!"

The "cow-boys" walked onto the set and delivered their few lines. It seemed to Bobby to take forever. Then the cue was given. The "Earps" and "Holliday" walked onto the set to a crowd of what seemed to Bobby to be thousands. After standing in a shaded area for several minutes the glare of the bright spring sun, dazzling blue sky, and having hundreds of pairs of eyes on him was bit overwhelming and Bobby hesitated for moment. Then he caught himself and moved on, walking from "Hafford's Corner" to where he would say his lines – provided he remembered them! It seemed like a dream come true. "I'm Wyatt Earp!" he thought to himself.

The "Earps" and "Holliday" moved into the OK Corral. Bobby delivered the first Earp line as Wyatt, "You boys have been looking for a fight. Well now you can have it!"

Harold then spoke as Virgil, "Throw up your hands. We're here to disarm you!"

As they had rehearsed, the next few moments were tense as both sides eyed each other with their hands on the pistols. The crowd stood perfectly still, enthralled with the action, and most full knowing what was about to happen.

Pistols were cocked providing the hushed crowd with the distinctive "click-click" which everyone who had ever seen a western movie knew meant flying lead was imminent.

Harold, acting as Virgil, and holding Doc's walking stick in his left hand, held the stick high over his head and spoke those famous final words before the shooting started, "Wait...that's not what I want!"

The cue had been given.

A few shots were fired. Henry Sills, a member of The Gunfighters playing Ike Clanton ran up to Bobby "begging for his life." "Wyatt – don't shoot me. I'm not heeled!"

Bobby thought for a moment, and then remembered his line, "The fighting's commenced. Get to fighting or get away!" and pushed Henry to one side. Henry regained his feet, and then ran off, just as Ike had done.

Bobby began firing his pistol, pulling back on the hammer and then pulling the trigger, one-handed as he thought Wyatt would have done. He tried to "aim" at his "assailants", but also tried to aim down and to one side of the opposing man as he was trained to do for a reenactment.

With the loud noises, some younger children in the crowd began to cry. But most people were into it... some men smiling as this would be the closest they would get to an event that had only read about or seen on TV or in the movies.

Suddenly, Bobby felt a sharp pain in his chest. His first thought was that he had taken a direct hit from a blank; but all the others were far enough away, at least 15 feet. Even if he had taken a direct hit, the "cow-boys" were too far away for the blast to really hurt him... not like this!

"What the heck...?"

His free left hand went instinctively to his burning chest as he looked down. *"Blood! "My blood!"*

Bobby hit the dirt with a dull thud... and then everything went black.

Just as it had in 1881, the action lasted for about 30 seconds, the air being filled with acrid gun smoke. Ike had run off, the three remaining cow-boys lay wounded, Morgan was on his knees, and Doc and Virgil nursed some minor wounds. Everything had gone as planned – almost. The crowd cheered and applauded as Harold yelled "Clear" marking the end of the skit and a signal to the "dead" that it was ok to stand up.

In all the excitement, Harold hadn't noticed that Bobby had gone down. As he turned about to survey the area and take his bow, Harold saw Bobby lying on the ground. At first Harold was miffed. Bobby had practiced the skit many times and knew that Wyatt didn't go down in this one. In fact, Bobby knew as well as anyone that Wyatt was the only combatant that walked away unscathed. Harold walked over to Bobby, "Hey Bobby – are you trying to re-write history?"

It was then that Harold noticed, much to his horror, a spreading red stain on Bobby's shirt and a distinctive hole in his vest. Harold knelt down for a closer look. Yes... it was a bullet hole and yes... it was blood!

The crowd's applause was dying out as Harold turned quickly about and sprang to his feet. "Is there a doctor about! We need a doctor! This man's been shot!"

Thinking it was all part of a continuing skit, several in the crowd began to chuckle and some applauded again.

Angry at the response from the crowd and lack of response from his fellow reenactors, tears began to stream down Harold's face. He turned to Bobby, and then turned again to the audience, "This is not a joke. This is not part of the show. This man's been shot. We need help... now...is there a doctor...?"

The next moment was one that everyone experiences at least once in their life where it is obvious that a severe trauma has occurred, and because it happens so seldom, no one knows how to deal with it. Everyone, including the audience and reenactors were trying to come to grips with the situation, and decide what, if anything, they should do.

Harold's mind went back to a few moments just before they walked out on stage. "Bill!" Harold yelled out angrily, "Bill Salter... lemme see your damn gun!" Turning his attention back to Bobby, Harold yelled, "Where is Sills? Somebody find Henry Sills! Tell him to get his medical kit!"

When not involved in old west reenacting Henry Sills was a Riverside County firefighter and paramedic... besides being an antique railroad buff.

Bill had broken out of his Frank McLaury character and was now on his feet. As he heard Harold yelling and saw Bobby lying on the ground with an ever-widening bloodstain on his shirt, a cold chill ran down his spine. His head began reeling as he thought of what the only explanation could be – one of his shots – or somene's shots was not a blank! Had he replaced all his live ammo with the blank, plastic cartridges?

Bill walked over to where Harold was standing, near Bobby's feet. His hands shaking uncontrollably almost knowing what Harold would find, Bill handed over his pistol, a blue-steel replica of an 1873 Colt .45, arguably the most popular firearm in the old west. Harold grabbed the pistol brusquely, jerking it out of Bill's hand. By this time, Henry Sills emerged from the crowd, medical kit in hand, and began attending to Bobby. "It doesn't look good for Bobby!" was the initial prognosis.

Looking at Bill in disgust, Harold opened the loading gate on the pistol and began to eject the spent shells. The first one was a spent plastic cartridge – a blank that had exploded harmlessly into the air. Bill gave a brief sigh of relief but knew that there were five more cylinders to go. The second, third, fourth and fifth cartridges were ejected – all spent plastic blanks. Bill held his breath. Harold spun the cylinder one more notch and pushed the ejector rod expelling cartridge number six – a spent brass shell which a few moments before had contained a lead slug which now was embedded in Bobby's chest. The brass casing fell to ground and came to rest against the heel of Bobby's boot. Bill's head was reeling as tears welled up in his eyes.

Henry Sills, kneeling beside Bobby turned his head and looked up at Harold. In a low and somber, barely audible voice he declared, "Legally, I can't declare a death, but.... my medical training tells me.... this man is dead."

Looking at Harold's now tear-stained face and the tears starting to trickle down Bill's cheeks, Henry also began to sob. *"I'm a trained professional!' he thought. "Trained professionals don't cry. Doctors and paramedics save people and lose people every day. This is another patient... and other person I am supposed to help. I'm just doing a job... a job I was trained to do! Trained medical professionals don't do this! They don't cry!"*

At that moment, Bobby's wife and son arrived. Nobody had to tell the audience that Kate and Greg were Bobby's wife and son. They could all tell from the incredulous look on her face. Many turned away, knowing the horror she now faced.

Henry Sills looked up at Kate from where he knelt on the ground. "I did what I could. I believe death was instantaneous. He never knew what hit him... never knew..."

Greg stood motionless, his 10 year old mind unable to comprehend the gravity of the situation. Now sobbing uncontrollably, Kate sank to her knees and held Bobby's head in her trembling hands.

Henry Sills stood, turned, and walked away, the crowd who had gathered around Bobby parting to let him through. As he emerged from the crowd he could see the Riverside County ambulance just arriving, bouncing over the rough ground, people pointing to where Bobby lay. *"Too late!"* he thought.

Head down and with his mind spinning, Henry walked slowly, resolutely down the short Main Street. He had no idea where he was going or why. He simply had to get away from the melee around Bobby and be alone.

Finally, as he reached the end of the Main Street he looked up to find someone... and something he had never seen before – a bright red circus-style wagon drawn by four fine-looking horses, driven by a man dressed in 1880's period clothing with long, flowing white hair. Fancy lettering spread boldly across the length of the wagon's sides in yellow, gold leaf, and blue as if it were an advertising poster for the Barnum and Bailey circus read, "E.T. Thornton – Mercantile."

Partly out of curiosity and partly as a diversion from his grief, Henry stared up at the man sitting on the driver's seat wearing a top hat and black frock coat. "Obviously" he thought, "This man is a reenactor although I've never seen him before."

The two men looked at each other for just a moment – then the man on the wagon broke the ice. "I'm Ezra T. Thornton... and that was an unfortunate incident. Such a tragedy – that young man – leaving a widow and a young son."

Henry looked up at Ezra, pushing his wide brimmed hat to the back of his head, wiping his sweating forehead with his sleeve. "I lost a good friend today – a fellow reenactor. I lost Bobby – I lost Wyatt Earp. I did what I could... which wasn't much... did what I could but..."

Ezra cut in, "Henry Sills, you are a Riverside County paramedic, a medical professional – not God! Medical professionals lose patients every day!"

Henry wiped his running nose with his sleeve, "Patients – yes. But this was a friend – it was Bobby Dumas – it was Wyatt Earp!"

Ezra leaned down from his seat high on the wagon and extended his hand to Henry urging him to climb aboard. Henry grabbed Ezra's hand, placed one foot on a step made for that purpose and swung up onto the seat next the Ezra. He wasn't quite sure why he was climbing aboard a wagon with a man he didn't know, except that this person was obviously a fellow reenactor, and he now needed a friend... and Ezra seemed like a friend impartial to the day's events.

Once seated, Ezra turned to Henry, "I watched the whole thing from here. A shot to the chest with a .45 slug at about 15 feet... Wyatt was dead before he hit the ground. There was nothing you could do after that. Nothing! Nothing anyone could do!"

"But...!" came the reply.

"But I know you... Henry Sills. You are a good man - a conscientious man. You are a man who will beat himself up forever over this... unless.."

"Unless what?"

"Unless you find a way to redeem yourself – to feel whole again."

Henry's mind left Bobby Dumas for moment and concentrated on his new "friend." It seemed that this man whom he had never met seemed to know him as well or better than he knew himself. Henry's concentration was broken with Ezra's words, "Well? What do you want to do? Do you want to spend the rest of your life haunted by today's events? Or do you want a chance to... save Wyatt Earp?"

Henry thought for a moment. Henry was a young man but old enough to know that he would not feel this bad forever. But he also knew that this would haunt him unless he found a way to deal with it. He decided to humor his new friend and maybe help himself. "Sure... show me how to deal with this. And by the way... how do you know my name?"

Ezra smiled and the two men shook hands. "Just call me Ezra. Now climb in the back of the wagon and change your clothes. Those chaps and spurs and your "Boss Of The Plains" hat won't work where we're going. There's a period men's business suit back there – your size. Put it on. There's a small cot back there too. You might want to lay down and rest a bit. We have a long way to go! But don't worry – I'll have you back here in time for supper!"

Tuesday October 25, 1881 7:45AM Benson, A.T.

Henry Sills awoke with a start as Ezra's wagon hit a bump in the road, then came to a stop. Henry rose from the small cot where he had fallen asleep, what seemed like minutes ago, and poked his head through a curtain to see Ezra Thornton pulling his wagon up in front of a Wells Fargo office on a dusty street. "Where the hell are we?"

Ezra turned to his incredulous friend, "We are on our way to your redemption my good man. Welcome to 1881 and Benson, Arizona Territory. I have booked passage for you on the Wells Fargo stage at 8AM to Tombstone. Once you arrive, check into the San Jose House. They will have a room waiting for you in your name – all paid for. In the room you will find additional clothes. You'll need them. You'll be in Tombstone about five weeks."

Henry's eyes opened as wide as saucers. "Five weeks? Tombstone? 1881? I thought you were going to have me back before supper! What the hell is going on?

Ezra could only smile at his friend's amazement. "If you're looking for redemption... if you want to save Wyatt Earp, get on the stage. Oh... and if anyone asks... you work for the Atchison, Topeka and Santa Fe railroad, on vacation in Tombstone. Once you get situated, meet me at my store, on the corner of Sixth and Allen Street. I'm sure you'll have no trouble finding it. Hurry... you don't want to miss the stage. You have a date with destiny... and redemption."

Still despondent over his friend's death – and not knowing what else to do, Henry Sills boarded the stage.

Tuesday October 25, 1881 Noon Tombstone, A.T.

The Wells Fargo stage made an unscheduled stop in front of the San Jose House, specifically for Henry Sills and the driver gave him a friendly send-off. He checked in, and entered his room where he found plenty of clothing, all neatly stacked and folded on the bed... all in his size. Henry's head began to swim. Was it all a dream? "Maybe I'm the one who is dead!" he thought. "Maybe I was the one who took that bullet instead of Bobby!" Not knowing what would happen next, and having no other choice, Henry headed toward the corner of Sixth and Allen Street, and Ezra's store.

Henry entered the store, greeting Ezra. "Well Mr. Thornton... I'm still not sure what's going on here. This place looks like Tombstone... seems like the early 1880's... but I still don't know. If it's a movie set, it's a darn good one!"

Ezra smiled, "Mr. Sills... this *is* Tombstone. And as for the date; just look at the calendar."

Henry turned to a calendar hanging on the wall. The year said 1881, the month was October, and each day was crossed out, up to and including the 24th. Henry turned to Ezra with an incredulous look on his face, "Are you telling me this is October 25th, 1881... the day before the OK Corral gunfight?"

Before Ezra could answer, Henry heard the door open behind him. Knowing that what he and Ezra were about to discuss would not make any sense to anyone else... and should probably not be overheard by anyone else, Henry simply turned to see who was entering.

Ezra raised his hand in greeting, "Good day Wyatt!" "Good day Ezra!" came the reply.

Henry was stunned. It was Wyatt Earp... WYATT EARP! As Wyatt moved closer into the darkened recess of the back of the store, Henry could see Wyatt's face more clearly. All Henry could do was stare at the tall man with the regal moustache and piercing blue eyes. Henry and Wyatt exchanged glances, but not a word was said. Henry couldn't bring himself to speak!

Wyatt smiled at Ezra, "I don't suppose you have any more of your home-brew do you, Mr. Thornton?"

Ezra returned Wyatt's wide smile with his own, "Wyatt, you know I'm never out. You know where it is. Please help yourself!"

Wyatt turned and reached into the large wooden barrel in the middle of the floor retrieving an ice-cold bottle of sarsaparilla. Ezra followed with, "And as always Mr. Earp... for my friends, my bottled brew is always on the house!"

"Well" said Wyatt, "I have business to attend to. I'll see you later, Ezra... and thanks" Wyatt turned and quickly left, leaving Henry with his chin on his chest.

In a moment, Henry was able to compose himself and found his voice, "That looked just like...my friend Bobby Dumas! Or does Bobby Dumas look like Wyatt Earp? Man! What the hell is going on here? Ezra...?... Mr. Thornton?"

Ezra smiled at Henry's astonishment, and reached into the ever-present ice-filled wooden barrel in the middle of his store. "Henry, you look like you could use a drink! Here... have a sarsaparilla – on me!"

Henry reached for the cold bottle, leaned back against the wooden sales counter, and tried to make sense of his day. Ezra gave him a moment to collect his thoughts, and then looked very intent, more so than Henry had yet seen him, and began to address the sarsaparilla-sipping reenactor, "Now... if you want to redeem yourself, if you want to stop feeling guilty about Bobby Dumas, if you want to save Wyatt Earp, here's what I need you to do... and you must follow my instructions precisely...."

Wednesday October 26, 1881   1:50PM   Tombstone, A.T.

Henry Sills had been wandering around Tombstone all morning, taking in the sights and sounds of what appeared to him to be... Tombstone. It sure looked like a new mining camp in southeastern Arizona Territory – new for 1881! It all looked so real... the buildings... the people... the way they dressed and talked. If it was a hoax, he thought, it was a darned good one. He walked to the edges of town, north south east and west, perhaps hoping to find some trace of the twentieth century that would tell him it was all a sham. But there were no traces – only endless desert beyond the town's fringes. All he could do was play along for the time being.

Henry checked his pocket watch – it was 1:45PM, and he remembered Ezra's instructions about where to be on Fremont Street in just a few minutes. He hurried to his assigned spot, still not believing what he thought he was about to see. History was going to happen right before his very own eyes.

Moments later he arrived and stationed himself on the north side of Fremont Street across from the alley at the back of the OK Corral. He witnessed four men in the empty lot, one with a bandaged head. "That must be Ike!" he thought. Ike had received a rap on the head earlier in the day courtesy of the Earps. The men were obviously irritated, and spoke loudly, vowing to kill Virgil and Wyatt if they "dared show their faces" in the street.

Henry listened for a few more minutes, then turned and walked back up Fremont Street, stopping a man on the street and inquiring about who Virgil Earp was, and where he could find him. Henry felt foolish asking the question. "Hell" he thought, "I've read so much about the Earps, I feel I know them personally. Why would I have to ask such a foolish question?" But he somehow felt irrevocably compelled to follow Ezra's instructions to the letter.

The man pointed out Virgil standing at Hafford's Corner – the northeast corner of 4th and Allen. Henry went over to Virgil, just as Ezra had advised him to do, and told him a small band of angry men were planning to gun down him and his brothers... along with Doc Holliday. Virgil thanked him for the information, then turned to his brothers Wyatt, and Morgan, and Doc Holliday and said, "We have business to attend to!"

The four men turned and began walking up Fourth Street to Fremont. Henry followed thinking, "I can't believe I'm going to see the actual OK Corral gunfight! And Bobby Dumas... or at least it sure looks like Bobby, is playing the part of Wyatt. Man, what is going on here? This is too real to be a dream. I'll just play along and see where this goes."

A few tense moments later, the Earps and Holliday approached the empty lot behind the OK Corral between Fly's photography studio and Harwood's boarding house. Henry could see the Clanton and McLaury brothers waiting and knew what was going to happen next... and crossed Fremont Street for a better view.

The Earps and Holliday spread out. He could tell there were words being said but couldn't hear them. Then he saw Virgil' s arm go up, holding Doc's walking stick, and knew Virgil was trying to stop what was inevitable. But it was too late and the fighting was on. The air filled with lead and acrid smoke. Ike Clanton ran up to Wyatt pleading for his life - right on cue. Wyatt threw him off yelling, "The fighting's commenced. Get to fighting or get away" and with that, Ike ran off.

In thirty seconds, it was over...just as Henry Sills had played the re-enactment so many times before... except that this was the real fight... or it sure seemed like it. As he stood in awe of what he had just witnessed, it occurred to him that someone was just behind him and to one side. He turned to see Ezra watching him, a slight smile on his lips.

Ezra stepped forward to address Henry, "So... what's next Mr. Sills? How does history play itself out?

Henry thought for a moment, "Well... the Clantons and McLaury's will want the Earps and Holliday tried for murder. There will be a coroner's inquest in Judge Spicer's court... and the Earps and Holliday will be exonerated... right?"

Ezra smiled, "You are assuming that is what will happen. You are assuming that history... this episode of it anyway, is a foregone conclusion; that everything will play out exactly as you have read about it and re-enacted it. You are assuming that life is pre-ordained, that destiny cannot be changed."

Henry looked puzzled, "Isn't it?"

Ezra looked at Henry with a stern countenance, "Is it... isn't it? We'll see. And...oh yes... there is still the matter of your redemption!"

Henry had almost forgotten about that and grinned at Ezra, "Well, I see Wyatt Earp didn't get killed in this version of the OK Corral shootout. In fact, he wasn't even touched. So far, everything seems to have gone as I have always read about... but that says nothing about my redemption!"

Ezra smiled again, "Mr. Sills, your redemption will come soon enough. And that inquest...it'll be lengthy! The Clantons and McLaury's have a lot of friends around these parts... who will testify to anything that suits them. Make a mental note of everything you have seen and heard here today. You will need the information later. For now, just enjoy the sights here in Tombstone... but stay out of Spicer's courtroom. We'll talk again soon."

Saturday November 19, 1881   11:50AM   Tombstone, A.T.

For weeks, Henry Sills had been following the progress of the coroner's inquest in the local papers and from what he could pick up from talking to people on the street. He spent his time strolling around town and watching life go by in 1881. His room had been paid for ahead of time by Ezra, and whenever he felt hungry, he stopped by the Can-Can restaurant on the corner or Fourth and Allen Street, and enjoyed a meal – each time adding the cost to Ezra's running tab.

At Ezra's request, he had not gone to any of the courtroom proceedings. And he kept thinking that as he and Ezra pulled away from the field in Riverside, California where Bobby Dumas had died, Ezra promised to have him back in time for supper. It seemed like eons ago. He wasn't sure how long he would be stuck in 1881, but it seemed that certain events simply had to play themselves out... and he, Henry Sills, old-west reenactor, railroad buff, and Riverside County Fire Dept paramedic would be an integral part... although he wasn't sure how he fit in.

Henry walked along the boardwalk on Allen Street, on his way to a lunch meeting with Ezra at the Can-Can Restaurant. When Henry arrived, Ezra was sitting at a table along with two other men.

The three men stood as Henry approached. Ezra spoke, "Henry, I would like you to meet Attorneys Tom Fitch and Webster Street. Gentlemen, may I present Mr. Henry Sills..."

The men shook hands and sat down, the restaurant abuzz with miners, businessmen, and people of all stations taking their mid-day meal. Henry looked at both of the men he just met, "You are the lawyers defending the Earps and Doc Holliday!" Henry caught himself as he almost blurted the half statement, half question posed to his new acquaintances.

Tom Fitch gave a passing glance to Ezra, the words not spoken, but the eyes asking, "Who is this man... and why are we meeting." Fitch addressed Henry, "Indeed we are – and what do you do, Mr.

66

Sills."

Before Henry could answer, Ezra spoke up, "Mr. Sills is an old friend of mine – came here from Las Vegas, New Mexico. He's a locomotive engineer – taking a little vacation here in our fine city."

Henry had no idea how to respond or where Ezra might be going with his story. But he didn't have much time to think about it when Webster Street chimed in, "I see...have you been here long? I supposed you have heard about the affray out on Fremont Street a few weeks ago?"

Again, Ezra spoke for Henry, "He arrived here the 25th of last month – the day before that awful affair on Fremont Street. In fact, oddly enough, Mr. Sills was present... right across the street when the fighting started. He saw everything, didn't you Henry?"

Henry looked puzzled and glanced at Ezra, not quite knowing what to say. But Ezra's eyes told him now was the time to speak, and to speak about what he saw on October 26th. "Indeed I did" reported Henry. "Although I couldn't hear everything that was said immediately prior to the street fight, I certainly saw everything!"

Henry Sills spent the next several minutes describing in great detail what he saw and heard – how Virgil Earp had raised his arm trying to stop the fight – how Ike Clanton pleaded for his life and was thrown off by Wyatt. He even described the wounds sustained by the Earp party, Morgan being shot across the shoulders and the two minor wounds sustained by Doc and Virgil.

The two attorneys looked at each other in amazement. Tom Fitch looked at Ezra, "Yesterday Ezra, I thought this case was sunk... and the Earps and Holiday would be on their way to jail. As I told you yesterday, we needed a miracle! I thought you were kidding when you said you could deliver one. Mr. Sills is indeed a miracle!"

Webster Street looked directly at Henry, "Mr. Sills, you are going to testify for the defense!"

Henry looked at Ezra with a look of surprise – and horror. Ezra smiled his usual all-knowing smile, "Don't worry Henry. It will be alright. We'll go to my store after lunch. I have some knowledge of the law. I'll prompt you on what to say... and how to say it. You'll be fine!"

Tuesday November 22, 1881 9:15AM   Judge Spicer's Courtroom Tombstone, A.T.

On the morning of Tuesday, November 22nd, Henry Sills and Ezra Thornton walked into the courtroom of Judge Wells Spicer and sat just behind the table where Attorneys Fitch and Street were sitting.

As Judge Spicer entered the court, all rose, and the Judge called the court into session, looking at Tom Fitch. "Call your first witness, counselor!"

Tom Fitch stood again and turning called out, "I wish to call Mr. H.F. Sills to the stand!"

Henry looked at Ezra as he rose. Ezra gave Henry one of his all-knowing smiles and said softly so only Henry could hear him, "Your redemption is at hand."

Henry wasn't sure what Ezra meant but made his way to the witness stand. After he was sworn in, Attorney Fitch began.

Fitch: "Please state your name and home city for the record."

Sills: "My name is H. F. Sills. My home is in Las Vegas New Mexico."

Fitch: "And what is your present occupation?"

Sills: "I am a locomotive engineer."

Henry looked at Ezra for reassurance. Ezra had spent a good deal of time coaching Henry on what to say... and how to say it. Ezra returned a reassuring glance and a very subtle nod.

Fitch: "How did you happen to come to Tombstone?"

Sills: "At the present time I am on lay-off from the Atchison – Topeka and Santa Fe railroad."

Fitch: "When did you arrive in Tombstone?"

Sills: "On October 25th."

Fitch: "Were you a witness to a street brawl on Fremont Street on the afternoon of October 26th of this year?"

Sills: "I was indeed."

Fitch: "Can you please describe the events of that afternoon?"

Sills: "I saw four or five men standing in front of the OK Corral on October 26th, about two o'clock in the afternoon, talking of some trouble they had had with Virgil Earp, and they made threats at the time that on meeting him they would kill him on sight. Some one of the party spoke up at the time and said: 'That they would kill the whole party of Earps when they met them.' I then walked up the street and made inquiry as to who Virgil Earp and the Earps were. A man on the street pointed out Virgil Earp to me and told me he was the city marshal. I went over and called him one side, and told him of the threats that I had overheard this party make. One of the men that made the threats had a bandage around his head at the time, and the day of the funeral he was pointed out to me as Isaac Clanton. I recognized him as one of the party I had seen at the OK Corral. A few minutes after I had spoken to the marshal. I saw him and a party start down Fourth Street. I followed them down as far as the post office. Then I got sight of the party that I had overheard making those threats. I thought there would be trouble and I crossed the street. I saw the marshal go up and speak to this other party. I was not close enough to hear their conversation, but saw them pull out their revolvers immediately. The marshal had a cane in his right hand at the time. He throwed up his hand and spoke. I did not hear the words though. By that time Billy Clanton and Wyatt Earp had fired their guns off. The marshal then changed his cane from one hand to the other and pulled his revolver out. He seemed to be hurt at the time, and fell down. He got up immediately and went to shooting. The shooting became general."

Fitch: "Did you know Wyatt, Virgil, or Morgan Earp or Dr. John Henry Holliday prior to this time?"

Sills: "No sir"

Again Henry looked at Ezra. Again, Ezra gave an approving nod. Henry felt like he was lying through his teeth. He had read so much about the Earps, and knew so much about them, he felt they were his own brothers – in 1994. But here, in 1881, H.F. Sills had just arrived in Tombstone the day before the fateful fight – and had no prior knowledge of anyone in town.

Fitch: "Did you know Frank or Tom McLaury prior to this time?"

Sills: "No sir."

Fitch: "Did you know Ike or Billy Clanton prior to this time?"

Sills: "No sir."

Fitch: "Prior to arriving in Tombstone, were you aware of any animosities – any troubles between the parties in question?"

Sills: "No sir"

Fitch: "Do you have any idea why these two parties would want to shoot at each other?"

Sills: "I only know that I heard the Clanton and McLaury parties talking among themselves about some trouble with Virgil Earp on the afternoon of October 26th."

Fitch: "And what time was that?"

Sills: "About 2PM."

Fitch: "Thank you Mr. Sills. You may step down."

Tom Fitch called his next witness as Ezra and Henry exited the courtroom and headed toward Ezra's store, long since overdue in opening for the day's business. When they were out of ear-shot of the courtroom, Ezra turned to Henry and said, "So how does it feel to be redeemed?"

Henry paused for a moment. "I don't feel redeemed. I mean... what did I really do in there? I thought you were going to have me use my medical skills to save someone here in 1881 to redeem myself. What I did was I told a pack of lies. With all the books I've read over the years, I feel I know the Earps better than I know many of my friends. I knew about all the troubles between the Earps and the cow-boy faction! I know about Wyatt's political aspirations and Ike's dirty dealings! I know the whole damned story and I lied about it... and I don't feel any better. In fact I feel worse!"

Ezra stopped in his tracks, "And what do you know about the outcome of Judge Spicer's hearing?"

Henry stopped short, "I know that the Earps and Doc Holliday will be exonerated."

Ezra replied, "And do you know why they will be exonerated?"

Henry slid his hat back on his head and furrowed his brow, "No, not really... a combination of things I suppose."

Ezra beamed, "Trust me; you'll feel better about yourself in a few days!"

Henry Sills was called to testify several more times and was cross examined by attorneys for the prosecution. But he stuck to his story and would not be rattled or intimidated – even by Attorney Will McLaury, brother to the slain siblings, Frank and Tom, who was determined to see the Earps and Holliday hung.

Wednesday November 30, 1881 2:00PM Judge Spicer's Courtroom

Despite the fact there was standing room only; one could have heard a pin drop as Judge Wells Spicer entered his courtroom. After a month-long inquest, with a veritable parade of witnesses and a flurry of conflicting testimony, and with all principals waiting breathlessly, Judge Spicer began a rather long and laborious reading of his decision, expounding on the many legal points involved.

As he reached his conclusion he noted, "In view of these controversies between Wyatt Earp and Isaac Clanton and Thomas McLaury and in further view of the quarrel the night before between Isaac Clanton and J.H. Holliday, I am of the opinion that the defendant, Virgil Earp, as chief of police, by subsequently calling upon Wyatt Earp and J.H. Holliday to assist him in disarming the Clantons and McLaury's committed an injudicious and censurable act; and although in this he acted incautiously and without proper circumspection, yet, when we consider the condition of affairs incident to a frontier country; the lawlessness and disregard for human life; the existence of a law-defying element in our midst; the fear and feeling of insecurity that has existed; the supposed prevalence of bad, desperate and reckless men who have been a terror to the country, and kept away capital and enterprise; and considering the many threats that had been made against the Earps, I can attach no criminality to his unwise act. In fact, as the result plainly proves, he needed the assistance and support of staunch and true friends, upon whose courage, coolness and fidelity he could depend in case of emergency."

Judge Spicer went on for a few more minutes with additional points and concluded with, "There being no sufficient cause to believe the within named Wyatt S. Earp and John H. Holliday guilty of the offense mentioned within, I order them to be released."

As would be expected, the courtroom was abuzz with excitement. Above all the commotion Henry turned to Ezra and said, "So... I knew this was how it was going to turn out. I still don't get it... and still don't feel any better about Bobby's death!"

Ezra stood and simply replied, "Follow me."

The two men walked behind the judges bench and rapped on the door to the Judge's chambers seeking entry. Ezra called out, "Wells... it's me, Ezra Thornton. May I have a moment sir?"

The door opened, "Ezra... for you? Sure come on in. What's on your mind?"

Ezra and Henry entered the room and the three men shook hands and exchanged pleasantries. Then Ezra spoke, "One quick question, Wells... if I may. Was there a turning point in this hearing where you were convinced one way or the other about the Earps and Holliday?"

Judge Spicer paused, looked at Henry for a long moment, then looked again at Ezra. "Those Clantons and McLaurys and all their cronies are bunch of thieves, liars and cut throats. I didn't believe a one of them. In fact, every damn person in this hearing seemed to have their own agenda, either for or against the Earps; everyone except Mr. Sills here. He is the only person that seemed genuinely non-partisan; the only person without an agenda, the only one with no axe to grind. How did you happen to find Mr. Sills, Ezra?"

Ezra smiled broadly, "Oh... he's just an old friend!"

"Well, I hope the Earps and Holliday bestow that honor upon Mr. Sills" replied Spicer. "If it wasn't for Mr. H.F. Sills, and given the local sentiment, this probably would have gone to trial. And had it gone to trial, I believe Will McLaury would have had a good chance to win; not fair and square mind you, but he could have won. That could have put Doc and Wyatt at the end of a rope... and I would be powerless to stop it. It's my job to execute the law; and the law says I have to hang murderers!"

Ezra moved to depart the room, "Thanks Wells. We'll leave you to your thoughts. I know it's been a tough day. Stop by later for a cold sarsaparilla... on the house!"

Ezra and Henry stepped outside into the cool November air where Ezra turned to a visibly shaken young man, "Well, you've done it. You've saved Wyatt Earp... and Doc Holliday!"

Henry stood in the middle of the courtroom not knowing what to say, and tried to grasp what had happened over the past few weeks, and especially what had happened in the last few minutes. Just then Wyatt Earp, the man himself strode by, walked right up to Henry and extended his right hand saying, "Thanks friend. I could tell by the way Judge Spicer looked at you when you were on the stand that you were about the only person he believed in there."

Henry looked down at their clasped hands, then looked into Wyatt's eyes, but saw the eyes of his friend, Bobby Dumas, and then Wyatt turned and just as quickly as he had come, was gone.

Ezra then headed down the street to his store and motioned to Henry, "Come on. We have quite a journey ahead of us. I promised I'd get you back to Riverside before supper so we have to hurry!"

Ezra and Henry walked to the OK Corral where Ezra retrieved his horses, hitched them to his large red wagon, and headed north to Benson. "Why don't you crawl in the back, change back to your other clothes, and take a little snooze, Henry" said Ezra. "You deserve it!"

Henry crawled into the back of the wagon and was soon fast asleep only to awaken what seemed like just a few moments later to the sound of Ezra's voice. "Here we are Mr. Sills, Riverside, California... at the same event we left a little while ago... and just in time for supper!"

Still somewhat dazed from his deep sleep, Henry hopped down from the tall perch of a seat where Ezra remained sitting. "Thanks for everything Ezra. I do feel better now! Will I ever see you again?"

Ezra snapped the reins to get his horses moving and simultaneously looked down at Henry, "If you ever get to Tombstone again, look me up! I'll have a cold bottle of sarsaparilla waiting for you!"

Henry replied, "Sure thing!" And Ezra was off; his horses' hooves making a loud clopping noise on the hard asphalt of the street.

Henry looked at his pocket watch. According to his watch, about an hour had passed since he and Ezra had left – "But I've been gone for over a month! How can that be?" he thought.

Just then Harold, the leader of Henry's reenactor group approached him. "Sills, where have you been? I've been all over looking for you! Are you alright? You were a mess when they took Bobby away. There was nothing more you could have done. Bobby was dead when he hit the ground. You did everything you could have done. Don't beat yourself up over this!"

Henry turned to his friend and with a faint smile replied, "You're right... I did everything possible to save Wyatt Earp!"

The Real Story Behind "The Man Who Saved Wyatt Earp"

There are great men who perform great deeds – such is the stuff of history books. Then there are ordinary men who perform extraordinary deeds – also history-book material, and also the stuff of lore and legend.

And then there are the uncelebrated, obscure men who go about their daily lives, leaving barely a minor impression in the sands of time. Perhaps they are only a footnote in a scholarly book, known only to armchair historians or patrons of the genre. But if not for their contribution, however seemingly insignificant, history may have taken a decidedly different turn. Mr. H.F. Sills was such a man.

Tombstone, in 1881 was a city divided. On one side stood the Earps - Wyatt, Virgil and Morgan and their friend, Doc Holliday. The Earps, like everyone else in Tombstone at that time, were trying to get rich off the silver that was being pulled from the ground surrounding that wide-open "mining camp." The Earps worked in law enforcement, gambling, security, and mining speculation.

On the other side stood a faction known as "The Cow-boys", a group of former Texas ruffians who were widely suspected of rustling cattle on one side of the Mexican border and selling it on the other. Despite that, and other suspected depredations, there were those in town who supported the cow-boys knowing that, despite their dubious legal veracity, played a role in the city's commerce.

There were professional and political differences as well as personal animosities. The whole business came to a head on the afternoon of October 26, 1881 as the two factions met in an alley behind the OK Corral in Tombstone. An attempt to disarm a contingent of Cow-boys by Town Marshal Virgil Earp and his deputized brothers and Doc Holliday ended in a shooting spree leaving Frank and Tom McLaury and their friend Billy Clanton dead. Virgil Earp and Doc Holliday sustained minor wounds. Morgan sustained a more serious but not mortal wound. Wyatt was unscathed. The *Tombstone Epitaph* of the following day announced, "Three Men Hurled Into Eternity In The Duration Of A Moment."

But it was not the end of the months-long bickering and sniping. It was only the beginning.

Prior to the gunfight, the Earps were viewed, if not favorably, at least socially acceptable. Holliday was tolerated. Thirty seconds of flying lead changed that. Many then considered the Earps and Holliday not much more than thugs and accused them of pre-meditated murder. It was no secret that the two parties had had words. The day of the gunfight, Ike Clanton (who ran as soon as the gunfight started) was seen prowling the streets of Tombstone armed (illegally) with a rifle, looking for the Earps and Holliday – ready to shoot them on-sight.

Others, thought the cow-boys got what they had coming to them.

But neither side welcomed the violence and bloodshed – and the negative publicity that it caused. Bad publicity was bad for business. It scared away new business capital from the east and upset the rhythm of growth – so important to those who stood to benefit from it.

Days after the shootout, an inquest was opened in Judge Wells Spicer's courtroom to determine if there was enough evidence to conduct a trial for murder against the Earps and Holliday. The proceedings sometimes referred to as the OK Corral Inquest or the Spicer Hearing lasted nearly a month. It had all the trappings of a modern-day media event with conflicting testimony and high drama.

On November 22, 1881, Mr. H.F. Sills, an engineer on leave from the Atchison, Topeka and Santa Fe railroad took the stand for the defense.

Arriving in Tombstone via Wells Fargo coach only a day before the gunfight, Sills had no knowledge of either party, or their on-going feud. Unlike the local residents, Sills had no ax no grind – no ulterior motive – no business to support - no political ally to mollify. He had only the truth to tell.

But some did not believe Sills and considered him part of an elaborate conspiracy – an Earp ally, cleverly placed and tactically maneuvered to support the Earp side and discredit the Cow-boys. And it is not hard to see how some would come to that conclusion. Little is known of Sills prior to the hearing. And afterward, it was as if he simply vanished – disappearing into the anonymity of time except for one brief mention in a newspaper three months later.

Despite grilling from the prosecution, Sill's testimony was seen by Judge Spicer as honest and truthful. Earp fans point to Sills' testimony as an island of integrity in a sea of partisan mudslinging and half-truths. Some might even see Sills as the Earps' savior. Cow -boy partisans decried Sills' testimony and tried to discredit him.

Some consider Sills the only true non-partisan witness at the Spicer hearing. Some might call him a "dream witness", a man with all the right answers. Others contend that he was simply a solid citizen, doing what any other upstanding citizen would do

Corroborating virtually all of the Earp testimony, Sills testified that he had been standing in front of the OK Corral and heard threats made against the Earp party.

Upon discovering who Marshal Virgil Earp was, Sills promptly found him and warned him of the impending danger. He told Virgil that a "party of armed men" had been making threats against him. Sills, at the time, did not know that the party was cow-boys, only that they were armed and posed a threat.

Sills then told how he had witnessed the confrontation itself.

He stated that on the afternoon of October 26th, he had witnessed four or five men standing in front of the OK Corral talking about trouble they were having with Virgil Earp and that they planned to kill him on sight if they should run into him. He noted that one of the men had a bandage around his head. This would have been Ike Clanton, the bandage covering a wound inflicted by the Earps earlier in the day.

He told how Virgil Earp had raised his cane, and spoke to the other party although he, Sills, did not hear what was said. It was at that time that Virgil called for the cow-boys to disarm themselves and cow-boy Billy Clanton and Wyatt shot first – almost simultaneously. After that, the shooting "became general."

Some note that Sills "remembered" minute details about the gunfight, details that someone close enough to watch and yet close enough to be in harm's way, would probably not remember given the commotion caused by 30 rounds being discharged in as many seconds. Yet despite being able to cite, in perfect order those details crucial to the Earps' defense, Sills remained imprecise about his arrival in Tombstone. He arrived from Benson in a Wells Fargo coach with two other men, the driver and another passenger although he could not identify or describe either of them.

Sills seemed too much to be the right person in precisely the right place at precisely the right time and... for precisely the right reason to hold any credibility. Sills had virtually no reason to be in Tombstone. He had neither family, nor friends, nor business in Tombstone. He could not identify the men he arrived with in Tombstone. He heard threats that no one else heard.

On the other hand, would the Earps risk their careers at the least, their lives at the worst, on a perjured witness? Maybe - given the consequences. But maybe not since Will McLaury, attorney for the prosecution, a talented and determined man, was a brother to two cow-boys slain at the OK Corral.

Further, would the attorneys knowingly risk such a venture? Maybe. But maybe not since this was only an inquest, not a trial, and there was plenty of opportunity and time to discover a conspiracy.

Or was it just a big, elaborate hoax?

How does a person suddenly appear at a particular time and place, play a key role in a life and death legal struggle, and then suddenly vanish without a trace? Researchers and genealogists have tried in vain for years to find what happened to mystery-man H.F. Sills.

Given today's technological ability to gather, store and disseminate personal data, it's pretty hard to simply "disappear." But in 1881, disappearing; falling from the public record, or changing one's name was not difficult. Ben Sippy, Tombstone's first city marshal left town when cow-boy antics began to be too much for him. He was never heard from again. And when the man we now commonly refer to as Curly Bill Brocius was arrested for the shooting of Tombstone lawman Fred White in October, 1880, he gave several different fictitious names to throw-off officials. At first, they had no idea who they had arrested.

Sills testified that he had been born in Canada and was 36 years old at the time. A search of Canadian birth records of the 1840's, covering his time period, did not reveal an H.F. Sills – although there were several close approximations. One, an H.N. Sills was born in 1848, meaning a three to four year difference existed; unless Canadian officials recorded the year incorrectly.

Exhaustive reviews of local newspapers from Sills' hometown in Canada for late 1881 and 1882 show no indication that he returned home during that time. One would expect that had Sills returned home, there would have been some mention that a "local-boy" had made national headlines during such a celebrated inquest – but there was no such story.

Present-day interviews with families using the Sills name in that area proved fruitless.

It is possible that a Henry F. Sills (spelled "Cills" in the 1880 census) originally from Canada was married in May, 1878 in Iowa, and gave his occupation as Railroad Fireman could have been this person? But he disappears after the 1880 census. Further, Sills did not mention in his testimony that he was married.

Perhaps Sills wanted to disappear at the conclusion of the inquest and made a conscious effort to hide his tracks. A crowd of angry cow-boys who had again unsuccessfully attempted to bring legal pressure to bear against the Earp party was a good thing to hide from. Or... maybe he wasn't quick enough to hide and the cow-boys made short work of him, the local coyotes assisting in making the body disappear forever.

Despite virtually saving Wyatt Earp, his brothers and Doc Holliday from what certainly would have been a lengthy trial and possible murder conviction; Sills was never again mentioned by any of the involved parties. Sills' name was never mentioned in Stuart Lake's landmark tome, *Wyatt Earp – Frontier Marshal.*

It would seem that someone who played such a pivotal position in a high-profile legal proceeding would write about it. Or at least, relate the story to someone who would publish the memoirs – somewhere – at some time. No Sill's memoirs exist.

For those who consider Sills a phony or a conspirator, there is only supposition and conjecture. For those who believe Sills' testimony, he provides enough verifiable truth to convey veracity.

The only thing we can be sure of is the testimony of H.F. Sills resulted in Judge Spicer's decision, which read in part, "I do not believe that any trial jury that could be got together would, on all the evidence taken before me find the defendants guilty of any offence".

Other Details

The Can-Can restaurant mentioned several times in the story was indeed one of Tombstone's favorite eateries.

The San Jose House opened for business in Tombstone in January 1879. It continues to serve (March, 2010) as a lodging house for guests.

William McLaury was indeed the brother of the McLaury bothers slain in the gunfight – and he did arrive in Tombstone from Texas with vengeance on his mind, and hatred in his heart.

Addie Bourland did in fact own a dress shop across Fremont Street from the OK Corral from where she witnessed the gunfight. She testified as well.

Tom Fitch, Webster Street, James Howard, and T.J. Drum were the actual lawyers for the defense.

The name "Henry" is pure conjecture. No records actually show Sills' first name. He was always listed as H.F. Sills. He was however, according to the Earp inquest court records, a locomotive engineer on vacation in Tombstone. Why someone would vacation in a mining camp, having no family or friends or any other contact there is beyond comprehension. Beyond reason... beyond...

Chapter 4: THE STAGE DRIVER

"I sell a number of products, sir. But mostly I make dreams come true and occasionally... I dispense justice."

Ezra T. Thornton March 15, 1981

Tuesday, March 8, 1881, 8:55AM Tombstone, Arizona Territory

The sun shone brightly as Ezra T. Thornton rounded the corner of 6th Street onto Allen Street completing the short walk from his home. He stepped onto the wooden boardwalk and under the protective canopy above, his hard-heeled shoes making a distinctive clumping sound against the wood.

He unlocked the door, stepped into his mercantile store, and walked to the back where he hung his frock coat and high top-hat on a wooden peg near the pot bellied stove. Ezra brushed back his long strands of white hair, a white that matched his closely cropped beard. His dark maroon cravat tie provided striking complement to his bright red, brocade vest.

"Another day!" he thought as he straightened his tie and pulled his vest taut to his waist. Ezra was always well dressed, well groomed, a man of station. "Another day to..."

A ringing bell attached to his front door interrupted Ezra's thought. Phin, the local manager for the Kinnear Stage Lines entered the store. Usually, Phin was dressed in the business fashion of the day, a sack suit topped with a high-crowned derby. However, today he was dressed in rough corduroy pants tucked into tall boots, "gus" shirt, and a bright red bandanna. His long, dirty-blond hair was sticking out of big black Stetson. Usually jovial, Phin wore a very stern look on his face this morning. Phin walked to the center of the store as Ezra moved behind the counter, ready to serve his first customer of the day.

"Mornin' Mr. Thornton!"

"Good morning Phin. What can I get for you today?"

"Got any shotgun shells?"

"Certainly... will one box do?"

"Sure... I don't expect any more trouble than one box of shells can handle. And just put it on my account."

Ezra turned to a shelf behind him, grabbed a box of shells and handed it to Phin. "You aren't driving the morning stage to Benson are you, Phin?"

"Yup....got to" came the reply. "I lost another driver last night and don't have anyone to fill in on short notice. Last night it seems my driver, John, was chased by highway men. They shot at him but he got away. He's got a family.... doesn't want his children to grow up without a father so he's taking a job in one of the mines."

Phin took his box of ammunition, thanked Ezra, and turned to walk out. As if hitting a brick wall, Phin stopped in his tracks, and turned back to Ezra. "Say, you know a lot of people don't you?" he said.

"I do indeed sir." came the reply across the store's curved glass display case. "I know practically everyone here in town, and have contacts all over the country due to the people I purchase products from. I know people in New York, Boston, St. Louis, and Chicago. And... I know the distributors in San Francisco and Prescott. I know people all over. What is your point?"

A faint smile crossed Phin's lips, "With all those contacts you have, do you suppose you can find me a stage driver? I mean... someone that will stay more than a few weeks? Hell...maybe you can order me one from one of those suppliers of yours?"

Both men chuckled at the strange thought of simply "ordering" a person through a mercantile supplier.

Ezra leaned over the display case and with a sly smile and wink replied, "Well, with my contacts, I can get *most* anything. I'll see what I can do!"

Tuesday, March 15, 1981 Tucson, Arizona

The calendar said early spring. But the weather said summer as the sweat began to trickle down Buddy's back. Or maybe it was just that he was nervous as he and his friend, Peter, sat in Buddy's old Buick near the end of a strip mall, Buddy behind the wheel smoking incessantly. With every puff, he was reminded of his mother as he was growing up... telling him to stop smoking, or stop doing this or that. His mother always told him he was a naughty boy and would never amount to anything.

After sitting quietly for the entire ride to the mall, Peter finally spoke up. "Do we really have to do this Buddy? We can find another way to get back at them! This is just going to get us in deep trouble. We'll never get away with it! We might even get killed!"

Buddy, unshaven for several days, his dark beard seen strikingly against his white tee shirt flashed a frustrated frown at what had been his route partner and remained a long-time friend. "Pete, you know the score. Since those good-for-nothings fired us three years ago, all I can get is crappy, minimum wage jobs that nobody wants. And you've been unemployed for months. I'm sick of it. I think that breathalyzer test was wrong. We only had two beers before work that morning! Not the 5 or 6 they said we had!"

Buddy stared out the window at the entrance to the mall. The entrance he knew would be used by the Tucson Armored Security truck as it entered the mall lot – the same route he had driven three years before. Buddy knew the truck would stop at every store, make a pick-up, and head directly to the bank. This was the last stop for the route. The truck would be loaded. "I figure, by hitting a Tucson Armored Security armored truck, we can get back at them. Hurt them! And we can make off with the money and start over again in Mexico! I hear American dollars go a long way down there. We can live like kings and snub our noses at Tucson Armored Security!"

Pete turned to Buddy, wiping the sweat from his forehead with a stained handkerchief. "Are you sure Buddy? Don't you want to think this through?"

Buddy took a long drag on his cigarette. Then, pulling it slowly from his mouth, held it between his forefinger and thumb. "I've thought about it long and hard and made up my mind."

Buddy pointed out the windshield with his cigarette hand at the armored truck entering the lot. It pulled up in front of the first store. Buddy smiled at Peter, "Here comes destiny!"

The truck made several stops as it moved along the curb. Each stop was the same. The driver remained inside the truck at the wheel. Two guards exited the truck. One stood outside, his hand on his holstered gun while the second man went inside the store.

Finally, the truck pulled up at what Buddy knew was the last stop. Buddy and Peter watched as the two guards exited the truck, one stepping briskly into the convenience store. Buddy started the Buick's engine, the tailpipe belching smoke and soot, and looked intently at the door to the convenience store. Inside, he could see the guard taking the cash bag from the store clerk. The two seemed to be chatting giving Buddy the extra minute he needed. Buddy jammed the Buick into Drive. "It's now or never baby!" he yelled.

The Buick quickly accelerated and wheeled to a screeching stop at the back of the armored truck. Buddy threw the shifter into Park, flung open his door and pulled his revolver all in what seemed to

Peter to be one smooth action.

The guard standing at the truck tried to pull his gun from its holster. Buddy could tell immediately that the guard was every bit as scared as he was. In what seemed like an eternity to both Buddy and the guard, the guard's gun finally cleared its holster only to be dropped. The guard looked at Buddy in a grimace that said, "It's my time!" But Buddy wanted to hurt the company, not the guards. Buddy's .44 spit lead and the guard went down with blood gushing from his thigh, his pistol now totally out of reach.

Buddy then turned to the store's door to find the first guard coming at him with his gun drawn, ready to fire. Time seemed to stand still as Buddy tried to get his pistol into a firing position. But the guard already had his gun at the ready. Buddy winced, almost knowing that the guard had him and could get his gun into play first.

Just when Buddy thought he was dead, a shot rang out from behind him and the guard went down, his gun and money bag flying out in front of him right towards Buddy. Buddy looked around quickly to see Peter standing in the parking lot near the Buick, still in the military firing stance he had been trained to use in the Marines, smoke coming from the barrel of his pistol.

Buddy then looked towards the truck and a very nervous driver staring out the window at his co-workers lying on the ground, their life oozing onto the pavement. He recognized the driver, Ronnie. Buddy called out, "Hey Ron, is that you? I thought you were going to retire back when I worked this route?"

"I was – but I enjoyed the work too much! Isn't that ironic!" The guard's muffled voice was barely audible through the thick plating of the truck.

"Well, how do you like the work now, Ron? Your friends are bleeding to death out here. Open the door, give me the bags, and I won't finish off these two losers!" growled Buddy.

"You, of all people know I can't do that, Buddy!" came the muffled reply.

A tense moment went by. Then Buddy looked intently at the guard who had dropped his gun. "I'm pullin' back on the hammer, Ronnie. Mr. Fumbles here is going to be the first to go! You can be the hero who saved these two. Or you can be known as the first Tucson Armored Security guard who forced the death of two co-workers. What's it going to be?"

Ronnie removed his hat, running his hand over his balding head. "Ok...Ok... don't shoot them. I'm coming out!"

The door began to slowly open. Buddy could see his former friend; his white moustache and paunchy form began to light from the truck. Suddenly, the one hand that he had been pretending to steady himself with by using a pull-handle inside the truck emerged into the sun-light holding a shotgun.

"Damn you Ronnie!" Buddy quickly brought his pistol into firing position and squeezed off two rounds in quick succession, one hitting Ronnie in the neck and the other right between his eyes.

Peter, hearing on-coming sirens had already jumped back into the car and was now screaming at the top of his lungs at Buddy. "Hurry Buddy! Hurry! The cops will be here any minute. Let's go, dammit!"

Buddy quickly looked back at Peter, then looked at the dead and dying guards. People in the convenience store began to peer out the window, staying low enough in case more shots were fired. All over the parking lot, people could be seen peering from around parked cars and light poles. It was as if time suddenly stopped.

Buddy shoved his pistol into his belt, threw open the armored car door and grabbed two bags within easy reach. Peter yelled at him again, "Buddy... damit... let's go!"

Buddy ran back to his car, threw the bags into the back seat and slid behind the wheel. "Next stop, Mexico!"

Robbing an armored car near an interstate highway was part of Buddy's "master plan." The Buick pulled onto Interstate 10 and quickly blended into the heavy traffic.

******

Forty-five minutes later, Buddy left Interstate 10 and headed south, down Highway 80. Buddy looked pleased with himself, and turning to Pete said, "In about another hour or so, we'll be in Agua Prieta, Mexico! I don't know how much money we have in those two bags. But if we need more, we'll get more. The same way we got this!"

The look on Peter's gaunt, pallid, face had been stoic up to this time adding years it seemed to his 35 year-old features. Now, his countenance changed to worry and grimace as he looked at Buddy in disgust. "If you are going to rob someone else, fine. Rob a vacant house or store. But for goodness sake let's not shoot anyone else, Buddy. That was never supposed to happen. You said we wouldn't shoot anyone. You said the guns was just to scare people. Damn Buddy! If we get caught, we're gonna hang!"

Buddy looked at his friend, his long hair blowing in the wind coming through the open windows as the car cruised easily along the state road. "You are just as guilty as me, old pal. We both pulled the trigger back there. But forget all that! Now how many cops do you see around us? The answer is - none! We got away just as free and clear as can be. Man, we were long-gone by the time the first cop showed up at that mall. They have no idea where we are."

"Yeah no cops..." Peter said with a frown as if he almost wished they were being chased. "It's almost too easy... like we were supposed to get away with it or something. It's creepy!"

Just as the words finished coming out of his mouth they passed a police cruiser obviously waiting for speeders as they came over the top of a rise in the road. Buddy watched the cruiser in his rearview mirror as they eased away from it. "Now ya see. That cop has no idea. He's not following us. He's not calling us in on his radio. We are f-r-e-e, free, baby! Free!"

They rode along silently for another few miles until they came across a sign promoting Tombstone and the OK Corral. Buddy smiled and looked over at Peter, "The shootout at the OK Corral – now that was a shootout. I haven't been down here for years. Since the cops apparently aren't on to us, whatdda ya say we take a quick break and get something to drink in Tombstone?"

"Sure."

In a few miles, the Buick eased off the state road and onto Sixth Street. stopping to park just short of Tombstone's main thoroughfare, Allen Street. Buddy and Peter stepped out of the car stretching and yawning. As they stepped onto the curb Peter noticed the huge, bright red wagon parked in an alley behind the building. "Wouldja look at that wagon! And look at the lettering, E.T. Thornton – Mercantile. They must use this for parades and such."

As they rounded the corner onto Allen Street, they noticed a similar but smaller sign suspended from two lengths of chain under the sidewalk overhang, signaling that they were in front of Thornton's store. They both stopped for a moment to look down Allen Street. "Well..." noted Buddy, "this really does look like the old west. Everyone is in their old-west clothing. It must be some sort of special event!"

The streets were filled with people dressed in 1880's clothing. Men wore boots, frock coats, wide brimmed hats, and vests. Some looked like businessmen in top hats. Others wore chaps, gun belts and carried lariats. The women dressed in polonaise dresses, long skirts, and blouses buttoned to the neck accompanied by fancy velour hats with feathers. Peter gave Buddy a little shove. "I'm thirsty! Let's see if Mr. E.T. Thornton has any cold drinks!"

Just as they were about to enter the store, Ezra T. Thornton stepped outside and stood in front of the door. "Good afternoon gentlemen. Welcome to Tombstone and the first annual Gathering Of The Gunfighters event!"

Buddy looked at his friend and smiled wryly. "Gathering Of The Gunfighters, huh?"

Buddy then turned to Ezra. "You must be E.T. Thornton?"

"I am indeed. Call me Ezra.... and can I call you Buddy?" came the reply.

Buddy's jaw dropped to his chin. "How do you know my name? Have we met before?"

Ezra smiled, "The last time you were in my mercantile, you were filling your pockets with rock candy. Your mother called you a naughty boy. It cost you your next-week's allowance. Do you remember that day?"

Buddy rubbed his chin, "Ah yes... I do remember that day! You were there... and here you are again... and you don't look a day older. How in blazes..."

Buddy was interrupted by his partner, "What do you sell in this mercantile store of yours?" asked Pete.

Ezra smiled and became animated. "I sell a number of products, sir. But mostly I make dreams come true and occasionally... I dispense justice."

Buddy and Peter looked at each other in amazement. Peter spoke up. "What the hell are you talking about? Dreams and justice?"

Ezra smiled again. "Precisely! Step into my store and I'll tell you all about it."

"Ya got anything cold in there ta drink?" Peter inquired.

"Sarsaparilla!" came the reply. "The best in town – bottle it myself. And it's the same price as it was in 1881 – only 5 cents per bottle!"

The three men stepped into the store, which was like stepping back into time. The deep but rather narrow mercantile space was typical of stores of the late 19th century. Products of all types and descriptions lined the walls on deep shelves. In front of the shelves stood glass display cases with curved glass exhibiting everything from fine jewelry to hand guns. The store seemed rather dark inside to Peter but he figured it was because they had just come in from the bright sunshine of the Arizona desert. Ezra walked over to a barrel in the middle of the store, reached in, his long white hair falling over his shoulders, and retrieved two bottles of sarsaparilla and handed them to the two men. The bottles dripped water as they had been sitting in ice. Buddy and Peter each took a long swig from their bottles.

Buddy wiped his mouth with sleeve, then turned to Ezra, "Now what's this about makin' dreams come true and dispensin' justice?"

"Precisely. Look around sir. The dreams are all around you!"

Ezra began to walk around the store and point at various items for sale. "There are dreams in the picks and shovels piled in that corner for the prospectors hoping to strike gold or silver. There are dreams in the playing cards in the display case for those who want to try their luck in games of chance. There are dreams in the large pots and pans that I sell to restauranteurs whose dream it is to have their own successful business. There are dreams in the women's dresses and men's boots, hats, and other clothing items I sell, that clothe the people of this fair city. And there are dreams in the foodstuff I supply to help keep everyone fed in a mining camp such as this. I try very hard to give people what they want – and what they deserve – to make their dreams come true. Of course, gentlemen, not all dreams come true. But I try."

Buddy and Peter looked almost disappointed as if Ezra was going to tell them something magical. Peter spoke up, "I didn't know people were still prospecting out here. And how many games of chance can there possibly be here in Tombstone. This is a tourist town – not Las Vegas!"

Ezra winked at the two men who continued to sip their drinks, "You'd be surprised what goes on here in Tombstone... quite surprised."

Buddy spoke up again. "And what about the part about justice? What's that about?"

Buddy was almost afraid to ask about justice knowing that he and Peter had just shot three men. But Buddy figured that Ezra would have some other mundane explanation for his version of justice so there was no harm in asking.

"Ah yes, justice." Ezra started. "Well, you see Buddy, justice comes in many forms. So it's hard for me to say exactly what form it will take."

The words no sooner fell out of Ezra's mouth when a voice amplified through a bull-horn filtered into the store from the center of Allen Street, "Buddy and Pete... we know you are in the mercantile store... This is the Arizona Highway Patrol. Come out with your hands up!"

Buddy's amiable demeanor turned suddenly sour and Peter was visibly rattled. Ezra's voice turned dark and solemn, "Word travels fast here in the desert. I know that you two had a very interesting and potentially profitable morning in Tucson. Too bad you won't be able to cash-in on your endeavors. I think the men outside the door in the blue uniforms have a different vision for you two."

Buddy and Pete had had their backs to the store's front door the whole time they had been talking to Ezra. Suddenly, they turned around to see four Arizona Highway Patrol cars parked on Allen

Street with patrolmen crouching behind the cars for cover, guns drawn. All the period-dressed people walking on Allen Street had disappeared or were peeking around the corner of the Bird Cage Theatre, hoping to catch a glimpse of some modern-day mayhem in a yester-west town.

A voice from a bullhorn again penetrated the front of the store, "This is the Arizona Highway Patrol. Buddy Philpot and Peter Roering, we know you are inside the store. We have the building surrounded. Drop your weapons and come out with your hands up and nobody will get hurt. You have 5 minutes to comply!"

Peter was visibly shaking. "Dammit Buddy. I told you this was gonna happen. Someone in Tucson must have gotten a description of the car or the plate number. Now what are we gonna do!"

Buddy pulled his pistol from its hiding place in his belt under his shirt and stuck it directly in Ezra's face. "I'll tell you what we're gonna do Petey. We are going to take Mr. Thornton here as a hostage and walk right out of here. Those cops may want to shoot us, but they won't shoot a hostage... especially an old guy like Thornton. Come on Thornton. We're going to take a little ride to Mexico!"

Despite Buddy and Pete being extremely agitated, Ezra kept his cool. Even with a gun in his face, and a hot breeze blowing through the screen door, Ezra never broke a sweat.

Buddy grabbed Ezra's arm, put the gun to his head, and began to lead him to the front of the store. Ezra, very calmly and assuredly offered an alternative to Buddy's plan. "Not that I wouldn't love to take a ride to Mexico with you gentlemen but I have a better idea."

"What could be better than a hostage?" growled Buddy.

"The Arizona Highway Patrol gave you five minutes to come out" explained Ezra. "That will give you time enough to put on some of my old-west costume clothes. I'm sure there are sizes to fit you. You tell the cops there are two customers in here that you are going to set free, then take me as a hostage. Meanwhile, you tie me up in a chair. Getting dressed will be easy. You probably noticed that you can't see in the front of the store in the daytime because of the way the sunlight shines on this side of the street. Once you are dressed, go out the front door. The cops won't shoot because they will think you two are the customers. The wide-brimmed cowboy hats will hide your faces if you keep your heads down. Then you go blend in with the crowd, wait a while, then head for Mexico. In fact, if you go down to First Street, at the other end of Allen, go to the Kinnear Stage Lines. Ask for Phin. Phin runs a transport service back and forth to Mexico for products sold all over the southwest. Tell him you want a job driving to Mexico. Tell him I sent you. He'll understand. He'll make sure you get what you need."

Pete looked at Buddy with fear and panic written all over his face. "Whadda ya think, Buddy? At least this way, we can get out of here. If we take a hostage its gonna be more difficult. With Thornton's plan, we can just high-tail it out of here. I like the idea."

Buddy flashed a solemn face to Pete, then Ezra. He thought for half a moment, then smiled at Ezra. "Show us those clothes old man!"

Buddy and Pete followed Ezra's plan pulling on corduroy pants, high, leather boots with Cuban heels, blue and brown bib shirts and the widest brimmed hats they could find. Once dressed, the two "cowboys" tied Ezra to a chair with rope from his own store stock.

Their readiness came none too soon as the bull horn from Allen Street blasted another message, "Time's up! Come out with your hands up! We don't want anyone to get hurt. Come out now. Don't make this any tougher! Don't make us come in there after you!"

Buddy edged closer to the screen door knowing that anyone outside could not see in. He could see the four police cruisers and a growing number of blue uniforms crouching behind the cars. He yelled out, "We got three hostages in here – two customers and Thornton! We're gonna let the two customers go and take Thornton with us! The two customers are guys dressed like cowboys. Don't shoot them!"

A tense moment passed. Then came the reply. "This is Sergeant Taylor of the Arizona Highway Patrol. Let the two customers go. Then we'll talk about you and Mr. Thornton!"

Buddy looked at Pete, both now dressed as if it were 1881. It was a crazy idea he thought. But no more crazy than thinking he and Peter could get away with robbing an armored truck. And for what - revenge? It seemed like this would be his last desperate act. In his heart, Buddy didn't think he and Pete were going to be able to pull off this stunt. But – there was really no other choice. Hostage situations rarely have a pleasant ending for anyone. Buddy called out, "Okay – the two customers are coming out! Don't shoot!"

Pete took one last look at Ezra, sitting tied to his own chair and looking so forlorn, except for an almost imperceptible smile on his face. "Why are you doing this for us old man?"

"I told you" came the reply, "I make dreams come true. Your dream is to get out of here - to be free. I'm only making your wish come true."

Buddy and Pete adjusted their black Stetsons to make sure they were on secure, bowed their heads so that the wide brim would hide their faces, swung open the screen door, and stepped out onto the covered boardwalk.

Ezra smiled as the men exited.

Keeping their heads bowed and eyes cast downward, Buddy and Pete turned right outside the door and hurried west along Allen Street's boardwalk. All they could see was the heavy timbers of the boardwalk. All they could hear was their boot-heels thumping against the heavy wood, and sensation of their hearts beating relentlessly in their chests. They tried to walk quickly, but not too quickly so as to draw attention to themselves. Almost expecting to be "made" by the Highway Patrol the two walked all the way to the end of the block, the corner of Fifth and Allen, before they even looked at each other.

Reaching the corner of Fifth and Allen Streets, the wooden boardwalk gave way to a dirt street. Suddenly Buddy and Pete were no longer focused on the sound of their boots on the wooden timbers, or the pounding of their own hearts. They became acutely conscious of the tinkling sound of an upright piano wafting through the air from the Oriental Saloon on their immediate right and the muffled sound of hoof beats on a dirt street, a distinctly different sound, Pete thought, than if the street had been paved.

The two men looked at each other, and then looked up. All the people that had been in the street before, dressed in the 1880's attire were still there. Only – everyone was dressed that way! Gone were the tourists in the shorts, tee shirts and sandals. Gone were the little children in strollers and young moms and dads carrying knapsacks full of diapers and baby bottles. They were all gone - vanished – replaced by men in derby hats and sack suits. Women were dressed in frilly dresses that fastened to the collar and high shoes with low heels. Across Fifth Street was the Crystal Palace Saloon where men with long moustaches moved in and out of the distinctive corner door. The smell of cigar smoke and horse manure produced a very distinctive aroma.

Buddy and Pete looked at each other again in disbelief. Buddy whispered to his partner, "This can't be. This feels like the 1880's. It's so real! But it has to be something put on for the tourists!"

Pete replied, "There's one sure way to find out. Turn around!"

The two men bowed their heads again to hide their faces, then slowly turned to face the other end of Allen Street where they had just come from. Slowly, they raised their heads, each suspecting that an officer of the Arizona Highway Patrol would be right behind them with a gun stuck in their faces. When their heads were straight they peered down the covered boardwalk. The street seemed much the same as far as the stores were concerned. And the Bird Cage Theatre was right where it should have been, on the corner of Sixth and Allen. But the police cruisers and all the blue uniforms were gone –

replaced with horse drawn buggies and coaches of all sizes and descriptions.

Buddy was the first to speak, "I don't get it. This is some type of elaborate trick. And I'm not sure why. Let's go back and get that old man!"

Are you sure the Highway Patrol won't be there?" offered Pete.

As the two men talked, they looked at their surroundings and spotted what obviously was a businessman lounging in front of the Crystal Palace, reading a newspaper. The two looked at each other, each having the same idea at the same time. They walked across Fifth Street and up to the man with the newspaper.

"Pardon me, but is that today's newspaper?" asked Pete.

"Yes" came the gruff reply. "What of it?"

"We sure would appreciate a quick look at the front page, sir" said Buddy as he reached for the paper and held it up slightly so he could see the date on the front page. It read, Tuesday March 15, 1881.

"I still don't believe it!" exclaimed Buddy. "It's gotta be some kind of trick!"

Pete replied, "Trick or not, I don't feel safe going back to see the old man. Let's go to that place he was telling us about – Kinnear's Stage Company on First Street I think he said. What do we have to lose?"

"Only our minds if we can't figure this out pretty soon" quipped Buddy.

The two men continued to walk down Allen Street to First Street where they saw the Kinnear Stage building, just where Ezra said it would be. They stood in front of the place on the opposite side of First Street for several minutes trying to decide what to do, feeling foolish about asking for a job doing something they knew nothing about, and being sent by a man who may or may not exist, at least in 1881. But, they thought, despite the confusion and absurdity of their situation, it was better than being on their way to a long jail sentence.

Finally, they found the courage to cross the street and move toward the large stable door. As they approached, a man stepped from the darkness of the building into the late afternoon sunlight. He was dressed in rough corduroy pants, not unlike the pants worn by the two bewildered would-be cowboys and tucked into tall boots. The man wore a bright red bandanna that matched his complexion, set off by long blond hair and a big, black Stetson. "Are you boys Buddy and Pete?"

The two looked at each other. It seemed to get weirder and weirder. Here was another person whom neither one of them had ever met, but who obviously knew their names. "Yessir" came the terse reply.

Phin smiled. "Well good. My name is Phin. I run this stage line. Ezra told me you boys would be along today. He sure has a way of delivering whatever his customers order. He said Bud was good with the ribbons. Which one of you is Bud?"

Buddy, trying not to look too bewildered not really sure what Phin was talking about decided to just play along and replied, "I'm Buddy, and I guess I'm ok."

"Good" said Bob. "Bob Paul is going to ride shotgun on tonight's stage to Benson. Bud, I want you to drive and Pete, you ride along to learn the route. Where are you boys from anyways?"

"Tucson" Pete replied.

"Well then, I guess you know your way to Benson since you had to come through there to get here" grinned Phin. "We'll have a large shipment of bullion tonight, worth $80,000. I see neither of you is heeled. Pete, why don't you commission a shotgun from the office? With that much money on board, it doesn't hurt to have another gun on board! The stage leaves Tombstone at 7PM. I have other business to tend to. See you boys in a bit."

Phin walked back into the building leaving the two men standing on the boardwalk even more confused than before.

Buddy looked at Pete in a quizzical manner. "Ribbons?"

"Reins" Pete replied. "Ribbons are reins – just think steering wheel for a stage coach. Evidently, you are going to be the stage driver and this other guy, Bob Paul, is going to ride shot gun."

"But Benson is north!" Buddy protested. "We want to go south – to Mexico!"

Pete looked at his partner, the confusion and disorientation taking its toll on his facial features. "Look – north, south; does it really matter? At least we don't have the Highway Patrol to deal with any more. Let's just take this job going to Benson and back, and we'll see how far this hoax, if it is a hoax, extends. Then, we'll know. When you think about it, what other choice do we have?"

"I guess you're right – what choice do we have...?"

Buddy and Pete perched on a bench in front of the office to ponder their fate.

******

Stable-hands brought the stage out from the barn, completely hitched to a four-horse team. The stage coach was resplendent in its bright red paint with the words "Kinnear Stage Lines" in yellow and gold over the door on both sides. The color of the huge wooden spoke wheels matched the yellow lettering and the black leather boot on the front and back of the stage glistened in the setting sun.

Pete climbed onto the dickey seat on the back of the stage. Seven other passengers boarded the stage. Buddy took his place in the driver's seat and Bob Paul introduced himself to Buddy as he climbed to the "shotgun" seat. Buddy cracked the whip, and the stage lumbered down First Street and headed north to Benson with a brilliant Arizona sun setting over the mountains.

The Stage Driver

Bob Paul directed the route. The stage made several stops along the way and had just pulled out of Contention City at about 10PM. The sky was black with just a hint of faint moonlight. Despite a warm day, the night air was frigid. Bob Paul and Buddy swapped seats so that Buddy could warm his hands while Bob drove the stage. Just north of Drew's Station, the stage slowed for a grade. At the top of the grade, and before the stage could resume speed, several dark forms emerged from the surrounding rocks and brush.

"I can't believe this!" thought Buddy. "In the morning, we're robbing the 20th century version of a stage coach. In the evening we're protecting the 19th century version of a Tucson Armored Security truck – and now it looks like we are about to get robbed ourselves!"

A muffled voice could be heard from the side of the road. It appeared to be a man with a bandanna over his face, wielding a shotgun. "Stop the stage! Throw down the box!"

Bob Paul growled, "I stop for no one!"

Several shots rang out, the highwaymen aiming for what they thought was the shotgun messenger who should have been Bob Paul but, warm hands and all, was Buddy. Buddy took one shot to the chest, and slumping over, died instantly. His limp body hung forward and onto the hooves of the wheel horses that now broke into a dead run.

As the stage sped forward, the highwaymen fired upon it. Pete, facing backward on the top of the stage could see bright flashes as the six-guns and shotguns roared. One slug found its mark and Pete slumped forward and off the back of the stage and onto the cold road – dead.

Bob Paul courageously slipped down to the tongue of the now fast-moving stage to retrieve the reins that were dragging on the ground. Finally, Bob was able to pull the stage under control and continued on to Benson where he telegraphed Tombstone about the incident.

The following day, a posse found the bodies of Eli "Bud" Philpot and Peter Roering lying where they fell.

******

Buddy and Pete found themselves standing on Tombstone's First Street on the opposite side of the street from the Kinnear Stage Lines. "Something feels very strange about this, Pete" said Buddy. "Very strange and bizarre – but somehow oddly familiar. It feels like... feels like I have lived this moment before!"

Buddy and Pete looked at each other is disbelief. A page from a newspaper, carried by the seemingly constant breeze got stuck against Pete's leg. He bent down, picked it up and checked the date – Tuesday, March 15, 1881.

A man appeared from the large barn on the opposite side of the street and called to them, "Are you boys Bud and Pete?"

"Yes" came the reply, barely audible across the street due to the rising wind and blowing dust.

The man on the opposite side of street cupped his hands around his mouth to amplify his voice. His form stood almost in silhouette against a setting sun. "Ezra told me you would be coming. I have jobs for you. Come on over!"

The Real Story Behind "The Stage Driver"

On the evening of Tuesday, March 15, 1881 the Kinnear stagecoach, running between Tombstone and the city of Benson was robbed. (Benson is about 20 miles north of Tombstone.) The stage driver, Eli "Bud" Philpot and a passenger, Peter Roering, were killed.

Famed old west lawman, Bob Paul, who was supposed to be riding "shotgun" but who was driving the stage at the time, barely escaped with his life. Paul drove the stage on to Benson where he wired Wyatt Earp who was dealing faro at the Oriental Saloon.

Wyatt Earp formed a posse which read like a who's who of the old west. It included Wyatt's brothers Morgan and Virgil Earp, Bat Masterson, Cochise County Sheriff Johnny Behan, Behan's Under Sheriff (Deputy) Billy Breakenridge, George Parsons and Dr. Emory Goodfellow. A man named Luther King was arrested and named Harry Head, Bill Leonard and Jim Crane as accomplices in the attempted stage robbery.

King was captured. Behan returned King to Tombstone where he allowed the would-be robber to easily escape. It then became quite evident that Behan was playing both sides of the law. This later became a point of contention between Wyatt Earp and Johnny Behan and developed into just one of the incidents that led up to the most famous gunfight in history, the Shoot-Out at the OK Corral, some seven months later.

Chapter 5: THE WRITER

"I know who knows the truth – and they can tell you – and you can tell the world. But are you ready to do that? Are you ready to stand up for the truth? Are you the lawyer, the seeker of the truth you think you are?"

Ezra T. Thornton October 11, 2003

Monday, October 11, 2003 8:00AM Tombstone, Arizona

"Your first time in Tombstone, I presume?"

Rod Livingston had been standing for several minutes in front of Ezra's Mercantile store on Tombstone's Allen Street, staring at the Bird Cage Theatre across the street. It was an early Saturday morning and the throngs of tourists in shorts and baseball hats had not yet ventured out to taste the heat of a rising Arizona sun.

Ezra stood in the doorway of his store, impeccably dressed as always in his usual 1880's-style attire, boiled white shirt, red brocade vest festooned with a rich gold-watch chain and high-top shoes.

The man standing before him, just off the boardwalk, turned about, knowing that he was the only one on the street at this early hour. Facing the well-dressed man, he suddenly felt under-dressed and out of place in his blue jeans and ragged tee shirt. Moreover, carrying a lap-top computer under his arm, as opposed to the usual camera carried by Tombstone's tourists, the man seemed particularly out of place.

Stepping up onto the board walk to shake Ezra's hand, Rod replied, "Why, yes. It's that obvious, huh?"

The two men smiled warmly.

"Ezra T. Thornton. I'm a merchant. This is my store – and welcome to my town."

"Rod Livingston from Los Angles. Seeker of the truth."

Ezra pressed his hands into his vest pockets, "Seeker of the truth, huh? That's a pretty broad statement Mr. Livingston. I believe we are all seeking some sort of truth. But it sounds as if you are on some sort of crusade – being here in Tombstone from Los Angeles and all."

Rod smiled again, "Broad statement – yes – well – you see, I'm a lawyer, a District Attorney in Los Angeles to be more precise. Truth is my stock-in-trade. I also dabble in fictional short stories with an old-west theme. Been a hobby of mine for twenty some-odd years, most of my adult life. I even produced a couple of paperback novels. Sort of fancy myself as a Louis Lamour – with a law degree!"

Ezra removed his top hat and mopped his already sweating brow with his handkerchief. "So what brings you to my town, Mr. Livingston? Are you seeking some sort of *truth* here in Tombstone?"

Rod's face began to beam as he went into an explanation. "While doing research for my western stories and books, I continually find books, magazine articles, and web sites that all proclaim to provide the *truth* about Wyatt Earp or the *truth* about what happened at the OK Corral – or the truth about the death of Johnny Ringo. With all the information out there, not all of it can be the truth. As a lawyer, it's my job to find the truth. Ultimately, there must be one, true version of what happened. Everyone seems to provide a slightly different take or a slightly different angle on the same stories that have been written about for over 100 years. What I want to do, Mr. Thornton, is find *the truth* for myself. I intend to write the end-all, be-all book about Tombstone. And I intend to start right here where Tombstone history began – right here where the Earps and Clantons once walked. I want to dispel all the rumors, half-truths, and outright lies. I want to de-bunk the legends. Maybe Wyatt Earp wasn't the brave law-man that he was purported to be - maybe Johnny Ringo was shot by his own men. Hell... I don't know. But I intend to find out! But I plan to make this the end-all, be-all book of Tombstone history!"

As Rod finished his explanation, he thought he could hear sounds emanating from the Bird Cage Theatre – almost as if a show was in progress and the entire audience was laughing at the punch line of a joke just delivered by an on-stage comedian. The sensation of a laughing audience was so vivid, that Rod turned about and looked over his shoulder. But all he saw was a still-empty Allen Street, and a once bawdy theatre, now-turned tourist attraction awaiting it's doors to be opened to a sneaker-clad public for another's day's admission fees.

Rod again faced Ezra, thoughtfully removed his sunglasses and began to speak, "Did you hear that? I could have sworn I heard...."

The Writer

Not allowing the would-be debunker to finish his sentence, Ezra started, "That's a pretty tall order, Mr. Livingston. You look to be about 40 years old. If you live to be 80, you may get a good start on things. But I doubt you'll ever finish. Why, a good friend of mine, a Mr. Jeffery Stone of California recently wrote a biography of Wyatt Earp – the latest one you know – and it took him 15 years just to write about one man! One man! Jeffery traveled all over the country finding the information. Much of it is in Arizona. But the Earps traveled all over. The information about the Earps, and Tombstone, is spread across libraries, university archives, historical societies, and housed in private collections all over the country! So how can you do justice to the entire history of Tombstone in just 40 years, Mr. Livingston? That is assuming that you live another 40 years!"

The two men looked at each seriously for a moment, and then laughed. Having written only fictional stories all his life, a relatively "quick-write" when compared to non-fiction, Rod Livingston had not realized until this moment how much work would be required for a non-fiction book. It would be like preparing for the biggest legal case of his life – with a large list of witnesses, all of them now long-dead – and evidence spread across 100 years and countless locations. Rod laughed the nervous laugh of a man who just realized that he had blundered badly and made himself look rather foolish.

Ezra laughed, knowing full well that Rod had not realized how big of a job he had undertaken, and was now trying to find a way to get out of the conversation gracefully.

Again, Rod heard the faint yet distinct sound of laughter coming from the Bird Cage across the street. He began to turn his head when Ezra again began to speak with a tone more serious than before. "The truth needs to be told, Mr. Livingston. But the truth will not be found in some library or university archives or even at the Arizona Historical Society. No sir. You have to go right to the source if you want the truth."

Rod looked at the white haired man in a most quizzical way. "The source, Mr. Thornton? The source is the people who lived during that period... and they are all dead. Long gone. Now if this were 1925 or so, there would be enough of them still around to ask. But here, in 2003, I'd be hard-pressed to find a grandchild of those that lived here in the 1880's. And they may know nothing. So...what the heck are you talking about?"

"The libraries, archives and such carry a lot of information" started Ezra, "mostly true material. But they don't tell the whole truth, the complete truth, the truth that historians and others want to hear, the truth that those who lived here in the early 1880's want to have told. For years, they have waited for someone brave enough, and talented enough to tell all."

Ezra paused for a moment as he watched the Los Angeles lawyer wallow in his words, and then continued, "The truth is a powerful thing. And people want to know the truth – they deserve the truth. And those who lived here during the palmy days of the camp want the truth to be told. Writers, historians, and armchair theorists will forever contemplate the question of who fired first at the OK Corral incident. That story needs to be told. Armchair forensic 'experts' want to know how Johnny Ringo died. Someone needs to tell that story. Conspiracy theorists want to know precisely whom the would-be assassins were who shot Virgil Earp in December, 1881. I know who knows the truth – and they can tell you – and you can tell the world. But are you ready to do that? Are you ready to stand up for the truth? Are you the lawyer, the seeker of the truth you think you are?"

The two men just looked at each other for a moment. Rod wasn't sure if Ezra was serious or just kidding him.

Rod pondered: If Ezra was serious, if he knew who knew all this information, then why had it not been told before now? Rod could only surmise that Ezra was having a little fun with a "would-be historian."

Ezra's line of conversation seemed ludicrous to Rod. It was almost as if the two men would simply walk around town and visit the Earps, the Clums, Doc Holliday, the Clanton's and McLaury's and all the rest in a sort of Sunday-like visit.

"Wait here a moment" said Ezra. "I'll be right back."

Ezra disappeared into his store and Rod wondered why. Was there something in the store that would shed some light on Tombstone's past? Were the Earps and Clantons hiding in his store? Ezra seemed so serious, the thought crossed Rod's mind.

A moment later, Ezra appeared with two brown bottles, freshly pulled from a barrel of ice, condensation dripping from them onto the wooden planks of the sidewalk. "Sarsaparilla Mr. Livingston?"

The offer of a cold drink broke the intensity of Rod's pondering mind and the two men chuckled again, walked over to a bench in front of Ezra's store, and sat down.

Ezra continued, "Several writers have tried to get it right – the truth that is. The only problem is" Ezra's voice evoked force and conviction, "all the documents and old newspaper accounts and diaries that can be dragged up and located here in 2003 does not tell the whole story. You have to talk to the people that lived it!"

The two men looked at each other again, serious for a moment, and then broke out into another laugh. Rod still was not sure if Ezra was serious or not. Perhaps Ezra was simply an odd old man, playing mind-games with him.

"By the way, Mr. Livingston", queried Ezra, "why *do* you want to learn the truth? Why is *the truth* so important to you anyway?"

Rod looked straight as Ezra. "The truth is my job and my life, Mr. Thornton. It is what I am about. It is what I do. I find the truth and make it public. I live for the truth!"

Ezra downed another swallow of sarsaparilla. "And does the truth ever get anyone into trouble?"

"Sure!" came the reply. "In my business, most often times, it means trouble for someone!"

The two men just looked at each other for one poignant moment. Rod took a last swig from his bottle, then handing it to Ezra, stood up a readied himself to leave. Rod feigned seriousness; "You have an interesting take on this town, Mr. Thornton. But I don't think Wyatt or Doc or Johnny Ringo will be stopping by to tell their story – especially to me - the neophyte historian!"

Ezra stood and straightened his vest and his tall, black top hat. "Well I suppose I do have an interesting take on the town. And some people would consider me odd. But I suppose that is how one becomes when one lives in a small town for a long time. And I have lived here for a very long time."

Rod replied, "What is a very long time? How long have you been here?"

Rod had been sitting on the bench facing Ezra, looking east up Allen Street; his back toward the west, and the main portion of the historic district. Seconds before, Rod had heard footsteps – heavy, boot-clad footsteps - clomping along the wooden sidewalk approaching from behind him. At that moment, the footsteps stopped. Ezra looked up and smiled.

"Good morning Ezra!" came a deep, booming, authoritative voice.

"Good morning Wyatt!" came the reply.

Rod turned his head to see a handsome man, probably in his mid-thirties with sandy-blond hair and regal moustache, and except for his sparkling white shirt and dark red cravat tie, he was dressed all in black. But the thing that caught Rod's attention was his blue eyes; piercing, deep – as if they could see right through a person.

Ezra stood up, shook hands with the man in black, and then turned to Rod. "Mr. Livingston, I would like you to meet Wyatt Earp!"

Rod dutifully stood, and shook hands with his new acquaintance. "Good morning Mr. Earp. It is indeed a pleasure to meet you."

Rod smiled and seemed delighted. But he could not help but notice that Wyatt's hand was cold – cold as ice. Although the outside air was somewhat cool, it really wasn't that cool – not cool enough it seemed, to have hands that felt like they had been handling ice cubes.

Ezra began to speak. "Wyatt; Mr. Livingston here is a writer – from Los Angeles. And he says he is here in Tombstone seeking the truth".

Wyatt and Ezra smiled knowingly at each other.

"Well" replied Wyatt, "perhaps there is a truth to be told. Exactly what truth are you looking for?"

Rod got the impression that Wyatt was feigning sincerity and simply shining him on. Not sure what to make of the whole scene, Rod quickly figured that Wyatt was simply a local reenactor, albeit a darned good one, and that they were just simply having a little fun with yet another garden-variety tourist and wanna-be historian.

Continuing with renewed sincerity, and fully resolved in his quest, Rod replied, "I want to know the truth about Tombstone, Mr. Earp. I want to know all about the OK Corral shoot out. I want to know exactly how Marshall White was shot. I want to know if Johnny Behan really was a compatriot of the cow-boys. I want to know...."

Wyatt cut him off in mid-sentence. "Whoa. That's a pretty tall order my boy. And from what spring will all this truth flow?"

Rod fumbled for words, having been distracted by Wyatt's interruption. "I plan to do some research, Mr. Earp. Lots of research."

Wyatt and Ezra looked at each other and again smiled at each other. Wyatt spoke again. "Well, if you really want the truth, Ezra is your man. He can point you in the right direction – that is if..." Wyatt's face became very stern and serious. "...if you have the stomach for it."

All three men looked at each other. For a few seconds, a time that seemed like an eternity, a look of seriousness had come over all of them, as if they had just heard that a close, mutual friend had died.

Suddenly Wyatt broke their trance with another wide smile, which again brought smiles to Rod and Ezra. Rod turned to look at Ezra and as he did, out of the corner of his eye, he caught Wyatt giving a wink to Ezra.

"Good day gentlemen!" announced Wyatt, "A card game awaits!" Rod and Ezra watched Wyatt walk across Allen Street and disappear behind the Bird Cage Theatre.

Rod looked quizzically at Ezra; "Is he a local reenactor? I know a lot of those guys come here from California. Interesting fella...?"

Ezra, finishing a swallow from his own bottle replied, "Oh he's originally from Monmouth, Illinois. But I guess you could say he's now a local."

Rod pondered for a moment about how Ezra had replied to his question, knowing that Wyatt Earp was born in Monmouth, Illinois.... in 1848! Was it a coincidence?

Rod continued, "So...getting back to what Wyatt said about you pointing me in the right direction to find the truth. Can you really do that? And... how can you do that. I mean... I don't understand... Do you know people at the Arizona Historical Society, or.....?"

Ezra downed his last swallow of sarsaparilla. "If you really want to know the truth, meet me here at my store at 11:45 tonight."

Rod looked incredulously at Ezra, then smiled. Rod figured that both Ezra and Wyatt had been toying with him and his idea about the truth. Sarcasm now dripped from Rod's words, "Yeah right – 11:45. Got it. Well, anyways...thanks for the drink. What do I owe you?"

"You can pay me for the drink by being here at 11:45 tonight" was the reply with a crafty wink.

Rod shook hands with Ezra, tucked his lap-top computer securely in the crook of his arm, turned, and started to walk west on Allen Street trying to make sense of his encounter with "Wyatt Earp", and a strange man who seemed mysteriously out of place, yet very comfortable with the oddity of it all. Before he had gone 10 steps, Rod heard Ezra's voice calling to him; "Eleven-forty-five! Don't be late! I'll take you right to the source!"

Rod turned to acknowledge the old man. But when he turned, Ezra was already gone.

Monday, October 11, 2003 11:35PM Tombstone, Arizona

Rod Livingston stepped from his motel room on the corner of Fremont and Fifth Street and headed south down Fifth Street to Allen Street. He zipped his coat against the chilling breeze and pulled his baseball cap tighter on his head. Fremont Street, being a state-maintained road was well lit; light also emanating from the motel's advertising sign. As he moved onto Fifth Street and walked past the office of the *Tombstone Epitaph*, the shadows got deeper and more ominous.

He carried his lap-top computer with him... with a fully-charged battery. Being an excellent and fast typist, he was determined to capture every word. That was... if there were words to capture! Skeptical, his "lawyer mind" fought with his creative mind, each arguing with the prospect of meeting anyone on the empty streets of Tombstone at quarter to midnight, who would provide him with some usable information. He steeled himself against the brisk breeze.

Rod moved along silently, now approaching the front door of the Crystal Palace; his sneakers making barely a sound against the wooden planks of the sidewalk. Had this been a Friday or Saturday night, or a Monday night in 1881, the sounds of live music and the tinkling of beer glasses could have been heard coming from the Crystal Palace Saloon. But tonight, all that could be heard was the breeze rustling the advertising flyers discarded by the day's tourists as they blew across the intersection of Fifth and Allen.

Rod started crossing Fifth Street on Allen and midway across Fifth he stopped. "This is right where Virgil Earp was shot, and almost killed at the hand of an assassin, or assassins – December 28, 1881 – probably a night just like this one." Rod thought to himself. A chill came over him. He looked up at the Arizona sky, and then continued his trek up Allen Street, the dim glow of the street-lights guiding his way.

Rod looked up ahead to Ezra's store, half expecting to see the well -dressed gent standing there - and half expecting no one to be there. He walked a few more steps, stopped in his tracks, and looked down at his sneakers in disgust. "Boy am I stupid. I feel so dumb. Out here at mid-night, looking for a crazy old codger who was just jerking me around – probably the same way he jerks all the other tourists around. I'm going back to my room and going to bed!"

Rod raised his head to look one last time down the street toward Ezra's store – just to prove to himself how ridiculous this situation was.

As he focused in eyes in the dim light, he could see a figure standing in front of Ezra's store. It was Ezra! Ezra called to Rod, his voice echoing down the empty street, "Hurry! We'll be late for the show!"

Rod now moved quickly toward Ezra and replied, "Show? What show?"

Ezra, still dressed in the same elegant clothes he had worn that morning, yet with nary a wrinkle for a whole day's wear replied, "Every evening there is a variety show at the Bird Cage. Everyone who is anyone in Tombstone attends. They will tell you everything you want to know. Everything."

Ezra secured his high top-hat against the strong breeze as he started across Allen Street. "Come with me."

As the two men walked across Allen Street it was painfully obvious to Rod that the Bird Cage was closed and dark. Had it been an evening of that hour in late 1881 or 1882, throngs of people would have been milling about outside waiting to get into the place. The sound of music would have been readily heard. Thirsty patrons would have been seen through the open doors securing drinks at the mahogany bar. Laughter and frivolity, the by-product of silver mining would have been the prevalent sounds.

Instead, a steady wind blew causing Rod to shiver as he watched his own reflection in the darkened windows on the doors of the Bird Cage. But it was his reflection....only. Did he miss Ezra's reflection as they moved quickly across the street? Or... did Ezra not cast a reflection? Rod quickly put the odd thought out of his mind as he turned his attention to where they were headed.

Ezra and Rod moved around to the west side of the Bird Cage and to the back of the building to a small door, which Rod expected would be locked. Interestingly, the door was unlocked and the two men entered to what was obviously the Bird Cage's famous stage – behind the curtain.

The light inside was extremely dim, it's source seemingly incorporeal. Somehow, Ezra knew just where to reach for an oil lamp, and lit it.

Ezra pulled a prop chair and table from the corner and placed the oil lamp in the center of the table. The flickering glow threw eerie shadows on the dark, water-stained walls.

Bending at the waist and with an outstretched hand, he beckoned the bewildered writer to sit down. "They're all expecting you – the lawyer and writer from Los Angeles. The show will begin in about 10 minutes. Have a seat here for now. You will know when it's time to go out front!"

Rod sat down resolutely at the small table and chair opening his laptop computer and plugging in the mouse, thinking more and more that a joke was still being played on him. He wondered just how far it would go. Suppose it was a ruse... suppose it was real. He just didn't know. Rod asked, "Exactly who am I going to meet? How will I know when it is time to go out in front of the curtain? Ezra, this is nuts!"

Ezra turned about and began to leave. Rod spoke up. "Wait! Where are you going? Don't you want to be here with me?"

"No" came the reply. "This is your time. You want to be a writer? You want to be a historian? You want the truth? Listen, and take notes. It's all here my good man. Forget about the Arizona Historical Society. Forget about the University of Arizona archives. Forget about taking years to find all the information, disseminate it, and write about it. It's all *right here*! Right here... right now! You'll see!"

Ezra spun about on his heels and left the bewildered man in the baseball cap and sneakers to his own thoughts. It took about 30 seconds after Ezra left for Rod's thoughts to turn to distaste for the whole affair. "I'll bet Ezra and that Wyatt Earp guy are standing right outside that door laughing their heads off at me!"

His curiosity got the better of him and Rod stuck his head around the edge of the stage curtain to gaze upon the main audience area. What he saw, was what he expected to see – a dark, dusty and dank museum – a testament to a time long past. It became painfully apparent that no one was coming to a dark, dusty museum at midnight in Tombstone.

Rod walked over to the door where he had previously entered and poked his head outside only to be met by the cold breeze and a dark, deserted street. Expecting Ezra and Wyatt to be around the corner in the front of the building, Rod stepped outside and moved to that direction. But neither Ezra nor Wyatt could be seen.

Disgusted, and convinced that he had been taken advantage of, Rod returned to his small prop-table, retrieved his laptop computer, and emerged again into the dark street. He turned his coat collar against the wind, and walked briskly back to his motel room – to sleep – and wonder.

Tuesday, October 12, 2003 10:00AM Tombstone, Arizona

After having breakfast at a café on the corner of Third and Allen, Rod again found himself meandering east on Allen Street, laptop at the ready. Thoughts of the previous evening swirled in his head. He could not help but think that Ezra, and whoever that "Wyatt" guy was had had a field day with him. Getting him to go sit in an empty theatre at midnight must have been a load of laughs for the two.

On the other hand, Rod could not help but think that there was *some sincerity*, at least with Ezra. He wasn't sure yet about "Wyatt". Suppose Wyatt was sincere. "Suppose... suppose" he thought.

But suppose Ezra was right. Suppose there was a truth to be told... and he had missed the opportunity to discover that truth? Suppose...?

Rod rarely used the word "suppose", but found himself using it quite frequently within the last 24 hours. He didn't know what to make of it.

Rod strolled past the Tombstone Territorial Book Store on the corner of Fourth and Allen and stopped momentarily to gaze into the display window. There, propped upright next to a black, wide-brimmed hat and a fake Colt revolver was the landmark book by Alford Turner entitled, *The Earps Talk*.

Rod stared at the book, his mind wandering back to the previous evening and what to make of his most inauspicious start as a non-fiction writer and historian. He was not sure how long he had been standing there with a blank stare on his face when he suddenly became conscious of someone standing beside him. Rod turned his head to see Ezra Thornton standing right next to him.

Ezra smiled, "Well Rod, it looks like you are interested in Mr. Turner's book!"

Rod smiled sardonically. "Isn't it ironic – the name of the book I mean".

Ezra replied, "How do you mean?"

Rod turned to face the smartly-dressed mercantilist, "What I wouldn't do to hear the Earps talk! Suppose I could here them talk. Suppose..."

Ezra pulled a pipe from his pocket and began to load it with tobacco interrupting Rod. "Ah yes, I was looking for you – hoping to find you out here on the street. You were missed last night. A lot of people wanted to meet the writer and lawyer from Los Angeles. They wanted to tell you their story. Where did you go? How long did you wait backstage? You disappointed a lot of people."

"Very funny Mr. Thornton" replied Rod with a distinctive note or sarcasm in his voice. "You and that 'Wyatt' guy have had your fun – your little joke. You were probably right around the corner from the Bird Cage laughing your butts off as I sat in that musty, old theatre. Well, I hope you had a good laugh. But now it's over. Good-day!"

Rod pushed past Ezra and started east down Allen Street, his sneakers moving quietly along the wooden boardwalk.

Ezra called after him, "As a professional... as a lawyer... Mr. Livingston, to what length do you go to seek the truth?"

Corner of 4th and Allen Streets ~ July 2008   **K. Davis photo**

Rod had only gone a few steps when he spun around, "To any length – any length for the truth!"

Ezra's face took on a look of seriousness. "And do you still seek the truth about Tombstone? Do you still want to tell the *real* story?"

Rod made no audible sound, but his stern face and set-jaw told Ezra that Rod was a man with a mission. – determined – the way a good lawyer should be when seeking the truth.

Ezra returned the determined countenance, "Eleven forty-five this evening in front of my store. Your last opportunity..." Ezra gave a long pause and then continued, "...to hear the Earps talk!"

Rod was not sure how to take this last invitation. Was Ezra continuing to play with him or was there any truth to this seeming relic of a man? Suppose Ezra was telling the truth? Rod tightened his grip on his laptop with his right hand and shoved his left hand resolutely into the hip pocket of his jeans, putting his head down to ponder an appropriate response to Ezra. His head was only down for a moment and came up with the words, "Well...we'll see" coming out of his mouth.

But Rod Livingston, seeker of the truth was speaking to no one, Ezra having already vanished. Wondering how the old man could move so quickly, Rod turned about and continued his stroll east on the south side of Allen Street, past the growing numbers of tourists, past the restaurants and show hawkers dressed in 1880's cow-boy garb, and stopping to peer in the door of Big Nose Kate's Saloon.

At 10AM it was too late for breakfast for most people, too early for lunch, yet a few people, mostly the reenactors he had seen on the street yesterday, sat at the tables talking. One in particular stood out. Standing at the bar with a steaming cup of coffee, was Wyatt!

Not quite sure what to say to his new "friend", but wanting to "feel him out" a bit more, Rod pushed the swinging saloon doors opened and approached the man dressed all in black – a wide-brimmed pork-pie hat with a slightly lower crown than most of the other reenactors covered his sandy-blond hair. Rod gave Wyatt a good look. From his blond, handle-bar moustache to his black, cravat-style tie to his spotless boots and back up to snow-white shirt, Wyatt looked like; well – Wyatt!

Wyatt saved Rod the trouble of breaking the ice and spoke first, extending his hand to Rod, "Well Mr. Livingston, have you found the truth yet?"

Standing at the bar, the two men shook hands. Like the previous day, Rod found Wyatt's hand cold – cold as ice – most inconsistent since Wyatt had, just a moment before been holding a hot cup of coffee.

"Not yet, Mr. Earp" came the rather terse reply.

Before Rod could think of the next thing to say, Wyatt continued, "I understand from talking to Ezra that you had your opportunity last night but didn't stick around long enough to learn the truth!"

Rod took on a discerning tone, "You look every bit the part of Wyatt Earp... er... Mr. Earp. But my guess is you're one of the local reenactors... or maybe you're with one of those reenactor groups from California or New Mexico. My guess is that you and that Ezra guy are just having fun with a neophyte historian – just poking fun at me."

"Are we?' came Wyatt's quick reply. "As a lawyer, you seek the truth. And to determine the truth, you require evidence – isn't that right, Mr. Livingston?"

"Absolutely correct Mr. Earp! You know that better than anyone. It takes evidence and testimony from credible witnesses. You, of all people know that since it was evidence and especially the testimony from Mr. H.F. Sills that exonerated you, your brothers and Doc Holliday during Judge Spicer's inquest after the OK Corral gunfight!"

Wyatt smiled, "You do know something about your history don't you Mr. Livingston. Well... if you want to learn about the whole truth, meet Ezra tonight at 11:45 in front of his store. He told me he would give you one more chance. After that – well – you'll be relegated to reading books and poring over the dusty archives throughout Arizona... and other far-flung places."

Rod pondered Wyatt's statement and as he did, he happened to look past Wyatt at the large mirror over the back-bar and for the first time noticed that Wyatt did not cast a reflection in the glass! Rod could see everyone else's reflection – the reenactors in their wide-brimmed hats sitting at the tables drinking coffee, the small stage where the single singer-guitar player would perform each night, and the many stained-glass windows on the front of the saloon. But he could not see Wyatt's reflection. More odd, was that he was the only one who seemed to notice!

Dismissing the phenomenon to some odd dispersion of light through the stained-glass windows, Rod finally replied, "Well – we'll see. Have a good day Mr. Earp – or whoever you are!"

Wyatt just smiled, unfettered by the would-be writer's cynicism, "Good day Mr. Livingston!"

Rod turned, pushed past the swinging doors and continued east on Allen Street.

Soon, Rod was approaching the west-facing wall of the Bird Cage Theatre – a bare wall. Rod stopped and stared at the wall – the *bare* wall! A chill ran down his spine and he felt his stomach clench into a

knot. The previous evening, this now-bare wall had had a door in it –
the door Ezra had taken him through to the back-stage area. Yes!
He was sure of it!

Rod turned his head to look across Allen Street and Ezra's store.
Through the large windows, Rod could see Ezra had several
customers he was waiting on. But Rod had not seen Ezra pass him
on the street. Rod wondered how Ezra could have walked the whole
length of Allen Street undetected by him, and now be waiting on
customers in his store?

Rod stood fixated on the store, watching Ezra's every move. After
a moment or two, Ezra looked up and noted the lawyer watching him.
Ezra gave a smile and brief wave. Rod did not smile but waved back,
then turned has attention again to the bare wall – that *bare wall* –
and distinctly heard the sound of a crowd of people laughing.

Tuesday, October 12, 2003 11:35PM Tombstone, Arizona

Not convinced that he would learn anything by again going to the
Bird Cage Theatre at midnight, but feeling that he had to satisfy his
own curiosity, and being still baffled by the "disappearing" door on
the side of the theatre, Rod, clutching his laptop in the crook of his
right arm, headed out of his hotel room to meet Ezra. Just as before,
as Rod turned off Fifth Street onto Allen Street and headed east,
Ezra's form, straight and lean, could be seen at the end of the block
in front of his store.

As Rod approached the store, his sneakers moving almost silently
over the wooden boardwalk, Ezra spoke, "You're just in time - the
crowd, and the show awaits - and all are expecting you."

Showing no emotion - not quite sure what emotion to show; Rod
silently followed Ezra across the street to the Bird Cage. Rod
wondered if he was a pawn in some elaborate hoax – but why anyone
would go through this much trouble to dupe some lawyer from Los
Angeles was beyond him. But if he were going to meet people who
would reveal the truth about Tombstone, who would they be? It all
seemed too strange.

Rod was lost in thought as he crossed Allen Street a half-step
behind Ezra. Again, as before, Rod caught his own faint reflection in
the door windows of the Bird Cage – but did not recall seeing Ezra's
reflection. Maybe he missed it he thought, because his brain was
swirling with thoughts of what the next few minutes would bring.

Suppose Ezra was on the level... What then?

The two men rounded the corner of the Bird Cage and there,
again, was the door that would lead them inside - the door that had
not been there just a few hours before. They stepped inside and Ezra

again found the oil lamp and lit it.

Rod looked about. A black Mariah, an ornately trimmed funeral-wagon used to haul the dead to the cemetery, or Boot Hill, occupied one corner. Various antiques, and an old store display case lined the back wall. The stage curtain was down so that they could not look out into the audience area. Despite the dim light, Rod could see that the place was quite old, dingy, and drab – just the way an historic building in a state of "arrested decay" should be.

"Stay with me this time" Rod whispered.

"If you wish..." Ezra replied. "...but in a few minutes, you'll have no need for me. You'll have more people to talk to than you'll know what to do with!"

Rod didn't reply but sat down at the small prop table and chair in the center of the back-stage area, unzipped his jacket, and opened his laptop, poised to write – *the truth!* Ezra stood silently nearby, pulling his pipe from his pocket and began to fill it with tobacco from a small pouch secreted in a vest pocket.

Rod looked at his watch – 11:59:45. As he gazed at the watch, the second hand clicked past the hour. At that precise moment, the sound of heavy footsteps could be heard just on the other side of the stage curtain. Rod knew from pictures of the Bird Cage that two short stair cases graced either side of the stage allowing performers to step down off the stage into the audience. Now, it sounded like someone; someone with heavy boots, was climbing up one side of those stair cases approaching the back-stage area.

Rod's heart practically stopped as the curtain on stage-right moved and a man, dressed all in black with a wide-brimmed, pork-pie hat appeared. Instantly Rod recognized the man, and thought that he had again been made a fool of.

"Good evening Wyatt!" said Ezra delightedly.

"Good evening Ezra!" came the reply in the same tone.

Wyatt looked directly at Rod. "They are all waiting for you – all with a story to tell. I trust you are ready? Come, let me buy you a drink!"

Rod remained in his chair. He looked at Ezra who was smiling broadly, almost beaming. Rod then looked at Wyatt, also sporting a wide smile, his piercing blue eyes glistening in the faint light of the oil lamp, his royal moustache bristling as he spoke. "Come along... the night awaits you!"

Rod, now somewhat frightened of what might be on the other side of the curtain finally found the courage to speak and addressed Wyatt. "Who is waiting for me? Who are you talking about? I can't hear anything. I don't think there is anyone on the other side of this curtain!"

Wyatt extended his hand, "Well, you won't know unless you go out front and look now will you?"

Rod hesitated, and then, deciding there was nothing else to do but go out front, or run, he decided this would mark either the start of some mystical journey, or the end of the entire, elaborate hoax. Rod rose, grabbed his computer, and followed Wyatt around stage right.

Wyatt pulled the stage curtain aside and the two walked into what a moment ago had seemed like a darkened room but was now bright with the light from crystal chandeliers – revealing a room full of reveling patrons. Rod gasped. Instead of being musty, dark, dull and dingy, everything looked new and fresh. Rod imagined that this was how the theatre looked on opening night in December of 1881!

A small oak bar toward the front of the room had people lined up for drinks – whisky, beer and cigars. A small dumb-waiter just to one side of the bar hoisted drinks to "waitresses" serving male patrons in the boxes high above the main floor while cigar smoke and the sound of a tinkling piano permeated the air. Everyone was in high spirits, laughing and cajoling each other, the ladies in their fine evening gowns and the men all dressed in their finest clothes.

Rod stood staring at the scene with his eyes fixated and his jaw open. It was too elaborate for a hoax, he thought. It could be a movie set or television show set was his next thought, but there were no cameras, no mike-booms, no "techno-clutter" around. It looked like the real thing!

Rod, Wyatt and Ezra walked down the short stairway onto the main floor. Nobody seemed to notice that Rod was dressed in blue jeans, a tee shirt, light jacket and sneakers and stood out like a sore thumb. Not to mention the computer now neatly tucked in the crook of his arm, partially concealed, but still visible. People would give him a glancing look, then return to whatever they were doing.

The three stopped at the bottom of the stairs when Wyatt turned to Ezra, "Would you like me to introduce him around?"

"A capital idea!' Ezra replied. "Meanwhile, I believe I'll have a drink at the bar. Join me later won't you?"

Ezra then looked straight at the dumbfounded lawyer, "Well, you wanted the truth. Here are the people that can give you the truth. Everyone you ever read about in every story ever written about Tombstone... is here tonight! And like I said, you don't need me to talk to anymore. Show him around Wyatt!"

As the two men prepared to walk about the main floor, suddenly the stage curtain opened revealing a huge, fully decorated Christmas tree – which Rod could not believe was not there a moment ago.

Moreover, all the clutter, including the prop table and chair was gone – as were the brown water stains on the back stage curtains and walls – and the black Mariah. A finely-dressed man walked to the center of the stage and as he approached the center, everyone in the theater stood and applauded.

The man removed his black top-hat, and raised his hands in acknowledgement of the crowd's appreciation. As the applause began to subside, the man began to speak, "Happy Holidays everyone – and welcome to the Bird Cage Theatre. I am your host, Billy Hutchinson. Please enjoy yourselves! Let the revelry begin!"

The crowd again applauded as Rod turned to Wyatt, "Happy Holidays? Isn't he kind of early? Why, this is only October!"

Wyatt smiled, "Mr. Livingston, it is December 26, 1881 – opening night here at the Bird Cage. In fact, every night is opening night here at the Bird Cage – every – night!"

As Rod tried to fathom what Wyatt was saying, a man dressed in black pants, a grey vest, grey frock coat and grey Stetson approached. The man's long, drooping moustache and pasty complexion gave the impression that he was a very sick person – looking older than his chronological age. Wyatt and the man-in gray shook hands. "Good evening Wyatt! Who is your friend?" A southern drawl was distinctly present in the man's voice.

"Good evening Doc" came Wyatt's reply. "I'd like you to meet Mr. Rod Livingston, attorney, writer, and seeker of the truth. Mr. Livingston, may I present Doctor John Holliday."

Doc and Rod shook hands and Rod could not help notice that's Doc's hands were every bit as cold as Wyatt's had been. Rod could not help himself and blurted out, "Doc? Doc Holliday - *the* Doc Holliday?"... seeming every bit a nervous schoolboy on his first date, not a Los Angeles District Attorney.

Doc winked at Rod as he replied, "Do you know any other Doc Hollidays?"

Rod stood in utter amazement not quite knowing what to make of everything. The people, the music, the cigar smoke and meeting Wyatt Earp and Doc Holliday on the Bird Cage's opening night all seemed like a dream. He half expected to wake up to find it was all a dream... but for now it seemed so real.

As their hands parted Doc took a step backwards and looked Rod up and down, "Seeker of the truth huh?"

"Indeed Mr. Holliday – and I plan to write about it and let the world know what really happened in Tombstone." Rod replied with an air of authority – as much as he could muster still not quite sure who he was really talking to.

Doc stared at the lawyer for just a moment, then stepped right up to him placing his left hand on Rod's right shoulder saying in a low tone, "If you want to know the truth about that street fight a few weeks ago out on Fremont Street, sit down here at my table and I'll tell you."

The two men sat down at a nearby table. Rod placed his laptop on the table, opened it and turned it on – half expecting the 21st century contrivance not to work... seeing that he was now in the 19th century – and he wondered what he would do if it did not work. But with a couple of beeps and a few flickering pilot lights, the computer came to life.

Rod was suddenly painfully aware that his dress and mode of note taking were hideously incongruent with the rest of the scene. But lacking any further insight, he decided to simply continue and see what happened.

Once seated, Doc began to open up and Rod Livingston, seeker of the truth, began to write, "Now... historians have tried to make me the perpetrator of that whole sad affair. The fact is, one of the McLaury brothers – and I'm still not quite sure which one – neither one of those curs will admit it - but one of them cocked their revolver first, getting ready to fire. Hearing that, I let go with the first shot from Virgil's shotgun, and then..."

Rod and Doc sat talking for several hours as Rod tapped away at the keyboard. Every few moments Ezra or Wyatt would approach the two and introduce Rod to a host of people. Mayor Clum, Johnny Ringo, Curly Bill, and Ike Clanton as well as all of Wyatt's brothers were present.

Rod listened to Doc, his fingers flying across the keyboard as the party roared. A variety of singers, dancers and other interesting if not bizarre acts graced the stage, all to the tune of a small orchestra poised directly in front of the stage. If it was a dream he thought, it was the best one, and most realistic he had ever had!

Then amidst the furor and seeming calamity of it all, Billy Hutchinson once again took the stage and all suddenly got quiet – as if on cue. Billy walked to center stage and announced, "First light! First light!"

Ezra hurried to where Doc and Rod had been sitting all evening. "Mr. Livingston, it is first light. We must be going!"

"First light?" Rod protested. "What is first light? And Doc and I are just getting into it. And I haven't even talked to any of the others yet! I need more time, Ezra! More time!"

"There will be time later." Ezra assured. "But for now, its time to go. We have to leave before the tourists begin arriving."

Rod and Doc shook hands again – that same, cold, clammy hand of Doc's – and headed up the stage steps and out the door through which they had entered hours ago. The two men walked to the front of the building and out onto Allen Street. Looking east toward Sixth Street, Rod could just see the first slivers of daylight on the horizon.

Rod looked at Ezra again with a quizzical look on his face and said, "First light... what's the deal with first light anyway?"

The two men stopped in the middle of Allen Street and Ezra turned to face Rod, a serious look on his face. "I'm sure you have read the accounts of people hearing or seeing things – strange things – metaphysical things - in the Bird Cage?"

"Of course" replied Rod. "Many people have had strange experiences in there. I've read several... and seen a few photos purportedly of ghosts in there. What of it? Certainly you are not saying that..."

Rod stopped in mid-sentence, suddenly grasping the gravity of what he was saying.

Ezra smiled and quickly replied, "Mr. Livingston, the Bird Cage is, well, what you might call a repository of the essence of Tombstone. If the essence becomes, or in this case, remains in concentrated form, as it is most nights with a full party going on, the essence tends to bleed over into the corporeal world and thus, the anomalies occur that you read about! Too much of that would cause too many people to come snooping around. That kind of snooping we don't need. But when there is less concentration of the essence, like during the day and early evening hours, all is in balance."

Rod tried to grasp Ezra's explanation, his mind spinning. The two continued walking across the street and stopped in front of Ezra's store. Ezra said, "I believe I will get a jump on the day and start early. Will I see you again tonight?"

Wednesday, October 13, 2003 11:30 AM Tombstone, Arizona

Rod awoke from a fitful sleep and had to re-orient himself. "Yes," he thought; "I am in a motel room in Tombstone, and yes, it is 11:30 in the morning, a bright, shining morning and..."

Rod thought quickly back to his night of interviewing Doc Holliday then thought about all the notes he had taken. Jumping out of bed, he quickly went to the dresser where he had placed his laptop, turned it on, found the file, and read the pages and pages of text. Yes... it was all there. Doc's own words! The truth about the OK Corral gunfight from non other than Doc Holliday himself!

Closing the file, Rod collapsed back onto the bed and proclaimed to no one in particular; "Doc Holiday himself! Listen to me. Who is going to believe that?"

Seeking affirmation of the night before, Rod dressed and walked down Fifth Street, onto Allen and down to the Bird Cage Theatre. As before, the door he and Ezra had used to enter the night spot was just a blank wall during the day.

As Rod stood staring at the blank wall he heard a voice behind him, "Hello Mr. Livingston. I trust you had a good time last night?"

Rod turned around to see Mayor John P. Clum approaching him, looking every bit as dapper as he had the night before in his finest brown, pin-stripped suit and derby hat, and as chipper as if he had had a good night's rest.

"Indeed, I did have a good time!"

"And will we see you again tonight?"

"You can count on it. In fact, I would like to interview you tonight if I may, Mr. Mayor. Or even better, how about if we do an interview right now? I'll run back to my hotel room, get my computer..."

Rod heard someone call his name from across the street. He turned away from the Mayor to see a man standing in front of Ezra's mercantile store. He was dressed in fancy, hand-stitched boots, sporting a pair of ivory-handled Colts holstered butt-forward, a bright blue and white striped shirt, large red bandanna around his neck and a white Stetson capping long, brown, curly locks of hair – Curly Bill!

Rod turned back to continue his conversation with Mayor Clum. But in the second it took to turn his head in the direction of Curly Bill and turn back again, the Mayor was gone.

Befuddled, but getting somewhat used to people coming and going so quickly, Rod walked across Allen Street to greet the gunman. The two shook hands and as before with the other characters that he met, Curly's hand was cold – ice cold. The two men began to talk and in a moment, Ezra emerged from his store with two glistening bottles of cold sarsaparilla, handing a bottle to the Los Angeles lawyer and the gunman.

"Mr. Livingston here is going to write the story of Curly Bill Brocius!' Curly announced to Ezra. "And he's going to tell the truth – that I am not a heartless killer – but a rancher and a business man."

Ezra smiled and the three men stood talking and sipping on the sweet beverage for several minutes. Periodically, people would walk by and say a brief hello or wave from across the street as they passed by; people who Rod had met the night before, and he now knew at least by sight. Morgan and Virgil Earp, Sheriff Johnny Behan, Billy Breckenridge, Big Nose Kate, George Parsons... all people whom Rod had first been introduced to through his reading of Tombstone events, then introduced to the night before, all made their presence known. Rod thought, "Were they really good reenactors? Were they the real thing?"

After waving to Billy Claiborne, the youngest of the cow-boy faction, Rod focused his attention on Ezra with a quizzical look – a look Ezra had seen before on the Los Angeles attorney. Before he could even ask the question of the mercantilist, Ezra had the answer for him. "As you can see, Mr. Livingston, they are all around us. The tourists and even the locals think they are reenactors when in fact, they are the originals - still here after all these years - still waiting for someone to tell the truth about Tombstone and the lives they led here. They are all hoping that you will be the one, Mr. Livingston - the one to tell the truth."

"But I have a further question about some of them". Rod replied. "I knew the majority of the people you and Wyatt introduced me to last night. If I had not seen their picture at least I knew the names. But there were several people that I did not recognize at all! I didn't recognize their face or their names. Who are they?"

Ezra took on a dark countenance, "Pray that fate does not let you learn their identity. Some truths are better left undiscovered."

Rod had been intensely focusing on Ezra while he talked forgetting about Curly Bill. "Well Ezra," he started, "Curly Bill had begun to tell me his story. And I'll be sure to get it right."

Smiling, Rod turned to where Curly Bill had been standing, looking for approval from his new-found gunfighter friend. Instead, he stared at an empty sarsaparilla bottle; sitting on the wooden boardwalk, still wobbling from being hurriedly placed in its spot.

******

Rod Livingston spent the next 9 nights at the Bird Cage – every night an opening night – every night everyone was greeted by Billy Hutchinson wishing them Happy Holidays. Rod interviewed everyone, typing furiously on his laptop. Gunfighters, lawmen, soiled doves, miners, merchants, shop-keepers, politicians, and bankers came to Ezra to tell him their story – and he wrote down every word filling page after page with – the *truth*.

Rod was thrilled. Of all the authors, the countless authors who had penned stories about Tombstone, his would be recognized as the truth. He would come to be known as the undisputed authority about Tombstone as well as the Earps, Holliday – everyone. The truth would be told – and the lawyer, come-historian would tell it.

******

Saturday, October 23, 2003 2:00PM Corner of Fourth and Allen Streets, Tombstone, Arizona

A lone reenactor, dressed in chaps, a blue non-descript shirt and red bandana stepped into the center of the intersection of Fourth and Allen Streets, fired off three rounds of blanks from his Colt .45 to get everyone's attention, and began to speak loudly, so the gathering tourists could hear him. "Welcome to Tombstone's 74th annual Helldorado Days, folks. My name is Bob King, and I'll be your host for today's festivities. In just a few moments, the Wild West Gunslingers, a fine group of reenactors from California will be putting on quite a show for you - to show you what really happened at the OK Corral so many years ago!"

A crowd of tourists gathered on the corner of Fourth and Allen Streets to await the mock gunfight, a staple of Tombstone's annual Helldorado Days celebration since it was first held in 1929. With cameras around their necks sporting pseudo cowboy hats all waited patiently.

Of all the events held in Tombstone to generate tourist traffic, Helldorado is the "grand-daddy" of them all, attracting tourists and would-be gunfighters, lawmen and soiled doves from all over the US and several foreign countries.

Waiting for his next night of note-taking and revelry at the Bird Cage, Rod sauntered onto Allen Street to take-in the festivities, arriving just in time to hear Bob King, Master of Ceremonies ready the crowd for yet another gun battle. Rod carried his laptop with him, just in case he should run into one of his new friends on the street that had time to talk.

As he emerged onto Allen Street from Fifth, a stagecoach drawn by two horses carrying tourists on a tour of Tombstone approached. The reproduction Wells-Fargo stage coach was fully loaded with six tourists inside, six riding on top, and a driver and shot-gun messenger "on the box." The horses were spirited, this being the first full day of Helldorado festivities and with a large crowd on hand.

The stage pulled up at the curb and was about to start letting passengers off when suddenly, a tall, thin cowboy, one of the reenactors dressed in a long, dirty, white duster and worn chaps walked out onto the street and let go with a double shot gun blast. This was normal fare – a way for the reenactors to announce that a show was about to start – but they usually waited for the stagecoach to reload with passengers and get down the street before they discharged a shotgun.

With all the other commotion on the street, it was all the impetus the horses needed. Before the driver knew what was happening the team bolted and began running down Allen Street.

Rod Livingston had just stepped from the curb, lost in thought, thinking of the night before and who he might interview this night – or the next, when he suddenly looked up to find two wild horses and a stagecoach full of screaming people bearing down on him at a rapid pace.

Before he could react, the stagecoach was upon him, knocking him to the ground. As he went down he lost his grip on his computer – which went flying – bouncing on the street and trampled by careless hooves. The last thing Rod saw just before the huge, yellow wagon wheel crushed his chest, was pieces of plastic and circuit boards flying everywhere. And then... all went black.

Sunday, October 24, 2003   4:30AM The Bird Cage Theatre, Tombstone, Arizona

Rod was suddenly conscious that he was sitting at table in the Bird Cage, the same as he had been for the past several nights – but this was different. Very different – and it just suddenly occurred to him that things were... well... different.

He had spent the past several hours talking to Tombstone's most famous female entrepreneur, Nellie Cashman, and taking notes with a pad of paper and a pencil!

Rod excused himself on the pretext of going to the bar for a drink, but his real agenda was to look around and try to decide what was different and why. Something just didn't feel right.

Arriving at the mahogany altar of liquor, Rod looked up to see his friend Ezra tending bar, "What'll it be Mr. Livingston? Ah... I know... I have just the drink for you!"

Ezra reached behind himself and produced a cold bottle of sarsaparilla, handing it to the incredulous attorney. Before he could blurt out a question, Rod happened to look beyond Ezra to the mirror at the back-bar and could not see his own reflection – or the reflection of anyone else in the room for that matter! The theatre lobby reflected in the glass was old and dingy with long streaks of water stain running down the brown walls, a picture of Fatima, the exotic dancer, in the background complete with tears and rips, the way it appeared in 2003!

Turning around, Rod saw a different lobby, fresh and new, the picture of Fatima undamaged and in vibrant color as if just painted. The red brocade wall paper looked as expensive and lavish as the red velvet curtains gracing the stairways leading to the second-floor show boxes. The mirror reflected an empty lobby of the 21st century but looking across the crowded room full of cigar smoke and the smell of whisky it was opening night – all over again.

Rod looked down at himself to see what he was wearing. A blue, pin-stripped suit complete with gold watch and chain stretched across a four-pocket vest was completed with a boiled-white shirt, smart red cravat-style tie and high-topped shoes. On his head sat a smart, brown derby-style hat. Rod looked every bit the part of a "dandy-dude" and could have passed for a business man, attorney, or newspaperman in 1880's Tombstone – although he was completely unsure where the clothes came from they fit well, were quite clean and unwrinkled – although it occurred to him that he may have been wearing them for many hours prior to his being conscious of wearing them.

Just then another rather dapper man, similarly dressed approached the bar. Ezra addressed the two men, "Mr. Livingston, I would like you to meet Mr. Harry Carson, also of Los Angeles – also a writer – or – would-be writer."

Rod turned to Ezra then to his new acquaintance, "Would-be writer?"

Ezra replied, "Yes…you see…"

His sentence was interrupted when proprietor Billy Hutchinson took the stage, as he did every morning at about this same time announcing, "First light! First light!"

With a sudden look of consternation on his face, Rod looked at Ezra, "Well… I guess its time to go. Will you be leaving with me Ezra?"

Ezra just smiled, first at Rod, then at Mr. Carson. Carson turned and smiled at Rod. Then Ezra spoke, "Mr. Livingston – there is no rush. You have all the time in the world. Stay here if you like, or take a stroll down Allen Street to enjoy the Helldorado festivities. It doesn't matter. For you – it just doesn't matter anymore. You are now where you are *supposed* to be – in Tombstone."

More perplexed than ever, Rod alternated his stare between Ezra and Mr. Carson. Finally, Carson spoke, "You see Mr. Livingston, back around 1950, I too wanted to write the truth about Tombstone and Wyatt Earp. I ran into Ezra here who gave me the same unique opportunity you had. And like you, my time on earth was cut short – too short to get my material published. It's the same story for about 20 of us here – the people you didn't recognize – well – that's us. Or more precisely, that's now… you! If you take a walk down Allen Street to Fourth, you can still see where the street is stained with your own blood. It was one of the worst accidents ever on Allen Street."

Ezra walked around from the back of the bar, grabbing his frock coat and top hat from a rack behind the bar. Donning both so as to appear "proper" in front of the patrons, Ezra moved into the main part of the lobby and past Carson and Rod, noting, "I have an announcement to make."

Ezra walked to the back of the room and took the stage, Billy Hutchinson having just vacated it. In a loud voice so everyone could hear, Ezra announced, "Ladies and gentlemen - in the parlance of the 21st century, we have some bad news and some good news. The bad news is that we have lost yet another writer, and would-be teller of the truth about Tombstone. The good news is that the mystery, mystique and romance surrounding Tombstone is alive and well and as long as that persists, people will come to Tombstone and keep it's memory, if not it's truths, alive. Writers will continue to write books and magazine articles telling what they know, and what they believe to be the truth. Someday, maybe they will know the truth. But for now, the public must settle for the legend and the romance that is Tombstone. You see... Mr. Rod Livingston, former Los Angeles attorney, and would-be teller of the truth will now be joining us for opening night... every night."

The Real Story Behind "The Writer"

The Writers

In 1914, it looked like things couldn't get any worse for Tombstone. The mines were flooded, most of the residents had fled, and business in general was at low ebb. But things did get worse.

State prohibition in 1914 forced the closure of all Tombstone's saloons, the town's only draw for the meager cadre of soldiers that ventured the 18 miles from Fort Huachuca for a cool drink. Some saloon owners turned their places into full fledged restaurants, others became movie theaters and others simply shuttered their windows and doors and left. Tombstone continued to limp along as best it could.

The summer of 1919 saw journalist Frederick Bechdolt in southern Arizona, covering miners' labor disputes and gathering historical data for a series of stories he wanted to write. At the time, Bechdolt had the unique opportunity to talk with old-timers, people who had come to Tombstone and the surrounding areas in the 1880's and had lived through the Earp era, had seen the Bird Cage during it's glory days, and sat side by side with the Clantons and McLaury's at the Crystal Palace Saloon. He even interviewed "Texas" John Slaughter, long-time rancher and one-time Cochise County Sheriff. It only interview Slaughter ever gave.

..r the title, Stories of the Old West", Bechdolt's series of stories began running in the *Saturday Evening Post* in November, 1919. He described Tombstone as a "roaring town" that "had a man for breakfast every morning".

The legend, as it is known today, had begun.

Gradually, Bechdolt's stories garnered interest in Tombstone and with the advent of the automobile, people began journeying to Tombstone to see the places they had just read about.

In 1922, Bechdolt cobbled his stories together in book form and released, *When The West Was Young.* It was an instant hit. The book went on sale in Tombstone. With a stroke of the journalists' pen, the world was introduced to a series of characters that might have been forgotten, but today have become practically household words.

Other writers and books would soon follow.

One of the most seminal works was writer Walter Noble Burns' *Tombstone – An Iliad of the Southwest* released in 1927. Much of the material was sourced from the pages of the *Tombstone Epitaph* newspaper, piles of which could then be pawed through at the Arizona Pioneers Historical Society.

Old copies of the *Epitaph* also served as the primary source for Douglas Martin's *Tombstone's Epitaph* released in 1951.

"Helldorado", a tell-all book written by former Cochise County Deputy Sheriff Billy Breckenridge was released in 1928. The book slammed the Earps and is one of the few ever published that does not treat the Earps kindly, or at least on even footing with other contemporaries. Breckenridge along with his boss, Sheriff Johnny Behan were on opposite ends of the social and political stick facing the Earps and Doc Holliday.

In October, 1931, Stuart Lake's "Frontier Marshal", an early effort covering the life of Wyatt Earp was released and became an instant success starting what could be considered the first wave of Earp-mania.

Early writers had nowhere to go to source material other than contemporary newspaper accounts and interviews with old timers, perhaps the purest way of sourcing historical material.

Over time, many other writers, sometimes due to carelessness, sloppiness, time constraints, political pressures, or just plain maliciousness began to get their facts wrong. Other writers, using the same bad material as a source also got the facts wrong, and the mis-information and bad information, no matter its impetus, was perpetuated.

In one such case, a well known writer, claiming to have access to a myriad of materials from Tombstone's past began to pen stories that were rich in detail and seemed readily plausible. But under severe scrutiny, the writer finally confessed that he was a "novelist", not a historian, and that much of his material was contrived based on few verifiable facts. His career as a writer was over, but his material lives on.

Gradually, the information, from that writer and others, was debunked by more careful research and emerging facts. Each writer subsequently wanted to be known as the provider of the "truth" about Wyatt Earp, Tombstone, and the OK Corral shootout. Each proclaimed to reveal what *really* happened in Tombstone in 1881.

The Writer

Rod Livingston is purely a fictional character – but he could be based on any number of writers known to *this* writer.

Rod kept using the term "Suppose", as he pondered the sincerity of Ezra and Wyatt; a term he otherwise rarely used. The last words uttered by Wyatt Earp as he lay dying in a rented bungalow in Los Angeles on Sunday morning, January 13, 1929 were reported to be, "Suppose... suppose..."

The Bird Cage

In July 1881, Billy Hutchinson and his wife Lottie purchased a plot of land on the southwestern corner of Sixth and Allen Street for six hundred dollars. Their dream, financed by a San Francisco liquor distributor was to build a place of entertainment and culture – where Tombstone's elite could while away their leisure hours in an exciting yet refined atmosphere. They wanted "respectable" citizens to feel at home in the place, unthreatened by some of the rougher elements that frequented places like the Crystal Palace, or the Oriental; two of Tombstone's favorite "watering holes."

The Hutchinson's vision was for an entertainment mecca that would rival the best theatre house from the east coast to the Barbary Coast. The *Tombstone Epitaph* of the times proclaimed that the new Bird Cage would be "dedicated by Hutchinson's Variety troupe in an entirely new and original series of plays, songs, dances, etc. that will serve to interest and amuse the audience.

Just prior to the theatre's opening Billy Hutchinson traveled to San Francisco to secure a bevy of talent. He wanted the best for his opening night. Appearing that night was a comedy team of Burns and Trayers who "kept the audience convulsed with laughter."

Billy found all sorts of talent to appear at his inaugural night festivities including piccolo player Harry Lorraine and Miss Irene Baker who was described as "pretty" with "a sweet voice" and was a "clever actress."

Other acts included the "woman with the iron jaw: who could pick up heavy objects in her teeth. In stark contrast was serious opera singer, Carrie Delmar. It was a veritable cornucopia of talent.

On the evening of December 26, 1881, dust-covered miners sidled with formally dressed ladies and businessmen, each paying their fifty -cent admission fee to see the latest show in town. Drink-hawking hostesses flitted about the room easily making friends with all they came into contact with inviting men to have a drink – the expensive stuff – and to continue imbibing. "Drifters and droolers", miners and muckers, clerks, cashiers, bankers and bad-men all "slaked their thirst" for both booze and women at the Bird Cage.

For many years after it opened the Bird Cage ran full-blast, twenty -four hours a day, seven days a week – such was Tombstone's hunger for entertainment and diversion.

Unfortunately for Billy Hutchinson, the Bird Cage never achieved the social status he sought - a place for Tombstone's elite. That honor would go to Schieffelin Hall, one block north and two blocks east of the Bird Cage. Though not far away geographically, it was a world apart in terms of social status.

This could have evolved because of the Bird Cage's close proximity to the "cribs' of ill repute along Sixth Street, or simply because of the entertainment offered. While Schieffelin Hall was host to professional acting troupes in what would today be considered "PG" rated shows, the Bird Cage catered to a stronger element with such wild events as masquerade balls featuring "raunchy ballad singers" and men impersonating women – and vice versa.

While the town roared, so went the Bird Cage. But like most boom-towns, Tombstone was destined to go bust. The mines began to fill with water as the miners dug deeper and deeper. Large pumps were brought in to drain the water – and the plan worked for a while. But fire destroyed the pumps in 1886. That, coupled with the declining value of the silver that was being taken from the ground spelled the beginning of the end for the west's most famous honky-tonk.

Later Bird Cage owners, Joe and Minnie Bignon, tried in vain to drum up business but Tombstone's silver allure had been tarnished. The place would not attract either performers or audiences. The Bignons closed shop in 1892, returning briefly sometime later for a short stint, but shuttered it again.

In an effort to revive Tombstone as a tourist attraction, the town's citizens developed the idea for "Helldorado Days", a celebration of the town's history, lore and legend. The first Helldorado celebration was held in 1929 as it continues today, on the third weekend in October.

After being boarded up for almost 40 years, the old bawdy house was again reopened for 1929's Helldorado, inadvertently becoming one of the main attractions for the entire event. Appearing on stage in 1929, as she had in the mid-1880's was singer Annie Duncan, the "Tombstone Nightingale."

And watching the show, as they had done almost 50 years prior, was former Cochise County Deputy-Sheriff under Johnny Behan, Billy Breckenridge, and former Tombstone mayor, John P. Clum – both men from Tombstone's Earp era in the early 1880's.

Today, the Bird Cage is still a big attraction in Tombstone, as a museum and one of the few original buildings, large portions of the town succumbing to two major fires. Locals and tourists alike, hundreds of them, have experienced paranormal activities in the musty confines of the Bird Cage's adobe walls.

This writer has personally seen photographs taken by a Clanton descendant showing eerily floating balls of light in the otherwise darkened theatre. Being inside the theatre, even during the day, one can sense a presence. Standing on the boardwalk in front of the place late at night, this writer has experienced an eerie and bizarre phenomenon – as if someone were watching! Perhaps, it was Rod Livingston, or Ezra Thornton – or even... Wyatt Earp himself!

Chapter 6: THE IMMORTALS

"You two will have a stage act. Lester will be the star. We'll call him The Fastest Man Alive."

Ezra T. Thornton February 1882

February 1882 5:00PM Tombstone, A.T.

Ezra T. Thornton locked the heavy wooden and glass door of his mercantile store, turned, and began the short, one-block walk west down to the corner of Fifth and Allen Street and the Crystal Palace Saloon. A cool breeze caused small dust-swirls in the dirt street. Ezra's long, white hair stuck out from his top-hat and the breeze made the locks stream out behind him. Ezra buttoned his black frock coat against the oncoming cold of the night as the sun set in a brilliant red at the western end of Allen Street.

Finely dressed women with children in tow who had been shopping throughout the afternoon began to vacate Tombstone's main thoroughfare. A loud blast from the steam whistle at the Consolidated Mine Works signaled the end of a shift. Soon, the street would fill with dirty, tired miners looking for a respite from their daily toil. Cow-boys with broad-brimmed hats, businessmen in sack-suits, Chinese coolies, soiled doves, nattily dressed card sharps, men and women of all stations lived and worked here in Tombstone, one of the biggest boomtowns of the west. In the wake of the OK Corral incident and the national attention it brought to the town giving it a reputation for be a rowdy place, people continued to pour into the city from all over the country, looking for that one opportunity to strike it rich and make a name for themselves.

The heels from Ezra's shoes made a distinct clumping sound as he strode down the covered boardwalk toward the Crystal Palace. The clumping stopped as his heels hit the dirt of Fifth Street. Ezra crossed the street, stepped into the Palace, and strode directly up to the bar. He ordered a beer, then took a table near the door where he could look outside onto Allen Street. Despite the few people in the saloon, the air was still heavy with the smell of acrid cigar smoke, tobacco juice and cheap perfume. A single piano near the back of the large room plinked out some imperceptible tune played by a non-descript piano player.

As Ezra sipped his beer, he heard the Kinnear Stage pull up to a stop across the street in front of the Grand Hotel. He stepped just outside the saloon's front door to get the first glimpse of Tombstone's latest visitors or... newest residents. The dust was still swirling around the stage as two passengers emerged from opposite sides of the now dark recesses of the coach.

The first man to light seemed to be about 35 years old, slight build, almost boyish complexion topped with long blonde hair and finely dressed in a brown sack suit, overcoat and a black derby. He sported a neatly trimmed moustache, blond, but slightly darker than his hair. As his foot hit Allen Street he looked around, almost in amazement and somewhat incredulously. It seemed to Ezra, from the look on the man's face, that he was amazed at what he saw. What was the man to expect from a raw and still growing mining camp?

The second man had emerged from the opposite side and was walking around the back of the coach. This man was considerably younger, early 20's, Ezra figured. He was tall, lanky, with short-cropped brown hair, clean shaven, and dressed in fine blue corduroy pants, matching blue vest, white starched shirt with dirt in the sleeve creases from the 20-mile ride from the train station at Benson. His collar was open; the sign of what had likely been a long trip, probably being several days in the same clothes.

Two men from the Grand Hotel greeted the older man, helped him retrieve two rather large trunks from the top of the stage, and the three of them disappeared along with the trunks into the hotel. "Another easterner!" Ezra thought. "Looks like a business man. But what can he be carrying in those huge trunks? Hmmm? "

Former Tombstone mayor, John Clum, pulled up behind the stage driving a spring wagon. The younger man stepped over to greet Clum shaking hands. He helped the young man load his two small bags onto the wagon and the two of them headed north on Fourth Street toward Clum's house.

Clum had not run for reelection the month before. His alignment with the Earp – Holliday faction, once a positive influence in Tombstone had turned sour. Many residents blamed the Earps and Holliday, rather than the Cow-boys for the street-fight behind the OK Corral the previous October. The Earps, especially Virgil were seen as the perpetrators of the mayhem and anyone who was aligned with them carried the same stigma. Although Clum continued to run the *Tombstone Epitaph* newspaper it was difficult for him to sell local advertising and some of his staff had left his employ over the affair.

Ezra stepped back into the "Palace", sat down, and engaged in some light conversation with some of the other Tombstone businessmen as they came in for their afternoon thirst-quencher before heading home for dinner.

It was almost 6PM. Ezra was gulping the last of his beer and was just about to stand and leave when the older man from the stage strode in. His overcoat and suit coat now missing, he stood in his shirt-sleeves and vest although his black, brocade cravat style tie and black derby were still in place. Standing just inside the door, the stranger looked about the room with the same incredulous look as when he lighted from the stage an hour before. It almost seemed like he was looking for something or, perhaps not believing what he was seeing. At any rate, it was apparent that he was disoriented.

Ezra remembered the two large trunks the man had recently unloaded from the stage. Curious, and being that they were now physically so close, Ezra spoke up from where he sat extending his hand to shake the other man's hand. "Good afternoon sir. And welcome to Tombstone! I am Ezra T. Thornton."

The stranger looked down at Ezra, smiled, and shook Ezra's hand. "I'm Lester."

Ezra returned the broad smile. "Well Lester. What do you say I treat you to a beer and you tell me how you like our little town?"

Lester pulled out a chair opposite Ezra and sat down as Ezra motioned to one of the hostesses to draw two beers. The noise level of the "Palace" began to rise as more and more people came through the front door looking for their evening's pleasure. The clicking of the roulette wheel now seemed incessant and the flap of shuffling cards could barely be heard above the now constant tinkling of the piano.

Ezra looked at Lester to see who, or what he was watching as Lester continued to look about the room with a quizzical look on his face. "Are you looking for someone?" inquired Ezra. "I know just about everyone in town."

Lester leaned forward in his chair and looked intently at Ezra, "I've come to Tombstone to make myself immortal, Mr. Thornton. Immortal!"

Ezra looked back at his new friend in great surprise. "Immortal? Hmm? That's a pretty tall order for any town, let alone a relatively new mining camp. Is there something here that I don't know about? Special spring waters perhaps? Or perhaps some special mineral is being extracted from the ground along with the silver that has that capability? Or perhaps... there is someone here, maybe in this very room that has the ability to make you immortal?"

Lester smiled at Ezra's amazement. The hostess set the two beers on the table. The two men eyed each other as they simultaneously drew their first quaff of the golden brew.

Lester wiped the foam from his moustache with his sleeve. "Well, you might say there is somebody here who can make me immortal, Mr. Thornton. You see, I have this desire, not to live beyond my years as the term immortal might infer, but to have people remember me for all time. I am an educated man having attended college in Massachusetts. I traveled west to find what I wanted to do. I spent several years as a bank clerk in San Francisco and knew that would not bring fame or immortality. I went to Virginia City to open a mercantile store with a business partner, which didn't pan out. I have been in practically every cow-town and mining camp from St. Louis to the Barbary Coast looking, looking... trying to find myself and my fate. My last job was not far from here as a Well Fargo station agent over in Naco. And then it hit me!"

"What hit you, Lester?" Ezra asked taking another sip of beer.

Lester leaned forward. There was a twinkle in his eye. "For years I have been reading in the newspapers about the troupes of entertainers traveling throughout the west. And the same names keep appearing, first in this town, then that. When they appear on stage people applaud. Men in the audience throw roses at the actresses on stage. After the show, members of the audience buy drinks for the actors. They are lauded wherever they go and people adore them. They are famous. That's what I want to be, Mr. Thornton – famous. And with fame will come immortality. People will remember my name long after I'm gone!"

"I see" said Ezra rather thoughtfully. "And do you have any training in the area of acting? Have you appeared in any local productions? How about school? Did you perform with the students in any Shakespearian plays perhaps?"

The twinkle went out of Lester's eyes and he looked downward into his beer. "Well, you see... that's the damnation of it Mr. Thornton. Now that I know what I want to do; now that I know what will make me immortal, I don't know if I have the talent for it. I have never performed in a play. I have never acted before."

Ezra sat back in his chair and crossed his arms. "It seems you have an interesting dilemma, Lester. So, this person you are seeking. What role will they play in your quest for immortality?"

"Oh yes!" The twinkle returned to Lester's eyes. "Despite my lack of training, I feel I have the talent. Talent, like the silver ore being pulled from the ground around Tombstone, has to be refined and developed to make it shine. I read about the recent opening of the Bird Cage Theatre here in Tombstone and that Billy Hutchinson, the theatre's owner is beginning to attract many of the best troupes and acts in the country. I am hoping to join an acting company here in Tombstone and tour with them. I am looking for someone... anyone who appears to be an actor or actress. Once I identify them, I'll introduce myself and maybe...just maybe..."

Ezra choked back a smile thinking that his new friend had fanciful ideas that could never be realized. "And what makes you think an acting company would enlist your, er... talents, Lester? What do you have that an acting company would want?"

Lester looked at Ezra and took on a serious tone. "Costumes, Mr. Thornton, costumes. Buying or making costumes is always a challenge for an actor. Over the past few years I have been collecting costumes in every town I have visited. I brought two trunks of costumes and more are on the way. When the manager of the acting company sees my costumes, and knows that I am ready for any play, any part, it will be my ticket in. Then, I will have to prove myself. But prove myself I will! I will be immortal!"

"You sound quite serious, Lester."

"I am indeed, sir!"

Ezra sat back in his chair, gulping the last of his beer. He sat the mug on the table and looked intently at Lester. "Well, if you are that serious, I happen to know Billy Hutchinson quite well. His Bird Cage Theatre is across the street from my store on the corner of 6th and Allen. Stop by tomorrow at precisely noon. I'll take you over and introduce you to him."

Lester smiled, "I will Mr. Thornton. Thank you!"

"Until tomorrow then...!" Ezra rose, donned his coat and hat, and headed out onto Allen Street.

******

Ezra stepped from the warm light of the Crystal Place into the now -cold darkness of Allen Street. The children of Tombstone and most of the ladies, except those who were escorted by their husbands or paramours, had vacated Allen Street. At night, Allen Street belonged mostly to the male constituency.

Many miners had just completed a day of backbreaking work to earn a few dollars of pay. The card sharps, gambling cheats, and ladies-of-the-night had started their hard-nights work to separate the miners from their earnings.

The street was dark except for the light coming through the windows and open doorways of the many saloons up and down the street. Cow-boys and business men, miners and military men from nearby Camp Huachuca, ladies of negotiable affections, and people of all station roamed Allen Street, going from saloon to saloon, looking for that next encounter that could make them rich... or famous... or both!

Ezra stopped for a moment on the boardwalk in front of the Crystal Palace Saloon to take in this scene. "How wonderful a time this is." He thought. "A time of such great opportunity!"

His musings soon gave way to the hunger in his stomach. Ezra stepped off the boardwalk and headed across the street to the Grand Hotel and a hot meal.

The Grand Hotel was as the name implied; the grandest hotel in Tombstone and one of the best between St. Louis and San Francisco. The décor was magnificent with red brocade wallpaper, shining brass handrails, elegant furnishings, and a mahogany bar that rivaled any in the country. The dining room was always well appointed with fresh, white linen tablecloths, fine china dishes and crystal glassware. This was not a place for the rowdy and unrefined, although those occasionally found their way inside. This was a place for Tombstone's elite – politicians, business owners, and high-rollers.

Ezra opened the heavy door, stepped inside and was greeted by a young hostess. "One for dinner tonight, Mr. Thornton?"

As the young lady spoke, Ezra looked about the dining room. Every table was occupied with well-dressed men with cigars and ladies in the best fashions of the day. Every table held a different conversation which created a din, almost a buzz, above which could be heard the occasional burst of laughter. As long as silver continued to come from the ground around Tombstone, there was reason to be optimistic, and jovial.

John Clum, sitting with the man he had picked up at the stage earlier in the day occupied a table near the back of the room. Clum happened to look up, saw Ezra, and motioned for him to join their table.

As Ezra approached their table, they both rose to greet him.

Clum smiled broadly. "Good evening Ezra!"

Ezra smiled warmly. "Good evening John."

Clum looked proudly at the young man at his table, "May I present my nephew, George; my older sister's boy."

George and Ezra shook hands, smiled politely, and sat down. Clum continued. "George just completed his first year at Rutgers. My dear sister wishes George to learn a trade – the newspaper trade. She wants him to ultimately become a writer – a famous writer. I'm not sure that I know of any newspapermen who became famous. But perhaps learning to write in the newspaper trade will lead to bigger things." Clum now smiled broader still and leaned toward Ezra. "Maybe his writing skills will make him immortal. As immortal as Shakespeare himself!"

Both men chuckled, and looked at George who smiled sheepishly and spoke in the same manner. "Writing newspaper copy is fine Uncle John. And I will try my hardest to do a good job for you at the *Epitaph*. But there is little creativity to newspaper writing. I need to be more creative. I want to exercise my poetic skills, my acting skills... I want to do something creative! If I am to achieve immortality, I should like it to be for something other than writing newspaper copy!"

Clum looked back at his nephew with a slight smile, but a decidedly sterner demeanor. "Acting... being on-stage is no life for a person – traveling from town to town - and living out of a trunk. What kind of future could you have? And this fixation with poetry? It would lead to a life of starvation I'm sure. Writing is the key my boy... prose and newspaper copy... and politics. A skilled politician and writer can go places, my boy!"

George seemed crushed. "Well, I promised mother – and you that I would give this a try. And try I will."

A waiter wearing a clean, white apron and a bushy, handlebar moustache approached their table, took their dinner order, and left. In the ensuing moment prior to the restart of conversation, Clum noticed a man and woman sitting at a table across the room and motioned to them. Clum began to rise from his chair. "I need to discuss a matter with Mr. Fly. I'll be back in a moment. Ezra – why don't you tell George about your store?"

George turned to his new friend. "You have a store here in town Mr. Thornton?"

Ezra spoke proudly, "E.T. Thornton – Mercantile; right on the corner of Sixth and Allen Street. It's a general mercantile with all sorts of products from all over the country. From pots and pans to the latest fashions for men and woman to guns and ammunition; I have it all. And what I don't have, I can usually get within a short time. I have contacts with major merchandise distributors and manufacturers in all the major cities of the union."

George thought that operating such a store was even more mundane than writing newspaper copy. But to be polite he replied, "That sounds very interesting, Mr. Thornton."

Ezra, who had been sitting forward in his chair looking directly at George now sat back in a more contemplative posture. "Interesting? Perhaps... sometimes..." Ezra paused for a moment, somewhat hesitant to make his next statement. "What makes life interesting for me - is helping people. Occasionally, I help make a dream or two come true."

George chuckled. "Now that *is* interesting, Mr. Thornton. And just how do you do that? Can you make my dreams come true?"

Ezra leaned forward in his chair again and moved closer to George. His countenance took on an eerie, fiendish grin and he spoke in a low tone so that no one could hear. "You'd be surprised at what I can do. Be at my store tomorrow at precisely noon. Don't say anything to your uncle. I'll make both your dreams come true."

George was shocked, almost stunned at the claims made by his new friend. It seemed impossible that this man, just a man... could make dreams come true. Mr. Thornton was a merchant; nothing more.

Before George could collect his thoughts and comment on Ezra's wild claims, Clum returned and again took his place at the table. "And how are you gentlemen getting along?"

Ezra smiled and replied, "Splendidly!"

******

It had been a busy morning at E.T. Thornton – Mercantile. Ezra's cash register jingled all morning long. As the noon hour approached and many businesses were getting ready to close for the mid-day break, Ezra rang up his last sale of the morning, a bolt of linen material for Mrs. Prichard.

Just before the large clock on the back wall struck 12 noon, George and Lester approached the front door. Each recognized the other as their traveling companion on the previous day's stage and they exchanged polite greetings. But neither knew exactly why they were to meet with Ezra, or that their business with Ezra had anything to do with the other man.

The bright, Arizona sun of the outdoors made the faint light indoors even weaker. The back of Ezra's store looked almost dark. The two men walked about one quarter of the way into the store and stopped, looking about. Lester called out Ezra's name.

Ezra's voice could be heard from the darkness of the store's inner-reaches. "Good day gentlemen. Please close and lock the door behind you. It is noon-time and I should be closed. Besides, we have important business to discuss!"

George turned, closed the door and locked it behind him. As he turned to again face the back of the store, Ezra appeared from the shadows looking somewhat mysterious in his black top-hat and long, opera cape. Before the two men could say a word, Ezra flung open his cape. His right arm, at first down by his side, rose quickly to become perpendicular to his body revealing a pistol. Ezra pulled the gun's hammer back to cock it and fired once directly at the two men. The sound of the blast inside the confines of the store was deafening and acrid gun smoke filled the air.

George and Lester ducked behind the merchandise cabinets on either side of the store, cowering in fear. Fear that they had misjudged Ezra's seemingly benevolent intention and fearing that for both of them, the western frontier was not the place to be.

Ezra leaned back on his boot heels and roared with laughter. "Gentlemen, gentlemen – come on out. I sincerely mean you no harm. If you don't believe me, check your person. You will find no holes. And take a look at the window in the door. It is fully intact. Nor are there any bullet holes in the adjoining walls. Gentlemen, what I fired at you, was a blank charge - a brass bullet casing stuffed with gun powder and wadding – no projectile! You were never in harm's way!"

George and Lester crawled out from their hiding places, somewhat relieved, but still suspicious of this man that they still hardly knew. Lester spoke. "Alright, so you didn't mean to harm us. But what was the purpose of scaring us half to death! Have you taken leave of your senses?"

"Senseless? Perhaps." Ezra replied. "But I am the senseless man who is going to make you both immortal. That is what both of you want isn't it – immortality?"

George and Lester looked at each other in disbelief. It seemed odd that both of them, with the similar desires, and similar dreams, had come together in this place and time. It seemed even more bizarre that they had both befriended this strange man only the day before who was now promising them immortality.

Ezra turned to step deeper into the store and motioned for the two men to follow him. In the back they found a small table with three chairs. On the table were sandwiches set neatly on china plates, and bottles of sarsaparilla, a sandwich and bottle for each man. They all sat down to eat lunch as Ezra explained his plan.

"There are many sophisticated and educated people here in Tombstone." Ezra started. "And there are many who are, shall we say, not as bright as you two. The more sophisticated people generally attend shows at Schieffelin Hall over on Fremont Street. The rest, usually the miners and ruffians, frequent the Bird Cage... although" Ezra now smiled slyly, "Although Tombstone's sophisticates have been known to visit that bawdy place on occasion!"

The three men chuckled. "So what does that have to do with us... and immortality?" Lester queried.

Ezra continued, "You two will have a stage act. Lester will be the star. We'll call him *The Fastest Man Alive*. Here's how it will work. Since few people in Tombstone know you yet, I will introduce you as an act I found through an entertainment broker in Europe. With my many connections, this will seem perfectly plausible and will give you an air of mystery and intrigue. Lester, you will then walk out onto the stage and stand on one side facing the opposite side. George, you will walk out onto the side opposite Lester. Prior to walking out onto the stage, Lester will conceal in his mouth two spent lead slugs which I have already secured for you."

Ezra reached into his pocket producing four lead slugs explaining that two would be held in Lester's mouth and one each in the palms of his hands. He went on, "At a prescribed signal, George will fire this gun loaded with blank rounds at you, Lester. You will pretend to catch the lead with your mouth and catch one in each hand. After firing four rounds, I will walk back out onto the stage and ask Lester to reveal the lead which he will produce, one from each hand and two from his mouth! The crowd will love it!"

Lester and George looked at each other in disbelief, and then looked back at Ezra. "This is all very interesting." Lester commented. "But how is this going to immortalize us?"

Feeling rather resolute after having traveled a great distance in the past few days, and now being subjected to what he thought was questionable idea at best, George spoke up, "This is an interesting idea. But sooner or later people will catch on, even the slower ones. And what of the more sophisticated and educated people in the audiences – won't they see right through this immediately?"

Ezra took his last swig of sarsaparilla and looked slyly at both men, "Trust me. Just trust me. Folks here in town have been doing that for some time now. And besides, what have you got to lose? You both want a creative outlet for your energies – well here it is. And with any luck, you'll both be famous... maybe even immortal. Now, let's take a ride outside of town and give this a few practice runs shall we? When we return, I'll talk to Billy Hutchinson and find you a place in his line-up for tonight."

******

It was a typical night at the Bird Cage Theatre. Despite the rather chilly February night air, the three large doors of the Bird Cage were wide open to relieve the building's interior of cigar smoke and the heat generated by so many people crowded into a rather tight space.

The Bird Cage Theatre - June 2009 (K. Davis photo)

Cow-boys in wide-brimmed hats and coarse pants with red shirts stood three and four deep at the lobby bar next to businessmen in sack suits derby hats. The two bartenders meted out all the finest liquors of the day, beer and cigars.

People began to move from the lobby to the theatre area where they took their place on wooden benches. Those people of seemingly higher station, and with more money to spend, walked up the steps at the far end of the lobby to the "cages" or boxes on the upper level.

Below street level, in the inner bowels of the west's most wicked entertainment establishment, a card game was being played. Hundreds, perhaps thousands of dollars changed hands there every night. And when the men tired of cards, women of the night, poised in their "cribs" on the other side of the room, were ready to take a man's money.

At precisely 9ᴾᴹ, Billy Hutchinson, owner of the Bird Cage appeared on stage. The crowd applauded wildly as Billy had brought to the frontier a brand of entertainment that seemed perfect for a mining camp. He spoke loudly trying to be heard above the crowd, "Ladies and gentlemen – I give you our own, Ezra T. Thornton!"

Ezra stepped out from behind the stage curtain as Billy walked down the stage stairs and into the audience. "Ladies and gentlemen! I bring to you tonight an act that is utterly amazing. These two gentlemen have performed all over Europe and are here now, for your entertainment pleasure. Prepare to be surprised and astounded as you witness, the Fastest Man Alive!"

Lester, dressed in a regular sack suit and hat, street clothes of the day, then walked out onto the stage and stood at Ezra's left. Lester, in seeming preparation for his demonstration, handed Ezra his coat and hat. Lester then removed his tie, handing it to Ezra, and opened his collar as Ezra explained to the audience, "The Fastest Man Alive has been practicing his craft for years. He has the reflexes of a scared cat and the agility to catch live rounds fired from a pistol at close range. He will not be harmed in any way, nor will anyone in this room for he... is the Fastest Man Alive!"

Ezra turned to the opposite side of the stage and called to George, "Shooter! Are you ready!"

"Yes... I am ready!" came the loud reply.

Lester stepped to the far right side of the stage and faced the opposite side. Ezra walked down the stage stairs into the audience. By the time his foot hit floor of the Bird Cage, the audience was silent, not really knowing what was about to happen.

Ezra called to George, "Shooter, all is ready!"

George, dressed all in black complete with a fine, beaver top hat and full-length opera cape stepped from behind the curtain on the left side of the stage. Mimicking Ezra's moves from earlier in the day, George threw open the cape and raised the pistol to shoulder height pointing directly at Lester. The crowd gasped!

George fired once and Lester raised his right hand very quickly pretending to "catch" the "flying lead." With the second shot, Lester repeated the action but with his left hand. With the third shot, Lester quickly bent at the waist slightly to his right opening and closing his mouth, "biting into the air" as if to catch the round in his teeth. With the fourth shot, Lester repeated this move but to the opposite side. George dropped his arm to his side, pulled his cape around him, turned, and quickly exited the stage.

Ezra, standing at audience-level looked out over the stunned crowd. Filthy miners sat on the bench seats with their jaws dropped in amazement. Well-dressed ladies in the raised boxes clutched their handkerchiefs over their mouth expecting to be repulsed with the seemingly inevitable splatter of blood. Ezra smiled. The audience was convinced that George had just fired four times... four live rounds at Lester.

Ezra then bounded up the stairs to the stage and approached Lester. With the audience still virtually silenced, Ezra acknowledged Lester, then turned to address the sea of bulging eyes and shocked expressions, "And now, the Fastest Man Alive will produce the lead fired at him. Show us the first round!"

As Ezra called for each piece of lead, Lester produced them, first from each hand, then two slugs from his mouth. Ezra held each one up as the crowd now cheered with glee! As soon as the last slug was produced the band in front of the stage, began to play a rousing tune. Ezra, Lester and now George stood on stage with their hands raised in triumph.

In the front row, watching this spectacle was a drunken soldier from nearby Camp Huachuca. The man had been drinking heavily and had been seen quarreling with the bartenders earlier in the evening. The soldier stood up drawing a revolver from concealment. "See if you can catch this!" he growled as he rapidly fired four shots directly at Lester.

All four bullets found their mark and Lester dropped where he stood. The band played and the crowd roared thinking it was all part of the show. George could only look on in horror. Ezra was stunned.

******

The following morning, rather than opening his store, Ezra went to the undertaker's office to arrange for a funeral service for Lester. It was the least he could do whereas he had gotten Lester into this situation... and the fact that Lester apparently had no family nearby. At the undertaker's he ran into George who was sadly looking at Lester's body lying in a pine coffin.

Ezra found the courage to speak, "I didn't mean for this to happen. I only wanted to give you boys a chance at what you wanted. Many people who will play that stage at the Bird Cage will go on to be famous the world over. But now, ironically, you will have another chance. Not the chance you wanted... not exactly - but a chance just the same!"

George looked at Ezra incredulously, "Chance, chance for what? Certainly not a chance for fame as a stage act when my partner is dead!"

"This is your chance for the immortality you sought." replied Ezra somberly. "This man needs a tombstone. Tombstones usually last a long time. The engraving on a tombstone becomes the essence of the man. Maybe it is not immortality, but it is as close as you can get. Here's your chance – be a writer – be a poet. Come up with something for this man's gravestone. You can be known forever as the man that wrote this man's epitaph."

"You bastard!" George cried out. "You planned this didn't you! You knew that soldier would be in the front row. You planned the whole thing!"

137

"I planned to make you famous as a performer. I am only a storekeeper... a mercantilist... and now a one-time stage manager. Lester's epitaph – he needs one – a good one. One that will long be remembered." Ezra replied.

"But I hardly knew him. I didn't even know his last name!" George had the look of a man who was taking on an impossible task.

Ezra handed George a key. "Here is the key to Lester's room at the Grand. I'm sure he has some kind of identification with him... documentation of some sort with his full name on it. See what you can find and have the undertaker write whatever you want on his tombstone."

George took the key and headed down Allen Street to the Grand Hotel.

******

It was late afternoon as Ezra closed his store and headed west on Allen Street to Boot Hill to attend the service for Lester. He buttoned his frock coat against the wind and increasing cold as the sun set on another day, the last day Lester would be above the ground.

A short time later he arrived at Boot Hill to find the service had already begun - a small number of people stood by while the pine box was lowered into the ground. It was then that Ezra noticed George's handiwork on Lester's tombstone. He had apparently found Lester's full name... and put his poetic energies to work.

Ezra stayed until the service ended. After the last person left, Ezra walked right up to Lester's grave marker, looked on the front, then walked around to the back and examined in thoroughly. "What a shame..." Ezra thought to himself. "George never signed his work. I would have thought that if he wanted immortality, signing what could be his best work would be the way to do it. Oh, well. Maybe there is hope for him yet.

The tombstone read:

Here Lies Lester Moore

Four slugs from a .44

No Les No More

The Real Story Behind "The Immortals"

Lester Moore's tombstone, inscribed as above, has, for years, been a curiosity at Tombstone's Boot Hill cemetery. An extensive search on the internet for Lester's history reveals little. Suffice to say that he was a Wells Fargo station agent located in Naco, Arizona Territory in the 1880's.

Arizona historian Marshall Trimble, in a reply published in the August/September issue of *True West* magazine to my question about Lester Moore wrote the following: "Les Moore was a Wells Fargo agent at Naco, Arizona, during the 1880's. His life had been pretty non-descript until he met Frank Dunston. Dunston was impatiently expecting a package. When it arrived damaged, Dunston argued his way into an Old West shootout, firing four times and fatally wounding Les Moore. Before he went down, Moore fired a fatal round into Dunston. Les Moore's friends brought him to Tombstone for burial. According to Tombstone historian Ben Traywick, nobody seems to know if Les' friends inscribed the poem, or if some clever scribe did it later.

Grave of Lester Moore   **(K. Davis photo)**

John Clum, mentioned in the story, was the city's mayor during its heyday in 1881. Clum also operated the *Tombstone Epitaph* from May, 1880 to May, 1882. The paper has been through many owners but still exists today and is located on Tombstone's Fifth Street between Allen and Fremont.

Mr. Fly, also mentioned in the story was Tombstone's premier photographer. His photography studio, located on Tombstone's Fremont Street formed one side of the alley where the OK Corral Gunfight was fought.

The Grand Hotel, located on Tombstone's Allen Street was indeed one of the best hotels in town during the 1880's. The building still stands. However, the second floor of the building has been removed. The first floor now houses "Big Nose Kates" Saloon, a favorite "watering hole" for locals and visitors to Tombstone.

The Crystal Palace still stands, as it always has, on the corner of Tombstone's Fifth and Allen Street. You can visit it today and belly up to the bar for a beer, just like the Earps and Doc Holliday did over 100 years ago.

Camp Huachuca, a US Army base located 18 miles due west of Tombstone originally founded in March, 1877 to protect settlers against Indian attacks and guard the US-Mexican border still exists. It is now known as Fort Huachuca and still houses military personnel who occasionally visit Tombstone for fun and recreation, just like they did over 100 years ago.

The Bird Cage Theatre was, in its prime, known as one of the wickedest places on earth. It stands today, on the southwest corner of Tombstone's Sixth and Allen Street as a museum and is said to be haunted. It was not uncommon for rowdy cowboys, and others, to fire guns in the theatre as evidenced by many bullet holes in the ceiling and stage-front that can still be seen.

In his book entitled, *Desert Honkytonk*, author Roger Bruns describes several odd stage-acts performed at the Bird Cage including a "bullet-catching" act, very similar to the one described in the story.

Billy Hutchinson was indeed the Bird Cage's first owner.

Some of the terms used in the story may be unfamiliar. Today, we refer to a person who cheats at a card game as a card shark. Card sharp was the original term. Also, today when we hear the term cowboy, we think of the men who drove cattle to market on the long trail-drives of the late 1860's and 1870's. During that time, the same term was used, only it was typically spelled cow-boy and had a decidedly different connotation, especially in Tombstone. If you said the word cow-boy in 1880's Tombstone, it had the same meaning as "gang-member" in modern-day Los Angeles.

Chapter 7: BRUNCKOW

"I have the perfect spot for you to stay where you will be warm, comfortable and secure. I own a cabin a short way outside of town – the old Brunckow place. You'll stay there as my guest! You'll be just as snug as can be! Don't worry!"

Ezra T. Thornton October 24, 1929

March 10, 1871 Southeastern Arizona Territory

Somewhere between Camp Grant, a military outpost in the Arizona Territory, and the Pinal Mountains, Indians attack a pack train carrying supplies to military personnel. Two men are murdered and sixteen mules stolen. The Camp Grant Apaches, a group of peaceful Arivaipas living at the reservation, are blamed. US Army Lt. Royal Whitman, the commanding officer for the post, and in charge of the peaceful Arivaipas, and oddly enough, an Army officer who is sympathetic to the plight of the Indians living on reservations, questions the Arivaipas' leader, Eskiminzin. Whitman believes the story that Eskiminzin tells him, and satisfies himself that all Arivaipa Apaches were present and accounted for at the reservation at the time of the attack and professes their innocence.

But the local Caucasian community would not accept Whitman's explanation. Public sentiment is such that no distinction is made between good Indians or bad Indians or one tribe from the other. All everyone knew was that the only good Indian was a dead Indian and all Indians were wished dead.

The incident also brought criticism for Whitman's policy of caring for the Indians at government expense. Whitman was doing his job the best way he knew how, at the behest of the federal government, but was politically chastised for it.

March 20, 1871 Tubac, Arizona Territory

Indians on the warpath raid ranches around the small town of Tubac, Arizona Territory. Tubac rancher L.B. Wooster is murdered along with a Mexican woman. Tucson's *Arizona Citizen,* a local newspaper proclaims that recalcitrant Indians were sweeping the area, killing and committing depredations at will. The Camp Grant Indians are again blamed. And again, Lt. Whitman conducted his own investigation only to account for every reservation Indians at the time of the attack.

Still, locals do not accept his explanation and things begin to heat up. The Caucasian community in and around Tubac and Tucson, call for death to all Apaches and the dismantling of the Camp Grant reservation.

On March 25th, the *Arizona Citizen* asks in an editorial if the murderers would continue to be allowed to roam at will, fed by the supplies purchased from the "people's money" – meaning the Camp Grant Apaches living off government supplied foodstuffs.

April 10, 1871 Outside Tucson, Arizona Territory

Indians attack a farm and make off with nineteen head of cattle. A posse is dispatched from Tucson and chase the band for 50 miles. They finally catch up with a straggling Indian, kill him and, post-mortem, identify the straggler as an Arivaipa Apache from Camp Grant.

Locals begin to "build a case" against the peaceful Camp Grant Arivaipa Indians, despite their declared innocence by Lt. Whitman. Nobody wants to hear about peaceful Indians anyway; there were economic reasons to wage war against the Indians. As long as there were Indians to fight, there would be soldiers in the area. And as long as soldiers were stationed in southern Arizona, there would be a need for an infrastructure to provide food and other supplies to the soldiers, paid for with a seemingly endless stream of government funds. The infrastructure meant jobs, income, and a number of ways for the unscrupulous to scam the system. Whitman's noble experiment was a threat to this lifestyle.

But it was a tenuous balance of power. Violence and the occasional Indian depredation was necessary to keep the soldiers in the Territory – but no white man wanted to get hurt in the process.

Many contractors who worked within this infrastructure made their money, and then headed out of the Territory with their bags of loot. Some went to the east coast, some on to San Francisco - but none really cared for Arizona all that much, only in the income it could afford them. These people would eventually come to avoid reservations with working and prosperous Indians because it meant less business.

In the waning days of April, 1871, a band of renegade Pinal Apaches steal into San Xavier Mission, near Tucson, and make off with four horses and six head of cattle. What is most disturbing to the locals is a white man is killed in the process.

Instantly, the Arivaipa Indians at Camp Grant are blamed. Locals want the Apaches, all Apaches, good or bad, no matter what tribe they belong to, exterminated, wiped from the face of the earth. They demand that General George Stoneman, then in command of the military in Arizona, to march to Camp Grant and eradicate the territory of the red menace.

Stoneman makes an inquiry of Lt. Whitman who again attests to the whereabouts of his Arivaipas during that night. He states that they were all in the vicinity of Camp Grant and had not traveled to San Xavier.

General Stoneman advised the citizens of Tucson that the Arivaipas were not at fault. But the Tucsonans would not be placated. They wanted revenge. They wanted blood. They wanted all Indians dead. Despite having no proof or even any indication, Tucson's *Arizona Citizen* howls that the perpetrators must have come from Camp Grant. Newspapers of the latter half of the 19th century were powerful organs for raising the consciousness of the public for good... or not.

April 27, 1871 Tucson, Arizona Territory

Local Tucson luminary William Sanders Oury had had enough of Indian depredations and talk of peaceful Arivaipas. On the evening of April 27, 1871 he gathers together several local citizens and declares that if the military will not handle things then it is up to the citizens to quell Indian disturbances. He then calls for volunteers to rid the area of the Camp Grant Apaches. Only a handful of volunteers step forward – not enough to attack a whole tribe of Apaches.

More meetings are held, speeches given, resolve stated, and breasts beaten – but to little avail. Despite the outcry about the crimes and the general hatred of Indians, only six white men step forward – along with forty-eight Mexicans. Oury is disappointed to say the least. Fifty-four volunteers were not enough to do the job. Oury needed more people.

He finds more volunteers in the Papago Indians, hereditary enemies of the Arivaipas. They are only too willing to spill Arivaipa blood... and at the insistence of a Caucasian leader, their actions are somehow validated. The Papagos feel that they can now kill their hereditary enemies with impunity... and they are emboldened.

Despite all the rhetoric pouring from Arizona's Anglo community, Oury is able to garner little support from them, having not the stomach to perform such a heinous act as actually killing an Indian – another human being. It was one thing to talk about, quite another to complete the act. Yet, they were only too ready to supply guns and ammunition to the party-of-death and so it was that many leading citizens quelled their own burning conscience yet exacted a terrible toll using the hands of others.

In the early morning hours of April 28, 1871 Oury, together with a band of Mexicans armed with rifles, and Papago Indians, armed with their silent but deadly war-clubs, one-hundred and forty-six people in all, head out of Tucson. To avoid raising suspicion, they travel in small bands, gathering in a wash a few miles outside of Tucson. Nobody suspected the band's blood-thirsty plans. The soldiers at nearby Fort Lowell went about their business, totally unaware of the carnage about to happen.

Oury and his band of would-be murderers marched south. Just in case someone in Tucson noticed Oury, or any of the then-known war-mongers missing, they sent six riders along the road from Tucson to Camp Grant to intercept anyone who might be sent to Camp Grant to sound the alarm.

But one messenger was sent. Corporal Clark of the Twenty-First United States Infantry, was on his way to Camp Grant at top speed when he was intercepted by the six riders sent by Oury. They managed to detain Corporal Clark for two hours; then sent him back to Fort Lowell, his mission un-accomplished.

While the six riders were entertaining Corporal Clark, the main body of Oury's death squad marched onward. That night; they camped almost within sight of the Arivaipas. Here they waited until just daybreak. Attacking the Indians at night could be dangerous – without being able to see there was good chance Oury's men could kill each other and they did not want another white man to die over this affair.

About 2AM they rose, readied themselves for a bloody battle, and marched so close to the camp they could see the smoldering embers of the camp fires that had burned during the night. They crept ever closer, moving from shadow to shadow, rock-to-rock, staying low, staying quiet. They wanted surprise to be on their side. The Papagos, the Mexicans, and the six white men lay on the ground, hearts pounding, clubs and rifles at the ready.

April 30, 1871 5:00AM Arivaipa Encampment at Camp Grant

Noglee awoke with a start to the sound of footsteps just outside of his wikiup; the traditional Apache home. He looked over at the other members of his family, mother, father, and two sisters still sleeping soundly. The steps outside, especially because of their quick pace, were not normal at this hour – unless there was trouble. If there was trouble, his mother and father would have been up, fully awake, and ready for whatever would happen. But they were asleep, still unsuspecting, still unknowing.

Noglee could not help but wonder about the footsteps. He sat up, pulling his blankets aside. Even inside the wikiup, the cool morning air was apparent, and he could feel it against the bare skin of his chest.

He listened intently – more footsteps. Still his parents slept.

Although he had only seen 10 summers, Noglee was wise ahead of his time. He knew something was not right. He had heard stories of attacks on Apache camps by whites – by Army soldiers – by Mexicans – by Papago Indians. Could this be another surprise attack? As the thought ran through his mind, his blood ran cold and every muscle in his body pulled taut. He was ready to jump at a moment's notice – to run – or to fight – he wasn't sure.

At that moment the flap to the opening in the wikiup was abruptly pulled open. In the early morning sunlight he saw a Papago Indian in silhouette, war paint streaking his face, a huge club, stained with the blood of past battles upraised ready to strike.

In an instant the Papago was inside the wikiup, his first blow striking Noglee's father in his first waking moment. A quick second blow crushed his skull, the Arivaipa brave died in his bed.

Noglee reached for his knife, a recent gift from his father on the occasion of his 10th summer, and began slashing the Papago, blood spurting from each wound.

The Papago howled waking Noglee's mother and two younger sisters. Seeing the carnage and blood, both siblings and mother began to wail, his mother trying desperately to fight off the Papago, Noglee slashing at his back.

Despite his wounds, the Papago managed to momentarily push Noglee aside, raise his club again and bring it down with ferocious force – through the skull of Noglee's mother abruptly ending her high -pitched cries.

The Papago then spun around and turned his attention to Noglee. Their eyes met. Noglee could see the hate, pain, and intensity in the Papago's eyes. Noglee's eyes widened with terror as another Papago and a Mexican wielding a pistol entered the wikiup. Three armed men, two with clubs and one with a pistol was no match for a boy with a knife. As much as he did not want to leave his sisters, he knew he was no match for the men. He could only hope that they would spare his two sisters. Then, as was the Apache custom, he would live to fight another day, freeing his sisters and taking revenge on those responsible for the attack.

In one smooth, swift motion, Noglee slipped under the outer wall of the wikiup to the outside – and the most horrific scene his young eyes had ever witnessed.

While he fought off one of the first Papago attacks, others were exacting their bloody carnage in adjoining wikiups. Once the screaming began there was no longer any need for stealth. Their presence had been announced and those with guns began filling the air with lead. Mexicans and Papagos used their rifles and pistols with deadly accuracy as the Arivaipas tried to flee to the mountains – just as they had done so many times before.

Noglee ran, as fast as he could, toward the hills where he would be safe. He dodged Papago clubs and Mexican bullets. He avoided the white men, figuring they would be the most vicious of all.

Gun smoke from the pistols began to fill the air, the acrid smell permeating Noglee's nostrils. As he ran, his bare feet touched on puddles of blood – Apache blood – drawn from his friends, his family, and other children – people he had known all his life and who were now either dead or dying. Inherently, Noglee knew that nothing would be the same after this day. Nothing!

The camp became a shambles. Bodies of women, children and Arivaipa warriors were strewn everywhere. Wikiups were pulled down. The wounded cried for mercy. Children cried for their mothers. Mothers ran about, trying to find their children, screaming and crying. Blood, Arivaipa blood poured into the desert sand.

Above the smoke, gunshots and screams, Chief Eskiminzin stood, tall and proud, issuing the Apache call to arms. But there was no one to answer his call. All were either dead, or fleeing to the mountains. He called once more – and a Papago club silenced Eskiminzin. He crumpled to the ground, as if dead – the peace-loving Eskiminzin.

Moments later, it was over. Papagos and Mexicans began looting the place, taking souvenirs of their "good deed", ridding Arizona of a few more Apaches. They set fire to the wikiups, threw the rest of the Arivaipas belongings about, and took into captivity, twenty-seven Apache children. They looked upon what they had done and took pride in a job well done. Over one hundred Apaches were dead, the rest had been "taught a lesson", and nobody from Oury's party had been killed. It had been outright murder – a bizarre spectacle of death.

Noglee joined with others from his band as they climbed into the mountains, a place where white – and Mexicans – usually did not pursue them. They could only hope that the Papago's would take the lead from the white and Mexican confederates and confine their killing to the desert floor.

News of the "good work" spread quickly. One hundred and eighteen Arivaipas had been killed – of those, only eight were men. The rest were women and children.

December 1871 Tucson, Arizona Territory

In December 1871, 104 members of Oury's "posse" were arrested and indicted for the attack and murders at Camp Grant. The testimony given during the perfunctory five-day trial was confusing, evidence flimsy, and the prosecuting attorney obviously inept. It was painfully clear that even the prosecution was in sympathy with the Indian-hating populace. Once again, the Indian side of a legal matter was not properly represented. It was nearly impossible, in those times, to be arrested, tried and convicted for killing an Indian.

The jury deliberated only nineteen minutes, the jury foreman, then-future Tombstone resident John B. Allen, gave Judge John Titus a verdict of "Not Guilty", exonerating the entire lot. William Sanders Oury just smiled.

September 30, 1881   Tombstone, Arizona Territory

It was mid-day in Tombstone and Ezra T. Thornton was closing the door to his mercantile store on the corner of 6th and Allen Streets as a prelude to securing a light lunch. On this last day of September, the streets were filled with people, wagons, and horses, all kicking up a choking amount of dust.

The still-warm sun shone brightly. Ezra locked his door, and then turned to look at the lot across Allen Street and the rising adobe walls which would become the Bird Cage Theatre, his eyes squinting against the brightness compared to his rather dark store.

Before he could take his first step toward the Can Can Restaurant and lunch, four loud whistle blasts were issued from the steam engine at the Vizina Hoisting Works on the corner of Fourth and Toughnut Street.

Since it was not yet time for a shift change in the mines, the blast could only mean one thing – trouble was afoot. The signal was issued again and men brandishing pistols and rifles were seen hurrying toward the center of town.

Ezra quickly unlocked his door, secured a pistol from behind the counter, stuffed it into his coat pocket, locked the door, and proceeded down Allen Street. Taking a right on Fifth and a left on Fremont Street he was soon standing in front of *The Tombstone Epitaph* newspaper office, it's founder and editor, who was also the city's mayor, John Clum, already present. Clum stood on a box, rifle in hand, preparing to address the assemblage – the Citizen's Safety Committee, a group of local businessmen and citizens who could be counted on, at virtually a moment's notice, to provide additional police support against an "aggregation of cattle thieves, and stage robbers, all-around-bad-men and blustering gun fighters."

"Members of the Citizen's Safety Committee", Clum began, "Thank you for your usual expedient response. I have just received telegraphic reports from the San Carlos Indian reservation that the renegade Apache, Geronimo, and a band of his followers have broken out of the reservation and are headed in this direction. As many of you know I have had several experiences with Geronimo and know him to be a devil of the most devious sort – capable of killing, stealing; and committing general depredations upon men, women and children. I once captured Geronimo at gunpoint, put him in shackles and delivered him to the authorities – who promptly let him loose. He is not to be trusted, is a known killer and must be stopped. Reports indicate that he is on his way south and will likely come through the area on his way to Mexico – his usual hiding place when pursued by the army. To protect our city, our women, and our children, I propose to ride across the country, track down Geronimo and his band, and bring them to justice. Who is with me?"

Several businessmen stepped forward. In the forefront were the Earp brothers, Wyatt, Virgil and Morgan followed by Cochise County Sheriff Johnny Behan and his deputy, Billy Breckenridge; twenty-eight in all.

Clum then turned has attention to a few others in the crowd who had not yet volunteered and cajoled them into riding with him. Clum figured he could use as many men as he could get, not knowing how many braves Geronimo had taken with him.

Finally, Clum looked at Ezra. "What about you Ezra Thornton? Will you ride with us this day?"

Ezra looked up at Clum, still standing on the box. "I have no fight with Geronimo. I know that you have a special vendetta against him, and perhaps rightfully so. But I think, seeing that they are on the run from the military and other posses, he will want to get to Mexico as soon as possible – probably not stopping to loot Tombstone. I will demur Mr. Clum, saving my energies for trouble closer to home."

Disgusted, Clum said not a word to Ezra but stepped off his box and proceeded to the OK Corral, directly across the street, to secure a horse for his vendetta ride against Geronimo. A few moments later, the Citizen's Safety Committee galloped down Fremont Street and out of town leaving a trail of dust behind.

Ezra, along with many other citizens dispersed to pursue their daily routine.

Ezra completed his day's work, took his dinner at the Grand Hotel dining room, joined friends for a few after-dinner libations, and then headed to his small house.

Ezra walked down brightly-lit Allen Street into the red-light district of Sixth Street and turned north. As he passed Fremont Street the city-light was behind him and the shadows grew darker, his hard-soled shoes crunched over rocks, and the night air, only slightly cooler than that of the hot day, filled his lungs.

As he rounded the corner of his house, Ezra stopped abruptly, face-to-face with an Indian – and as healthy a specimen as Ezra had ever seen. In the pale moonlight Ezra could instantly tell that the brave was in his late teens or early twenties, with strong, square facial features, as if chiseled from stone. His long, black hair fell over a white shirt tucked into white pants – typical of those worn by reservation Indians. In his waist-band was the handle of what appeared to be a large knife. But other than the knife, the Indian was not armed, nor did he carry any other weapon or anything in his hands.

In the brief instance it took to realize what was happening, or what he envisioned happening, Ezra cursed himself for not having ridden on Clum's "Vendetta Posse." At least, he wouldn't be in this predicament and at best, he might have killed or captured this Apache who stood before him.

Ezra's mind raced. Where was the pistol he had had earlier? "Ah", he thought, "...returned to the shelf under the counter in his store – fearing a robbery but not an assassination at the hands of a red-man... not in a cosmopolitan city like Tombstone!"

But did he have anything to fear from this young warrior? Was he from Geronimo's band? He made no aggressive movements; his face was calm – not as he imagined a passion-crazed Indian would look on "the warpath."

All this thought went by in the blink of an eye.

Before he could contemplate his options; run, fight, or... the red-man spoke in reasonably good English. "I am called Noglee from the tribe you call Arivaipa Apaches. My name means 'Runs with Coyotes'. I will not harm you." With that, Noglee raised his hands, palms open to show his good faith. Ezra breathed a little easier, but was still faced with a person who was armed, while he was not.

Noglee went on, "As a boy, I was at Camp Grant when the Papagos, Mexicans and six white men attacked us. I managed to escape but my family - mother, father and two sisters were all killed. Other tribe members took care of me as a child. We moved onto the

San Carlos reservation where we have lived for many years in peace. Sometimes times were good, sometimes not. The reservation was run by a Nantan – a white leader who was not always effective, but we did not have to fear for our lives while the Nantan was in charge. Now things have changed. The soldiers are back on the reservation and in charge. Those who lived there years ago when the army ruled the reservation remember how we were treated; no better than dogs. Now, the soldiers have returned and we will not live that way. I, with many others chose to run with Geronimo. We are unsure of where we will go – but we will not stay at San Carlos."

Ezra contemplated what the young brave had said. Removing his top-hat, Ezra reached for a handkerchief and mopped his sweating brow. It seemed obvious that he was not going to be summarily executed, but he was not sure why this tortured soul would come to him. Ezra moved to the steps leading up to his house and sat down on them.

Noglee continued to stand, tall and stoic – as he had led most of his life, as a prisoner of war, living on a reservation – totally dependant on government rationing, and government rules and regulations.

"I can appreciate the pain and suffering that has been inflicted upon you." Ezra said in a calm voice, looking up at the brave. "But why do you come to me? What is it you want from me?"

Noglee replied, "We know that over 100 men, including the leaders that brought death to my people at Camp Grant were put on trial. The trial was very short. Much was said but fell on deaf ears. Those men walk free today. They were not punished. Many of my people – my parents – my sisters are still dead."

Noglee then crouched down on his haunches to be at the same level as Ezra and spoke softly – imploringly, "My desire is to find the leaders who attacked us at Camp Grant, especially the man they call Oury. I want revenge for what he did. But I am not sure how to find him now; it has been so many years. And even if I did find him and take my revenge, it could lead to my own death. I now have a family of my own to think of. But you have contacts in the white-man's world. You could find him for me."

Noglee then moved closer to Ezra and said, almost in a whisper, "It is said that you are big medicine – that you have powers that go beyond other men. Will you use that power to help me – to help my people – to make right was has been wronged?"

Neither denying nor confirming any power that he may or may not have, Ezra looked squarely at Noglee. "It is true that a great injustice has been inflicted upon you and your people and I am sympathetic to your cause. Oury is a criminal who unjustly walks the streets while you continue to suffer a great loss."

The two men looked at each other in the dim moonlight, Noglee hoping for a positive response, Ezra, sympathetic to the young brave but unsure how deeply to get involved with a politically and socially explosive situation.

After a long pause, Ezra finally spoke, "In my culture – in the white man's culture – we would bring Oury and his band to justice in a court of law. But that system has failed you." Ezra made another long pause while, in his mind, he reviewed his options and finally finished with, "I will see what I can do. How can I contact you?"

Noglee's stern face broke into a faint smile, "I will contact you."

At that moment, a slight rustling of the hard-packed desert dirt that surrounded his house distracted Ezra's attention - footstep perhaps. He turned his head to see what it was and was surprised to see five to six human forms standing in a shadow, only a few feet away – no doubt, part of Noglee's band. They had obviously been present the entire time he and Noglee had been speaking.

Ezra turned back to Noglee to ask about his friends, but saw only a coyote, slinking away into the darkness. Then Ezra remembered Noglee's words describing his name, "Runs With Coyotes."

Ezra quickly turned back to address the other Indians standing in the shadows, but they were gone as well. Ezra walked over to where they had been standing. The ground seemed undisturbed.

It had been a strange and mysterious evening.

1929, September 15 3:15PM

A slow, mid-week afternoon saw Ezra T. Thornton staring out the large front window of his mercantile store at the Bird Cage Theatre across the street.

Shuttered for many years, the Bird Cage was once the hottest night-spot west of the Mississippi and east of San Francisco. Workers were busy pulling down the shutters and boards, and sweeping out the dust, getting ready to re-create the Tombstone of another era, this, on the 50th anniversary year of the town's founding. The celebration would be called Helldorado.

With the silver long gone, mining operations shut-down, and the population reduced to about 1500, city officials hoped to revive the town as a tourist destination. With the advent of the automobile, and roads getting better, people were traveling more. The speed and efficiency of the modern car made places formerly not easily accessible, like Tombstone, quite easy to get to. Helldorado was to mark the beginning of what city officials hoped would be a steady stream of vacationers and history buffs – people who would spend money in Tombstone and revive the economy.

The town was abuzz with activity as carpenters, painters and other craftsmen created old-west style store fronts over modern storefronts – and painted old store fronts to look new. Lights were strung throughout the city to allow night-time festivities. A huge arch at the far west end of Allen Street, the town's main street, where the majority of people would enter the city, announced a hearty welcome.

Ezra watched the activity and thought back to a time; it seemed like only yesterday, that Tombstone was in its hey-day, the epitome of western boom-towns. As a prominent town businessman, Ezra had attended many of the organizational and planning meetings. He knew there would be many "old-timers" invited, now in their 70's and 80's – people who had lived in Tombstone during those "palmy" times, destined perhaps to see the old camp one last time before "tossing in their cards" for the end of their game.

But Ezra was – still Ezra – forever dapper in his top hat crowning a long, flowing head of snow-white hair. His white shirt with the tall collar was spotless, adorned, as always, by a cravat style tie, today it was red. This was partially covered by the vest he always wore, today's choice was also red, a four-pocket style, out of which draped a bright gold watch chain. His black and white striped pants, perfectly pressed, and high-topped shoes completed his ensemble.

Ezra always dressed this way. During the 1880's, he was certainly in vogue. During the 1890's and into the early twentieth century, some locals thought he simply was not doing well financially (although his store was always busy) and continued to wear the same clothes. For the past 20 years, some simply considered his attire eccentric. Now, with the advent of the Helldorado celebration, and a call by city officials for everyone in town to dress "in 1880's costume" to give the illusion that a tourist was stepping back in time, Ezra was once again in vogue.

As Ezra stared across the street, thinking about times past, he was somewhat startled by a man who suddenly stepped into his line of vision, and stared intently into the window, back at Ezra.

He was an older man, and by his outward features, Ezra figured him for an Indian, seemingly in his late 70's or early 80's. His face was wizened and lined with the type of wrinkles that give ample evidence of a life lived with much worry and anguish. He wore a suit, a modern suit of grey flannel, which covered a clean, white shirt topped with a green necktie.

In his hand he carried a medium-sized leather satchel - well worn. Obviously he was traveling – and had traveled extensively.

On his head, despite the warmth of the day, was a wide-brimmed hat topping thick tufts of snow-white hair. The old Indian, removed his hat, and seeing his reflection in the window, noticed sweat coming from his brow. He reached in his pocket for a handkerchief, mopped his brow, then returning his hat to his head, turned and watched the activity across the street at the Bird Cage.

Ezra poked his head out the door and called out to the old Brave, "My good man – you look like you could use a cold drink! May I offer you a sarsaparilla? It's on me – compliments of the E.T. Thornton – Mercantile."

The old Indian turned to see Ezra standing in the doorway of his store, one hand holding the screen-door open, the other extended holding a brown bottle, water dripping from it, Ezra having just pulled it from a barrel of ice inside the store.

The Indian slowly reached for the bottle, his gnarled, brown hand slightly trembling with age. The two men looked at each other, their eyes meeting, and a warm smile breaking over each other's face.

"Thank you. You are very kind."

"My pleasure".

The Indian put the bottle to his lips and closing his eyes, drew his head back and took several deep swallows, obviously quite thirsty. Pulling the bottle from his lips, and opening his eyes, the old Indian looked straight at Ezra; "You have not changed at all, perhaps the effects of your powerful medicine. I am old and feeble – not the great brave I was in my youth."

Ezra looked quizzically at the old man standing before him with a sense that he should have known him...but could not place the face or voice or any instance where he would have run across such a man. The Indian spoke again, "You are Ezra Thornton. I remember you as if we met yesterday. But do you remember me?"

Ezra's quizzical look turned suddenly into a faint smile and almost in an instant, into a wide grin, "Of course. Noglee – Runs with Coyotes – orphan of Camp Grant and Geronimo confederate. I was wondering if I would ever see you again."

Noglee's grin widened as his eyes, at first dim, began to sparkle, "And I thought the same thing about you. Do you remember a late night meeting at your home – almost 50 years ago?"

"I do indeed" said Ezra quick and certain. "...like it was yesterday."

Ezra's face then lost much if its wide smile. "And I also remember a request you made of me all those years ago. I have not acted upon it, but have not forgotten it either."

Noglee's countenance also turned serious. "In my many years, I have learned to read the white man's language and have read many books and newspapers. I have learned that the killing at Camp Grant was one of many fights between whites and Indians. Sometimes the Indians attacked the whites. Sometimes the white attacked the Indians. The fighting has been going on for many years. Now – and even then, almost 50 years ago, it was impossible to right all the wrongs. But my heart is still heavy from the loss of my parents and sisters."

The two men sat down on a bench in front of Ezra's store, shaded from the warm mid-day sun by the canopy that hung over the sidewalk for the length of the street. The activity of the Helldorado preparations went on all around them – hammers banging nails, saws cutting wood, supervisors yelling directions to workers. Yet the two men were in their own world, not hearing any of the commotion around them, trying to reconcile a past and wonder what do with a future that seemed all too short.

The two paused for a moment. Then Ezra spoke, "And what of your own family. Are they with you?"

Noglee's eyes turned decidedly sad and he spoke very softly. "When I saw you last, I was running with Geronimo, my wife and baby still at San Carlos. Later, we reunited in Mexico but it was a hard life. We ran from place to place, plundering ranches and small white settlements wherever we found them; anything to survive. We had one other child but it was no life for a family – for anyone – to be on the run all the time. Eventually, after so much running, we were tired and surrendered to General Crook along with Geronimo in 1887. We were shipped off to a place called Mount Vernon Barracks in Alabama. It was very hot there – but different from Arizona. There are many diseases there. My two sons died from a fever. Apache medicine and white medicine could not save them. My wife died not long after, from a coughing sickness. The soldiers there called it consumption. I miss my families – both of them – and wonder why I am still alive."

Both men paused again. Then Ezra asked, "It would appear, from your clothing that you are doing well now?"

Noglee thought for a moment, and then replied, "By some standards, yes, I suppose I am. For many years, because I speak and read the white man's language, I have taught the language to children at the San Carlos reservation. For those times when I travel, I wear a white man's suit of clothes. It seems to command more respect from whites that I meet. After all these years, there are still those that look upon an Indian with scorn."

Noglee looked straight at Ezra, "But I am getting too old to travel much any more. And my age makes me wonder why Usen, the father of all Apaches, has allowed me to live this long. Perhaps I am meant to seek justice for all of this. But I am old and unsure how I would go about seeking justice."

Noglee looked out into the street at the workers preparing for Helldorado. "We heard about your celebration here in Tombstone. I was not sure if you were still alive or what I hoped to find here. I had a vision... the vision told me to come to Tombstone – that I would find answers here – answers to a lifetime of anguish over my lost family. Finding you gives me hope – but I am unsure for what."

Ezra looked down for a moment in deep thought. Then, shifting in his seat, he again looked at Noglee. An unusually cool breeze began to blow and ruffled the men's clothing as Ezra started to speak. "I must first apologize for having not taken action based on our last meeting. But neither have I been totally inactive. I have been following Oury's whereabouts all these years from stories in the newspapers. He has become a powerful "Nantan", a leader in Arizona politics. Helldorado is the kind of event that politicians like Oury like to attend. It gives them prominence and allows voters to see them taking part in local events. I have a plan and will put it into motion immediately. Why don't you check into the San Jose House hotel on Fremont Street? Tell the clerk to send the bill to me. We will talk later."

The two men rose and shook hands. Noglee looked squarely at Ezra. "I will trust in your judgment. It seems that you and Usen are working together." The two men smiled at each other.

Thursday, October 24, 1929 5:15PM

Ezra locked the door of his store, righted his hat, buttoned his black frock coat against a cool breeze, and headed for the Crystal Palace Saloon, as the autumn sun sank into the desert at the west end of the city.

Ordinarily, Allen Street would be practically deserted at this hour with all the shops closed and the locals heading home to their dinners. But tonight was different. It was the end of the first day of the city's Helldorado celebration and the streets were alive with color, music and excitement!

For weeks, the local paper, *The Tombstone Epitaph* had been running articles about the city's preparation citing the re-opening of the Bird Cage Theatre and the "resurgence" of the Crystal Palace Saloon, sure to be a "favorite watering hole" for locals and tourists alike.

Other newspapers around the country picked up the story and before long, everyone in America was aware of Tombstone's golden anniversary celebration.

Several articles in *The Epitaph* talked about the people who were expected to show up for the celebration. One article specifically talked about a "Parade Of Old Timers" to be on hand for the festivities, naming former Tombstone mayor and founder of *The Tombstone Epitaph*, John P. Clum and former Cochise County Deputy Sheriff, Col. William Breakenridge as two "old-timers" of note. It claimed the "...silence in the old buildings for two generations would be broken at last by the surging throngs of visitors...".

Ezra walked along the covered boardwalk to the Crystal Palace Saloon and stepped inside. It was almost as if he had returned to 1881. The place was filled with thirsty customers. The long, mahogany bar along the west wall, shined brightly with renewed luster, the product of much polishing by workers.

At the far end of the building a piano played songs popular 50 or more years ago – some from the Civil War period. A few couples danced but mostly people were sitting at tables or standing at the bar, just as they had done 50 years ago, sipping whisky, beer – and some sarsaparilla.

Not immediately finding an open table, Ezra moved towards the bar. Passing a table a hand came up and grabbed Ezra's arm. A deep, baritone voice could be heard above the din of the tickling piano and the incessant clinking of beer mugs being carried by the waiters. "Ezra. Ezra Thornton – is that you?"

Ezra looked down at the hand and followed it along the arm to which it was attached and finally to a face, which he was not sure he recognized. It occurred to Ezra that this may be one of those "Old

Timers" mentioned in *The Epitaph* and that probably he should know or recognize the person. But, just like Noglee, time had painted the man's face with so many lines and removed so much of his hair, it was hard to tell.

The deep baritone continued, "Clum – John Clum. Surely you cannot forget the city's first mayor?"

Ezra turned to face the former mayor and the two shook hands warmly and smiled. "Of course – Mayor John P. Clum – how could I forget? And I understand you will be honorary Mayor again for a few days!"

With a wide grin, pleased that he was remembered, Clum replied, "That's what they tell me."

Calling Ezra's attention to another man sitting at the table Clum continued, "And of course you remember Deputy Cochise County Sheriff Billy Breckenridge. Billy is here to promote his new book, most aptly named *Helldorado*."

Ezra reached across the table to shake hands with the old Deputy, "Of course. Colonel Breckenridge, how are you?" The two men shook hands warmly and Ezra was invited to join the two in talks about "the old days."

A short time later, the old friend's laughter and frivolity were broken when a man, seeming to be in his 60's, slightly younger than the men at the table, approached. He was out of breath, sweaty, and obviously under duress. His thin, gray hair matched the rest of appearance, totally out of place and wild.

"Mr. Thornton – I need to talk to you!" the man gasped. "Something is horribly wrong. I... I don't know how to explain it. But... well... I just need to show you... and talk to you. Now Mr. Thornton! It's important!"

Ezra ignored the man's imploring behavior and introduced him to the others at the table, "Gentlemen, may I present Mr. Michael O'Rourke."

As soon as Clum and Breckenridge heard the name they looked at each other in disbelief, obviously both with the same thought, but said nothing.

Ezra continued, "And Mr. O'Rourke, may I introduce John Clum and William Breckenridge, former residents of the city."

As soon as he heard the names, O'Rourke stopped all motion, and stood perfectly still, riveted in place, as the blood drained from his face. Obviously, he was scared, so much so that he momentarily froze in his tracks.

It was a tense and bizarre moment. Ezra, stood smiling as if he had just introduced three old friends who were dying for a reunion,

O'Rourke staring at Clum and Breckenridge as if he were looking down the barrel of a loaded shot gun, and Clum and Breckenridge alternating looks between themselves and O'Rourke trying to make sense of the whole affair.

After a short time - that seemed like hours, Ezra spoke up. "Well Mr. O'Rourke, what did you want to talk about? Please sit with us and have a drink. You look like you could use one!"

Now wide-eyed with a crazed look on his face, O'Rourke turned to Ezra, "Maybe later. Right now there is something I need to do!"

O' Rourke turned and headed out the door as quickly as he entered. Ezra regained his seat, as Clum spoke up addressing both men, "Was that who I think it was? Was that *the* Michael O'Rourke – Johnny-Behind-The-Deuce? "

Ezra smiled fiendishly, "It most certainly was!"

Breckenridge broke in, "O' Rourke... O' Rourke... isn't he the man who shot the mining superintendent back around 1881? I believe Schneider was his name. Yes... that was it! Schneider!"

The men all nodded in agreement. Breckenridge continued, "Everyone thought he was dead! After he broke out of jail for killing Schneider, he was never heard from again! I always figured someone who was such a hot-head would kill again and we would hear his name – or see it in the papers. But nothing! I would have thought him dead!"

Clum nodded in agreement. "He should be! He got away with murder and was never punished! And what is he doing here anyway? You would think he would know enough to stay away from Tombstone! But after all this time, he probably figured there would be nobody left who knew or remembered him – and he can now walk the streets of Tombstone with impunity! Of all the nerve!"

"Well gentlemen" Ezra said, "Mr. O'Rourke is here at, what you might say, the request of a higher power. One might also say he has a date with destiny. Before long, justice will be served, and Mr. O' Rourke will be redeemed – in a manner of speaking."

Clum and Breckenridge looked at each, and then Breckenridge looked straight at Ezra, "What the hell does that mean?"

Before the question could be addressed, an approaching man caught Ezra's attention and again Ezra stood. Grasping the man's shoulder he turned to address Clum and Breckenridge, "We seem to be at no loss for former Territorial friends today. Gentlemen, may I introduce Noglee, of the Arivaipa Apaches. Noglee is a teacher at the San Carlos Reservation."

Clum immediately stood to shake the old Indian's hand, "If we lived another 50 years I would still recognize your face. Good to see you old friend!"

Noglee extended his hand and with a broad smile proclaimed, "Nantan-Betunnykahyeh!"

Clum looked at Ezra, "That was – or is – my Apache name. The name bestowed upon me when I served as Indian Agent there from 1874 to 1877. I remember Noglee as a very young boy."

Noglee sat down and the four men began to talk about times past, about Indian affairs, Geronimo, and the current state of the Indians. They talked of early days in Tombstone, of cow-boys, gunfights, and what became of the "Earp boys."

They talked about how times had changed, and how the automobile was causing things to change even faster. Clum related how he and his adult son, Woodworth and wife, Florence had driven from Tucson to Tombstone via motorcar and found the experience quite pleasant.

About 45 minutes passed when suddenly another person walking towards the table caught Ezra's eye. Ezra did not recognize the man, but the man obviously spotted Ezra. As the man approached, all discussion ceased.

"You must be Ezra Thornton."

"I am indeed sir."

"You look exactly as described. I stopped at your store. Finding it closed I inquired from some men painting a store-front. They said I could probably find you here – and you look exactly as described."

The stranger extended his hand, "I am William S. Oury."

Instantly, the frivolity at the table moments before turned to tension so thick one could almost taste it. Clum and Breakenridge knew the name and knew what he had done... and gotten away with. Clum knew, and Breakenridge calculated, that the Indian sitting before them had been a victim of Oury's raid on Camp Grant on an April morning so long ago. Both men felt embarrassed for the Indian, having to suffer the indignity of being civil, if not cordial, given the social setting they were in, to a man who had caused him a lifetime of grief and anguish.

Blissfully, Oury did not acknowledge the Indian.

Oury continued, "I received your invitation via telegram, I appreciate your invitation and as such... here I am. I never thought I would be lauded as an 'old-timer', but I guess that's what I am now!"

The entire party chuckled at the opportunity to lighten up a bit – that is – all except Noglee.

Oury's chuckle turned suddenly serious, "Unfortunately, the reservation you made for me at the San Jose House hotel did not hold, or there was a mix-up. They told me at the hotel that a man named O' Rourke took their last room three days ago. That doesn't really matter except now, with all the other hotel rooms taken by arriving tourists, I am without a room. I have slept under the Arizona skies on many occasions, but now, being almost 80 years old, the hard ground is not a place I care to lie for several hours."

Ezra looked up and smiled, "Don't concern yourself, Mr. Oury. I happen to know that Mr. O' Rourke will be departing shortly. But in the meantime, I have the perfect spot for you to stay where you will be warm, comfortable and secure. I own a cabin a short way outside of town – the old Brunckow place. You'll stay there as my guest! You'll be just as snug as can be! Don't worry!"

Breakenridge turned to Clum, "The Brunckow place? As I recall the roof burned off that place years ago and the adobe walls have been melting with each summer rain ever since. That place can't be habitable... is it?"

Ezra smiled and stood up addressing all present, "Nonsense... the Brunckow place is as good as new!"

Ezra turned specifically to address John Clum, "Mr. Mayor, do you suppose you and your son could drive Mr. Oury out to the Brunckow cabin?"

Clum hesitated for a moment, knowing his son would not necessarily mind the short drive, but helping this man that murdered so many Indians – men women and children - seemed despicable.

Ezra sensed the consternation in Clum's face and knew exactly what he was thinking. "Mr. Mayor, I really don't want to impose upon you and your son, but it just wouldn't be right to have Mr. Oury sleep under the stars at his age now would it? And I know you want to make things right for a fellow old-timer now don't you?" Ezra gave Clum a little wink.

Clum wasn't quite sure what Ezra was referring to, but he knew Ezra well enough to go along with him and comply.

A few moments later, Clum's shiny Dodge motorcar sputtered down Allen Street, Woodworth Clum at the wheel with John Clum in the front passenger seat, and Oury and Ezra riding in the back. The tail lights disappeared into the darkness.

A few moments later the car turned off the Charleston Road onto a dirt road, the headlights focusing on a small adobe cabin only a few yards from the pavement, fully intact, complete with a roof, two glass -enclosed windows and a chimney.

The car pulled up at the front door, Woodworth keeping the headlights trained on the front of the modest cabin while the men went inside, and lit the kerosene lamp which sat on the table in the

160

middle of the cabin. The soft glow of the lamp revealed a sparsely appointed but clean single-room cabin with a single bed complete with several blankets, a table with two chairs, and a small fireplace.

The escort party made ready to leave and Ezra addressed Oury, "Woodworth will bring us out here tomorrow morning, around eight o' clock to pick you up. I'll bring some supplies from my store for breakfast, we'll have a good meal, and be in Tombstone just in time for the celebration to begin! Have a good evening, Mr. Oury!"

The party all shook hands and said their good-byes.

Friday, October 25, 1929 8:00AM

The Clums, father and son, occupied the front seat of the black Dodge, and Ezra again occupied the back seat as the car motored down the road towards the Brunckow cabin to retrieve William S. Oury – Indian killer. The bright Arizona sun glinted off the chrome and glass sometime blinding the men as they wheeled their way along, the car's conversation turning to the celebration of the "old-timers" who would make what would likely be, their last visit to Tombstone.

"And what of your Indian friend, Ezra?" asked Woodworth. "Will he be staying the week for the whole celebration?"

At that, John Clum turned in his seat. Ezra and the former Mayor passed a knowing glance at one another. Ezra answered, "In all likelihood, Noglee has already gone. He got what he came to Tombstone for."

Woodworth look perplexed, but drove on, a few minutes later turning off the Charleston road onto dirt, following the short road to the Brunckow cabin – or what was left of it.

Unlike the prior evening, the cabin looked like it had been abandoned for a long time – a very long time. It was as it had been previously described – roof burned off and the walls melting back into the desert floor with each passing rainfall. The three men emerged from the car, Woodworth with an incredulous look on his face, but Ezra and John Clum understanding the situation – and saying nothing.

As they moved around the partial walls of the cabin, they noticed a body lying on the floor inside – William S. Oury – with a single arrow penetrating his chest, his white shirt soaked with blood. But even more gruesome were the deep, fresh gashes in his body, the clothes in those spots torn away by coyotes who had feasted on his flesh, gnawing on each extremity.

Woodworth took one look at the hideously gruesome sight, turned, and supporting himself with one hand on the partially melted adobe wall, proceeded to empty his stomach contents on the ground.

John Clum and Ezra heard a rustling of brush behind them and turned to see a lone coyote staring at them. Woodworth was too busy soiling the landscape to notice the two men pass a knowing smile at the wild beast.

A sad smile came over John Clum's face as he looked the coyote square in the eye and said almost inaudibly, "Good-bye old friend... good-bye."

The Real Story Behind "Brunckow"

Camp Grant

The story of Oury's killing of 118 Arivaipa Indians in the early morning hours of April 30, 1871, and it's aftermath in December of that year, is entirely true and has come to be known as the Camp Grant Massacre. The dates and people mentioned are accurate including Chief Eskiminzin, who would live until the fall of 1894 and was a lifelong friend of John Clum's. Only Noglee is a fictional character.

Tombstone

John P. Clum was indeed mayor of the city of Tombstone from January through December, 1881 – and there really was a Citizen's Safety Committee, also referred to a vigilance organization or group. In those days "vigilante" or "vigilance committee" had a positive connotation, rather then the negative connotation it has today.

The first Helldorado celebration was held the third week of October, 1929 and has continued ever since. John Clum and Billy Breckenridge attended the first Helldorado and in fact, together with fellow frontiersman Anton Mazzanovich, led the opening day's parade. John Clum was joined on that trip by his son Woodworth, wife Florence, and *Los Angeles Times* newspaper reporter Harry Carr. History records that the first day's festivities were hampered by rain.

Billy Breakenridge indeed penned a book called *Helldorado*. Some see it as an anti-Earp slam. It debuted a few months before October 1929 but is still available and quite popular today among students of the old west.

San Carlos

In the fall of 1872, General Oliver Otis Howard founded the San Carlos Indian reservation primarily for the Arivaipa Apaches.

162

Eventually, several other tribes were consolidated on the reservation. In some cases, the different lifestyles and cultures clashed causing dissention among the various tribes. But mostly, their problems were based in the fact that, except for the period between August 1874 and July 1877 when John Clum (the same John Clum who later became mayor of Tombstone) operated the reservation under a strict code of civil rule, there existed a clash between civil and military authorities. The civilian, politically-appointed Indian Agent was supposed to manage the administration of the reservation while the military was supposed to maintain law and order. Sometimes the two entities would get in each other's way, issuing conflicting orders confounding and demoralizing the Indians.

After seven years of primarily civilian rule, and peace; a miscommunication and misunderstanding caused the military to return to San Carlos resulting in an outbreak of Indians, primarily led by the famed Geronimo.

Mount Vernon Barracks, Alabama

In the late 1880's, many Indians were captured or forced to surrender and were warehoused in places like Alabama, Arkansas and Florida, places totally unsuited to their lifestyle, culture or ability to cope with the environment. Mount Vernon Barracks was a miserable place inasmuch as it was always humid; a great departure from the arid Arizona desert the Indians had been used to. A usual accompaniment to humidity was mosquitoes and Mount Vernon had their share and what was worse, they carried malaria, typified by a high fever, which killed off many Apaches. Tuberculosis, also known as "consumption" or coughing disease also affected many.

Administrators and politicians attributed the high mortality rate of the Indians during this period as "homesickness' or "melancholy" or simply being depressed. It was all that, but the fact was that germs and viruses, not encountered in the dry deserts of Arizona, were now killing off a people that had no resistance to the infections carried by the mosquitoes.

Eskiminzin, Chief of the Arivaipas and a small band of his followers were finally allowed to return to their beloved San Carlos reservation after much politicking by sympathetic army leaders and John P. Clum, a life-long friend of Eskiminzin. They were removed to San Carlos on September 14, 1894.

Usen

Usen is the Apache's Supreme Being.

The Brunckow Cabin

The Brunckow cabin is now a slowly melting mound of dirt that once was a small adobe hut, two-hundred yards from the Tombstone-Charlestown Road, just half-mile from the San Pedro River. Today, it looks innocuous, just a remnant of a time gone-by, its deteriorating walls still standing vigilant against passing time. But if the walls could talk, they would tell some fierce tales of murder and mayhem, greed and double-crossing.

From its very beginning, Brunckow's cabin was in a very desolate area of the Arizona desert, and is associated with many deaths.

Frederick Brunckow

Frederick Brunckow was born in Prussia around 1830. He was an educated man, being schooled at the University of Westphalia and fluently spoke German, French, and English. About 1849 he emigrated to the United States landing at New York and eventually, about 1856, found his way to Texas.

He was working as a shingle-maker when he was invited to join the Sonora Exploring and Mining Company, outfitting for a mining expedition into Arizona Territory. The party ventured to El Paso, Texas and eventually to Tubac, Arizona where it established a base of operations. Brunckow was versed in geology and knew how to assay rock, determining what ore had promise, and which was simply – worthless rock.

In 1858, Brunckow and others from the party returned to New York to provide information about what they found. Since the claims they had uncovered looked promising, the party returned to Arizona.

Brunckow, together with William and James E. Williams, and a chemistry professor named Morse formed a partnership and began working a claim in what was soon to become the Tombstone Mining District. To house themselves, they built a small adobe hut near the claim. To help them perform the back-breaking work of moving tons of ore, the party hired a dozen or so Mexicans to do the heavy labor. They lived nearby hoping that a show of numbers would ward-off marauding Apaches.

On July 23, 1860, William Williams headed to Fort Buchanan, some 35 miles distant, to purchase supplies. When he returned around midnight on July 30th, the place had a strange quietness about it. Ordinarily he would have been greeted by barking dogs. But no dogs barked – nothing stirred – not a sound. As he got closer, he noticed an awful stench about the place.

Entering the small mine store, Williams struck a match. There, on the floor, lay the body of James Williams, riddled with bullet holes. The store had been completely ransacked, items stolen, and the place turned upside down.

With no sign of any of the workers or his comrades, and not knowing if the murderer or band of murderers were still in the area, Williams quietly backed away from the scene, mounted his horse, and quietly rode back to Fort Buchanan where he reported the heinous deeds.

The next morning, a squad of soldiers accompanied Williams back to the scene where they discovered that Frederick Brunckow had also been killed. Missing were all the Mexican laborers, a cook named Brontrager, the company's livestock, and about $3,000 worth of goods. That evening, Brontrager stumbled into Camp Jecker, headquarters for the Sonora Survey Commission. He told how two men had held him prisoner while other white men killed the rest of the party. They took Brontrager as a hostage in case anyone should chase them and they headed for the Mexican border. Once over the border, and safely away from US authorities, they let Brontrager go and split up to further avoid being followed.

The soldiers dutifully buried the bodies. The killers were never caught.

A Short Civil War

During the Civil War, US troops were pulled from the frontier to fight battles against the Confederacy in the east and south. During this time, western commerce practically ceased, there being no protection from the Apaches that roamed the area.

Four brave souls found the diggings at Brunckow's and decided, despite the danger, that they would become rich from the findings of others. The Apaches found them before they found riches. It was the death of them.

Duffield Versus Holmes

In 1873, US Marshal Milton Duffield claimed the old Brunckow diggings, as did Joseph Holmes. Duffield was not well liked - had a violent temper – and always went about heavily armed. Not a good combination, especially for a man charged with upholding law and order.

On June 5, 1874, Duffield showed up at the mine site to evict Holmes. As he approached, Duffield began waving his arms and shouting like a mad-man as was his manner. This immediately caught Holmes' attention. Knowing Duffield's character, and suspecting that he was "armed to the teeth", Holmes walked out of the little adobe cabin armed with a double-barreled shotgun, one of the most feared weapons of the west, and without hesitating, shot Duffield dead. Strangely enough, Duffield was unarmed.

Duffield was buried at the site. Holmes was tried for the murder and sentenced to three years in prison but escaped before he had a chance to serve any time. Authorities didn't spend a lot of time or effort looking for him. He was never seen again.

Miscellaneous Deaths

Over the next few years, several others were found dead at Brunckow's site. A man and his son camping overnight were found dead. Later, a lone prospector taking shelter there was found with a bullet in his back by unknown parties. A man named Rogers next claimed the cabin only to have Apaches claim his life. An early settler to the area told in his diary of finding a family of four massacred at the cabin. Their bodies were also buried at the site.

The *Prospector*, a Tombstone newspaper carried an article about Brunckow's cabin in their May 20, 1897 edition. Among the recounts of previous episodes of mayhem, they cited an instance where five robbers fought over the bullion they had recently stolen from a Wells Fargo bullion wagon. Apparently, they could not determine how to best divide their ill-gotten riches. The five of them were found dead – with the bullion load still intact.

The article also tells of a ghostly apparition seen walking about the place at night. As soon as someone approaches, the apparition vanishes, only to be seen at another location at the site – but still out of reach. Nightly visitors also reported hearing the sounds of mining coming from the shaft – pounding on drills, pickaxes pulling away rock, and the sawing of lumber for trusses.

A Tombstone Connection

Tombstone founder Ed Schieffelin spent a night at the cabin in the company of other miners, and soldiers from Fort Huachuca. The fireplace in the small hut was said to have served as a furnace by which Schieffelin and his business partner, Richard Gird, assayed local silver ore. Fortunately, no harm came to the party and their short stay was uneventful.

But fate would chalk-up one more death to the Brunckow cabin – by remote-control.

On October 26, 1881, just a few miles from Brunckow's in the city of Tombstone, Wyatt Earp, together with his brothers Morgan and Virgil and their friend Doc Holliday shot it out with Frank and Tom McLaury and Billy Clanton in what has come to be known as the OK Corral gunfight. The McLaury bothers and Billy Clanton were killed triggering a series of events over the course of several succeeding months leaving Virgil Earp maimed for life and Morgan Earp dead. Blaming cow-boy Frank Stillwell for Morgan's death, Wyatt Earp tracked Stillwell to a Tucson rail yard where, on the night of March 20, 1882, Stillwell died of "lead poisoning" at the hands of Wyatt Earp. At the time, Stillwell was the owner of the Brunckow property.

William S. Oury

Mr. William S. Oury was born in Virginia on August 13, 1816 and went to Arizona in 1856 engaging in stock raising and trading. He indeed was the principal instigator in what has come to be known as one of the most heinous crimes against Indians by a civilian party, the Camp Grant Massacre.

Oury went on to become an Arizona politician and was the first president of the Pioneers Society at Tucson. He died at Tucson in March of 1887, of natural causes, never having paid for his crimes against Indians, and against humanity.

Chapter 8: JUSTICE AND REDEMPTION

"My good man – I can tell you are really troubled. If leaving Tombstone is what you want, I can arrange that. When would you like to leave?"

Ezra T. Thornton October 25, 1929

Monday, August 26, 1929 7:30PM The Gem Boarding House Dallas, Texas

Michael O'Rourke had a made a life for himself, such as it was, over the past 48 years in Dallas, Texas. Starting out as a sometime saloonkeeper, sometime stock handler, and occasionally performing odd-jobs, O'Rourke was only consistent about one thing – he was a gambler – and a darned good one at that. Being careful who he "fleeced" he wanted to make sure that he never cheated or angered the locals. He had made a mistake a long time ago – angering people in the place where he lived – and didn't want to repeat that portion of his life.

Sometimes O'Rourke would win big, but he never flashed his money about. He dressed conservatively and lived frugally in a clean but non-descript boarding house in Dallas. He had few possessions save his clothing and a few personal items. If other boarders greeted him, he would simply smile, say hello, and move on, never bothering to get to know anyone in the building. Everyone figured that Mr. O'Rourke just liked to keep to himself. The only person O'Rourke ever saw with any regularity was his good friend John Barbower, Attorney At Law. The only other diversion he had was occasionally acting in local amateur theater. But he never did more than a few performances, not wanting to get to know any of the other actors.

At 66 years old, O'Rourke was still in good shape and quite spry having worked hard all his life and being a physical person. Lean, and standing almost six feet tall, his graying hair and moustache was the perfect match for his piercing blue eyes.

On this particular evening, Michael O'Rourke walked home to the Gem Boarding House. Prior to ascending the worn, wooden staircase to his second floor room, he stopped to check his mail box finding a single envelope.

He noted the return address, "E.T.T Mercantile Allen Street Tombstone, Arizona." The enclosed note read:

Dear Mr. O'Rourke,

You are cordially invited to join your fellow Arizona Territory frontiersmen by attending Tombstone's Fiftieth Anniversary Show – Helldorado – to be held in Tombstone, Arizona October 24 – 27, 1929.

You will attend as my guest. Rail tickets are enclosed and a room has been reserved in your name at the San Jose House hotel starting Tuesday, October 22, 1929. Pack light. I will provide appropriate clothing for the event.

Sincerely,

Ezra T. Thornton

O'Rourke looked at the invitation again and thought to himself, "An all expense paid trip back to Tombstone.... it's been almost 50 years since I was there last. I wonder if there is anyone there, or who would attend, that would remember."

Sitting on the edge of his bed in his dingy room, staring at the waning daylight through a single, grungy, streaked window he thought to himself, "Fifty years... FIFTY YEARS! They must all be dead by now. Well... I'll go. It will be a welcome respite from my tawdry existence here!"

O'Rourke looked at the invitation one last time, "I wonder who this Thornton guy is... and how he got my name and address? Oh well... a free trip is a free trip – and I sure could use a few days away from this place!"

Tuesday, October 22, 1929 9:00PM

Michael O'Rourke checked into the San Jose House hotel, one of the oldest buildings and the oldest hotel in town, a remnant from the

1880's, and entered his room. There he found a hand-written note on top of a neatly folded pile of clothes. It read:

My Dear Mr. O'Rourke,

To better enjoy the spirit of our Helldorado event, please attire yourself with these clothes, reproductions of the clothing perhaps you yourself wore during Tombstone's rip-roaring 1880's era. In the closet you will also find a variety of hats and boots. Don whatever is to your liking, and meet me, tomorrow morning at 8AM, at my store on the corner of Sixth and Allen Street.

Sincerely,

Ezra T. Thornton

Wednesday, October 23, 1929 7:55AM

The next morning O'Rourke rose, dressed in a pair of brown corduroy pants, held up with leather suspenders, tucking the legs into a pair of brown mule-ear boots. He chose a rather non-descript red shirt, topped-off with a red bandana around his neck. As his crowning piece, a black "boss-of-the plains" Stetson covered his salt-and-pepper hair.

Moments later, he arrived at the E.T. Thornton – Mercantile, precisely at 8AM, just in time to see Ezra opening the door to his store. Ezra turned to look at O'Rourke and smiled, "Mr. O'Rourke, my name is Ezra T. Thornton. Welcome *back* to Tombstone!"

The two men shook hands, but O'Rourke looked at his new-found benefactor with a jaundiced eye. "How did you know I used to live in the area? Not that I don't appreciate the train ticket and the hotel room being paid for... but I am quite curious!"

Ezra smiled again, and handed O'Rourke a fresh bottle of sarsaparilla from the ever-present and always full keg in the middle of his store. "Drink Mr. O'Rourke?"

O'Rourke reached for the bottle as Ezra began to speak, "You might say I am Tombstone's ambassador. Through my contacts, I was able to find many of the old-timers. Former Mayor John Clum is here as well as Johnny Behan's former deputy Billy Breakenridge, Billy Fourr and a host of others. I hope we all can get into the spirit of things and recreate Tombstone of 1880's!"

171

O'Rourke's blood ran cold! There could be many people in town that remembered him... and remembered an incident that he tried to forget for almost 50 years. But... that was a long time ago... and there was a statute of limitations for most crimes – he wasn't sure about this one.

Before Ezra could detect the blood running from O'Rourke's face giving him a pallid color, a tall man with sandy-blond hair, and a regal moustache dressed in very distinguished looking suit as was the style of the 1880's walked into the store.

Ezra immediately acknowledged him and said, "Michael, I'd like you to meet Wyatt Earp. Wyatt, meet Michael."

The two men shook hands, and O'Rourke could not help but notice that Wyatt's hand was ice cold. Then Ezra continued, "Wyatt is with a local reenactor group here in Tombstone. They will be performing throughout the weekend, recreating various episodes in Tombstone's history. Michael, I thought it would be a good idea for you to join Wyatt... have Wyatt show you around... maybe get involved in a skit or two?"

Wyatt and O'Rourke looked at each other. It seemed to O'Rourke that when Wyatt looked at him, it was as if he knew something but did not want to let on what it was. The thought occurred to him, just for a split second, that this could be the real Wyatt Earp... seeing that John Clum and Billy Breakenridge had returned to Tombstone. But that was impossible. The real Wyatt had died in Los Angeles on January 13, 1929 at 80 years old. It was in newspapers nation-wide. This Wyatt was in his early thirties. Still, O'Rourke had an uneasy feeling about this "reenactor."

Wyatt grabbed a bottle of sarsaparilla from the oak barrel and looked at O'Rourke once again. "Our little group has a skit practice in a few minutes in an empty lot down on First Street. What do you say we take a walk down Allen Street and see the sights? Then perhaps you can join us... maybe play a small part in a re-enactment?"

Unsure of what to do or what was going on, and still feeling very uneasy, O'Rourke could think of nothing else to say but "Sure!"

Wyatt Earp and Michael O'Rourke said good-bye to Ezra, and then walked west on Allen Street. Even at the early hour of 8:15AM, the town was abuzz with preparations for the upcoming Helldorado celebration. Everywhere one turned, people were painting, hammering nails, and sawing wood or stringing electric lights. As they walked, their boot-heels made a distinctive clomping sound against the wooden boardwalk. Smiling, Wyatt turned to O'Rourke, "Michael, isn't this great? It sure feels just like 1881 doesn't it?"

O'Rourke felt a chill run up his spine and replied, "Yes... it certainly does... Wyatt!"

Moments later the two arrived at an empty lot on First Street where others, also dressed in period clothes were waiting, obviously friends of Wyatt's and part of the reenactor group. After some cursory introductions, Wyatt turned to O'Rourke, "Mike, Would you like to participate in a skit?"

Again, not sure what to do, and growing ever more curious about what Wyatt may... or may not know about him, O'Rourke replied, "Sure... I guess so. I did participate in some amateur theater in Dallas. I guess you could say I was a seasoned actor. What part do you want me to play? What is involved?"

Wyatt called out to members of the group, "Fellas... would you please raise the false-front building?"

Four members of the group approached a wagon that had been left on the lot and pulled from it a mock-up of a building, a false-front supported by two legs on hinges. O'Rourke watched as the building was "raised." The sign over the "door" said "Vogan's." Again, O'Rourke felt the blood drain from his face and he felt faint – but he was determined not to let his new "friends" know of his distress. After composing himself a bit, he turned to Wyatt and asked, "What part am I going to play? What are we re-enacting?"

Wyatt took O'Rourke by the arm and had him stand in front of the door of the false fronted building and said, "This is real easy. All you gotta do is look scared... you hear me? Look really, really scared! Got it?"

"Got it!" came the reply.

Wyatt grabbed a shot gun from the wagon and stood beside O'Rourke in the doorway of the small false-front building and said,"Ok boys... do it just like we rehearsed yesterday. Try and remember your lines!"

The group of reenactors, 10 in all, retired to a spot several yards off. A moment later, Wyatt yelled "Action!" as a Hollywood director would, and the group marched on Wyatt and O'Rourke in a menacing manner.

When they were within a few feet of each other, the small group began their banter with:

"Give us Johnny!"

"Yeah... give him to us Wyatt. He's the guest of honor at a neck-tie party!

"Yeah... we want Johnny-Behind-The-Deuce!"

O'Rourke felt light-headed and another cold chill went up his spine as he thought to himself, "They know... they know about me...

but how could they? How could they know it's me? Ezra only told them my name was Michael. They can't possibly know! Are they just playing with me? Is Wyatt just playing with me? What the hell is going on here?"

Wyatt leveled his shot gun at the crowd and called out, "This man may have killed Phil Schneider and if convicted, he'll hang for it – but he won't be lynched by a wild mob. If any one of you are brave enough, come on up and get Johnny. It'll cost good men to lynch that tinhorn... Number One'll be Dick Gird!"

At that point a wagon pulled by two horses and driven by another member of the group swung onto the lot. Wyatt grabbed O'Rourke, pulled him onto the wagon, and the three men sped off down Allen Street, away from the still-yelling "lynch mob."

The wagon finally pulled up at the curb on the south side of Allen Street, just before Fifth, in front of what was originally Vogan's Saloon. Wyatt smiled at O'Rourke and said, "You did really well, Michael. You truly looked scared. It was almost as if you had done this before! Would you like to join us when we perform in front of the public on Friday? We'll be performing right here... right in front of this building where the event took place 48 years ago! You make a great Johnny-Behind-The Deuce!"

O'Rourke looked at the sign over the entrance to the building where they had just stopped. It read "Vogan's Saloon."

Whatever color might have returned to O'Rourke's face, again drained from his body as he leapt out of the wagon mumbling to no one in particular, "I gotta get outta here!" and walked briskly down Allen Street toward Sixth and entered Ezra's store.

As O'Rourke entered, Ezra turned from straightening some stock on a shelf and smiled, "Well... did you have a good time performing you first re-enactment?"

Clearly shaken, O'Rourke retuned with, "You fiendish devil... you're just torturing me! I don't know how you know... but you know!"

Half-feigning a quizzical look on his face, Ezra replied, "Know? Know what? What do I know?"

Now O'Rourke was so upset he began stammering, "You know... you know that it's me... Michael O'Rourke... better known as Johnny-Behind-The Deuce. I am Johnny-Behind-The Deuce! And you have just been toying with me all along. Yes... I killed Schneider 48 years ago. I was a damn hot-headed kid. And yes... I escaped prison. Some people think I never paid for what I did. But I have paid for it every single day Mr. Thornton... every damn day of my life I have paid for it! Maybe you think you have me now. Maybe you think you are going to send me to jail. But I'm too old for jail now! I'll hide where you'll never find me. You'll never catch me – not you – not even Wyatt Earp can catch me!"

Ezra just smiled as O'Rourke turned and left.

Wednesday, October 23, 1929 10:00AM

O'Rourke hurried west on Allen Street not really knowing where he was going or what he was going to do. He only had a sense that Ezra, and possibly Wyatt Earp and others knew he was really Johnny -Behind-The Deuce and that there may still be warrant out for his capture in Arizona.

As he walked along the boardwalk on the north side of the street he started to notice people looking at him – watching him – like they knew something. Like they knew he was still a wanted man – a killer. Men looked at him... women looked at him... even children watched him as he walked by. He walked faster... but it only meant there were more people who would look at him with that inquisitive stare. Now he was almost at a run... which made him look even more obvious.

The town was getting ready for Helldorado which meant almost everyone in town was outdoors, cleaning up their store front or home... and watching Michael O'Rourke. Many stopped what they were doing and watched him... followed his movement as he moved quickly by. Their stare was inescapable, penetrating... and disturbing.

Finally, after what seemed like an eternity, O'Rourke crossed First Street and was on his way out of town... headed for... for...Benson? He wasn't sure. All he knew was he had to get away. But he had no plan, no extra clothes, no supplies... and no way to survive the 25 miles of desert between Tombstone and Benson. All he knew was... he had to keep moving.

O'Rourke walked... and walked... and walked some more. Hours later, he calculated that he should have come across the small Mormon settlement of St David by this time. But there was no settlement and then it occurred to him that there was no one on the road except himself. Nobody coming from the opposite direction, headed south to Tombstone for the Helldorado event... and no one headed north to Benson. There was no one on the road but himself. No one!

Finally, by late afternoon, tired and with blistered feet, Michael O'Rourke sat down to rest. Off in the distance, he could see what looked like smoke, or possibly dust. Yes... it was a dust storm, a bad one, and it was headed his way! Moments later, the high winds and swirling dust was upon him. O'Rourke pulled his hat down around his ears, put his bandana around his nose and mouth and tried to hunker down as best he could out in the open. He closed his eyes to shut out the stinging sand.

A short time later, the storm dissipated as fast as it came on and all was calm again. Michael O'Rourke stood up, opened his eyes, and was startled to find himself standing in front of the door to his hotel room at the San Jose House – and it was starting to get dark. "I've lost almost this entire day!" he thought to himself. At that moment, Ezra Thornton appeared from around the corner of the building, "I trust you had a good day in Tombstone, Mr. O'Rourke?"

O'Rourke just looked at Ezra... it was as if he had never had the heated exchange with the old storekeeper that morning. "Was it all a dream?" he thought. But the blisters on his feet told him it was not a dream – but something he didn't understand. Finally he decided to "play along" with whatever it was that was going on and he found his voice, "I had a splendid day, Mr. Thornton but now I am tired, and believe I will turn in."

"Then I will see you in the morning" replied Ezra. "Tomorrow is the first official day for Helldorado. It should be fun!"

Michael O'Rourke removed his boots, and fell into bed fully clothed, exhausted, wondering what he would do next!

Thursday, October 24, 1929 10:15AM

The Helldorado celebration was in full swing by the time Michael O'Rourke decided to venture out onto Allen Street again. He still was not sure what had happened but the blisters on his feet were miraculously "healed" and the sand that had permeated his clothes from the day before was now completely gone. In fact, his clothes looked clean and fresh.

O'Rourke stopped at the Can Can Restaurant for breakfast. Dressed as he was in 1880's style attire, as many people were, no one gave him a second look and so he chalked-up the previous day's adventure as simply a bad dream.

After breakfast, O'Rourke moved up Allen Street through the throngs of people to a spot where people seemed to be gathering in anticipation of some event or show. As he approached, he could see they were gathering in front of Vogan's Saloon. Anticipating what was about to happen, O'Rourke tried to steel his mind against the agony of watching a recreation of his own sordid past – the day he shot Phillip Schneider and was almost lynched for it. He stood in the back of the growing crowd, trying to look inconspicuous.

A moment later, a horse and rider pulled up in front of Vogan's... just as it had 48 years prior. The "Johnny-Behind-The-Deuce" character dismounted yelling that he had "killed his man" and wanted protection from a lynch mob. Wyatt Earp, or rather, the same reenactor who was the official Helldorado Wyatt Earp appeared and took "Johnny" inside Vogan's – just as it had happened 48 years prior.

Moments later a group of reenactors playing the part of an "angry mob of miners" appeared in front of Vogan's – just as they had done 48 years prior. Wyatt appeared before the crowd, shotgun in hand, and the "heated" exchanges began - just as it had happened 48 years prior.

"Give us Johnny!"

"Yeah... give him to us Wyatt. He's the guest of honor at a neck-tie party!

"Yeah... we want Johnny-Behind-The-Deuce!"

Wyatt leveled his shot gun at the crowd and called out, "This man may have killed Phil Schneider and if convicted, he'll hang for it – but he won't be lynched by a wild mob. If any one of you are brave enough, come on up and get Johnny. It'll cost good men to lynch that tinhorn... Number One'll be Dick Gird!"

At that point the miners began to back-down. It was playing out, just as it had 48 years ago. O'Rourke tried to calculate if he was more scared then... or now.

A wagon, pulled by two horses, and driven by a reenactor, swung onto Allen Street and stopped in front of Vogans Saloon. O'Rourke figured Wyatt would walk out with the "Johnny" character, get into the wagon, and move off. Just as he had resigned himself to that outcome, and began to feel some relief with the end of the re-enactment at hand, and thinking that the prior day's misadventure was just a bad dream, the entire crowd turned and stared at him. It was as if time stood still as he stared back in wonderment and awe.

It was as if they all knew! They must know!" he thought. "Otherwise, why would they stare at me like that?" His mind raced! It was 1881 all over again!

O'Rourke scanned the crowd once more. Yes...they were all looking at him – all with grim looks on their faces. All except for one! Ezra Thornton stood in the back of the crowd – sporting a slight smile. But O'Rourke didn't have time to think about why the elderly storekeeper was smiling. He had more immediate business to deal with!

Looking for a quick escape, his heart pounding and sweat beading on his brow, O'Rourke leaped onto the wagon, simultaneously pushing the driver to the ground while wrenching the reins from his grip. He gave the reins a quick snap and the horses were off at a dead run – heading south for Bisbee, and the Mexican border.

Thursday, October 24, 1929 5:10PM

The Arizona sun was setting as Michael O'Rourke plodded along what he thought was the road to Bisbee and onward to the Mexican border. His horses were played out and barely moving, having only stopped to rest very few times throughout the day. The hapless driver calculated that he should have reached Bisbee long before this, but the road just continued on – a ribbon of asphalt in a hostile environment. His throat was parched not having run across water all day. But he knew he had to keep on moving. Somehow, it seemed like he was re-living 1881 all over again – and half the people in Tombstone wanted to see him hang – for a crime he committed almost 50 years ago.

Soon, off in the distance he spotted what looked like smoke. Soon, he could see it was actually dust – and lots of it - being stirred up by a howling wind. In a moment, the wind and dust swirled around the little wagon. O'Rourke stopped the horses, and slid under the wagon, pulling his hat down around his face to protect himself from the stinging sand. He closed his eyes, and tried to take the time to figure out what was happening to him.

Moments later, the howling stopped, just as quick and abrupt as it started. O'Rourke opened his eyes, expecting to be looking at the underside of his little wagon. Instead, he was looking up at a darkening sky and could hear music off in the distance, and the buzz of a crowd of people... off in the distance. He stood up, and found himself outside the San Jose House hotel; in front of the door to his room. He had the feeling he had been in this situation before but was not sure how or why.

Suddenly... he remembered. He remembered the crowd of people in front of Vogan's that morning. They all looked at him. They knew about how he had killed Schneider. They wanted to see him hang – HANG! He just knew that they knew!

All at once fear gripped him like never before. He had to get away from Tombstone at all costs. Looking around for a quick escape route, he looked west down Fremont Street and noticed, only a short distance away, a man getting into a car – a shiny new Model A Ford. O'Rourke bolted down the street and before the driver could close the door, O'Rourke was on top of him, threw the driver into the dust, and jumped behind the wheel. He spun the car about and headed south – again bound for Bisbee – but his escape was short lived. As soon as he passed the Tombstone city limits the car's engine sputtered and died.

Confused, enraged, and now desperate, O'Rourke walked back into town to find another car – or some type of conveyance. In a moment, another Model A approached him headed south. O'Rourke flagged down the driver. When the car stopped, O'Rourke yanked the driver from his perch, jumped into the driver's seat, and spun the car around heading north on Fremont Street. Once at First Street he took a left and decided this time, he would try his luck going down the old Charleston Road – but his luck was no better. As soon as the car came upon the city limits marker, the car's engine sputtered and died – exactly like the first car.

O'Rourke screamed at no one in particular, "It's some sort of conspiracy! Someone or something does not want me to leave! My past... its... its catching up with me! But how – and why?"

In a momentary flash of clarity he thought, "Ezra Thornton – the smiling merchant. He must have something to do with it – or know who does. I've got to find him – and right away!"

Thursday, October 24, 1929 5:15PM

Former Mayor John Clum and former Cochise County Deputy Sheriff Billy Breckenridge, having both recently arrived in Tombstone for the Helldorado event, sat at a table in the Crystal Palace Saloon on Allen Street, along with Ezra, quaffing beers and discussing the 'old days.' Clum had been the city's first elected Mayor under the new city charter in 1881. Breckenridge had been a Deputy Sheriff under Johnny Behan during the same period.

In those early days of the camp, Clum and Breckenridge were on opposite ends of the political landscape. Clum had aligned himself with the Earp-Holliday faction. Breckenridge, either by design or because of who he worked for, aligned himself with the cow-boy faction. Johnny Behan, Breckenridge's boss, was a crony of the cow-boys and Breckenridge may have gone along to remain employed... or he may have chosen his path. In either case, back then, there was no love lost between the two parties. In fact, Breckenridge's book, *Helldorado*, was especially unkind to the Earps and Holliday.

But the former differences seemed to be washed away by the beer they consumed, and the fact that Ezra, a neutral, non-combatant in the feud, showed kindness to both. Moreover, age had a way of mellowing things – and almost 50 years had passed since the conflict that led to the OK Corral shooting.

Clum and Breckenridge laughed, cajoled, and remembered the events of those times with Ezra egging each on in turn.

The men's laughter and frivolity were suddenly broken when Michael O'Rourke approached the table. He was out of breath, sweaty, and obviously under great duress. His thin, gray hair matched the rest of appearance, totally out of place and wild.

"Mr. Thornton – I need to talk to you!" the man gasped.

"Something is horribly wrong. I... I don't know how to explain it. But... well... I just need to show you... and talk to you. Now Mr. Thornton! It's important!"

Ezra ignored the man's imploring behavior and introduced him to the others at the table. "Gentlemen, may I present Mr. Michael O'Rourke".

As soon as Clum and Breckenridge heard the name they looked at each other in disbelief, obviously both with the same thought, but said nothing.

Ezra continued, "And Mr. O'Rourke, may I introduce John Clum and William Breckenridge, former residents of the city."

As soon as he heard the names, O'Rourke stopped all motion, and stood perfectly still, riveted in place. His blood ran cold.

It was a tense and bizarre moment. Ezra, stood smiling as if he had just introduced three old friends who were dying for a reunion, O'Rourke stared at Clum and Breckenridge as if he were looking down the barrel of a loaded shot gun, and Clum and Breckenridge alternated looks between themselves and O'Rourke trying to make sense of the whole affair.

After a short time - that seemed like hours, Ezra spoke up. "Well Mr. O'Rourke, what did you want to talk about? Please sit with us and have a drink. You look like you could use one!"

Now wide-eyed with a crazed look on his face, O'Rourke turned to Ezra, "Maybe later. Right now there is something I need to do! I gotta get out of here!"

O'Rourke turned and headed out the door as quickly as he entered. Ezra regained his seat, as Clum spoke up addressing both men, "Was that who I think it was? Was that *the* Michael O'Rourke – Johnny-Behind-The-Deuce? "

Ezra smiled fiendishly, "It most certainly was!"

Breckenridge broke in, "O'Rourke... O'Rourke... isn't he the man who shot the mining superintendent back around 1881? I believe Schneider was his name. Yes... that was it! Schneider!"

The men all nodded in agreement. Breckenridge continued, "Everyone thought he was dead! After he broke out of jail for killing Schneider, he was never heard from again! I always figured someone who was such a hot-head would kill again and we would hear his name – or see it in the papers. But nothing! I would have thought him dead!"

Clum nodded in agreement. "He should be! He got away with murder and was never punished! And what is he doing here anyway? You would think he would know enough to stay away from Tombstone! But after all this time, he probably figured there would be nobody left who knew or remembered him – and he can now walk the streets of Tombstone with impunity! Of all the nerve!"

"Well gentlemen" Ezra said, "Mr. O'Rourke is here at, what you might say, the request of a higher power. One might also say he has a date with destiny. Before long, justice will be served, and Mr. O'Rourke will be redeemed – in a manner of speaking."

Clum and Breckenridge looked at each, and then Breckenridge looked straight at Ezra, "What the hell does that mean?"

Before the question could be addressed, an approaching man caught Ezra's attention and again Ezra stood. Grasping the man's shoulder he turned to address Clum and Breckenridge, "We seem to be at no loss for former Territorial friends today. Gentlemen, may I introduce Noglee, of the Arivaipa Apaches. Noglee is a teacher at the San Carlos Reservation..."

Friday, October 25, 1929 8:00AM

Michael O'Rourke awoke with a start after a night of fitful sleep. The knocking on his hotel room door was insistent – but not overbearing. Bleary-eyed and still dressed in his clothes from the prior two days, he answered the door to find Ezra Thornton standing there straight and tall, neat as a pin as always. "Rough night Mr. O'Rourke?"

"Rough? That's not the half of it! You know don't you Mr. Thornton? You know about my past don't you? You know about Phillip Schneider – and you know why I need to get out of Tombstone!"

Ezra entered the room, "Yes.. yes Mr. O'Rourke. I've known all along that you were Johnny-Behind-The-Deuce. I know that you have made.. er... arrangements to redeem yourself with the Schneider family at some time in the future. Mr. O'Rourke – the future is now!"

O'Rourke's face took on an incredulous look. "What do you mean the future is now? Future... past... it's all a blur right now. And I've been trying to get out of Tombstone... for two days. I figure, if I can just get out of Tombstone I can clear my head and regain my equilibrium! I'll be able to think clearly again if I can just get out of Tombstone!"

Ezra put his hand on O'Rourke's shoulder. "My good man – I can tell you are really troubled. If leaving Tombstone is what you want, I can arrange that. When would you like to leave?"

"Now Mr. Thornton... right now! If you can arrange it, I'll leave this minute. I've had my fill of Tombstone! I've had my fill of that Wyatt Earp guy – and all those reenactors if that's what they really are! I'm done with the whole affair!"

Ezra smiled, "You have this hotel room for a few more days. It's all paid for. But if you want to leave, here's what you do. Pack your bags, and walk down to the Grand Hotel. There you will board a stage coach run by the Sandy Bob Stage Lines – they are running tourists around town in one of the original stagecoaches... giving guided tours of the town you know.."

O'Rourke broke in, "I don't need a tour of this damn town! I want to get out of it!"

Ezra smiled and restarted his instructions, "Don't worry, Mr. O'Rourke. The driver has special instructions. He'll see that you get out of Tombstone safely. Oh... you'd better hurry. The stage leaves in 15 minutes!"

Ezra stepped outside and was gone.

Michael O'Rourke wasn't quite sure what to make of things. All he knew was, he seemingly had a way out of Tombstone. He hurriedly packed his bags, and started running down Fifth Street to Allen Street, and the Grand Hotel. Moments later, he reached his destination.

The bright red stage with yellow wheels, freshly painted for the Helldorado event stood poised in front of the Grand Hotel, just as Ezra said it would be. The street was already crowded with people waiting for the Helldorado activities to start anew. A few looked at O'Rourke, but only in passing, not as they had the day before. O'Rourke smiled to himself, thinking the whole trip had just been a bad dream – and now he was on his way home to Texas.

The stage driver called down to him, "Throw your bags in the boot and climb in Mr. O'Rourke. We're about to leave!"

O'Rourke climbed into the stage to find one other man on board, well outfitted in an 1880's business man's suit, derby hat, and frock coat. The two acknowledged each other but said nothing. The driver snapped the reins and the four-horse team lurched forward, going west on Allen Street to First where it took a right, then out onto Fremont Street, heading towards Benson.

As the stage approached a sign marking the city limit, O'Rourke held his breath. "Will I get out of town this time?" he thought to himself. O'Rourke stuck his head out the window to watch as the wagon went past the sign when he noticed a familiar figure. It was Ezra Thornton, who only minutes before had been several blocks away, and who was now standing in front of the sign over a mile outside of the town-center – waving at the stage – and smiling. O'Rourke thought to himself that Ezra was smiling the same kind of smile as when he was standing in the crowd in front of Vogan's when everyone was staring at him.

A moment later, they passed the city-limit sign, and he realized he was outside of Tombstone – at last – he sat back and now took the time to look at his traveling companion. He was an older man, clean shaven, very well dressed in an 1880's period business suit with a red cravat tie, and a red vest to match his red complexion. Their eyes met, and the stranger spoke in a clear and calm voice, "Good morning Johnny. Sit back, relax, loosen your tie. You're going to be in here for a very long time!"

O'Rourke looked directly at his traveling companion with, "Long time? In 1881 a stage could make it to Benson in a few hours. I assume that's where we are headed. And now, on a paved road, we should get there a little quicker."

The other man smiled, "No Johnny, this time it will take longer – a lot longer. In fact, it will take an eternity! Look outside the window!"

O'Rourke grimaced and stuck his head out the window just in time to see the sign marking the Tombstone city limit go by for the second time. He stretched further to look up at the driver, who had disappeared leaving the reins lying limp on the seat, yet the horses trotted along.

Turning has attention back inside the coach, O'Rourke suddenly noticed that his traveling companion had also disappeared. A disembodied voice whispered, "Now leaving Tombstone..."

Friday December 24, 1929   3:00 PM   Home of Phillip and Marjorie Schneider, Manchester, NH

Marjorie and Phillip Schneider Jr. sat at their kitchen table wondering what they were going to do.

Forsaking the harsh life on the western frontier, and upon the untimely death in 1881 of her husband, Phillip Schneider Sr., Phillip's mother moved east to seek work and a means of supporting herself and her baby son. Mother and son eventually found their way to Manchester, New Hampshire where she was able to find work in the textile mills along the Merrimack River. The wages were meager but the company provided, at a very modest cost, a small cottage, a home for the two. Phillip's mother kept it clean and neat, a small brick place produced by the same brick masons who built the huge factories – made from the same dull-red bricks. It was almost a city within a city, one hardly able to distinguish between rows of homes and the huge facades of the factory buildings.

Young Phillip grew up in the shadow of the dull brick buildings and noise of the machines inside them. Eventually, after completing his schooling, Phillip followed in his mother's footsteps operating a machine in the same factory – but he had always wanted a better life.

He would invest a piece of each paycheck in the stock market – and over time, had watched his small fortunes grow. Eventually, he married Marjorie, a fellow machine operator.

But the recent stock market crash had wiped out everything that he had worked for. Now in their early 50's, the Schneider's were dead broke – and out of work. Despite their seniority status with the mill, they happened to be working a job that was deemed immediately expendable.

Now they wondered where their next meal would come from.

The couple's despair was broken for the moment by a knock at the front door. Marjorie stood to go answer it saying, "Well... maybe it's good news. Lord knows, things could not get worse!"

Phillip chimed in half-heartedly, "Perhaps it's Santa Claus with some new jobs for us. After all – it is Christmas Eve."

The open door revealed a postman standing poised in his clean, blue uniform, arm outstretched with a single envelope in his hand. "Good afternoon, Mrs. Schneider. I have a certified letter for your husband. I'll need a signature."

"I'll sign for it" she replied. Marjorie reached for the large envelope and looked at the return address. It read, "John Barbower – Attorney At Law   Dallas, Texas."

Marjorie could not imagine who might be sending her anything from an attorney, let alone one based in Texas. She signed for the envelope, said good-bye to the postman and closed the door behind her; a cold afternoon breeze finding it's way into the house.

Opening the large brown envelope, she found three smaller envelopes numbered one, two and three. A separate piece of paper said, "As per my client's instructions, I have been directed to ask you to open the letters in order." The paper was signed by Attorney John Barbower.

Sitting back down at the kitchen table, Marjorie looked at her husband, then opened envelope one, and read it out loud:

Dear Mr. Schneider,

You have been named as the sole beneficiary in the Last Will and Testament of one Mr. Michael O'Rourke of Dallas, Texas. Acting as his attorney and executor of his Will, and as per the stipulations of the Will, I have liquidated all assets associated with Mr. O'Rourke's estate. The residual amount is reflected in the enclosed check.

Justice and Redemption

Mr. O' Rourke has also seen fit to provide you with a private letter. I am unaware of its contents. I am providing it to you now as per Mr. O'Rourke's direction.

Please contact our office with any questions.

Sincerely,

John Barbower, Esq.

Marjorie looked at her husband who now had eyes the size of saucers! "Who is Michael O'Rourke?" she inquired. Her husband answered pensively, "Open envelope two."

Marjorie could tell that her husband was totally engrossed, and at the same time surprised and bewildered. She opened envelope two and began to read aloud the neatly, hand-written text..

Tuesday, August 27, 1929

To:
Mr. Phillip Schneider Jr.
Manchester, NH

From:
Michael O'Rourke aka Johnny-Behind The Deuce
Dallas, Texas

Dear Phillip,

I know you were too young to remember the events of January 14, 1881. Perhaps your mother told you the story, perhaps many times.

I have lived that day, every day, for the last 48 years, regretting every minute of it, hoping and praying that there would be some way I could redeem myself.

I have been invited to Tombstone to attend a fiftieth anniversary celebration at the behest of a gentleman I do not know.

I feel a strange foreboding at the thought of attending the affair, as if something dire will happen to me and yet, I feel I cannot miss the event. At 66 years of age, there is plenty of life in me. But I feel I must prepare for what could be a grave personal misfortune.

Subsequently, this day I have liquidated all my financial holdings and entrusted them to my attorney, Mr. John Barbower, with a directive to send the residual of my estate to you should I not return from Tombstone.

Whatever the amount is, it will not replace your father or the life you could have had as a child. I can only hope that it enhances your adult life, and somehow redeems, if only in small measure, the life of what was a young, impetuous, and hot-headed fool.

Sincerely,

Michael O'Rourke
Dallas, Texas

Marjorie stared at her husband for just a moment as tears began to run down his cheeks, and then opened envelope three. With trembling hands, she looked at the check. Yes... it was made out to her husband – in the amount of - $1,500,000!

Marjorie almost fainted. It took a moment to compose herself and she looked at the check again. The amount had not changed - $1, 500,000!

With eyes wide open in amazement she cried, "Honey! Who is Michael O'Rourke?"

The Real Story Behind "Justice and Redemption"

The phrase "Never a dull moment" must have been coined in Tombstone. From its very beginnings, fist-fights, gun-fights, robberies and mayhem of every sort were rampant so it seemed. Author Douglas Martin wrote, "...editors were busy men and death called frequently in Tombstone".

The year 1881 which would culminate in the attempted assassination of a town peace officer was off with a bang thanks to a card-playing 18 year-old tough named Michael O'Rourke– better known as Johnny-Behind-The-Deuce.

It was noon-time on Friday January 14, 1881 and O'Rourke was enjoying a lunch in a Charleston restaurant. W.P. (Phillip) Schneider, the 28 year-old chief engineer for the Corbin Mill, and a well respected individual, came into the restaurant and sat down for a mid-day meal. Schneider noticed a friend, A.E. Lindsey, and joined him at a table next to O'Rourke and his roommate, Robert Petty.

Schneider and his table-mate engaged in a conversation to which O'Rourke made some unwanted comments. Instantly, the situation escalated. Harsh words are exchanged as Schneider approached O'Rourke with a clenched fist.

Schneider's cabin had been broken into some time prior and O'Rourke was suspected but that could not be proven so something was bound to happen with O'Rourke and Schneider sitting in close proximity to one another.

Ladies were present in the restaurant during the exchange. Schneider was ashamed and embarrassed that they would have to hear such language in a public setting and it angered him.

O'Rourke headed for the door threatening Schneider as he left saying, "I will lick you when you come out."

A few moments later, O'Rourke and Petty ran straight into Schneider and more words were exchanged. A moment later, pistols were drawn.

Constable George McKelvey who had been watching the exchange saw the pistols being drawn and tried to intervene but he was too slow. O'Rourke fired hitting Schneider in the face killing him instantly.

O'Rourke dropped his pistol and began running. McKelvey gave chase on foot telling O'Rourke to give up and stop running. O'Rourke continued. A moment later, McKelvey fired a shot in O'Rourke's direction which stopped him cold.

At once, the miners were alerted – and wanted vengeance for such a heinous act from a young hothead. Schneider was well-liked by the miners.

Fearing the mob would grab O'Rourke and lynch him on the spot, McKelvey lit out for Tombstone with the young killer. It didn't take long for McKelvey to realize that the mob would soon overtake them. He sent O'Rourke ahead on horseback to save his own hide.

Shortly, O'Rourke arrived at the corner of Fifth and Allen Street "his horse reeking with sweat and dismounting in front of Vogan's saloon asked for protection, acknowledging that he had killed his man."

The street quickly filled with angry miners, cow-boys, on-lookers and the just-plain curious. With the mob from Charleston hot on the heels of O'Rourke, Allen Street became a pot ready to boil over.

There is no question that O'Rourke killed Schneider and it is uncontested that he ran from Charleston to Tombstone seeking refuge from a lynch party. However, it is here where history gets a little muddy.

The Tombstone Epitaph reported that Marshal Ben Sippy amassed a "well-armed posse of over a score of men to prevent any attempt on the part of the crowd to lynch the prisoner." Sippy was aided by Virgil Earp and Cochise County Sheriff, Johnny Behan.

The story more often told, is infinitely more exciting, and one that has made its way into more books and movies has Wyatt Earp, shot-gun in hand, single-handedly fending off the maddening crowd in front of Vogan's saloon. The 1994 movie, *Wyatt Earp* has Wyatt holding the crowd with a single pistol.

Biographer Tim Fattig notes that later in life, Wyatt Earp told three biographers – John Flood, Forrestine Hooker and Stuart Lake, that it was himself who defended O'Rourke. When the angry mob from Charleston approached Vogan's demanding the release of the young shooter, Wyatt stepped outside and leveled a shotgun on them, and gave a personal address to their leader, one of Tombstone's founders and most influential citizens, Dick Gird.

Wyatt called out, "It'll cost good men to lynch that tinhorn... Number One'll be Dick Gird!"

Ultimately, seeing the folly of their actions, and standing at the business-end of one firearm or another, the men soon dispersed. The heat was taken from the kettle – at least for the moment.

O'Rourke was placed in a light wagon, and accompanied by a cadre of "heavily armed men" was sent north to Benson and on to Tucson where he was placed behind bars. *The Epitaph* noted, "...he will repose at the county expense in a jail on whose walls are inscribed horrid mockery of justice blazoned within the names of other murderers who have partaken of county refreshment to be turned loose again to fasten themselves on the Tombstone public, a living curse."

Tombstone diarist George Parsons was in the thick of the excitement and left this record.

The officers sought to protect him and swore in deputies, themselves gambling men (the deputies that is) to help. Many

188

of the miners armed themselves and tried to get at the murderer. Several times, yes a number of times, rushes were made and rifles leveled causing Mr. Stanley and me to get behind the most available shelter. Terrible excitement, but the officers got through finally and out of town with their man bound for Tucson.

Tombstone had seen the last of Johnny-Behind-The Deuce, but they had not *heard* the last of him.

On Tuesday, April 18, 1881, the name of Michael O'Rourke aka Johnny-Behind-The-Deuce again graced the pages of *The Epitaph*, from a story taken from the *Arizona Mining Journal*. It seemed Mr. O'Rourke felt like he wouldn't get a fair trial in Tucson.

The headline, reproduced here as is was given in 1881 read:

A PRISONER TAKES FRENCH
LEAVE

The Murderer Of Schneider At Liberty

"Johny-Behind-the-Deuce" alias
O'Rourke is Tossed Over the Wall
By his Companions and Flies Like a
Bird to the Mountains – Over a Siz
Teen Foot Wall – Indians in Pursuit –
The Sheriff Hopeful, but Other Peo
Ple Not

After their evening meal, it was customary for prisoners to be let out into the prison yard for a short time prior to being locked-down for the night. O'Rourke and several other inmates made their way out to the yard watched-over by two prison guards, a Mr. Roach and a Mr. Hersy.

The wall surrounding the yard was sixteen feet high, too high to climb or leap over on one's own, but working together, it would be possible for two or more men to help one over the wall – which is probably what happened in a brief moment when the guards were distracted and the compatriots were in a corner of the yard not readily seen. O'Rourke had about a 20 second window of opportunity to make his escape.

As soon as the guards noticed something awry, they sounded the alarm and quickly herded the inmates back to their cells. It was then that they confirmed that O'Rourke had fled.

Guards and an Indian guide were quickly engaged in the search but they had no idea in which direction O'Rourke had gone – and he had several minutes in which to put some distance between him and the prison.

Johnny-Behind-The-Deuce had played a winning hand that day – and was gone.

Three weeks later, O'Rourke was spotted on his way to Texas – to disappear in the mists of time – never to be heard from again.

Other Details

Here are a few additional facts contained within the fictional story:

The date of O'Rourke's letter to Phillip Schneider Jr. is significant. The Stock Market Crash of 1929 is usually attributed to the last few days of October when in fact, the downward slide began on September 3, 1929.

The dates concerning Tombstone's Helldorado celebration are historically correct. During the celebration, there were many re-enactments commemorating various events in Tombstone. Former Mayor John Clum and former Cochise County Deputy Sheriff Billy Breakenridge attended and in fact were featured in the big Helldorado parade.

The San Jose House, one of the earliest hotels in Tombstone, continues to provide accommodations for Tombstone guests.

Billy Fourr was indeed a former and long-time Tombstone resident who attended Helldorado. He was a personal friend of John Clum.

Billy Breakenridge indeed penned the book, *Helldorado*, which is still available today. It has the dubious distinction of being perhaps the most prominent anti-Earp book ever written.

The Can Can Restaurant was a fixture in Tombstone for many years during the 1880's. It was revived for the Helldorado event in 1929.

The Sandy Bob Stage Lines indeed operated in Tombstone during its hey-days in the early 1880's.

Chapter 9: NANTAN

"If you could be anywhere else today, John, where would you like to be? What would you like to be doing?"

Ezra T. Thornton October 25, 1881

Tuesday, October 25, 1881   5:15PM   Tombstone, Arizona Territory

The blue sky of a crisp fall day was turning to crimson and gold as the sun set at the west end of Allen Street. Tombstone's stores and shops began to close, marking the time when most ladies, young girls and young boys went home to dinners and other bucolic pursuits while the miners, fresh off a shift in the silver mines began to filter onto the streets and into the saloons. Soon the street would be dark save the soft glow from gas lanterns that lit the saloons and bawdy houses.

John P. Clum was headed to the Can-Can Restaurant for dinner. He walked south on 6th Street and rounded the corner onto Allen Street only to run into two good friends. Ezra Thornton was just putting the key into the door of his mercantile shop to secure it for the night and as he did, he was carrying on a conversation with the former-failed San Francisco bank-teller now prominent mining claims agent, George W. Parsons.

Clum, who seemed to be in a hurry, now stopped dead in his tracks to greet his two friends. After their initial greetings the men shook hands; and then Ezra spoke, "John, you look like the weight of the world is on your shoulders. Is something bothering you?"

"It shows that much, eh?" came the reply.

The three men stood on the wooden sidewalk simply looking at each other for just a moment. They all knew Clum's situation. He was having a tough time of it given recent events and in light of that, both Ezra and George were at a loss for words.

Ezra broke the painful silence with, "I know what will make you feel better John... but you seemed to be in hurry. Are you in a hurry to get somewhere?"

"I was indeed in a hurry... for a little respite from my worries which I hoped to find at the Can-Can with a meal and a beer. But..."

Clum's words were stopped when Ezra broke in, "But a couple of friends and a cold bottle of sarsaparilla beats a meal at the Can-Can anytime doesn't it?'

Clum's face beamed, "You read my mind Ezra."

Ezra turned and opened the store again. The three men went inside where Ezra, always dressed impeccably in a red brocade vest, boiled white shirt, striped pants and elegant, black top-hat pulled up his right sleeve and reached into a large ice-filled barrel in the middle of the floor to retrieve three small brown bottles, cold water dripping from them as he passed them to his guests.

"This is on me!" Ezra proclaimed as he handed the bottles to his friends. Each took a sip from their respective bottles, and leaned on the long counters, which ran the length of the store on either side of the deep, narrow building. Ezra reached up to retrieve a kerosene lamp that was hanging from the ceiling, lit it, and replaced it on its hook, the soft glow from the light now filling the room.

"So tell us what's bothering you, John" said George, "As if we didn't already know about some of the things happening in your life."

Clum started in, "I continue to mourn the loss of my wife Mary. Although she has been gone for almost a year, my life is still empty without her. Her loss continues to be a big hole in my life."

He took another sip of the cool sarsaparilla from his bottle; then continued, "And this thing with the Earps and Holliday versus the Clantons and McLaury's is really wearing on me. We had political wrangling back at the San Carlos reservation when I was the Indian Agent there – but not like this – not to this degree! When I managed the San Carlos Indian reservation from 1874 to '77, things were a little more clear-cut, without all the political undertones felt in this town. It was me against the military, and my word was law at the reservation. We had our Apache Police and Apache court; but when you came right down to it, I had the last word. I was the authority. In fact, at times it was me and the Apaches versus the US Army. They were always trying to usurp my power, but I kept them in line pretty well."

"And what of the Earp – Clanton animosities, John" asked George. "Things have been pretty quiet the last few days. Maybe it's all blown over."

The three men looked at each contemplating George's words, all suspecting that the worse had not yet happened in the affair.

"If you could be anywhere else today John, "Ezra chimed in, "Where would you like to be? What would you like to be doing?"

Clum didn't have to think twice about that question and was quick with his answer, "San Carlos. I believe my best work was with the Apaches, as their Agent at the San Carlos reservation. Knowing what I know about the Apaches, and how they have been cheated and swindled by the white race in general, the US government in particular... and the US Army specifically, I was able to do my part to do what was right for the Apache – to start to make amends for many past sins. It was my way of making the world a better place. If the government – if the Indian Bureau had seen fit to give me a little more pay, seeing that my work load more than tripled in the three years I was there, and given me a few more resources I would have stayed. But they created just an untenable position – untenable for me...untenable for any man."

Clum stopped and realized the absurdity about which he was talking. George chuckled, then clarified to Ezra what the joke was about, "In the three years that John ran the reservation, there was never an uprising, never a break-out. Even after he left, things were quiet for a short time, then the depredations began anew. Why just a few weeks ago, we chased a band of depredators who had run off the San Carlos reservation not but a few miles from Tombstone! Didn't catch any of them though!"

Ezra took a last sip from his bottle, "So... you want to get back to San Carlos do you?"

"Yes" came Clum's quick reply. "But I have angered so many people during my administration – the Indian Bureau, the US Army – Arizona politicians. It seemed I was always at odds with them over the question of civil rule versus military rule of the Apaches. I wanted what was right for the Apaches – what would best serve their needs. And harsh, draconian military rule did not suit their needs or temperament – nor mine. I was so brash in my attitude towards the military and others that I fear the harm may be irreparable. Perhaps over time..." Clum's words trailed off as his thoughts occupied more of his psyche than his voice could transfer to words.

The three men stood looking at each other just long enough to allow Clum to have a moment to himself, and collect his thoughts. Ezra then broke the silence with, "Gentlemen, it's time for dinner! Let's treat ourselves to a sumptuous repast at the Grand Hotel tonight!"

Thursday July 10, 1882 8:45AM

John Clum sat on a wooden bench outside the office of the Sandy Bob Stage Lines. Two bulging suitcases sat on the wooden platform by his side, the contents of which represented everything he owned in the world.

Clum was dressed, as he always was, in a dapper business suit, clean white shirt and a derby hat – all of which had been perfectly crisp just a short time ago, but now began to look a bit wilted in the growing Arizona heat and dust.

"So... you're really leaving I see!"

Clum turned toward the familiar voice. It was his friend Ezra Thornton, standing at the edge of the waiting platform, holding a small, black leather satchel.

"Leaving...? Yes. Mostly because I don't have a reason to stay!"

Ezra walked up onto the waiting platform and sat down beside the man he met over two years ago, full of enthusiasm for the new mining camp, having a vocation in the newspaper business and ready to profit from it, and looking for a place to raise a family. But his dreams had been dashed by circumstance, and several turns of events over which he had no control. Ezra placed the black satchel at his side.

Clum took off his hat and mopped his sweaty brow with a handkerchief. "I never thought aligning myself with the Earp faction, despite the fact that I never approved of Holliday, would hurt me. It seems everyone in town – everyone – blames the Earps and Holliday for starting the street-fight back in October. And since then, everyone who was associated with the Earps, has been painted with the same dirty brush. In many ways, myself and other Earp confederates have been banished from the mainstream of Tombstone business and society. I have been finding it tougher and tougher to sell advertising in *The Epitaph*. My revenue source has seemingly gone the way of the dinosaur. The Earps and Holliday were exonerated by Judge Spicer but that doesn't seem to mean anything!"

Ezra placed his hand on his friend's shoulder, "I understand. But it's more than the Earps I'm sure!"

Clum continued, "My wife Mary, rest her soul, is gone and I have seen no prospects in town for a future companion. Because I considered Tombstone too harsh a climate for my son, Woodworth, I sent him to live on the east coast with my sisters, so I can no longer draw on his laughter for consolation."

Clum paused for a moment in reflection, and then continued. "And to top it all off, the attempt on my life, perpetrated probably by the Clanton Gang, the assassination of Morgan Earp and near-assassination of Virgil Earp makes it all very clear. There is no longer any room in Tombstone for John P. Clum!"

"Where will you go?"

"I'll start by going to Washington, D.C. to see my son and family" came the reply. "And from there, I'm not sure. Perhaps I'll get a job with the postal service maybe – or other government job. I'm not really sure."

Ezra smiled and asked the obvious question, "Now tell me what you really want to do!"

Clum returned the smile, "Of course you know the answer to that. We have discussed it many times. If I could go back to the reservation as Indian Agent, I would do it without hesitation. This is providing, of course, that the Indian Bureau would provide me with a salary commensurate with the work and responsibility. That may never happen – but I remain hopeful."

Ezra stood, straightened his vest and prepared to leave his friend. "Well, wherever your travels take you, you'll have some refreshment."

Ezra reached down retrieving the black satchel and handed it to Clum. "Here's a little traveling present from me – because I know you like the stuff!"

Clum reached in the bag and pulled out a small brown bottle – sarsaparilla – and it was ice cold. The best part was, there were five more

"How do you do that?" Clum asked. "It's ice cold! How can you keep a bottle of liquid ice cold in a leather bag in May... in Arizona?"

Ezra smiled, "Sometimes good things happen to us... and we shouldn't question it. Just accept it for what it is – a good thing."

Ezra let those be his parting words. He turned, and was gone.

Moments later, the 9AM stage arrived, and carried John Clum away from Tombstone.

Thursday March 8, 1912 6:30PM YMCA Gymnasium Concord, NH

"Where is the 'Trailblazer of Civilization'? I want to meet that person!"

John Clum, now a lecturer for the Southern Pacific railroad was busy readying his projector and other video equipment near the front of the large gymnasium when he heard a voice bellow from the back of the room. Clum looked up first to ensure that he had properly trained the light from his "magic lantern" projector onto the large white screen hanging from the ceiling. As he turned he looked past the rows and rows of wooden folding chairs, all perfectly aligned, waiting for his audience who would soon begin arriving.

They would come to hear about the wonders of the west and see photographs and moving pictures of the geysers of Yellowstone, the rapids of the Colorado River, the mesas of Utah, and the Indian reservations of Arizona as shown by John P. Clum, the "Trailblazer of Civilization" – a self-appointed sobriquet. The show would last an hour and at the end, people would be advised how inexpensive it was to get to "The West' via the Southern Pacific railroad! This was the railroad's way of building commerce and generating revenue for themselves through freight transfer and tourism.

Clum's gaze moved to the back of the large auditorium to see the last person he would ever expect to see in New Hampshire – Ezra T. Thornton – dressed exactly as Clum remembered him from 1882 with his red brocade vest and black top-hat. Thirty years had passed, yet Ezra looked exactly the same – as if time had passed him by.

"Why Ezra T. Thornton – what in blazes are you doing here in New Hampshire?" Clum blurted out.

"Hello to you too!" came the quick reply. "It is equally gratifying to see you!"

Clum then gave his old friend a quizzical look, "It is indeed good to see you Ezra. But here... in New Hampshire of all places? To what do I owe the honor?"

"I came to see the 'Trailblazer of Civilization'!" Ezra answered with a wry smile.

Clum feigned a serious countenance, "You could give this lecture every bit as good as I could; and you haven't even seen it yet. So what really brings you here?"

Ezra moved towards the front of the room and sat down in one of the wooden folding chairs as Clum resumed his fiddling with the projector.

Then Ezra took on a more serious attitude, "Ah, but I have seen your presentation – many times – in many different cities!"

Clum spun around and looked at his old friend in amazement.

Then, Ezra continued, "Oh yes – you've never seen me, but I was there; in Philadelphia, Boston, Baltimore, Atlanta – everywhere. I've followed your career fairly closely. But tonight is a bit different. You see, I know you have been writing to the Indian Bureau trying to get your job back at the reservation. You told them how you were as qualified as anyone in 1874 – and with your age and experience - you were even more qualified now. Of course, the Indian Bureau didn't see it that way. In their last letter to you, they said you were too old – that being an Indian Agent was a young man's job. They said that this would be the last word on the subject. That had to be devastating to you."

Clum looked at his friend in amazement, "That is precisely correct. But how did you know? How could you know? I've told no one, not even my wife about those letters! I..."

Ezra broke into Clum's quizzing with, "I have my connections my good man. It's all about connections! I just wanted you to know how sorry I was that you did not get the job and to let you know that, as your friend, I offer my sympathies."

Clum stood and stared at his friend in utter amazement, the only sound in the room was coming from the hum and whir of the idling projector.

Ezra rose from his chair, "But I do have something to make you feel a little bit better. It's outside. Come with me!"

The two men walked outside into the cold New Hampshire evening. Stepping around the corner of the building and into the street Clum was amazed at what he saw; a huge, enclosed wagon, bright red with yellow wheels and yellow axels. It looked like a circus wagon – it looked like Ezra's wagon he had seen parked behind Ezra's store in Tombstone. A team of four large draft horses was hitched to it, standing at the ready, looking more like they had just been freshly hitched.

As the two men moved to the side of the wagon, there, in bright bold yellow and gold letters on a strip of blue were the words, "E.T. Thornton – Mercantile" – it was indeed Ezra's wagon from Tombstone!

Ezra stepped up into the wagon while Clum stood on the sidewalk in sheer shock. Ezra emerged a moment later with a small, black, leather satchel and handed it to Clum saying, "Here's a little something I know you'll like - something in which to drown your worries over the letter from the Indian Bureau."

Clum opened the bag and reached inside to find six small, brown bottles – sarsaparilla! "You didn't come all the way here just to give me a few bottles of sarsaparilla did you? It's my favorite, and they are cold but... but I..."

Ezra broke in, "You'd better get inside and finish your preparations. I see your audience is starting to arrive!"

Indeed, people had started arriving and Clum knew he still had a few things to do to get ready. He looked at the door where his audience was filing into the building, then looked back at Ezra who just smiled, "Sometimes good things happen to us... and we shouldn't question it. Just accept it for what it is – a good thing. Go ahead in, I'll join you in a moment."

Without saying a word, Clum re-entered the building, smiling at members of his audience as he did. He made his final adjustments to the projector, turned about to face his now-sitting and waiting audience and was about to start when he heard the distinctive sound of hooves and the rumbling of hard, steel-framed wooden wheels against hard pavements and knew that Ezra was off once again. Clum started to make a comment about the sounds, but almost as he opened his mouth to make the comment, it was obvious that no one else had heard the sound – yet a small, black, leather satchel sat waiting for him under his projector table.

Clum began his talk, "Welcome to 'See America First', a fascinating travelogue of our great western states..."

Friday   October 25, 1929   9:30AM   Schieffelin Monument Tombstone, AZ

After months of preparation, Tombstone was ready to celebrate its 50th birthday with the first Helldorado celebration event.

But the old mining camp had seen better days. The mines had been flooded for years and although some mining operations still existed, it was no longer commercially viable the way it had been in the early 1880's. Businesses had closed and many buildings had been abandoned and boarded up. The building on Fremont Street that originally housed *The Tombstone Epitaph* had been long abandoned and was no longer habitable; the paper having moved to better quarters on 5th Street where it remained in business.

Even the venerable Bird Cage Theatre, a bawdy house that, during it's heyday had seen the likes of Wyatt Earp, Doc Holliday, Big Nose Kate, and every luminary west of the Mississippi at one time or another had been boarded up. A high-stakes card game that had gone on day and night, non-stop for several years had finally played-out years before.

But on this occasion, the city's 50th birthday, the Bird Cage had been reopened and actors, singers and dancers, dressed in the fashion of the 1880's again graced the Bird Cage stage to show visitors and tourists and members of the media what all the excitement was about all those years ago.

The city government, and other prominent citizens had hoped, prayed, that the city's birthday party, the first "Helldorado" event, would be the spring board to change Tombstone's economy to that of a tourist town. Since commercial mining was no longer viable, and the city had failed as a health resort (nobody desiring to try to regain their health in a place called Tombstone) the city decided to cash-in on it's reputation of gun-play and mayhem.

On this cool October morning, townspeople, tourists, newspaper men, photographers, film crews and honored guests made their way to the far west end of Allen Street and Schieffelin Monument, a large stone obelisk erected to the memory of Ed Schieffelin, the prospector who discovered silver back in 1877, for the event's opening ceremony. Some walked, some rode in wagons, and some traveled via automobile for the short 1.5 mile jaunt from downtown Tombstone to the monument.

Clum, being the city's first elected mayor under the new city charter in 1881 rode in an automobile as an honored guest along with former Cochise County Under-sheriff, Billy Breckenridge.

The car pulled up at the monument and Clum alighted, surprised that so many people had turned out for the celebration. Having arrived late the prior evening, Clum had not had a chance to tour the city or meet anyone. Looking around, he could see there were plenty of people to meet, some he thought he recognized, most were strangers to him.

As the ceremony began and the speakers commenced extolling the virtues of Tombstone, Clum sat scanning the crowd with an innate feeling that someone was watching him. Finally, he found the "watching eyes." They belonged to the one person he absolutely recognized of the hundreds present – Ezra T. Thornton – who still looked exactly as he had when Clum last ran into him in New Hampshire some 17 years prior – the same as when he left Tombstone almost 50 years before. The two men exchanged a smile.

When the speeches concluded, Clum and Ezra had a chance to talk only briefly, exchanging greetings and agreeing to meet later before Clum was whisked off to lead the grand parade down Allen Street.

Later in the afternoon, after the initial excitement had died down and the town began to engross itself in the festivities, Clum took the opportunity to slip away and take a brief walking tour of the town.

Being at the west end of Allen Street, he decided to walk one block over to Fremont Street to visit what remained of the building that once housed his newspaper, *The Tombstone Epitaph*, then head a few more blocks east, and one block south to the corner of Sixth and Allen Streets to visit with Ezra – that was – if his mercantile store still existed in the same spot.

A few moments later, Clum found himself standing on a concrete sidewalk in front of the former *Tombstone Epitaph* building, almost across the street from the now world famous OK Corral. He thought how strange it was to be standing on concrete where once a wooden boardwalk had existed.

All the windows had been broken out of the old office and the roof removed. The adobe walls were crumbling in many places making the building uninhabitable, perhaps not even repairable Clum thought. The brisk breeze through the many holes in the building made eerie whistling sounds. The tattered remains of what had been window curtains, bleached white by the Arizona sun fluttered in the breeze, the bigger curtains seeming like so many ghosts of the many people who had lived and died in Tombstone. The music, laughter, and sounds of the crowds only a block behind him was drowned out as Clum became buried in his thoughts and memories.

Clum had paused for only a moment in front of the building, but the many memories that flashed across his mind made it seem like he had been standing there for hours. He was just about to leave when he heard a voice, "I was wondering how long it was going to take for you to get here!"

At first, Clum thought his mind had gotten the best of him, but the voice seemed familiar. Suddenly, Ezra Thornton appeared from behind one of the crumbling walls. "I've been here quite a while!"

Ezra emerged from the building through an open doorway, the door laying to one side half torn from its hinges. He was dressed impeccably as always, white shirt, red brocade vest, striped pants and an elegant black top-hat. "Contemplating a return to Tombstone, John? Perhaps taking the helm of *The Epitaph* once again?

The two men chuckled and Clum replied, "The job of a newspaperman is a young man's job; and I'm 78 years old, Ezra - too old to be a newspaperman!"

Ezra stepped up to shake Clum's hand as he did he retorted, "The government told you that you were too old to be an Indian Agent again – but that never stopped you from trying!"

Clum thought for a moment, then replied, "Ah yes... that was back around 1912 as I recall – some 17 years ago. I was indeed younger then. Even at 60 I was still quite spry. But today Ezra, I feel like this building, a burned-out shell of my former self. I realize that there are more days behind me than in front of me and some of my dreams have never been realized. It is saddening really – but such is life."

Ezra then asked a question, to which he already had the answer, "And what dream have you not realized?"

"The dream I have always talked about..." Clum replied, "...to regain control of the San Carlos Apache reservation. I know it still exists. Times have changed... but interestingly; you haven't changed a bit Ezra! Did you dress in the fashion of the 1880's for the celebration?"

Ezra smiled, "John, I've always dressed this way. And now, it seems I am back in style again!"

Ezra then stepped back into the building behind the wall that had

200

concealed him only a few moments ago, and retrieved a small, black leather satchel. Emerging from the building, he presented it to Clum.

"It seems we've done this before. This seems familiar?" Clum mused.

Not acknowledging Clum's deja-vu, Ezra replied, "Open the bag, John. It's a little present for you."

Clum opened the bag. Inside were six little brown bottles – sarsaparilla! And, they were cold – ice cold! Clum looked at his benefactor in the most quizzical manner, just as he had done 47 years prior. His reaction was the same, "How do you do this Ezra? Keeping a drink cold inside a leather bag for an extended time –well – it doesn't seem possible. In fact... I remember now... that bag you gave me when I left here in '82 and again in New Hampshire around 1912 – I still have both bags! And I have tried placing other bottled drinks in the bags, but they don't get cold. But it kept the sarsaparilla cold all the way from Arizona to Washington D.C. How..?"

Ezra smiled, "Sometimes good things happen to us... and we shouldn't question it. Just accept it for what it is – a good thing."

The two men stared at each other for a moment, the weird whistling of the wind through the empty building being the only sound either of them could hear. Ezra broke the silence with, "And now... let us return to Allen Street to take in the festivities!"

Friday February 20, 1930 2:00PM The Clum Home Los Angeles

Now living in Los Angeles with his third wife, Florence, and being almost 80, Clum had long since given up his idea of returning to the San Carlos reservation and had pretty much forgotten about it. Up until two years ago, Clum busied himself visiting with his old friends Wyatt and Josephine Earp who lived close by, puttering in his rose garden, and having quiet dinners with his wife. With Wyatt having died a little over a year prior, Clum wrote magazine articles, tended to his roses, still had quiet dinners, and anticipated the daily mail.

On this particular day, he received a letter postmarked from Tombstone, with a return address of E.T.T. Mercantile.

February 17, 1930

To My Dear Friend John,

I read in yesterday's Tombstone Epitaph, with great anguish for you I might add, about the demolition of the old buildings at

San Carlos, in anticipation of the area being flooded by the new Coolidge Dam Project. As I read the article, I remembered you telling me that these were the buildings erected at your personal direction by the Apaches themselves. They had never built anything so sophisticated. But you showed them how to make adobe and they all became "brick artisans."

I know that you visited San Carlos when you were in Arizona on October last and saw the start of the demolition project. But now, according The Epitaph, the job is complete, and soon, the water over the San Carlos reservation will be safe for maritime navigation.

I understand the new reservation at Rice, AZ is quite nice and modern but no doubt, sans-character as it never had John P. Clum as an Indian Agent.

Your Friend,
Ezra

Wednesday   March 8, 1931   9:00AM   The New San Carlos Reservation at Rice, Arizona

Two cars pulled up in front of the shining, new administration building of the new San Carlos Apache reservation. One car carried John Clum and his wife, Florence, and was driven by John's son, 52 year-old Woodworth.

In the other car were two of Clum's closest friends, Dr. Clarence Toland and *Los Angeles Times* newspaper reporter Harry Carr.

Clum had wanted to visit San Carlos one more time in his lifetime, and his friend, Harry Carr, thought the trip would make excellent fodder for several newspaper features.

The troupe was greeted by Indian Agent James Kitch who advised that they still had about 2,600 Apaches living on the reservation, most of them still living in wikiups, the traditional Apache home.

Upon hearing this, Clum walked around to the back of the administration building to look out upon a wide-open expanse, and a number of wikiups. He would not have believed it had he not seen it with his own eyes.

Just then, Clum spotted an aged Apache riding his horse along a trail. Clum recognized him and called out to the old Indian, "Sneezer!" Clum motioned for the Indian to approach. The old

Indian looked at him in a quizzical manner, not knowing what to make of the situation – or who this "pale face" could be. Then, a younger Indian, who possibly had been told who Clum was, called out to the mounted rider, "It is Nantan Be-tun-ee-kiay!"

Nantan Be-tun-ee-kiay was the name given to Clum when he served as Indian Agent there; Nantan was the Indian word for boss or leader; Be-tun-ee-kiay was Apache for a person with a high forehead – Clum had been prematurely bald.

Instantly, and despite his age, the old Indian dropped from his mount and ran as fast as he could to greet his Nantan – his leader of more than 50 years prior. Many of the ordinarily stoic Indians smiled with approval. An old friend had come home and they were glad to see him – those who remembered. Sneezer and Clum exchanged greetings, Clum with the little Apache he remembered and Sneezer in very broken English.

Sneezer was anxious to escort his old Nantan around to meet the present day Apaches. The troupe including Florence, Dr. Tolland, Harry Carr, Woodworth, Agent Kitch and Sneezer walked around to the various wikiups and small groups of Apaches gathered around fires.

Many of the younger Apaches, too young to remember Clum as the reservation Nantan, related to him stories that they heard from their fathers and grandfathers. With the stories related, Clum knew who they were, and who their fathers and grandfathers had been.

The entourage finally came upon the last wikiup on the plain. Sneezer explained, in broken English, "Special meeting for Nantan only."

Everyone looked at each other. The look on Agent Kitch's face told them he had no idea what was going on. Florence turned to her husband, "Whoever is in here must be very special to you. Go ahead in. Enjoy your meeting. We'll see you back at the administration building."

Everyone turned to leave. Sneezer opened the deer-hide flap that served as a door and Clum and Sneezer entered the darkened room. Once his eyes got used to the darkness and he was able to focus, he could not believe his own eyes!

"Ezra T. Thornton – you certainly have a propensity for showing up in the most peculiar places at the most peculiar times!" Clum blurted, noticing that Ezra was still dressed as if it were 1881, except that today, he had a feather stuck into the band of his top hat. Ezra sat on a blanket on the dirt floor, cross-legged, Indian style,

"I thought you were here to see old friends. Am I no longer a friend?" was the wry reply.

"You are always a friend" said Clum, "...and after all these years, I shouldn't question where or why I see you, but I always do. And by the way, how did you know I would be here today?"

Ezra simply looked at Clum as the old Agent answered his own question, "Ah yes... connections – I remember now!"

Ezra thanked Sneezer for bringing Clum inside the wikiup, and then motioned for him to leave. Ezra rose and turned to Clum, "You are once again at San Carlos my old friend."

Clum looked down in disgust, "The name of this place may be San Carlos, and some of the same people are still here, the same people who were at San Carlos over 50 years ago. But this is not San Carlos. There are no adobe buildings built by Indians, there are no corn fields, no irrigation ditches..."

Ezra broke in, "And there is no military presence either!"

The two chuckled. Ezra continued, "You still long for your old job, don't you, Mr. Nantan? You look at Kitch and wish you were him! I can see it in your eyes, John Clum – Nantan Clum. You can't fool me!"

Clum's face saddened, "I wish it were 1874 again. There are some things I would do differently, perhaps not be so brash and impudent, as I was called.... But I would still look after the welfare of these people. I feel it was supposed to be my life's work, and I failed to see the calling when it was available. It is one of the great disappointments in my life."

Ezra reached down, and from under a blanket lying on floor in a heap, he pulled an ice-cold bottle of sarsaparilla and handed it to Clum who reached out to grab it saying, "I should have known this was coming!"

Ezra laughed. "And the next thing you are supposed to do is ask me how I happened to have a cold bottle of sarsaparilla in the middle of the Arizona desert."

Clum laughed and replied, "What was it you always said..? Sometimes good things happen to us... and we shouldn't question it. Just accept it for what it is – a good thing."

Ezra chuckled again then turned somewhat serious, "There is another saying that I have – that good things come to those who wait. You've not much longer to wait, John Clum. Now go enjoy your sarsaparilla, be with your wife and son and friends, enjoy your Indian friends - and I'll see you again pretty soon."

The deer-hide flap opened and a hand motioned for Clum to exit the wikiup. Not quite sure what Ezra meant, or what he should do or say, he followed the hand and stepped out into the bright sunlight. The hand was Sneezer's who now helped Clum keep his balance as he stepped out.

Clum stopped for a moment to look around and collect his thoughts. What had Ezra meant when he said good things happened to those who waited? Seeking an answer to his question, he turned and threw back the deer-hide flap and peered inside. But Ezra was gone, the little brown bottle he held in his hand the only memory of the meeting.

Clum and Sneezer returned to the administration building and Clum's party. Woodworth noticed the bottle and asked, "What do you have there, dad?"

Clum simply replied, "Perhaps a gift from a friend, perhaps a message in a bottle. I have not yet decided."

Monday   May 2, 1932, 9:20AM   The Clum Home   Los Angeles, California

On the morning of Monday, May 2 1932, John Clum rose, as he did every morning, dressed, and went out to the kitchen to greet his wife. May, in Los Angeles, is already quite warm. So, in his shirtsleeves, John Clum stepped out into his beloved rose garden to putter while Florence made breakfast for the two of them. The Clum home was on a corner lot so that the rose garden, although technically behind the house, also faced a street.

As Clum moved about the garden, pruning and digging, he heard the distinctive sound of hooves against hard pavement, and the rumbling wheels of a large heavy wagon – sounds he head not heard for years. At first, he thought back to similar sounds heard in Tombstone as the heavy ore wagons moved down Allen Street. Then he remembered hearing that sound since then – in New Hampshire when he visited that state's capital city to give a lecture for the Southern Pacific Railroad.

Ezra! Ezra? Could it be?

Clum stepped out onto the sidewalk just in time to see a huge red wagon drawn by four large horses pull up at the curb. The sign on the broad side of the wagon left no mistake in Clum's mind who was paying him a visit. There, looking as fresh as if it was painted yesterday, in yellow and gold-leaf lettering on a strip of blue, were the words, "E.T. Thornton – Mercantile."

And there in the driver's seat was Ezra, looking as he always did; his hair slightly longer and thinner than before but still trailing in abundance from under his elegant, black top-hat.

Clum laughed and called up to his old friend, "I have not seen a wagon like this for years! I would think you would have an automobile by now!"

Ezra returned the smile replying, "This is more my speed, and besides, it suits my purpose."

Clum was quick to quip, "And what purpose would that be?"

Ezra stepped down from the wagon and the two men walked into Clum's rose garden. Ezra then turned to Clum to answer his question, "My purpose, is to help my friends, and make things right wherever and whenever I can... and I also make a pretty good bottle of sarsaparilla."

Reaching into the deep pocket of his frock coat, Ezra produced an ice-cold bottle of Clum's favorite beverage and presented it to him. "Here you go my friend."

Clum and Ezra sat on a small bench in his garden, Clum taking the first sip of his drink. "Making things right? That's a pretty tall order isn't it? And just how do you go about making things right?" asked Clum.

Ezra replied, "Oh... I have my ways. And speaking of making things right, there is a wrong that has existed in your life for many years... a wrong that needs to be righted!"

Clum took a sip of the cold beverage and asked, "And what would that be?"

Ezra smiled, "Why to again see you as the 'Nantan' at the San Carlos reservation!"

Clum chuckled, "You'll see me again as the San Carlos Indian Agent when you explain to me how you keep a bottle of sarsaparilla cold in the pocket of a frock coat!"

"Well" Ezra said, "You know what I always say!"

Clum looked at his little brown bottle and replied, "Yes... "Sometimes good things happen to us... and we shouldn't question it. Just accept it for what it is – a good thing."

With that, Ezra reached into the inside pocket of his black frock coat producing an envelope and handed it to Clum.

"What's this?"

Ezra smiled, "Open it!"

Clum looked at the face of the envelope which was addressed, "John P. Clum   1958 W. 74th Street   Los Angeles, CA. It was his address all right; but the postmark was dated February 23, 1917. Clum mused, "Well, whoever wrote this got my present-day address correct, but I didn't live here in 1917 so how could anyone have known....?"

Ezra leaned over to his friend as they sat on the rose garden bench, "Look at the date John. What is the significance of the date? Do you remember?"

Clum thought for a moment, "It seems this was about the time I wrote my last letter to the Indian Bureau trying to get my job as Indian Agent reinstated. They never answered my letter and I gave up all hope. I was too old then anyway! That's what they told me in the previous letter."

Ezra smiled back at his friend, "Maybe this is the answer you were waiting for?"

Clum looked at his old friend in disbelief. Seeing Ezra, and having a letter with a 15 year old post mark on it was just too confusing. Clum opened the envelope, unfolded the letter and began to read:

Dear Mr. Clum,

Your bid for the position of Indian Agent at the San Carlos Apache Reservation has been accepted at a pay rate of $2,500 per annum. Please report to the reservation as soon as is practicable.

Regards,
E.W. Smith
Secretary / Indian Affairs
Washington, D.C.

As Clum was reading the short letter for the second time, in utter disbelief, Ezra stood up and straightened his vest and his hat, readying himself to leave. With a bit of a smile, but also being serious Ezra remarked, "Well... it is time for good things to happen for you old friend. Go tell your wife you are about to be the new 'Nantan' at San Carlos!"

Clum looked up at his friend replying, "Very funny Ezra. A cute joke. You know I'm too darned old anyway. I...."

Florence's sweet voice wafted through the rose garden disturbing her husband in mid-sentence, "Breakfast John! Come and eat while it's hot!"

John Clum rose from his seat, turned, and was about to call back to his wife that they would have guest for breakfast when he felt a sharp pain in his chest. Stumbling, he managed to make it to the doorway of the kitchen where he collapsed clutching his chest.

Florence, horrified at the scene, hurried to her husband's side, dishes dropping to the floor. She looked up to see Ezra standing a few feet from the doorway, smiling an incredulous smile – horrific in light of what was happening almost at his feet.

Florence thought how out of place this man seemed, the way he was dressed, that she had never seen him before, and that he only stood there, smiling, while her husbands life drained from his body. She screamed at him to do something – but Ezra only smiled.

Leaving her husband, Florence ran to the telephone to call for help. But it was too late. The old Nantan was gone.

Ezra turned, retrieved the half empty bottle of sarsaparilla from the small table where Clum had set it down moments before, mounted his wagon, and was gone.

Saturday August 8, 1874 11:00AM Arizona Territory

John Clum awoke with a start and was astonished to find himself, apparently, in the back of an enclosed wagon, lying on a bed of Indian blankets. The wagon was fairly dark inside but he could see through cracks in the wagon sides that it was daylight – very bright daylight.

The sound of the horses pulling the wagon told him that the team had to be four to six animals. The wagon creaked and groaned and bounced which told him that he was on a very uneven road – perhaps a dirt road – not the finely paved roads of Los Angeles that he had come to know.

Adding to the creaking and groaning was the tinkle of metal, pots, pans, and other metal objects hung inside the wagon. As he awoke fully, he could tell that the wagon served as both a living quarters, and as a mercantile wagon. "Nobody would travel with this much stuff" he thought to himself.

And then it hit him – mercantile wagon! The last thing he remembered was Ezra Thornton pulling up in front of his house in Los Angeles – but he couldn't remember anything beyond that!

Rising to a sitting position he came face to face with a mirror dangling from a string and took the opportunity to look at himself. His eyes and his face were young again! The lines and wrinkles of his 80 plus years were gone! Feelings of both horror and delight washed over him as he contemplated his next move.

As he looked toward the front of the wagon, he could see a heavy curtain marking the line between the wagon's interior, and the driver's seat. As the wagon lurched and swayed, the curtain moved enough so Clum could determine that one man, the driver, sat on the driver's seat. Hoping that the wagon's driver had some answers, Clum rose and poked his head through the curtains.

"Good morning young man!" came a cheery greeting.

"Ezra! Ezra Thornton. What in blazes is going on?"

"Do you remember me telling you that it was my job to right certain wrongs?" Ezra asked.

Clum thought for a moment, "Yes I remember that conversation. It seems like it was moments ago. But we couldn't get from Los Angeles to... where we are out here in the desert in a few minutes. And what happened to me? I'm young again! Why... just look at me!"

Clum climbed out of the wagon's cabin and took a seat alongside Ezra. He was dressed in a boiled white shirt, vest, cravat tie, short boots and striped pants.

Ezra reached behind himself producing a derby hat and handed it to Clum saying, "Here, don't forget this! Its part of your outfit you know!"

Clum looked at Ezra with an incredulous look on his face. "I don't get it, Ezra. Where are we? It's hot as hell here!"

Ezra gave a rather matter-of-fact reply, "My dear Mr. Clum; today is the day I get to right some wrongs for you. The correct question would be to ask where... and when are we! Where - is Arizona Territory, on the road from Tucson to San Carlos, a road I know you are fully familiar with. When are we? Today's date is August 8, 1874. Does that date stand out in your memory?"

Clum thought for a moment, still trying to comprehend everything, "Why yes, that is the day I arrived at the San Carlos reservation – almost 60 years ago!"

Ezra again gave a matter-of-fact reply, "Mr. Clum... depending on your perspective, today is 60 years ago. As I said, it is August 8, 1874. Today is the day you regain your title as 'Nantan Be-tun-ee-kiay; the Boss with the High Forehead!!'"

Ezra's wagon pulled alongside an open spring wagon and stopped. The wagon was loaded with supplies, and bags and packages of all description. A team of two fresh-looking horses, standing at the ready, were hitched up to it.

"Here is where we part ways, John" said Ezra. "As you know, the reservation is over that hill about two miles. Your Apaches are waiting for you. You can stay as long as you like."

Ezra handed Clum an envelope. "Here is your letter from the Indian Bureau. You left it in Los Angeles. I thought you would want it. It says you got a pay raise of $1,000 per year – compared to the first time you were here! More raises will come. I guarantee it. And the Indian Bureau stands ready to provide you with whatever resources you need. All you need to do is send them a letter requesting it. It's all here in this letter!"

"But what will happen to my wife, Florence? And what of my son, Woodworth? What will happen...?"

"Don't worry about them. Right now they are planning a funeral for John Clum, retired scholar, organizer, divinity student, football player, public office holder, newspaperman, postal inspector, postmaster, lecturer, and journalist. They will mourn your passing and life will go on for them. Your existence, such as it is, can go on here, at San Carlos, the way you always wanted it."

Having no choice but to accept what Ezra was saying, Clum climbed down from the huge red wagon and onto the seat of the smaller, green, spring wagon. He picked up the reins and was ready to head off when he looked imploring at Ezra for more answers.

Ezra saw the look on Clum's face, and knew the answer he had to give, "Young man, sometimes good things happen to us... and we shouldn't question it. Just accept it for what it is – a good thing."

The Real Story Behind "Nantan"

John P. Clum assumed his appointment as Indian Agent of the San Carlos Apache Indian reservation at noon on August 8, 1874. He was 22 years old, prematurely bald, and in charge of about 700 Indian – who a short time previously had shown their distaste for white rule by killing a young Army Lieutenant.

During this time, civilian Indian Agents were charged with the responsibility of managing the "good" Indians who stayed on the reservation. They provided for the general welfare of the tribes under their charge. When Indians ran off the reservations to commit crimes such as horse-theft and stealing from wagon-trains and remote ranches, the Army stepped in to capture and/or kill those Indians committing "depredations" against white settlers. There was a constant struggle between the military and civilian agent over who had the authority to do what – especially when it came to Clum's reservation.

His would be one of the most controversial, yet most effective and most celebrated tenures in the history of the reservation system. Clum established a form of Apache government with a court system and a very effective Apache police force.

Shortly after he assumed his position at San Carlos, he was able to convince his superiors and the Army that a military presence was no longer needed at San Carlos – that he would rule the place himself with his Apache Police.

After three years of constant struggle with the Indian Bureau in Washington, D.C. seeking more resources to help the Indians, out of utter frustration, John Clum left the reservation on July 1, 1877. Almost from the first moment he left, he regretted his actions. As he aged, matured, and mellowed, he realized that working with the Apaches was the only job he ever loved and his life-long regret for having abandoned his post at San Carlos.

From the Tombstone portion of the story, the Can-Can restaurant was a real restaurant, operating for many years in Tombstone. It served many different dishes but was operated by Chinese.

George Parsons really existed and was a life-long friend of Clum's, also serving as godfather for Clum's daughter, Caro. Parsons would later become famous as a diarist, his daily entries during his stay in Tombstone continue to serve as a valuable contemporary account of the period, still used by historians today.

The "street fight" referred to was the OK Corral gunfight that took place on October 26, 1881 between Virgil, Morgan and Wyatt Earp along with their friend, Doc Holliday against Frank and Tom McLaury and Billy and Ike Clanton. At the end of the 30-second "street fight", the McLaury brothers were dead as well as 19 year old Billy Clanton. Ike Clanton ran off when the fighting started. Morgan and Virgil were wounded. Doc received a slight flesh wound. Wyatt was unscathed.

However, as a result of that fight, assassination threats were made against many of Tombstone's leading citizens including John Clum and Judge Wells Spicer who exonerated the Earp party of any wrong doing. An attempt was made on Clum's life in December 1881, and made to look like a common stage holdup. John Clum indeed left Tombstone sometime around July or August, 1882.

For several years, Clum worked for the Southern Pacific railroad conducting lectures all over the east coast, trying to drum up business for the railroad through tourism. He indeed billed himself as the "Trailblazer of Civilization." It is unknown if he ever went to Concord, NH – but it is possible.

Beginning around 1929, the San Carlos Indian reservation was moved from its original spot to just outside of Rice, AZ because the original area was to be flooded with waters backed-up by the new Coolidge dam project. Clum indeed visited the new reservation on March 8, 1931 along with his with his wife, Florence, son Woodworth, Dr. Clarence Tolland and newspaper reporter Harry Carr. Harry Carr wrote several articles about the trip which appeared in the *Los Angeles Times*.

Sneezer was indeed one of the Indians at San Carlos during Clum's rein as Indian Agent, and he was also present during Clum's last visit in 1931. Clum could not pronounce the names of many of his charges in 1874, he not being fluent in Apache, and the Indians not being fluent in English. As a compromise, Clum named many of them based on either a phonetic pronunciation, or based on some of their physical or personal traits.

John Clum indeed died at his Los Angeles home at 1958 W. 74th Street Los Angeles, CA on May 2, 1932 at 9:30 in the morning. Prior to his death in 1929, Wyatt Earp and Clum visited each other often, Wyatt living not far away. Clum's house still stands today in 2010 and is a private residence.

For years after he left the Indian service, frustrated and disgusted with the constantly interfering Army and lacking the necessary resources (including his own pay) to properly care for the Indians, a seemingly uncaring and slow-moving Indian Bureau notwithstanding, Clum tried to get another appointment with the Indian service. He indeed wrote his last letter to the Indian Bureau on February 9, 1917. The appointment so long-sought, never came.

Chapter 10: RETURN TO TOMBSTONE

From an idea inspired by Lia Scott Price

"There was so much hate in that little boy... well... those feelings may still exist in that jar!"

Ezra T. Thornton March 25, 1953

August 1, 1952 City Post Office, Tombstone, AZ

It was a rather slow day at the Tombstone Post Office, slow enough that Postmaster Gray had the time to read a curious letter he had just received. It was addressed on the front only as "Postmastr Tumbstone, Az. The handwriting was scrawling and sloppy, as if someone very young... or very old had written it.

The letter read:

dear mr. postmaster

I am wondering if this is the Tumbstone town where the rich silver mines wer and the watter drounded them and before it did watter was sold for a dollar a glass? I am wondering if it is the town wher a man nameded ed gleeeson stil lives? I wnt to get in tuch with him becuz I owe him sumthng and if he iz ther I wil visit him Wil u pleez writ bac and tel me.

Thanc yew,

george ellis mcgurk aka arizona slim
albany, CAL

213

Postmaster Gray chuckled. He showed the letter to Mrs. Edith Landers, President of the Tombstone Chamber of Commerce and she agreed to follow-up with it. She replied to Mr. McGurk:

August 9, 1952

Tombstone Chamber of Commerce
Tombstone, AZ

Dear Mr. McGurk,

Thank you for your most recent letter inquiring about our fair city and one of its residents.

This is indeed the city to which you were referring. Ed Schieffelin struck silver ore here in the late 1870's starting a rush to the area and soon the boom-town of Tombstone sprouted from the dust of the desert floor. But by the mid-1880's water had flooded the mines effectively ending commercial mining on the grand scale that marked the town's beginnings.

The man you are seeking, Mr. Edwin Gleeson, still lives in Tombstone as he has for all his life. But he is quite aged now and very frail. I told him you were asking about him and he seemed to remember you but was not quite sure.

I am enclosing several brochures about Tombstone and the surrounding area. We have an ideal, healthy climate year around with plenty of sunshine and fresh air. We welcome former as well as new residents.

Sincerely,

Mrs Edith Landers
President / Tombstone Chamber of Commerce

A short time later, Mrs Landers received another letter from Mr. McGurk, this one addressed directly to her. The letter read:

dear missus landers,

thank yew for the infermashun   I am planning to go to tombstone very suun.   They call my son kid bronco becuz he wuz in a rodeo many yers ago.   I am called Arizona slim becuz I ust to liv ther in yur state   my son an me wil go to tombstone suun.   I owe somthng to ed gleeesun.   I am very ill rite now   I hop I mak it to tumbstone when I do I wil pay bac to ed gleesun wht I oweded him.

thnk yew

george ellis mcgurk aka arizona slim
albany, CAL

Mrs. Landers smiled – and filed Mr. McGurk's letter away in a desk drawer, not knowing quite what to do with it. She thought the father/son nicknames where quite whimsical, and wondered what these men looked like – and what Arizona Slim owed Ed Gleeson? It must have been some sort of serious debt to travel all the way from the San Francisco area! But it was not a matter for a busy person like the President of the Tombstone Chamber of Commerce to dwell on.   Life went on in Tombstone, and Arizona Slim and Kid Bronco were forgotten.

Wednesday March 18, 1953 Albany, California

George Ellis McGurk lay on his bed, in his small rented home in Albany, CA, wheezing and choking, his emaciated body showing every hard day of his 81 years. His grown son, best known as Kid Bronco was by his side waiting – waiting for the end that he knew was inevitable.

George Ellis McGurk never had any formal education, roaming from town to town throughout Arizona, New Mexico and California, working ranches, occasionally tending bar, but generally bumming aimlessly about. His son, a love-child of a short and tumultuous affair followed in his father's footsteps, holding only odd jobs here and there, settling for a while riding in a rodeo where he acquired his sobriquet.

The two seemed to just muddle along throughout their lives, keeping each other out of trouble – and out of jail most of the time.

If Kid Bronco didn't have anything that drove him in his life, Arizona Slim had enough driving force for the both of them.   He always talked about returning to Tombstone, to repay a debt, although his travels never seemed to head in that direction. Kid Bronco wondered about it sometimes and would occasionally ask his father about it. "Sometimes you wanna go...but you don't wanna go Poppa!" Kid Bronco would say. "It's like there is something there you are afraid of!"

Arizona Slim would growl back, "I aint' afraid of nothing. I just owe a debt I gotta pay. That's all!" Arizona Slim would then proceed to mutter under his breath for several minutes afterward.

The aged range-rider looked up at his son, unable to lift his head from his pillow, "Looks like I didn't make it to Tombstone, Kid! Looks like I won't be able to repay that debt I owe. Such a shame! I thought I had all the time in the world to do that. Now, it will go unpaid; forever I guess."

Arizona Slim rested a moment, gathering strength for what he had to say next:

"Kid, you are not the brightest son a man ever had. I blame myself for that. But I gotta say, you are the most devoted. All these years you took care of me, through my drunken binges, through my sickness. Thank you for all you've done! Now when I'm gone, here's what I want you to do. I've written a letter and I have things planned out..."

Father and son talked for several minutes. Finally, exhausted, Arizona Slim looked up at his son, and then closed his eyes... for the last time.

Wednesday March 25, 1953 9:30AM Tombstone Chamber of Commerce

"I have a package here for a Mrs. Edith Landers!" announced a uniformed messenger as he stood in the doorway of the Tombstone Chamber of Commerce building.

"I'm Mrs. Landers" came the quick reply.

"That'll be $1.92, ma'am. The package is COD!" the messenger said as he held out his hand.

Edith Landers thought for a moment, "I don't remember ordering anything either for myself or the Chamber that would have been sent COD. Where is it from, young man?"

The messenger looked at the package, then looked up slowly to the five Chamber employees, now eagerly awaiting his answer. "It's from... well... a crematorium... the Oakland California Crematorium! Isn't that where they cremate people... turn them into ashes?"

Everyone in the office looked stunned. Was it a cremated body... or something else? If it was a cremated body, whose was it?

Speculation went wild. Not knowing what to do, Mrs. Landers reached in her purse, found the amount due, and paid the messenger.

Edith Landers set the brown cardboard box on her desk and just looked at it for a moment. The speculative chatter of a moment ago was silenced as everyone looked pensively at the box. It was a complete mystery. Could this be someone's idea of a cruel joke – a joke that could only be played in a town called "Tombstone?"

Finally, curiosity won out over fear. Mrs. Edith Landers unsealed the mysterious box, and opened it. Not surprisingly, a well-packed urn containing the final remains of someone was inside. She carefully removed the urn from the box, set it on her desk, then stood back and looked at it in amazement. It was black... and dull. Dull... and black. It seemed as lifeless as the person it contained. It was devoid of any character or personality – almost a non-entity – just as the person within it had become. And yet, as she stared at it, it seemed there was something ominous about the little black jar. It almost seemed to mock her as she stared silently at it. As the head of the Tombstone Chamber of Commerce, it was Edith's job to bring people to Tombstone. And it was through her efforts that she brought one more person to Tombstone albeit someone who was grossly unwanted. It all seemed so bizarre.

Along with the urn came a letter. Edith read it aloud:

dear mrs lannders,

if yu are reading this leter I am dead and I am in tombstone in a jar I wanted to go to tombstone for alng time but did not mak it but I am here now i have a debt to repay to ed gleesun I owe him sumthng but can not pay bac to him now becuz I am dead now so ples bury me in boothill I alwys wanted tobe in boothill but I do not kno anyon in tumbstone excpt yu so pls help me be bureed in boot hill my son probly sent me cod becuz we hav litl monee so I must apalojiz for that I hope it is ok

sinseerly

george ellis mcgurk aka arizona slim

Edith Landers, along with the other women in her office were aghast, first that human remains in the form of ashes were in their office – and second, that they had come COD! Unwittingly, Mrs. Edith Landers had become the custodian of one Arizona Slim.

Standing silently, all eyes were fixed on the urn sitting on Edith's desk, Edith still holding the letter in her hands in a reading position.

The pensive silence was broken by a familiar voice, coming from the front office door which opened to Allen Street. "Hello!"

It was Ezra Thornton and as was his custom, and knowing everyone in town, he looked in the open door and gave a cheery greeting - but was met with silence. This was not the usual high-spirited reciprocation he was used to; prompting him to stop in his tracks, and then slowly enter the office.

Ezra moved slowly, pensively... his eyes fixated on the urn sitting on Edith's desk. "Is that what I think it is?" he asked.

Edith answered wryly, "Mr. Thornton, I'd like you to meet George Ellis McGurk, aka Arizona Slim. Mr. McGurk, meet Mr. Ezra Thornton."

Ezra continued in the same wry manner, "It would appear that Mr. McGurk just arrived in our fair city. To what do we owe the honor of his presence?"

Edith simply replied, "He's dead..." and handed Ezra the letter she still held.

Ezra took a moment to read the letter, then looked up at five pairs of eyes staring at him, hoping that he would have some kind of answer for them about what to do with Arizona Slim.

One of the women broke the short but poignant silence with,"Ezra do you know Arizona Slim? I'm sure you know Ed Gleeson, he's been here forever!"

Ezra thought for a moment, then sat on the edge of a desk, and began his explanation, "In March of 1885, a fight broke out in the Crystal Palace between a man called Windy Bill and Ed Gleeson. Ed was once quite a scrapper but you would never know it to look at him today as weak and frail as he is. Anyway, the two had had heated arguments for months over some real estate deal. Mostly it was a lot of yelling but on this one occasion it quickly escalated into fisticuffs. Windy Bill gave Ed a hard punch to the jaw that knocked him down on the floor. But Ed wasn't about to take a beating like that in front of his friends. He also knew that Windy Bill normally was armed with at least one pistol, and wasn't afraid to use it. When Ed came up off the floor he decided to be first on the trigger, pulled a small pocket pistol, a .32 I think, and let Windy Bill have a bullet right between the eyes. Windy Bill was dead before he hit the floor. The whole sad affair was witnessed by a young, 14 year old boy who was standing in the Crystal Palace doorway. Windy Bill's real name was Michael McGurk. And that 14 year old boy was George Ellis McGurk, now better known as Arizona Slim – the late Arizona Slim. Soon after the shooting, young George McGurk and his mother moved out of

Tombstone never to be heard from again – until now."

Ezra paused for a moment then went on, "Ed Gleeson was arrested shortly afterwards and went to trial. The Judge called it self defense although Windy Bill was, oddly enough, unarmed at the time. Gleeson was acquitted of all charges and set free. Some people thought it was more murder than self defense. As we all know, Mr. Gleeson remained here in Tombstone his whole life, but never again set foot in the Crystal Palace."

One of the office women spoke up, "What about the debt that he owes Ed Gleeson? If Arizona Slim left Tombstone at 14 years old, and hasn't been back here since, what could he possibly owe Ed Gleeson?"

There was another poignant silence. Everyone looked at each other and came to the same realization at the same time – all except the woman that asked the question. Ezra could tell from her expression that she still didn't get it and broke the silence with, "I believe what Arizona Slim feels he owes Ed Gleeson is a bullet – right between the eyes in retribution for killing his father 68 years ago."

With a quizzical look on her face Edith postulated, "I don't know why it took him so long to want his pay-back. I guess it just takes some men longer than others to work up the nerve to do something. But it doesn't matter now anyways because he's lost his opportunity. His debt will never be repaid!"

Ezra looked at Edith and smiled, "Are you sure of that?"

Edith looked annoyed at the off-hand remark and continued, "Mr. Arizona Slim wants to be buried in Boot Hill cemetery, but it's been closed for years. The City Cemetery would be just as good I guess."

Ezra took on a serious tone, "Not complying with the last wishes of a dead man is not something I would take lightly. If he wants to be buried in Boot Hill, then you should do everything in your power to get him planted there – and soon! If the son of Windy Bill and Mr. Ed Gleeson should meet... well... there's no telling what would happen!"

Again, Edith looked annoyed and assumed Ezra was just playing with her, and being facetious. "Now Ezra, "she started, "Arizona Slim is dead and just a pile of ashes, and Ed Gleeson is 92 years old and barely able to get around. What could these two possibly do to each other?"

Ezra continued in his serious tone, "None of you ever saw how bitterly these two men fought with one another, or how distraught Windy Bill's wife was when she left town, or how angry that little 14 year old boy was. In fact, he ran out of the Palace looking for a gun but was stopped by a few good citizens. I believe had he found a gun, he would have repaid Mr. Gleeson right there on the floor of the Palace. There was so much hate in that little boy... well... those feelings may still exist in that jar!"

"That ridiculous" Edith replied.

"Is it?" answered Ezra. He paused for just a moment and then went on. "Why don't you put Mr. McGurk in the City Hall safe and we'll see if we can get the Cemetery Commission to re-open Boot Hill for one more soul. I'll talk to the Mayor myself personally about the matter."

Edith tucked the urn under her arm, and headed out the door, for the City Hall.

Wednesday March 25, 1953   4:30PM   Ezra T. Thornton Mercantile

Ezra was busy placing some new merchandise in the window of his store when his eye caught someone walking by... very slowly. Ezra looked up and smiled at the gaunt, bent, silver-haired old man dressed in clothes that were too big for him, his open sport coat and mis-matched tie blowing in the rising wind. The old man returned the smile, showing a few missing teeth.

Ezra stepped to the door to invite the old man in; "Why Ed Gleeson, how have you been? Come on in. I have some news for you!"

Ed hobbled into the store where Ezra brought up a stool for the aged man to rest on. "Ed, would you like a cold drink?"

The ancient man smiled his tooth-bare smile again, "Sure, I'd love one!"

Ezra reached into his ever-present barrel of sarsaparilla, grabbed two, handed one to Ed Gleeson, opened one for himself, and then started with Ed's "news." "Ed, an old friend of yours arrived here in town this morning!"

Ed grinned again, "Really? Who is that?"

"George Ellis McGurk, aka Arizona Slim" was the reply.

Ed's face took on a quizzical look, trying to remember the name.

Ezra gave him a moment, then said, "You knew has father, Michael McGurk, better known as Windy Bill."

The quizzical look on Ed Gleeson's face turned to horror, and his complexion turned ashen. "What the hell is he doing here! I haven't heard that name in years!"

Before Ezra could gather a breath to answer, Ed blurted out, "I was acquitted of McGurk's shooting. I'm innocent! Innocent! There's nothing that boy can do to me now anyways."

Ed stopped and thought for a moment, then said, "Boy! He was about 14 years old back then. That was...let's see... over 65 years ago. He's not a boy any more... and neither are we, Ezra!"

Ezra piped in, "Would you like to meet him?"

Ed Gleeson paused and just stared at Ezra. "Meet the boy? What the hell would I say to him after 65-odd years?"

Ezra smiled, "Finish your sarsaparilla and I'll take you to see him! He's at the City Hall. We'll need to hurry to get there before 5PM!"

Ezra closed his store, and the two men walked to the City Hall.

Wednesday March 25, 1953   4:45PM   Tombstone City Hall

Ezra and Ed entered the Mayor's office just as he was ready to close the town safe and leave for the afternoon. All exchanged greetings, and then Ezra said, "Mr. Mayor, would you bring Arizona Slim out here to meet Mr. Gleeson?"

Mayor Reginald Johnson smiled and winked at Ezra, turned and bent down, reaching into the large safe, the same safe that had served the city for over 50 years! When he turned back around, he held the dull, black urn containing the ashes of Arizona Slim.

Ezra smiled, "Ed, meet Arizona Slim!"

Ed's jaw dropped!

Looking at Mayor Johnson, Ezra continued, "Mr. Mayor, did you know Ed Gleeson here was afraid of what to say to Arizona Slim if he met him?"

Mayor Johnson chuckled. "Don't worry about what to say to this 80 year-old boy. He can't hear you! Whatever happened between you and his father was years ago anyway. It's all water under the bridge now!"

Ezra took on a serious tone and said to the Mayor, "Are you sure?"

Mayor Johnson looked stunned at first. Then Ezra smiled and the Mayor returned the smile thinking that Ezra was only kidding. Ezra then asked, "So I assume you talked to Edith Landers about a final resting place for Arizona Slim?"

Mayor Johnson turned to return the urn to the safe. "We talked, but as you know, it's up to the Cemetery Commission to re-open Boot Hill for a new burial. They won't meet for several days. But I'll keep Arizona Slim right here, safe and sound! Nobody will bother him. He'll be fine until the Commission can decide what to do!"

Mayor Johnson closed the heavy safe door and spun the lock mechanism to seal it. He then turned to Ezra and Ed Gleeson saying, "You see? Safe and sound!"

Wednesday March 25, 1953 7:30PM   Crystal Palace Saloon

Word travels pretty fast in a town of 1500 people. Before long, a good number of people had heard about Arizona Slim and how he arrived in town, packed in an urn, and was waiting for the wheels of bureaucracy to carry him to Boot Hill and his final resting place. It was all the talk in the Crystal Palace Saloon, a favorite Tombstone "watering hole" almost 75 years after its founding.

Having finished his dinner at home, Mayor Johnson headed over to the Crystal Palace for a cool brew, and a little camaraderie after a long day. Dressed casually in blue jeans and button-down shirt, Mayor Johnson hadn't made two steps in the front door when the bartender hailed him. The place was fairly busy for a week night, most tables being occupied and several men at the mahogany bar, but not too busy to keep the Mayor from quickly approaching the waving bar-keep.

Mayor Johnson stepped up to the bar and smiled at the bartender, Fred Sandler, saying, "How are you doing tonight, Fred?"

Fred gave Mayor Johnson a dour look, reached down under the bar, and produced a black burial urn; "This turned up a little while ago. One moment it wasn't there, I turn around, and it's sitting on the bar. A few people said you would know about it. Since this is Wednesday night and I figured you would be in, I decided to just hold it for you."

Mayor Johnson looked at the urn in disbelief and touched it as if to reaffirm to himself that the urn was really sitting there on the Crystal Palace bar. He looked at the urn, then looked up at Fred. "How strange. I put this in the City Hall safe myself, closed the door, spun the lock and secured it. How the heck...?"

Fred interrupted the Mayor's thought. "And that's not even the strangest thing about it!"

Mayor Johnson looked quizzically at the bartender as he doled out drinks to the hostesses serving the tables. "How's that?"

Fred passed two more beers over the bar to a hostess, "That urn showed up not long after I came on my shift here at 5:30. There were only two people in the place at the far end of the room near the front door. There is no way in hell either of those men could have concealed this urn and placed on the bar in the blink of eye that it took me to turn around once; neither could anyone have come in, set the urn on the bar, then turned and left in that short amount of time either! I would have heard their foot steps on the hard wood floor. The damn thing just appeared out of thin air! That's the only thing I can figure!"

Fred started mixing a drink for another order. "I heard that this urn contains the remains of a former Tombstone resident?"

Mayor Johnson replied, "It does indeed. It contains one George Ellis McGurk, aka Arizona Slim. His father, Michael McGurk aka Windy Bill was gunned down right here... in the Crystal Palace, in March 1885 by..."

"Yes...yes.. I know" interrupted Fred, "...shot by Ed Gleeson. I am familiar with the story. I've heard it many times. And speaking of Ed Gleeson, I've seen him walk by several times this evening. He walks past, pokes his head in the doorway, but won't step in here, then keeps going. A few moments later, he walks by from the other direction, and does the same thing. Do you think there is a connection here?"

Mayor Johnson sighed, "Well... I don't know about that. Ed Gleeson hasn't set foot in this saloon in years. What would make him want to come in here now? And I have no idea how Mr. Arizona Slim made it out of the town safe, out of a closed and locked City Hall, and walked, without legs mind you, the entire length of a city block, and leaped up onto your bar! Somebody, and I don't know who but I *will* find out, is having some fun at our expense. Before I have my beer, I'm going to bring the urn back to the City Hall. Keep my place at the bar; I'll be right back!"

Ed Gleeson walked by the saloon's open door, poked his head in, but didn't allow his feet the cross the threshold, and just as quickly turned and walked away.

Thursday March 26, 1953   11:45AM   E. T. Thornton Mercantile

Ezra stood outside his mercantile store, watching tourists go in and out of the Bird Cage Theatre, waiting for his next customer. Although only March, the Arizona sun was beginning to warm the days quite nicely, and Ezra was thankful for the boardwalk's overhead roof which had shielded him from the sun's rays all these years.

A moment later, Mayor Johnson appeared from the corner of Ezra's building on the corner of Sixth and Allen Streets, on foot, and walking briskly. The two met and greeted each other.

"Ezra..." started Mayor Johnson, "I'm on my way to the Cemetery Commission meeting. Hopefully they will decide this afternoon if we can bury Mr. Arizona Slim in Boot Hill. Quite frankly, I don't care where they bury him, as long as he gets buried... and soon! He's become quite a nuisance."

Ezra was quick to reply, "Well, he really should be buried at Boot Hill. It's not right to deny a man's last requests – bad luck they say. And how can he be a nuisance? The urn is just sitting in the safe in your City Hall... isn't it?"

Mayor Johnson gave Ezra a look that said he probably had something to do with the urn showing up at the Crystal Palace. "Ezra, I hope you aren't the one playing games with me! Do you know Mr. Arizona Slim showed up at the Crystal Palace last night? Fred Sandler said one minute the urn wasn't there, a moment later, it appeared, as if out of thin air! It sounds impossible! And how could that urn have gotten out of the safe, out of a locked building, and walk a whole city block. I just don't get it!"

Ezra smiled a fiendish grin, "There's only one answer Mayor!"

Mayor Johnson gave Ezra and incredulous look, "How's that?"

Ezra replied, "That urn contains a very restless soul. I think you should get Arizona Slim planted at Boot Hill as soon as humanly possible!"

Mayor Johnson smirked, "Ezra, if I didn't know better, I would say you had something to do with these shenanigans! But right now, I'm late for the Commission meeting. I'll see you later!"

Thursday March 26, 1953   5:45PM   Crystal Palace Saloon

Bartender Fred Sandler had just started his shift and was cleaning some empty tables near the saloon's front door which opened onto Allen Street. Other than himself, the place was empty.

Suddenly, as he was looking down at one of the tables wiping it, he noticed a change in the ambient light and sensed someone standing in the doorway staring at him. Looking up, his eyes locked onto those of Ed Gleeson... ancient, bent, disheveled in ill-fitting clothes, tooth-bare Ed Gleeson. They just looked at each other for a moment, then Fred broke the uncomfortable silence, "Ed, you haven't been in here in over 65 years! In fact, I happen to know that there are those times, especially around this date, that you avoid this corner of town altogether. And now... well... yesterday I saw you walk by several times, poking your head in more than once. And here you are again. What gives?"

Ed suddenly looked wild-eyed as he tried to formulate an answer. "I don't know!" he stammered. "For some inexplicable reason, I'm drawn here... like a moth to a flame! In fact, I have a terrific urge to go inside, but I promised myself I would never go in here again. Never! And I intend to keep my promise!"

The two men just looked at each other for a moment. Fred sensed there was more at play here than the meanderings of an old man, but he couldn't put his finger on it! Ed Gleeson simply broke the stare, turned and was gone.

Fred bent over the table again, finished wiping it clean, then stood erect. Suddenly he thought he could feel someone staring at him, but nobody could have gotten into the place because he had been facing the only two doors that allowed the public to enter; and he knew nobody had been in the place a moment before.

Fred turned slowly towards the bar; where he sensed a person would be standing if they were staring at him. And there it was again! Sitting on the bar, for the second evening in a row, was the black urn... the dull, black urn containing the late George Ellis McGurk, aka "Arizona Slim." Fred shuddered in his white, starched apron!

He stared at the urn for moment, half expecting it sprout legs, leap off the bar, and run for the door. But it just stood there... silent, stoic, motionless... dull and black – black and dull! It seemed to Fred that the urn might even be mocking him, or perhaps daring him to guess how it got onto the bar.

Fred then caught himself, thinking that waiting for the urn to sprout legs was insane. The only answer was there had to be someone hiding behind the bar. He called out, "Ok... I know you're in here! Come on out! Come out from behind the bar!"

Getting no response, Fred quickly stepped up to the bar and pulled himself part-way over so he could see the floor on the opposite side. Nothing!

At that moment, Mayor Johnson happened to walk by the front door, and seeing Fred stretched across the bar, decided to poke his head in. "Lose someone Fred?" he quipped.

Fred scooted down off the bar and turned to face the Mayor saying, "No! I didn't lose anyone. But it would appear that you might have!" Fred then pointed to the black urn sitting on the bar.

Mayor Johnson walked to the urn and stared at it in disbelief. "Someone is playing a joke on us Fred! And they are pretty darn good at it... and I can't understand how they are doing it!"

Several people walked into the saloon, including Ezra Thornton, dressed as always, in his top hat, and 1880's wear. He walked over the where the bartender and Mayor were talking. "Well, Mayor..." Ezra started, eyeing the urn, "It would appear your friend just won't leave you alone!"

Mayor Johnson scowled. "That's not funny Ezra. Do you have anything to do with this? I put Arizona Slim in the City Hall safe myself... and here he is again."

One of the locals pulled up a stool at the bar adjacent to where the men were talking and overhearing their conversation chimed in, "He's obviously thirsty! Buy him a drink and maybe he'll go away!"

Nobody laughed.

Ezra replied, "I have no interest in moving poor Mr. Arizona Slim about the city. I didn't move him and I can't tell you how he got out here. What I can tell you is that Arizona Slim has a very disturbed soul... a very restless soul... a soul that needs something...something before it can rest. It needs to find an inner peace. I can feel it – I can sense it!"

"Well..." said Mayor Johnson, "...maybe Arizona Slim will find some peace tomorrow when we plant him at Boot Hill. The Commission approved his burial. They found one double lot left – and that's where he will be placed tomorrow afternoon."

Mayor Johnson picked up the urn and tucked it under his arm. "I'm going to return Arizona Slim to the City Hall safe and have the Marshal place a guard inside the City Hall all night! I've had enough!"

The Mayor turned and headed out the door. He no sooner stepped onto the sidewalk when Ed Gleeson approached. As the two men walked past each other, Mayor Johnson thought he felt the urn start to vibrate... then dismissed it as an overactive imagination, trying to figure out how the urn managed to get out of a locked safe, and down the street again.

Ed Gleeson stopped in the open doorway of the Crystal Palace Saloon, poked his head in, looked around, then continued his walk down Allen Street.

Thursday March 26, 1953 10:45PM Tombstone City Hall

Tombstone Deputy Marshal Flanagan wandered through the rooms and hallways of the Tombstone City Hall, muttering to himself, "I can't believe I'm on duty guarding a jar full of ashes! A jar full of ashes... of all things! Shheeesh!"

Earlier in the evening Deputy Flanagan had accompanied Mayor Johnson and Town Marshal Boyer as Arizona Slim was once again remanded to the confines of the Tombstone City Hall safe. All three men witnessed the event, and Deputy Flanagan swore to remain vigilant letting no one near the Mayor's office and the safe.

Now, several hours later, Deputy Flanagan was bored, and felt that guarding a jar full of human remains, especially those of a man called Arizona Slim, was beneath him. But he had his orders and had to remain inside the City Hall throughout the night.

He strolled into the Mayor's office one more time, and walked over to the safe. He grabbed the door handle and tried to twist it to release the door lock. The handle wouldn't budge. He pulled on the handle to try to get the door open, with the same result. Satisfied that the safe was secure, Deputy Flanagan took a straight wooden armchair from in front off the Mayor's desk, and dragged it out into the hallway. Locking the door to the Mayor's office, the deputy pocketed the key, and sat down in the wooden chair, propping it up against the wall. Moments later, Deputy Flanagan was dozing off, his eyes fluttering in a desperate attempt to stay awake.

After what seemed like only moments, Deputy Flanagan awoke with a start and came to the realization that he had been asleep. He looked at his watch – 11:40PM. He had been asleep for almost an hour!

Deputy Flanagan stood up to stretch and when he did, he felt that something was amiss, something he couldn't quite put his finger on. He put his hands on his hips and looked around, trying to determine why it seemed like he didn't feel "quite right." As his right hand hit his hip, it came to him – in .38 caliber! His service revolver was missing.

Thursday March 26, 1953   11:45PM   Crystal Palace Saloon

It was just about closing time at the Crystal Palace, and the end of Fred Sandler's shift. Alone, Fred stood behind the bar cleaning glasses when Ed Gleeson walked by, and once again, as he had several times during the evening, poked his head in the door.

Fred looked up from his glass-cleaning, "Ed, you're driving me nuts doing that. Stop poking your head in here and just come on in. Come on! I'll buy you a beer!"

Ed Gleeson's face took on a wide-eyed expression again – almost maniacal. "I... I can't go in there. I promised myself I would never again go in this God forsaken place. But I... I feel drawn to it. I feel drawn inside. I... I can't explain it" said Ed.

Fred chuckled and tried to make light of the scared old man. "Ed...give it up. It's been over 65 years since that incident. Face it... you have served your life sentence and then some...in a manner of speaking of course. Come in, sit down, I'll draw you a beer."

Slowly and cautiously, Ed Gleeson eased himself into the Crystal Palace Saloon. He moved as if he expected the floor to fall out from under him at any moment. Eventually, he approached the table closest to the door, pulled out a chair, and sat down. He sat stiffly, facing the east wall, the front door to his right, and the bar over his left shoulder. Ed noted, "I want to see if anyone comes in!"

Fred laughed, "Who the hell are you expecting at this time of night in Tombstone?"

Ed continued to sit stiffly and stare straight ahead at the east wall; the wall that was, during the 1880's, a wall of chance. It was the area of the saloon where games of chance were played. Night after night, men lined up at the poker and faro tables, and when they tired of cards, tried their chance at the roulette wheel. It was also along that wall where he got into an argument with Windy Bill resulting Windy's demise.

Fred pulled a beer mug from the rack behind the bar, filled it with beer, and brought it out to the table where Ed sat. "Here you go Ed. Enjoy it! I'm going to go in the back and get some items to restock my bar. If anyone wants to come in, just tell them we're closed. Ah... but you're welcome to sit and enjoy your beer while I clean up."

Fred turned, walked into the back room, and began stacking supplies to be brought to the front to restock the bar.

Moments later, Fred heard two people talking out front on the main floor of the saloon. He figured someone wanted to come in and Ed was telling them the bar was closed.

Although Fred couldn't hear what was being said, he could hear the voices. In a matter of a few seconds, the voices went from sounding amiable to irritated, to angry. The voices then seemed to rise in volume and intensity. He could make out Ed's distinctive high -pitched voice saying, "What do you mean I'm going to pay! Dammit, I've been paying for that mistake for the last 65 years! Don't you think I've paid enough? When does it stop?"

Ed's treatise was met with a muffled voice, and a loud bang. A gunshot!

Fred clambered over the boxes he had stacked in front of the door to the store room causing him to take precious extra seconds to reach the main floor of the saloon. He emerged to find a most incredulous sight. Ed Gleeson lay spread-eagle on the floor; his eyes wide open in utter horror, a gaping bullet hole right between his eyes.

Fred quickly scanned the room for a perpetrator, his eyes settling on a most bizarre phenomenon. There on the bar, for the second time of the evening, sat Arizona Slim's urn, the hideous black urn, the lid being screwed on as if the lid was being secured by an invisible hand, or from within! He watched incredulously as the lid finished twisting itself into place. It was only after the lid stopped turning that Fred noticed the .38 caliber police service revolver sitting next to the urn – acrid smoke still wafting from the muzzle.

Before Fred could gather his wits about him, people started to come in off the street to see Ed Gleeson lying on the saloon floor, his eyes still wide open in utter horror, blood tricking from a gaping hole in his forehead. Before long the place filled up with a sizeable crowd, enough that Deputy Flanagan had to push people aside as he shuffled to the scene of the crime.

Flanagan looked at the body of Ed Gleeson, then looked up at Fred. "Fred... what the hell happened here. Did you see who did this? What's the story?"

Fred stared at Deputy Flanagan, and opened his mouth. For a moment, nothing came out but a gurgle. Then, he murmured, "The urn... it was Arizona Slim... it was the urn! Look! There it is!"

Fred turned to the bar to draw everyone's attention to the urn – and pointed to where he had seen it last. Everyone turned and looked at the same time – and all stared at a freshly cleaned bar, devoid of all glasses, cups, bottles – and burial urns and firearms.

Fred exclaimed, "The urn! It's gone. Somebody has stolen Arizona Slim! Slim is the perpetrator. Find the urn and you'll find your man, Deputy!"

Deputy Flanagan took on an official-sounding tone, "Nobody leaves the building! Everyone is suspect. I want that urn found!"

As soon as he said it, Flanagan realized how silly he sounded – as if the urn could be held as a suspect in a shooting. As he was trying to figure out how to save face, and still solve the murder mystery, Ezra Thornton eased his way through the growing crowd.

"Deputy Flanagan!" Ezra called out. "I'll tell you exactly where that urn is!

Flanagan spun on his heels. "Ok... I'll bite. Where is it, Ezra?"

Ezra smiled, "Why it's right where it was left... in the City Hall safe!"

Fred replied agonizingly, "That's impossible Ezra. It was right here... sitting on the bar!"

Ezra replied, "Gentlemen, there is only one way to find out where the urn is. Deputy, call the Mayor and have him meet us at the City Hall directly. Tell him we need to check his safe!"

The entire crowd moved out onto Allen Street, and on to the City Hall, leaving poor Ed Gleeson to remain, unceremoniously, on the saloon floor.

Moments later the Mayor arrived and opened the safe. Inside, right where it had been carefully placed, were the remains of Arizona Slim...in his black urn... alongside Deputy Flanagan's .38 caliber revolver, a thin wisp of smoke still emanating from the muzzle.

Ezra smiled, "You see, Mayor? Arizona Slim is right where he is supposed to be!"

Mayor Johnson passed a dirty look first to Deputy Flanagan, then to Ezra, then back to Flanagan. "Flanagan...I'm not even going to ask how your pistol found its way into this safe... that I know you can't possibly open it since I know you don't have the combination. What I will demand however, is that you make sure Mr. Arizona Slim gets planted at Boot Hill no later than this afternoon. And take care of Gleeson too! I understand the lot that the Cemetery Commission assigned to Mr. Arizona Slim is a double lot... make use of it! Lord knows Gleeson does not have the money to pay for it himself."

"Oh... and Ezra?" Mayor Johnson continued.

"Yes?" said Ezra.

"You're in charge of headstones. I know you have a few in back of your store. Please supply one for each... appropriately engraved if you would! Send me the bill!"

Friday March 27, 1953   3:25PM   Boot Hill Cemetery

It was a small crowd that gathered to say goodbye to George Ellis McGurk aka Arizona Slim and Ed Gleeson. McGurk had been away from Tombstone for so long, he had no friends in the city. And Ed Gleeson had outlived most of his contemporaries... leaving him with few acquaintances and people that just felt sorry for the old codger.

Reverend Peabody provided two readings from the Bible for Ed Gleeson, and his body was lowered into the grave. No one provided a eulogy. The same sad ritual was repeated for Arizona Slim, as his urn was placed in a small box, and set at the bottom of the grave.

The crowd simply stood and watched as several grave-diggers began to refill the two holes. After a few minutes, the holes were nearly filled, and one by one, the small band of mourners trickled away leaving Mayor Johnson and Ezra Thornton alone with the grave diggers and the two headstones.

Mayor Johnson turned to Ezra and was getting ready to speak when muffled voices could be heard. In a matter of a few seconds, the voices went from sounding amiable to irritated, to angry. The voices then seemed to rise in volume and intensity. Ezra and the Mayor could make out Ed's distinctive high-pitched voice saying, "What do you mean I'm going to pay! Dammit, I've been paying for that mistake for the last 65 years! Don't you think I've paid enough? When does it stop?"

A cool, spring breeze wafted through the tombstones carrying away the anguished voice of Ed Gleeson.

Once again, Mayor Johnson turned to Ezra, afraid to admit that he had just heard the voice of Ed Gleeson, and nonchalantly said, "Very fitting epitaphs, Ezra!"

Ezra smiled and looked down at his handiwork. One read,

George Ellis McGurk aka Arizona Slim
Debt Repaid March 26, 1953

The other headstone read:

Ed Gleeson
Died of Unnatural Causes
March 26, 1953

The Real Story Behind "Return To Tombstone"

In August, 1952, the Postmaster at Tombstone received a bizarre letter, poorly written and badly spelled, from one Glen Efrom Will of Albany, California. He asked, "I am wondering if this is the Tumbstone town where the rich silver mines wer and the watter drounded them and before it did watter was sold for a dollar a glass." Mr. Will expressed a desire to visit the old mining camp, if it was indeed the Tombstone of fame and legend and asked if the Postmaster would write back and advise him.

Not sure what to do with the letter, the Postmaster forwarded it to the Tombstone Chamber of Commerce. Intrigued by the letter, the Chamber replied to Mr. Will forwarding brochures touting the area's mild climate, abundant sunshine and ideal elevation.

Soon after, Mr. Will wrote back to the Chamber thanking them for the information and expressing again a desire to visit the place. It was in this second letter that he identified himself as "Bronco Bill" and his son as "the "Rodeo Kid." Although amused by the letter, colorful writing, and fanciful names, the Chamber moved on to other matters and the "Bronco Bill" and the "Rodeo Kid" were forgotten – for a few months.

On March 19, 1953, the Tombstone Chamber of Commerce received notice of a package awaiting them at the Railway Express Agency office – with charges due - $1.92. Edna Landin, then-President of the Chamber agreed to pick-up the package and pay the charges due.

What she got was a complete surprise.

Her first clue that this would be the most bizarre package ever sent to Tombstone was that it came from the Oakland California Crematorium! Attached was an official notice allowing the contents of the box, a cremated human body - the body of one Glen Efrom "Bronco Bill" Will, to be removed to the "Tombstone Boothill Cemetery."

Aghast, Ms. Landin was not quite sure what to do with such a thing - a box of human ashes. And now, after accepting the package and becoming the "caretaker" of Mr. Will, Edna Landin had no idea what to do next. The box found its way into the City Hall safe until the Chamber could figure out what to do with Mr. Will.

Looking for an explanation as to why someone would send human remains to Tombstone, Edna Landin began looking for Mr. Will's son, the "Rodeo Kid". After many long distance phone calls she finally located him – in Berkeley, California.

When asked why he sent his father to Tombstone, his son replied that his father had planned on "going there about this time anyways – so I just sent him." The son explained that his father had been in Tombstone when he was 14 years old (around 1885) and that he always wanted to go back – so he sent him! When asked why he sent his father C.O.D., the son simply replied that he was broke!

With the mystery solved, arrangements were made to plant Mr. Will in his final resting place, among Tombstone's famous and infamous, in Boot Hill. The Hubbard Mortuary of Bisbee took care of the service – no charge. The Rose Tree museum, caretaker of the world's largest rose tree, provided white roses. Reverend William Barker of the First Baptist Church officiated.

Many of Tombstone's most prominent citizen's turned out on that day, March 27, 1953, to view the last burial at Boot Hill. The cemetery had been closed since 1883 when it was declared full. But its gates were opened one last time for "Bronco Bill" – his grave marker can be seen today. It reads:

1871   Glen Will   1953

HIS ASHES ARRIVED

COLLECT ON DELIVERY

About Boot Hill Cemetery/Tombstone City Cemetery

In the latter half of the 19th century, people moved west, and spread out across the American west. Those that lived on remote farms and ranches had a tough time of it. When they got sick or injured, home-remedies and make-shift emergency-care had to do. And when they died, a shallow grave on the family land became their final resting place.

In the towns that sprang up along rail lines, surrounded rail heads, and mining camps, health care fared somewhat better, but still, people died from disease injury and yes, the occasional gunfight or hanging – legal or otherwise. In the cities, graveyards became a necessity. Such was the case for Tombstone's Boot Hill Cemetery – which started in 1879 as the City Cemetery.

Started out of necessity, what has come to be known as Boot Hill is the final resting place for the famous and the infamous, sinners and saints, doves and demons.

Besides Mr. Glen Will, it is the final resting place for Mary Ware Clum, wife of Tombstone Mayor John Clum who died from complications of child birth. It is also the final resting place for Billy Clanton, Frank McLaury and Tom McLaury, victims of a "street fight" on October 26, 1881. And it is the spot of eternity for John Heath, lynched by a mob for his part in the Bisbee Massacre.

Many markers, most made out of wood and long since rotted, stolen or destroyed, noted how the person died – Murdered, Drowned, and Hanged By Mistake were just a few.

A pauper may be buried very unceremoniously, only the undertaker aware of his or her passing. Conversely, the funeral procession in December, 1880 for Mary Ware Clum, a most respected woman in the community, was one of the biggest the town had seen to date. Ironically, it was outdone, or at least equaled, by the funeral procession for Billy Clanton and the McLaury brothers in the wake of the OK Corral incident.

For more than four years, Boot Hill (an appropriate sobriquet as many buried there died with their boots on) was host to the noted and the notorious. But eventually, as Tombstone grew, so too did the list of deceased, and by 1884, more space was needed and so the City Cemetery opened on the far west end of Allen Street.

Over the years, and with the new City Cemetery in place, Boot Hill began to fall into disrepair. People actually dumped rubbish on the graves. When former Tombstone mayor John Clum visited Tombstone in 1929, he was dismayed that he could no longer locate his dear departed wife's grave.

In 1932, the "Broadway of America" highway (today's State Road 80) highway opened, going right past Boot Hill. Town officials thought Boot Hill would make an interesting place for a growing tourist trade to stop, and thus a clean-up, and the commercialization of Boot Hill began.

As the "outlaw graveyard" gained popularity, treasure seekers began carrying off valuable artifacts. A fence was erected, and care-taker assigned, warding off vandals and antique hunters.

Today, (2010) Boot Hill is run as a concession, taking in enough money to carefully maintain the graves and the surrounding grounds.

Ironically, the City Cemetery has fallen into some disrepair with crumbling grave markers, sinking grave sites, and decades-old weeds. Perhaps one of the most noted in the City Cemetery, with one of the most impressive markers, is famed Tombstone photographer C.S. Fly.

About the Crystal Palace Saloon

In 1879, Frederick Wehrfritz opened the Golden Eagle Brewery, an instant-favorite "watering hole" in Tombstone serving beer, whisky, sandwiches and gambling. The building was heavily damaged in one fire and wiped out in a subsequent fire. Wehrfritz erected another building on the same site, the corner of Fifth and Allen Streets – and on July 23, 1882, the Crystal Palace opened for business. The placed roared, as did the rest of the town, 24 hours a day, 7 days a week. Virgil Earp and Dr. George Goodfellow maintained offices on the second floor. And it was just outside the Crystal Palace on Fifth Street where Virgil Earp fell on December 28, 1881, the victim of an assassination attempt in retaliation for the OK Corral incident.

When the town began to die, most businesses died with it – or underwent traumatic changes. During prohibition, the elegant bar and back-bar that had graced the Palace for several years, were "removed for safekeeping" and shuffled off to a warehouse in Mexico. The warehouse eventually burned taking the bar with it. The "Palace" was reduced to showing movies and serving soft drinks. At some point, the second floor was removed.

In the 1940's and 1950's the Crystal Palace served as a hamburger joint and a bus station.

Then in 1963 a privately funded restoration project restored the Crystal Palace to its original splendor. A "faux" second floor was added and the elegant bar and back-bar were lovingly replicated from old photographs.

Today, the Crystal Palace operates as a saloon with live bands, whisky, beer and mixed drinks. It remains one of the premier "watering holes" in Tombstone.

About Tombstone's City Hall

The Tombstone City Hall, located on Fremont Street (now State Road 80) has served the city continuously since 1882. In 2006, the building was vacated with offices moved to temporary quarters to allow the building to be renovated. What will remain in the City Hall during renovation are many historical city documents dating back to the days of Virgil Earp, held secure in the City Hall safe.

Chapter 11: THE BAD MAN

From an idea inspired by Rachel Ledoux

*"Sir, you had better sit down. I have quite a story for you.
Major Tattenbaum indeed had to run for the rest of his life."*

Ezra T. Thornton May 3, 1882

Saturday, May 1, 1880 10:15AM Tombstone, A.T.

Ezra T. Thornton stepped out of his mercantile store onto the covered sidewalk along Allen Street where he observed a disheveled young man sitting on a freight box at the curb, two large travel trunks at his side. "You look like a man who has had a hard day..." said Ezra. "... and it's only a little after 10AM!"

The young man was facing Allen Street when he heard the voice behind him. Although it was only May, the summer heat of southeastern Arizona Territory was already quite intense. But sitting under the cover of the sidewalk overhang provided at least some shade for a few minutes.

The swirling dust churned up by the wagon wheels and horse hoofs moving up and down Allen Street settled on the clothing and the forehead of the young man. It was quite apparent that, although he was dressed in a suit and what had been a white shirt, he had been in his clothes for several days, his suit being quite rumpled and his shirt a light brown except for the creases. The sweat pouring down his temples and forehead from under his derby to his chin formed small rivulets on his dust-caked face and only added to his misery.

The young man turned to see Ezra T. Thornton standing over him, a person who looked different from anyone else on the street the young man thought. More refined, more elegant – even more so than any of the other businessmen he had seen in town. His long, white hair was clean, his shoes shiny, pants and shirt without patches, and his bright red, brocade vest gave him an air of flamboyance.

"I know most people here in town... but I don't know you. So I must assume you just arrived?" Ezra extended his hand to the man on the freight box. "Ezra T. Thornton's my name... and this is my store. Welcome to Tombstone."

The young man stood, turned and clasped Ezra's hand in return and in a heavy accent replied, "I am Major.. err... I mean... Mr. William Tattenbaum... at your service!"

Ezra raised one eyebrow, "Major huh? You are a military man I take it?"

Tattenbaum removed his derby revealing longish, somewhat shaggy blond hair, unkempt and matted, matching the rest of his body. The hairs of his moustache, long and blonde, stuck out in every direction. The only part of Mr. William Tattenbaum that was not disheveled was his piercing blue eyes. William pulled a matted handkerchief from his pocket, and mopped his brow. "I am.. er.. was a military man... Major William Tattenbaum... in service to Czar Alexander II of Russia."

Ezra stood back and looked the man over, up and down, and then said, "Well Major, you look to be man in his early 20's... so I don't think you retired from the military. And you don't look injured... so I don't think you received a medical discharge... so why..."

Ezra caught himself and decided not to finish his sentence. He could tell he had hit a nerve as the dirty ex-soldier stared down at his scuffed shoes.

Ezra smiled, "So why are you sitting on a freight box in front of my store?"

Tattenbaum's demeanor instantly brightened, "I was many weeks traveling to your country from Russia. I landed in New York; and now have been many more weeks coming to your city. I just arrived from Tucson on the stage... and now I need to decide what is next to do."

"Do you have a place to stay? Do you have any friends here in town? Some relatives perhaps?" asked Ezra.

Tattenbaum replaced his hat on his head, "I have no friends here... so I will need to find a place to stay. But I have other reasons to come to Tombstone. I have read about this place in the newspapers in New York – read about the mines, and how your town operates night and day. The newspapers said Tombstone is a 'wide-open' town. I wanted to see for myself what a 'wide-open' town looks like. I want to...how do you say... experience the American frontier."

"The San Jose House is short walk away on Fremont Street..." said Ezra. "It's a good place to stay. The rooms are clean and the prices reasonable. Tell them I sent you! I have an open account there if you are short of cash. Do you need…"

Tattenbaum cut Ezra short, "I have funds Mr. Thornton… but thank you for your generosity… and your kindness. I will count you as my first friend here in what I hope to be my new home… and my new country. If you can point me in the right direction, I believe I will secure a room in your San Jose House and try to make myself presentable."

Ezra watched the man pick up his two suitcases, and amble down the covered boardwalk along Allen Street. Before Ezra could turn and return to his store, Ike Clanton happened by. "Who is you new friend, Ezra?" said Ike.

Ezra looked at Ike and replied in a serious and inquisitive fashion, "Claims to be an ex-soldier… from Russia. But I don't know. He certainly sounds foreign, but not like the Swedes here in town, more like some of the German emigrants. Nothing about him really says 'military' to me though. I just don't know about him!"

Ike chuckled, "I'll get him into a card game. Then we'll see what he's really made of!"

Without saying another word, Ike moved on down Allen Street, and Ezra returned to his store.

Saturday, May 1, 1880 5:35PM Tombstone, A.T.

People filled Tombstone's streets as the day-shift miners headed home… and to the saloons and gambling houses to wash the mining-dust down their throats with whisky and beer. Shop owners, including Ezra T. Thornton were putting the lock on their doors while saloons and dance halls began receiving their early customers. The activity in Tombstone never ceased.

Ezra walked down Allen Street to the Oriental Saloon for a quick drink and perhaps some friendly conversation before heading home. As he stepped across the threshold and into the darkened room, he noticed the usual crowd at the bar and the tables. But at one table, a man sat alone, nursing a large mug of beer. The man stood out, different from everyone else – clean, well groomed, and impeccably dressed in what appeared to be a uniform. He wore dark blue, perfectly-pressed pants sporting a gold stripe down the outside leg, leading to perfectly polished, knee-high boots, most suitable, Ezra thought, for a cavalry officer. To finish the uniform, the man wore a bright red, high-collared tunic, also perfectly pressed and spotless, with horizontal gold braid across the chest. The man's long, blond hair was perfectly combed – every hair well-trained and in place, matching his long and regal blonde moustache.

Ezra stood for just a moment, looking at the man in the uniform, and could not help but notice that others were watching him too, occasionally "sneaking" a not-so-discreet peek at him, then turning back to their own conversations, snickering, and talking under their breath. Just then, it occurred to Ezra that someone was watching him! Ezra turned to see his friend, John Clum standing behind him in the doorway.   "Well...!" said Clum,   "Are you just going to stand there all night, or are you going to buy me a beer?"

Ezra replied with a chuckle and said, "John, I have someone I want you to meet!" The two men walked into the saloon, and right up to the table where the man in uniform sat.   Seeing the two men approach, the uniformed man stood and faced them, in a very military like manner, as if he were being approached by a superior officer. Ezra spoke, "Mr. Clum I would like you to meet Major William Tattenbaum of the Russian army. Major, meet Mr. John P. Clum of... er... *The Tombstone Epitaph,* a brand new newspaper... as of today!"

Ezra ordered another round of beers. The three men sat down to talk, and in minutes, it was as if they had been friends forever. Ezra talked about the founding of Tombstone. Clum talked about his time managing the San Carlos Apache reservation.   And Major Tattenbaum talked about life in Russia – the life of a privileged and elite upbringing - his life as the son of a wealthy Russian aristocrat.

The more Major Tattenbaum talked, the more it sounded like he was weaving an illustrious fairy tale; intricate in it's detail, expressed passionately by a man who believed everything he was saying was true – and yet it sounded so surreal. He talked of dancing with well-dressed ladies, ladies of station and elegance at glamorous balls. He talked about military ceremonies, and his station in life as a respected officer, "...in service to Czar Alexander II of Russia!" He spoke with an air of pomposity; yet there was a subdued streak of humbleness in his voice; as if some horrible truth bubbled just below the surface of his squeaky-clean veneer.

Two more cow-boys, members of the Clanton-McLaury faction walked into the Oriental and past the three men sitting at a table near the door. After they passed, they turned around and looked at Major Tattenbaum, and smiled slyly one saying to the other, "Why that's the prettiest man I ever saw!" The snide comment was not lost on the Major. Clum and Ezra heard it too; the cow-boy having no thought or respect for discretion.

Taking his cue, the Major looked first at Clum, then Ezra and said, "They mock me – yes I know. We are far apart culturally. I am clean, they are dirty. I am a member of the Russian aristocracy. And they are... well.. how you say... cow-boys. But I want to fit-in. I want to look and sound like I belong here – in America – in Tombstone."

Ezra chuckled and replied, "My good man, you may never sound like you belong here, but maybe we can make you look like you belong here. Stop by my store on Monday morning. We'll see what we can do!"

*****

Major William Tattenbaum spent Sunday wandering around town, in and out of the many stores, saloons and dance halls – still dressed in his finest uniform. Men, especially the miner and the cow-boy faction snickered at him... considered him a "dandy" and somewhat effeminate in the way he was dressed, groomed, and the way he carried himself.   Women saw him as refined, cultured and distinguished.

Men heard his stories of life as an aristocrat in a far-away place, and thought his stories were boastful at worst, or only partially believable at the least. In either case, they thought he was "too full of himself."

Women heard his stories and considered him a romantic; someone who could easily sweep them off their feet had their husbands not been present. He was a man who represented life on a plane far-above the dusty streets of a small mining camp in southern Arizona Territory.

Love him or hate him – Major William Tattenbaum was making a name for himself and it wasn't good – not really his fault... but that's just the way it was.

Monday, May 3, 1880 10:15AM Tombstone, A.T.

"I am here Mr. Thornton, here so you can make me fit in. Will you provide me with some new clothes maybe?" Major Tattenbaum exclaimed as he strode into Ezra's mercantile store, dressed in yet another perfectly clean and pressed uniform.

Ezra stepped out from the darkened back of the store. "Well... that will be a good start. I have quite a variety of clothes. Here..." he said pointing to an array of clothing he had laid out on the counter, "Do you see anything here you like? Everything here is in your size!"

William Tattenbaum smiled, picked out several pairs of pants, shirts, vests, suspenders as well as a couple pairs of fine leather boots, a double-rig holster, and two Colt .45's. It was obvious his eye was attracted to the brighter colors. If it was a choice between two items, one being a bright red, the other being bland beige, he would always pick the brightest, most colorful item.

Tattenbaum smiled as he paid Ezra for his pile of clothing saying, "Now I will look like I belong here in America!"

Ezra smiled, "Well, you are off to a good start. Clothes help define a man...but certainly don't make the man. But I'll say one thing for you... you're trying awful hard though!"

Ezra summoned two boys to help the Major get his large quantity of clothes back to his hotel room. As Tattenbaum left the store he noted, "I will change my clothes and be back... you will see!"

Monday, May 3, 1880 11:45AM Tombstone, A.T.

Major Tattenbaum emerged from his room at the San Jose House, crossed Fremont Street, and began his stroll down Fifth Street to Allen. He hadn't gone very far before he encountered John Clum headed in the other direction. "Mighty fine wardrobe, Major!" Clum exclaimed as the two approached each other. Major Tattenbaum smiled and continued on, happy with himself that he had made a good choice; black-striped duck pants tucked into black mule-ear boots, a white gus-style shirt, red suspenders, bright red bandana and a tan boss-of-the plains Stetson to top it all off.

"As long as I wear what everyone else wears, I'll fit right in" he thought to himself.

Tattenbaum rounded the corner on Fifth and Allen and headed east towards Ezra's mercantile when he spotted Ike Clanton and Ezra standing in front of his store conversing. As he approached, Ezra smiled, and Ike started laughing hysterically.

Tattenbaum started, "It must have been a very good joke Mr. Thornton told you?"

Ike replied, "You're the joke, Major! Why just look at you!"

Tattenbaum looked quizzically at his tormentor, What do you mean look at me? I am dressed very similarly to you – to everyone else on the street!" Getting more irritated he continued, "What is so different about how I am dressed?"

Ike removed his sweat-stained, hole-ridden, curled-brim boss-of-the plains Stetson and put it in front of Tattenbaum's eyes to make a point. "Now here's what a cow-boy's hat is supposed to look like!" Ike took a couple of steps back and looked at the now incredulous Major Tattenbaum, "Major... you are the cleanest, the prettiest, most perfect cow-boy I have ever seen! Nobody is that clean in Tombstone! Hell, nobody is that clean anywhere!"

Tattenbaum looked deflated and dejected replying, "I am just trying to fit in... to make a new home for myself. I'm..."

Ike interrupted, "Major, it sounds to me, the way you talk, that Russia was the perfect place to be... where you had a perfect life.

Why come all the way to Tombstone to start over? Why did you...?"

Ike was interrupted by a voice from a few steps behind him, "Why don't you stop making so much noise and come play some cards?"

Ike spun around to see an acquaintance approaching and smiled. As the man neared the group, Ike said, "Major Tattenbaum, meet Sandy King, an associate of mine.   Mr. Thornton, I believe you already know Mr. King!" All shook hands.

"Ike" said King, "We have a game starting in five minutes at the Oriental. Are you in or out?"

"I'm in" was the quick reply. Ike then looked at Tattenbaum, and then turned back to King, "And I believe we have a young 'cow-boy' here who wants to fit-in. Do you suppose we can fit him in?"

King looked at Tattenbaum, "Ever play cards before? Ever play poker or faro?"

"No, I have never played cards before." was the sheepish reply.

King looked at Ike, and then turned back to Tattenbaum. "You talk funny. Where are you from?"

Tattenbaum, straightened himself and pronounced proudly, "I am Major William Tattenbaum... in service to Czar Alexander II of Russia... and a nobleman!"

King smiled, looked at Ezra, then turned to Ike, then back to Tattenbaum. "Major huh? Not any more you're not. We don't have Majors in Tombstone. As of now, you're 'Russian Bill!'"

King laughed, and then looked back to Ike, "He'll fit in just nicely. Come on!"

Monday, May 3, 1880 3:45PM Tombstone, A.T.

Warm afternoon breezes wafted through the open doors of the Oriental Saloon slightly rustling the playing cards on the table. One flipped, and landed against one of the many empty mugs littering the table where five men sat, intently looking at the hand they were about to play.

Moments later, one of the five, Major William Tattenbaum, aka Russian Bill, threw his cards down on the table. "I am, how do you say, all-in. You gentlemen have taken a good amount of my money, mostly you, Ike Clanton, and now I am finished! I have no more money to play! And I fear I will never play good enough to make my money back! Somehow, I feel you have tricked me, but I don't know how!"

Ike replied angrily, "Nobody cheated you, Russian Bill!" But even before the words were completely spoken, Ike, and two other cow-boys at the table smiled that "knowing" smile that can only be shared by partners in crime. Major Tattenbaum didn't understand much about cards, or how to cheat at cards, or take advantage of someone who didn't know how to play cards, but he sure knew when he had been had.

Sandy King, the fifth card player didn't smile. It seemed he had been on the losing end as well, forfeiting his prize stallion to a high-roller from Shakespeare, New Mexico – one Mr. Harlan Grant card-sharp and lover of horses.

An eerie silence fell over the table. The cow-boys were not sure how Tattenbaum would react to being taken advantage of. They also knew that Sandy King had lost a prize possession, was known to be a hot-head at times, and un-armed, would not think twice about beating a man to death with his fists.

Then Tattenbaum found his "second wind", and turned to Ike saying, "Do you own a pistol?"

Ike suddenly had a bad feeling. "Of course I own a pistol. It's behind the bar. Milt Joyce – the bartender – he's holding it for me. Do I need to get it? Do you intend to shoot me over a card game?"

Tattenbaum smiled slightly. "Do not worry, Mr. Clanton. I am not armed. But I will get my pistols, and challenge you to a shooting contest! Maybe I can win-back some of my money! It is a contest where one cannot cheat. Either you are a good shot, or you are not! What do you say Mr. Clanton? You do know how to shoot don't you?"

Ike furrowed his brow and thought for a moment – quite worried. Ike considered that if Tattenbaum was indeed a military officer, chances are he could shoot pretty well. But so could he. The other edge Ike figured he had was that he knew the Major's pistols were brand new and he wasn't used to them. Ike wasn't sure he could beat the Major. But he was sure that his reputation was on the line and his pride stood in the way of discretion.

After some deliberation, Ike's face brightened, "Go get your guns. Meet us at the end of Fifth Street just outside of town in a half hour. Maybe you'll get you money back...maybe not. And maybe you'll lose a few more dollars!"

The men at the table, and all within earshot laughed out loud. Major Tattenbaum only smiled – that "knowing" smile that can only be shared by partners in crime. Major Tattenbaum did not have a partner in the place to share the smile with. But it wasn't wasted on Ike Clanton either... and he knew he could be in trouble.

Monday, May 3, 1880 4:30PM Tombstone, A.T.

Although late in the afternoon, the Arizona sun continued to draw beads of sweat from the two combatants, each taking turns raining lead pellets across the desert sand, plugging cans, fence posts, the occasional road runner, and anything else that they fancied as a fair target and the object of a bet. The shots from the heavy caliber pistols reverberated across the valley. The crowd that had been at the Oriental Saloon moments before had come to watch the spectacle, each unsure if they wanted to see Ike lose and the Major win, or vice-versa, or just to see what the clean and pristine Russian Bill was all about!

Ezra stood in the crowd taking it all in. Ike Clanton was getting beat handily as Tattenbaum proved to be an excellent shot. One would expect a beaten Ike Clanton to be a sore loser but it appeared that he was having fun – as if he didn't really expect to keep Tattenbaum's money anyway.

After about 30 minutes, and seemingly countless shots and numerous bets, Ike announced, "Well Russian Bill... I'm... how do you say it... all-in! I believe you have won back all your money... and then some! Let's call it square!"

Tattenbaum smiled as he pocketed the proceeds from the final bet. He then proceeded to eject the spent cartridges from his pistol when Sandy King approached him. "Bill... we could use a man like you. A man who is good with a gun is always a good man to have around... to have on your side... if you know what I mean! Why don't you stick around? Come on out to my ranch for dinner tonight. We'll talk!"

"Certainly" was the reply from Tattenbaum with a sigh of relief. Finally, it looked like he was starting to fit in.

As the crowd started to thin, Ezra approached Tattenbaum. "Major... it's nice that you are making friends. But are you sure these are the type of friends you want?"

Tattenbaum turned to Ezra, his face taking on a most serious countenance. "Ezra... Mr. Thornton..., you have helped me and I consider you a friend and appreciate your concern. But while I have lived a privileged life, I have also lived a very structured life; always doing what I was supposed to do, pleasing my mother and father, pleasing my teachers, trying to please my..." Tattenbaum's voice trailed off for a moment and he looked distant, but then continued, "... trying to please my superior officers. Now ... I want to please myself. If that means to live dangerously, I will live dangerously. But here, danger is a relative term, Mr. Thornton. Here...in your American west, one can lose themselves... or become someone else. As you can see, Mr. Thornton, just today I have been changed from Major Tattenbaum to Russian Bill. Anything is possible here in your West! I might even become known as a 'Bad-Man'"

Ezra retorted, "Why don't you stop by my mercantile store... have a sarsaparilla. We'll talk about it!"

Tattenbaum issued a quick reply, "I've made my decision!"

Ezra looked straight at Tattenbaum and said, "Indeed you have." Then he turned and walked away.

*****

Major William Tattenbaum - Russian Bill - had found his place in the west – or so it seemed; befriended, to a certain degree, by the cow -boy faction of Tombstone.

The days marched onward, summer approached, and Major Tattenbaum became friendlier with the likes of Curly Bill, Johnny Ringo, and the McLaury brothers. It was a strange relationship. It became plain to everyone, including Ezra, that the Russian immigrant was not really part of the "cow-boy inner-circle"; he was never consulted on any business or let in on any news of "business dealings." But Tattenbaum really had no use for any business the cow-boys may have had in mind. Money did not seem to be an issue for him.

Although Tattenbaum was now dressing like a "cow-boy", he could not shed his military bearing. His clothes, although the same style as everyone else, were always clean and neat, without patches or tears, and always perfectly pressed. His new friends alternated between chiding him for it, to egging him on to perform shooting tricks. Ezra was convinced that if it wasn't for Tattenbaum's shooting ability and quick draw, the cow-boys would have had no use for him and he would have been driven out of Tombstone as soon as he finished his first game of cards.

It was painfully obvious that they kept "Bill" around for their own amusement. The only person that seemed to have any respect for him was Sandy King. King and Tattenbaum talked constantly whereas others of the cow-boy clan only talked to the Major when it suited them. Tattenbaum would regale King with his stories of military maneuvers and riding a fine white stallion "...in service to Czar Alexander II of Russia!" King would brood about the fine stallion he had lost in the card game.

Saturday May 15, 1880 9:15PM Tombstone, A.T.

William Tattenbaum and Sandy King sat at a table in the Oriental Saloon, idly drinking beer and chatting, King still brooding over the fine horse he had lost at the same table two weeks prior. "I know he cheated me!" grumbled King. "That son-of a-bitch Harlan Grant! He already has more money, more horses, more of everything than anyone else in the Territory. Why did he need my horse? I know he cheated me somehow. And now he has my prize stallion! And I mean to get it back. Russian Bill... I need a plan! What I need to do is..."

King's vitriol was cut short as Curly Bill approached the table, smiling and pulling on his regal blonde moustache. Looking at Tattenbaum, Curly Bill blurted out to anyone who would listen, "Russian Bill... there he is... the cleanest man I ever saw!"

Curly Bill was smiling, but it didn't hide his contempt for Tattenbaum. Curly considered Russian Bill too feminine, too clean, and too full of himself. Tattenbaum looked at Curly with disdain, torn between his feelings of wanting to belong to the cow-boy clan, and at the same time, reviling most of them, especially Curly Bill, for their feigned friendship. He realized the only two friends he really had was Sandy King, and Ezra Thornton... and he wasn't quite sure about Ezra any more; given Ezra's disdain for his choice of friends.

Tattenbaum turned again to King, his face stern with resolve, "So... what is your plan? Whatever it is, I am in with you!"

King returned Tattenbaum's intense gaze, "I aim to get my horse back... and make that damn Harlan Grant wish he never cheated me! And you're going with me! I could use a man who is good with a gun!"

Tattenbaum smiled.

Wednesday May 19, 1880   11:30PM   Shakespeare, New Mexico Territory

An almost-full moon, cloudless sky, and bright stars gave King and Tattenbaum just enough light to pick their way through a thicket of waist-high brush after tying-off their horses a few yards behind them. They stopped just short of the corral containing King's former horse, and about 20 others. On the opposite side of the corral and a few yards off was Harlan Grant's house, large and stately. A few yards beyond that was a bunkhouse where his ranch hands stayed. King whispered, "Look at that place! Bought and paid for with gambling money from people he cheated from Tombstone to San Francisco! Well, he won't miss just a few horses. He has plenty! And he can always cheat a few more people and buy a few more horses. Russian Bill... how many horses would you like?"

Tattenbaum just stared at King. He couldn't believe he was doing this... about to steal horses... living the dangerous and adventurous life he had read about in the dime novels. The night air was warm and a slight breeze made things quite balmy; but Tattenbaum felt a chill run down his back!

Not waiting for an answer, and knowing they would need to move fast before anyone in the house woke up, King again whispered, "Here's three pieces of rope to lead your horses with. Take whichever three you want. I'm taking mine and two more. Hurry now!"

The two men moved into the corral, picked out their prizes, eased the nooses over the horse's heads, and led them out... and off into the night. Soon they found their own horses and were about to mount-up when they heard a dog barking in the distance. King looked at Tattenbaum with a look of concern, then mounted, and leading their stolen horses the two rode off at a walk, to make as little noise as possible.

Soon, they picked up the pace until they had put several miles between themselves and Harlan Grant's ranch. They came to a fork in the road and King pulled-up his horse saying, "I think it is better that we split up. I'll go left, you go right, and we'll meet at my ranch in a few days. Keep an eye out... but I don't think you'll have any trouble. See you in a few days."

Tattenbaum said goodbye to his friend, and began trotting down the road, his three prizes in tow.

Thursday May 20, 1880   2:30AM   Somewhere in New Mexico Territory

Major Tattenbaum had had a long day and needed some rest. He went a short way off the road, tied off his horses, collected some wood, and in a few moments had a fire going, heating a pot of coffee.

Clouds intermittently covered the moon, creating periods of almost utter blackness. A coyote howled in the distance and Major Tattenbaum felt quite alone... and quite safe, even with his ill-gotten horseflesh.

Tattenbaum was just about to doze-off when the horses began to stir, spooked by someone or some thing possibly approaching. Clouds covered the moon. Tattenbaum could not see beyond the soft glow of his small fire. Suddenly he became aware of a large object... a horse and rider almost directly in front of him only a few feet away. Tattenbaum reached for his pistol. As the gun broke leather, Tattenbaum heard a familiar voice say, "You make a lousy horse thief!"

The horse and rider moved closer, the rider saying, "You can put your six-gun away. I won't hurt you!"

It was Ezra, dressed as always in his city clothes and top hat. Tattenbaum looked up at him and said, "Mr. Thornton... how surprising to see you out here in no-man's land! Where did you come from?"

"Oh... you never know where I'm going to show up" was the quick reply.

Tattenbaum just looked at Ezra for a moment trying to figure out how Ezra could have traveled this far and found him. Tattenbaum continued, "How can you say I am a lousy horse thief? I was able to take three horses, and got away free!"

Ezra shot back, "You aren't very far from the scene of your crime and your fire can be seen for a quite a distance. You're not very hard to find at all...not for me... and not for the Grant ranch hands... tough men paid to protect Mr. Grant's livestock. I expect them to be here shortly! My guess is that if you abandon the horses here and move on, they'll retrieve the horses and forget about you! All they want is Harlan's horses. But if you stay here much longer, or continue on with the horses, I suspect they will eventually catch up with you and then..."

"And then what, Mr. Thornton?"

"Well" came the reply, "I'm not sure... but I do know it won't be good!"

The two men looked at each other in silence for a moment, each contemplating their next move.

Ezra broke the silence, "Leave the horses, and come back to Tombstone with me. I'll fix things up so... well... so that this just never happened. We'll have a sarsaparilla and laugh about it. Or you can stay here, and take your chances."

Tattenbaum remained frozen where he stood. He knew going with Ezra would have been the safe and easy thing. But he wanted to live dangerously. He wanted to live his own life in his own way, unfettered by others. He wanted to change his life! And if things got too hot for him, he figured he could just move to another area, change his name, and re-invent himself – from Major Tattenbaum to Russian Bill to... who knows what!

Ezra took Tattenbaum's silence to indicate that he intended to stay and face whatever would happen next. Without saying another word, Ezra urged his horse forward and in a moment was lost in the inky blackness of the night.

Tattenbaum took a bedroll from his horse, spread it near the fire, and went to sleep.

Thursday May 20, 1880   6:30AM

Major William Tattenbaum awoke with a start, and opened his eyes to bright daylight. Lying on his back, he was looking up the barrel of a shotgun. He had never seen the man on the other end of it, his finger on the trigger. But he suspected it was probably one of

Harlan Grant's men.

"On yer feet – Mr. Russian Bill – or whatever your name is!" came the gruff command from the man with the shot gun.

Once on his feet, Tattenbaum very much regretted Ezra's offer to take him back to Tombstone. There, high on magnificent stallion was Harlan Grant, flanked by ten of his men, all heavily armed, and all surrounding Sandy King, mounted on a horse with his hands tied behind his back.

All the men waited on Harlan Grant's orders. After looking at Tattenbaum for a moment, Harlan Grant announced, "Let's get these men back to Shakespeare. They'll need to stand trial!"

Thursday May 20, 1880   11:30AM

The party entered Shakespeare. Tattenbaum looked around for a tall, stately building – a courthouse – where he hoped he would be able to find a lawyer to plead his case, tell the judge that this was his first offense, that he had made a mistake, and was willing to make amends. But it soon became obvious that such a building did not exist in Shakespeare.

The party continued down the main street of town and pulled up to a large white building. A sign outside read, "Grant House Hotel." Suddenly it occurred to Tattenbaum that not only was Harlan Grant a very rich rancher; he probably owned the better part of the town of Shakespeare and was probably a very powerful man; and could probably do whatever he liked.

Grant announced, "Men bring out some tables and chairs. We're going to hold court right out here in the street!"

Saturday May 22, 1880 Tombstone, A.T. 8:00AM

Ezra had just put the key in the lock on the front door of his store, opening it for the day's business when John Clum walked by. The two men exchanged greetings, then Ezra began the conversation, "Will we see the next edition of your *Tombstone Epitaph* later this afternoon? Many people seem to prefer it over the Nugget. It's a great newspaper!"

Clum smiled and replied, "Yes, it will be out this afternoon... and I have quite a story for the front page; most tragic!"

Ezra gave Clum an inquisitive look. Clum continued, "It seems our friend Russian Bill has met his demise, the victim of a neck-tie party. Oh, certain people over in Shakespeare called it a legal capture and fair trial for two horse thieves – they got Sandy King too. But Bob Crouch happened to be there with his stage coach at the time and saw the whole thing. The trial lasted all of 30 seconds – Harlan Grant serving as judge and jury. Of course, he wouldn't get his lily-white hands dirty. His boys did the actual lynching - strung up Russian Bill and Sandy King side by side in the lobby of Harlan's hotel. Then they left them to hang there for a while; as a warning to others I guess. I suppose it will be a good long time before someone else tries to take horses from Mr. Harlan Grant! Well, I have a paper to get out. Good day Ezra!"

With a heavy heart Ezra trudged into his mercantile store, reached into the ever-present barrel of ice, and retrieved a bottle of sarsaparilla. Taking his first swig he thought to himself, "Russian Bill... Major Tattenbaum... whoever you are, or were, you could have had a decent life here in Tombstone! But instead, you just wanted to be a 'Bad Man.' Well, you didn't make a very good 'Bad-Man'".

Saturday, May 3, 1882 10:15AM Tombstone, A.T.

Working in the back of his store, Ezra heard the front door open, and the sound of heavy boots on his wooden floor. A deep and authoritative voice called out, "Is anyone here?"

Russian! The voice was distinctively Russian; something Ezra had not heard in two years! The accent sounded exactly like William Tattenbaum – Russian Bill.

Ezra stepped from the deep shadows into the light of his store front and was greeted by a well dressed, and obviously very refined middle aged man with a broad dark moustache and a walking stick. The man started, "Are you Ezra Thornton?"

Ezra extended his hand and replied, "I am... and I am afraid you have me at a disadvantage. You would be...?"

The man straightened his stance and replied, "My name is Yuri Chernak. I am an emissary, here in the United States on behalf of Countess Telfrin of Russia. Her son, Major William Tattenbaum has been missing for almost three years. She has commissioned me to look for him, and I have tracked him here, to Tombstone. I am told that you are a friend of his and may provide information as to his whereabouts."

Ezra was stunned. All the stories that Major Tattenbaum told, that everyone including Ezra thought were the tallest of tales, were apparently real. Ezra had a sinking feeling in the pit of his stomach, that he should have done more to save Major Tattenbaum from himself.

Not sure how to handle the situation and stalling for time to think, Ezra simply said, "William Tattenbaum huh? Sure... I know who he is!"

Encouraged that he felt he was nearing the end of his quest, and seeing that Ezra knew Tattenbaum, Yuri Chernak went on. "William Tattenbaum had been an ideal son, ideal student, and an ideal soldier. Then, one day, something happened. He was given an order by a superior officer, and refused to obey. When his superior officer told him to comply or face the consequences, Major Tattenbaum struck the officer so hard it knocked him down. Before the officer could regain his footing, Major Tattenbaum had run off, and apparently has been running ever since. He knew he had disgraced his family, his name and his reputation and couldn't face it. If he returns with me he will have to face consequences, but not as dire as running for the rest of his life! Where is he, Mr. Thornton?"

Ezra looked straight at the Russian emissary saying, "Sir, you had better sit down. I have quite a story for you. Major Tattenbaum indeed had to run for the rest of his life. You see, one day I happened to see a disheveled fellow sitting on a freight box in front of my store...."

The Real Story Behind "The Bad Man"

The story you have just read, is largely true.

In its hey-day, Tombstone just seemed to be a magnet for all sorts of colorful characters with colorful names. The most talented Hollywood screenwriter would be challenged to come up a cast that would include names like Curly Bill, Johnny Ringo, Buckskin Frank or one of the lesser known of Tombstone's inhabitants, but none-the-less colorful and charismatic; Russian Bill.

Russian Bill showed up in Tombstone around the mid-1880's claiming to be a noble man and an officer in the Czar's Imperial White Hussars. He further claimed that his mother was a wealthy Russian aristocrat, Countess Telfrin. He would go on endlessly with grandiose tales of daring-do and military exploits. But his was just one of many tales told around a camp fire or at a bar sipping beer or whisky. While many thought that Bill's tale was taller than most, it was just a tale – just a way to try to impress those around him and expand his own self-importance.

Naturally, and quite frequently, the question of his current state of affairs would come up. Given that it seemed that he had such an ideal life in Russia, fellow Tombstoners wondered why he wasn't still there. Bill would then go on to tell about how he had struck a superior officer in the heat of a moment and that he was now subject to a court martial. This would have not only meant prison time for him, but more importantly, an extreme embarrassment for his family.

After the incident, Bill fled Russia, wandered about, and eventually came to the United States to get lost in the westward rush.

Being an aristocrat, and being used to the finer things in life, such as good clothes and good grooming, Bill was always immaculately dressed – oddly enough, in cowboy clothing. Bill fancied himself a westerner and tried to look the part, complete with fancy gun-leather and a pair of fancy revolvers. He liked dressing in vibrant colors. And because the clothes were new, the un-faded colors made his stand out all the more and against the faded clothes most wore. His long hair was always neat and clean. Townspeople commented that he must have spent hours each day just grooming himself. Yes, Bill took pride in his appearance, as any respectable military officer would; and the townspeople chided him for it.

To exacerbate his already bizarre situation, Bill wanted more than anything to be associated with the cow-boy element in Tombstone. He tried to hang around with the likes of Curly Bill, Johnny Ringo, Ike Clanton and the rest of that faction. But it was painfully obvious that he just didn't fit in. It is thought that the Clanton-McLaury gang let Russian Bill hang around for their own enjoyment, laughing at his braggadocio and seemingly feminine mannerisms.

Eventually Bill had enough of his new friends and decided that if he wanted to make a name for himself as a Bad Man, if he wanted to become a notorious legend in his own lifetime and beyond, he would have to do it himself. He would have to actually commit some crime, some act of mayhem, some outlawry by which he would come to be known. Becoming an outlaw by association just would not do for Russian Bill.

Sometime late in 1880, Bill headed for New Mexico Territory where he would start over yet again in a new life of crime and the legendary status he so desired. It is here that accounts of Russian Bill's exploits differ slightly.

In one account, Bill encountered a man named Sandy King in Shakespeare, New Mexico. Bill knew Sandy King as he was also associated with Tombstone's cow-boy faction and the two of them were already acquainted with each other. The two men decided that they were going to make names for themselves outside the shadows of the Clanton's and McLaury's and go into the horse stealing business. Their new careers were short lived as they were both caught shortly after their first heist.

In another account, Sandy King, a former Tombstone cow-boy had taken up residence in Shakespeare, New Mexico Territory and was busy making a nuisance of himself as the town drunk and town bully. It was not uncommon for King to get rip-roaring drunk and start taking out his frustrations on the other bar patrons with his fists.

It was about this time that King, drunken and disorderly, had recently gotten into an argument with the clerk of a local general store, shooting the clerk's finger off when he didn't move fast enough to suit King.

In either case, the town's Vigilance Committee, which in this case was nothing more than a lynch mob, dragged Russian Bill, pleading for his life, into a makeshift courtroom. Within minutes Bill was tried and convicted of horse thievery and sentenced to immediately hang. The Committee dragged him to the lobby of the Grant House Hotel where a rope was thrown over the tall rafters in preparation for the sentence to be carried out.

Again, the stories vary somewhat at this point. One account tells of Sandy King being hung right alongside Russian Bill for horse thievery. In another account, only Russian Bill was hanged for stealing horses. The Vigilance Committee thought it was a good idea to hang Sandy King just on general principals being that he was a drunkard and a bully and the townspeople were sick of him.

When faced with the charge of shooting off the finger of the store clerk, King offered in his own defense that other people had done worse and gotten off with less. He cited a recent case where a man had entered the dining room of this same hotel and shot a man in a heated discussion over who was going to eat the last egg in the restaurant. The Committee didn't like King's defense and decided to string him up anyway.

In either case, the two were hung on January 1, 1881.

Russian Bill's Final Resting Place   **(H. McNeer photo)**

Reportedly, their dead bodies were left hanging for several hours as a warning to other miscreants who might be considering some form of mayhem or malfeasance that the Vigilance Committee meant business!

When news of his demise reached Tombstone, many people were upset that Russian Bill had reached such a cruel and unceremonious end. While they laughed at him, he was considered quite harmless – just another eccentric in a world of eccentrics – an amusing character with some great stories. While Russian Bill had talked a lot, and could swagger with the best of the cow-boys, prior to that time, he had never actually committed a crime.

For Sandy King, that was the end of the trail. But not for Russian Bill!

Two years later, a man showed up in Tombstone asking the whereabouts of William Tattenbaum aka Russian Bill. The man, with a heavy accent, finely dressed and with a highly refined demeanor was obviously from Russia and claimed to be working on behalf of the Countess Telfrin. It seemed the Countess was looking for her long lost son and was eager to learn of his whereabouts.

Tombstone residents were dumbfounded. For months they had laughed at this man, mocked him, and eventually had driven him out of town and to his death, never realizing that he had been telling the truth.

Shakespeare Cemetery   **(H. McNeer photo)**

The emissary headed to Shakespeare to confirm the story. After seeing the grave marker it was decided that, in order to save the Countess any more grief or embarrassment, the emissary would return to Russia with a story that Bill had met his end in an accident. The townspeople all agreed as they didn't want anyone else nosing around their town and discovering how quick "justice" came for the former Russian military officer, known as Russian Bill.

*****

Other notes about this story

Some of the story's early action takes place at the Oriental Saloon on May 1, 1880. This is out of historical context. The Oriental didn't open until June of 1880.

The Tombstone Epitaph newspaper indeed began production on Saturday, May 1, 1880 and was indeed founded by John P. Clum, and remains a viable periodical to this day. The *Nugget* preceded *The Epitaph* by about a year.

Chapter 12: THE DEATH OF JOHNNY RINGO

"Time is all relative here in Tombstone, Mr. Hickman...all relative. Believe me; you will have all the time you need to learn the truth about how Johnny Ringo died."

Ezra T. Thornton June 20, 2008

Friday June 20, 2008   12:05PM Tombstone AZ

"Good day to you Miss Lilly!"

"Good day to you Mr. Thornton!"

Ezra Thornton strode into the Tombstone Territorial Book Store on the corner of 4th and Allen Streets, and greeted the store owner, Lilly Putnam. It was a fine early-summer day; a few tourists milled about on Allen Street along with the usual cadre of local reenactors dressed in their 1880's wear.

Just inside the door of the bookstore sat a middle-aged man, also dressed in his 1880's-style finery.; a black sack suit with a boiled white shirt, high collar, and a cravat-style tie, all topped with a high-crown derby and period-correct eye-glasses. Before him on a table were spread a number of books – his books - entitled, *The Death of Johnny Ringo* by Martin Hickman.

Ezra stepped over to the table and the now-smiling man. Looking back and forth between the man and Lilly Putnam he said, "It would appear that we have a new author here!"

The man stood and reached out his hand, "Martin Hickman – truck-driver by day, author by night!" Ezra met his hand with, "Ezra Thornton, full-time mercantilist!"

"Can I interest you in a book today, Mr Thornton?"

Ezra looked at Martin, smiled, then turned to Lilly and gave her a wink. Turning back to the smiling author Ezra said, "The death of

Johnny Ringo is quite a controversy, Mr. Hickman – and has been since he died in 1882. Does your book dispel any of the rumors or controversy surrounding that unfortunate incident? Have you finally discovered who, in fact, killed Johnny Ringo? Or was it suicide? Do you reveal how that poor young man died?"

Martin Hickman smiled rather sheepishly, and suddenly looked boyish. "Well Mr. Thornton, there are many different theories as to how Ringo died. Are you familiar with them?"

By this time a few more tourists had wandered into the store and were picking-up on the conversation between the two men.

Ezra furrowed his brow, "I think I know a bit about it... but why don't you fill me in?"

With that, the customers in the store turned to look at the two men to better hear what Martin had to say. Seeing that he now had an "audience" and could do some selling of his book, Hickman started in with, "Well, as you know, Ringo was associated with the cow-boy element here in Tombstone, the Clantons and the McLaury's. And the Earp faction, Wyatt, Virgil, and Doc Holliday thought he had something to do with the assassination of Morgan Earp in March of 1882, in the wake of the OK Corral incident. There was bad blood between the parties."

More customers began to gather around the author and Ezra. Martin Hickman was on a roll! His years of research on Johnny Ringo, and the Tombstone legend was about to shine through.

Martin continued, "On July 2, 1882, Johnny Ringo was seen here in Tombstone, very depressed, and drinking heavily. I am uncertain what he was depressed about, but he was obviously in a bad state of mind. A few days later, he left, and was seen over in Galeyville, still hitting the sauce, and still feeling down. On July 11th, he left Galeyville. It was the last time anyone would see him alive. He had been on a drinking bender for over a week! Imagine the shape he was in!"

A voice from the growing crowd asked, "So when did Ringo die?"

Martin went on, "On July 14, 1882 a teamster, one Mr. John Yoast found Ringo sitting in the crook of a large tree with a single gunshot to the head, and a single round fired from the pistol he still held in his hand. His boots were off and he had wrapped torn pieces of his undershirt to his feet. Apparently, he had walked some distance with his feet wrapped. The other odd thing was, one of his cartridge belts was on upside down – which seems odd for a man who knew guns and would likely not make such an odd mistake!"

Again, a voice from the growing crowd called out, "So it was suicide then – right?"

"Not necessarily..." Martin noted, acknowledging the man in the crowd. "It looked like suicide, but then again, how can a person fire a pistol as powerful as a .45 into their skull, which would force the hand away from the body, and probably cause a man who would, in an instant, be dead, and be found still holding the gun in their lap? And why would he have his cartridge belt on upside down? And besides, there are a number of people who wanted to see Ringo dead, especially the Earp brothers!"

Ezra smiled at the growing crowd and widening interest and spoke up. "So... obviously you don't think it was suicide. But who do you think shot Ringo?"

Martin took on a more serious look and continued. "Well, there are many theories on that. Some say Buckskin Frank Leslie shot him. Others say it was Johnny-Behind-The-Deuce. A long-shot says Earp confidant Lou Cooley shot him. Of course, if you watched the movie, *Tombstone*, they had Ringo shot by Doc Holliday. But the most popular theory is that Wyatt shot Ringo."

Ezra piped in, "Yes... yes. Some say this, some say that... and it has been that way for 100 years. What do *you* say Mr. Hickman?"

Martin then smiled and scanned the small crowd in the store, and looking much like an 1880's "hawker of wares" salesman stated emphatically, "And of course... I cover each theory in grueling detail in my book. But you'll have to read it to find out who actually killed Johnny Ringo!"

With that, several men began reaching for their wallets to buy a copy and the book sales were on. Ezra watched the action for a few moments and then invited Martin Hickman to visit him at his store at 5 PM, then turned and left.

Friday June 20, 2008   5:05PM   Ezra T. Thornton Mercantile

Martin Hickman strolled the two blocks up Allen Street to Ezra's Mercantile and stepped inside. Ezra was standing toward the back of the store. "Quite a place you have here, Mr. Thornton! It has the distinct appearance of the early 1880's! In fact, dressed as we are, we really look like we belong here!" Ezra was always well dressed, looking like he just walked out of 1880.

Ezra stepped forward out of the shadows, "Then I have achieved my goal, Mr. Hickman. It is my intention to give the store the flavor of the late 19th century. This is your first time in Tombstone I assume?"

Hickman replied, "Indeed it is."

Reaching into the ever-present barrel of ice and sarsaparilla that held a prime spot in the center of his floor, Ezra said, "I thought so. I see just about everyone that comes through... and have for quite some time. Would you like a refreshing bottle of sarsaparilla? The first one is always on the house!"

"Sure" was the reply.

Ezra took a bottle for himself, took a deep draught of the sudsy brew, then turned to his new friend. "So...now that we are away from the crowd... who really killed Johnny Ringo? What is your take on it?"

Martin smiled, "Well... I have been researching Mr. Ringo for several years, looked at all the evidence, I have studied all the angles and... fact is... I still don't know! There are some things that still don't add up!"

Ezra took another sip from his bottle, then looked straight at the author, "How would you like to know exactly how Johnny Ringo died, Mr. Hickman? You would be known far and wide as the man who finally solved a 100 year-old mystery. In the world of Tombstone historians, you would be remembered forever! And isn't that what writers want... to be remembered long after they are gone?"

Martin thought for a moment, then said, "But how can that be? How can you have proof of an event that many people have researched for years? Assuming that you can produce the proof, how could you have held it hidden all this time? I don't get it!"

Ezra smiled, "Do you want to learn the truth?

With a quizzical look on his face the incredulous author replied, "Historians always want the truth. But how...?"

Ezra cut him off. "What is today's date?"

Hickman replied, "Ahhh... June 20th."

Becoming more animated, Ezra said, "And when was Ringo reported dead?"

Very authoritatively Hickman replied, "July 14th."

"So..." started Ezra, "From June 20th to July 14th... you have about three weeks to learn the truth about Johnny Ringo!"

"Three weeks?" said Martin. "I don't have three weeks! I have a book signing again tomorrow morning at the book store, then I have time for a brief stroll around town, and then I have to head back to my home in California... back to my regular job! And why will it take three weeks to find this evidence anyway?"

Ezra smiled his "all-knowing" smile, "Time is all relative here in Tombstone, Mr. Hickman...all relative. Believe me; you will have all the time you need to learn the truth about how Johnny Ringo died. Do you have a hotel room here in town yet?"

Martin downed the last of his sarsaparilla, "No, I stayed in Tucson last night and drove down here this morning – went right to the bookstore. There must be a room available here in town somewhere."

"There is indeed, Mr. Hickman" pronounced Ezra. "There is a room reserved in your name at the San Jose House at the corner of Fifth and Fremont – with three weeks all paid for. Park you car in the front on Fifth. There are some extra clothes in the room – period-correct - if you need them. Enjoy your evening – have dinner – have a drink at the Crystal Palace – and get a good night's sleep at the San Jose House. Tomorrow morning, come look me up. I'll be right here waiting for you – and ready to start you on your journey to the truth about Johnny Ringo!"

Martin Hickman wasn't convinced that he would learn the truth about Johnny Ringo. All he knew was that this strange but albeit friendly man was going to pay for a hotel room for him – for at least one night. Since he needed a place to stay anyway, Martin figured that he would stay at the San Jose House, do his book signing the next morning, and then head back to California. Although the whole arrangement seemed beyond bizarre, Martin figured he had nothing to lose.

The two men shook hands in agreement of Ezra's suggestion. Martin, left, had his dinner, parked his red SUV in front of his room at the San Jose House, and retired early. The day had been way too strange for him.

Wednesday Morning June 21 Room 3 San Jose House

Martin Hickman rose after a restful night's sleep, showered, and dressed in a fresh 1880's-era suit provided by Ezra. It fit perfectly! "As long as I'm in Tombstone, I may as well look the part" he thought to himself, tipping his brown derby into a jaunty position as he peered at himself in the full-length mirror.

It was a little after 8AM. Martin figured he would stop to see Ezra as requested, then have breakfast at a local café. Noticing that the room had become quite warm during the evening, Hickman tried to turn on the air conditioner, which refused to respond to a wild bout of knob twirling. Apparently, it had stopped working some time during the night. Resolving to ask the hotel manager to get it fixed, Martin headed out the door.

Before he could get both feet on the outside of the threshold he stopped dead in his tracks. His brand-new SUV which had been carefully parked in front of his door was gone! In fact... all the cars on the street were gone – replaced with horses and carriages!

The new hotel across Fifth Street was missing; replaced with Hoefler's General Store. Stepping out into the street, which he noticed was now dirt rather than asphalt, he noticed the large parking lot on the southeast corner of Fifth and Fremont, had been filled with a number of low, wood-frame buildings which housed several stores. Wide-eyed with amazement, Martin locked his room door behind him, and moved south on Fifth Street towards Allen Street. On the west side of the street, he noticed a grocery store, the Lenoire Furniture Store, a couple of assay offices, a jeweler and a barber shop. On the east side of the street was a few places he was more familiar with; the Tombstone Post Office, Spangenberg's Gun Store and on the corner of Fifth and Allen, the Oriental Saloon!

And then he realized something else peculiar... everyone... everyone was dressed in "period clothing!" No longer was there a definition between the sneaker-clad, baseball-cap wearing tourists and the reenactors. "But everyone here can't be a reenactor and not everyone is going to have clothes this authentic-looking!" he thought. The clothing was one thing – but swapping buildings during the night just couldn't happen!

Martin turned east on Allen Street and headed straight for, where he hoped, Ezra's store would be, on the corner of Sixth and Allen. As he approached the corner, he gave a sigh of relief when he saw Ezra step out onto the boardwalk and wave at him. Incredulously, Ezra and his store looked exactly as Martin had remembered it from the day before... but everything around it had changed!

Ezra smiled as Martin approached, "I can tell from the look on your face you have a lot of questions!"

The two men shook hands. "Well.." said Martin, "The first question is where am I... and it sure looks like Tombstone. I just walked by the Oriental Saloon... and there's the Bird Cage across the street. I guess the bigger question is 'When am I?' What is the date today?"

Ezra looked about and then reached down to retrieve a newspaper sitting on the bench in front of his store. He glanced at it momentarily, and then handed it to Martin.

"Holy smoke... look at the date!" exclaimed the astonished author. "June 21, 1882! Can this be correct... or is this some elaborate hoax? I mean... it sure looks like 1882. But you... and your store... looks like what I saw in 2008... if this is truly 1882!"

Ezra furrowed his brow in feigned concern. "Are you seeing a 2008 store in 1882... or did you see my 1882 store in 2008? As I told you yesterday, time... especially here in Tombstone... is all relative!"

The two men stood in silence for just a moment, Martin trying to make sense of it all. Ezra remained quiet, letting the incredulous author try to drink it all in.

Martin's head was swimming with a million thoughts – and then suddenly, his attention was diverted as a young, well-dressed woman, obviously a very refined lady, walked up to the two men. She smiled at Ezra, who returned the smile, and then turned to Martin. "Martin... may I present Miss Mary Parkhurst – a local, albeit relatively new local here in town. Miss, Parkhurst, may I present Mr. Martin Hickman who has *just* arrived in town!"

Martin gently took the woman's hand in his, their eyes met, and the sparks flew. Martin was stunned at her beauty, long, flaming-red hair pulled up on her head, topped by a fashionable green hat sporting a long peacock feather. Her brocade polonaise dress fit her shapely form perfectly, its dark green color matching her hat stood in stark contrast to her lily-white skin and long, demure eyelashes. Martin could not speak, but only stood there dumb-founded like a bumbling schoolboy.

Mary smiled at Martin's loss of words and although she too was instantly smitten, managed to keep her composure. She then broke the uneasy silence with, "Mr. Thornton, I should like to secure a few things from your store!"

"Certainly" came the reply. "Right this way!" Ezra and Miss Parkhurst disappeared into the mercantile

Martin was left outside in the morning air, the 1882 morning air, and his swirling thoughts! He wondered what, if anything he would or could say to Miss Mary Parkhurst when she exited the store. He stood at the edge of boardwalk, and watched people going in and out of the Bird Cage Theatre across the street. His thoughts darted back and forth between trying to make sense of his new environment – and how to approach Miss Mary Parkhurst. And what of his job he had to report back to in a few days?

Martin didn't have long to wait. A few moments later, Mary stepped outside, basket in hand full of freshly purchased items. He turned to see Ezra and Mary standing at the doorway saying their goodbyes. Martin spoke up, "Do you have a long way to walk, Miss Parkhurst? May I help you carry your items?"

Mary looked at Ezra, and then at Martin and said, "I only have a few blocks to go but yes, it would be a help if you could carry the basket! It's rather heavy."

Martin took the basket from her hand and then looked at Ezra, "I'll be right back!"

Martin and Mary walked east a few steps on Allen Street, then turned north on Sixth. After they had walked a short way, Martin spoke up, "I hope you don't think I am being too bold, Miss Parkhurst. I mean, we just met and... I'm uhhh... not from around here and I'm not really sure what the proper protocol is walking with a lady, or being seen with a lady... or even speaking to a lady.

I'm..uhh..."

Mary broke Martin's nervous stammer, "Don't worry... I'm still learning a bit about proper etiquette myself. You see, Mr. Hickman, I'm not from around here either... and, like you, have not been here very long myself."

Martin became even more curious about Mary's background. "How long have you been in Tombstone, Miss Parkhurst?"

"Only about a month...maybe five weeks" came the reply.

"And where do you come from?" asked Martin.

Mary thought for a moment, then replied, "Let's just say I have come quite a distance to get here."

Martin smiled at her and commented aloud, "Ah... she is attractive *and* evasive!"

Mary returned the smile. It was apparent that they were engaging in a cat and mouse game.

Martin continued with, "And what do you do, Miss Parkhurst?" asked Martin. "I mean to say... what is your profession? Do you work here in town? Have you even had a chance to find a job here in town yet?"

The two continued to walk up Sixth Street, turned onto Safford Street and headed east. Mary replied, "Well... by profession, I'm a writer, or to be more precise, a newspaper reporter. I know that seems rather odd in this day and age...but that's what I do. But at the moment, I am unemployed, and working on a personal writing project... a story you might say.. and uhhh... living with, what you might call, well...for lack of a better term, he is a benefactor. In fact, here we are, at my house." Martin's heart sank at the sound; "benefactor" not being sure what that meant.

The two had arrived at a small white house on the south side of Safford Street between Seventh and Eighth Streets, in the middle of the block. Mary turned to Martin, "And what do you do, Mr. Hickman?"

Without thinking, Martin started, "I drive a... err..." Martin caught himself just in time. If this was truly 1882, there wouldn't be any trucks for him to drive. Martin continued, "I drive a wagon... for a freight line... out of San Francisco. And I also write... part time... more for my own enjoyment more than anything else. In fact, I'm here working on a story myself!"

"And what is the story about?" asked Mary.

Martin took on a more serious look, "Well, let's just say at this point that it is under development."

Mary laughed, "And now who is being evasive?" Mary continued,

The Death of Johnny Ringo

"I would invite you in for some coffee, but I see my... err... benefactor, such as he is, is not home... and I'm not sure where he is or when he'll be back. It just wouldn't do if he were to find me here with you in the house."

Martin picked up on her train of thought, and then found a streak of brazen bravery, "So how about dinner tonight?"

Mary smiled, "I'll meet you at the Russ House at 6. Do you know where the Russ House is?"

Martin took her hand and smiled, "I think I can find it. I'll see you there!"

A few moments later, Martin was back at Ezra's mercantile store, Ezra again greeting Martin in front of his store. The two men stood on the boardwalk, the overhead awning shielding them from the bright morning sunshine as the city came to life with a growing number of people now busily walking about, and more stores opening for business.

As the two shook hands, Ezra commented, "Three weeks Mr. Hickman!"

"Three weeks?" came the reply.

"Yes" said Ezra. "As you recall from yesterday's conversation, it is three weeks to Ringo's death. Here is your chance to learn the truth about his unsavory demise. While you are here in Tombstone, whatever you need is on me. I have open accounts at every business in town. Just tell them to put it on my account. Never let it be said that I am not a patron of the arts! Trying to help a writer find the truth is my little contribution!"

Martin stood in silence trying to grasp the enormity of his situation. Then Ezra broke the silence. "And how did your little meeting go with Miss Parkhurst?"

"Oh... err... famously... I think." was the stammering reply.

"Well" smiled Ezra, "It never hurts to mix a little pleasure with business."

Still unsure of his surroundings and situation, Martin stood staring across the street at the Bird Cage Theatre. Just then, a well-dressed man stepped out of the theatre, and noticing Ezra and Martin on the opposite side waved at Ezra. The man looked somehow familiar to Martin... like he had seen him somewhere before.

"Good morning Ezra!" came the hail from across the street.

Ezra raised his hand in reply, "Good morning Mr. Mayor!"

Martin looked quizzically at Ezra.

Ezra smiled back in reply, "That's former mayor John Clum. I'm sure you've run across him in your research on Ringo? He'll be headed to Washington, D.C. in a few weeks to accept a desk job at the post office department, which he will hate."

Somewhat absent-mindedly, Martin replied, "Indeed I have seen Mr. Clum. He looks just like his photograph!"

Martin was then lost in thought. Maybe this really was 1882! And maybe time really was relative here in Tombstone. Ezra already knew what would happen to Clum when he reached Washington! Martin knew about it because he had read about it during his historical research. But Ezra was predicting, what in 1882, would be the future! It was all too confusing!

Wednesday June 21, 1882 5:50PM The Russ House

Martin strolled down Allen Street, on his way to dinner with Miss Mary Parkhurst, thinking about a conversation he had had earlier in the afternoon with Ezra. It seemed odd to Martin that Ezra existed, unchanged, in 2008 and here, in what certainly seemed to be 1882. He was still uncertain what was going on; it all just seemed so bizarre. But for lack of a better, more plausible explanation, he decided to simply accept what Ezra said was true, that he was on his way to dinner, with a woman he had just met, who lived with some man, which seemed odd in 1882 given the Victorian period and social mores of the time.

Martin and Mary met at the Russ House, on the corner of Toughnut and Fifth, exchanged greetings, and sat down at a table near the window. After a short, and tenuous silence, Mary spoke up, "I saw your face when I said 'benefactor' earlier, Martin... and I know you think he is a boyfriend and I understand your feelings. Actually, John is not really a boyfriend... really... he's... well... call him my support system... at least for the time being. He supports me... until uh... I can find a way to support myself. But then again... I may not be here too long anyway. If he needs a label, call him a land-lord. I rent a room from him in the back of the house."

Martin acknowledged her statement, and felt rather relived as he had strangely deep feelings for her. He had felt strongly attracted to women before, but only after getting to know them, not someone he had known less than an hour. He wondered if it was connected to being in 1882. He also wondered about Mary's choice of words; "support system" and "label" seemed out of context with the parlance he heard in the streets – here in 1882!

Mary continued, "Of course, John wants our relationship to be... well... more than what it is. He's nice... he's ok. And he *is* a benefactor. You see, when I got here, I didn't really know anyone. John and I met and before you know it, I had rented a room from him. He's helped me... that's all. In fact, he set me up in his home, was around for about a week, maybe 10 days, and then I haven't seen him for weeks. Every few days I find a few dollars on my dresser. I assume he comes by and leaves it for me. It's been keeping me going. Between that and... er... another benefactor, I'm doing alright."

The dining room began to fill with people – rough-looking miners, refined ladies, and well-dressed men prepared to take their evening meal. Sumptuous smells began to emanate from the kitchen area and shadows crept across the dirt street outside. The two ordered their meals.

Martin just stared at Mary for a moment, not quite sure of where to go next. He was torn between investigating her past and why she was in Tombstone, and verbalizing his feelings for her. The awkward silence was broken by an equally awkward instant where the couple both began to speak at the same time.

"Martin, when we first met at Ezra's ..."

"Mary, I was just wondering..."

Sensing where the conversation was going to go, Martin urged Mary to continue. "Martin..." she began, "when we first met at Ezra's this morning, I felt... I think we both felt... a very strong... well... attraction!"

Martin cut in, "Stronger than you have ever felt before... when first meeting someone?"

"Precisely!" came the quick reply. "You felt it too?"

Martin smiled rather sheepishly, "Yes... and I thought it was just me. I've felt a very strong attraction to a woman before, but only after getting to know them a bit. Mary, we have known each other a total of maybe two hours! This is crazy! Kinda nice... but crazy!"

Mary looked down at the table, "I agree. I feel exactly the same way. So... what do we do about it?"

Martin turned to look out the window, and wondered what Mary was really asking. Was she inviting him to advance their relationship – such as it was? Was she asking a rhetorical or a pragmatic question? Still unsure about his new friend and her background, he calculated that he should be prudent in his response.

Martin took a sip of wine in preparation of answering Mary's question and then replied, "Let's give it some time – sleep on it. Let's meet at the Can-Can restaurant for breakfast."

The two finished their meal, had coffee and casually spoke about life in Tombstone. Martin was still unsure of Mary's background, but after talking over dinner, there was one thing he was sure of – that Miss Mary Parkhurst was quite knowledgeable about life in Tombstone, Tombstone's citizens and characters, and Tombstone's brief history.

Mary had a similar feeling about Martin. Most people knew about the court inquest that followed the OK Corral incident between the Earp and cow-boy factions eight months prior. But Martin knew details – seemingly more details than were publicly released! In fact, he knew details about Morgan Earp's assassination in March, 1882, and Virgil Earp's attempted assassination in December, 1881 – all in the wake of the October, 1881 street fight. He knew about the ride across southeastern Arizona taken by Wyatt Earp and his compatriots seeking justice for the violence inflicted against his brothers, vowing to rid the country of the "cow-boy infestation."

Both diners were equally baffled – but tried hard not to let their astonishment show.

Finishing their coffee, they stepped outside onto the boardwalk, the hot breeze and deepening shadows a stark contrast to the bright lights and cooler atmosphere of the dining room. Martin took Mary's hand in his own. Martin whispered, "Can-Can restaurant – 8 AM?"

Mary whispered, "8AM!"

Thursday June 22, 1882 7:50AM

Martin walked along Allen Street headed for the corner of Fourth and Allen and the Can-Can restaurant. He was excited about again dining with Miss Mary Parkhurst. He wanted their relationship to blossom further. But he wasn't sure how long he would be in 1882. Ezra had said that he had about three weeks to discover who shot Johnny Ringo. He figured he had at least that much time. It might be time enough to develop some sort of relationship – but to what end? What would happen after he discovered who shot Ringo? What would happen after July 14th? Would he go back to 2008? If he went back, could he take her with him? It was all so overwhelming!

Shops began to open for business up and down Allen Street. A shift-change in the mines brought sweaty, tired miners into the streets and into the saloons, replacing miners who, a few dollars lighter, vacated their spots at the gambling tables and headed for the mines. The sun was already high in the sky, raising the temperature to near 90. A bead of sweat trickled down Martin's back.

Martin walked into the restaurant to find Mary already sitting at a table, a very distraught look on her face. Martin pulled out a chair and sat down asking "What's the problem?"

Mary wiped a tear from her cheek saying, "John... my land-lord... or whatever he is... he was home when I got in last evening. Somehow, he saw us together. He was angry. He says I'm his girl! I told him... on no uncertain terms... that I don't belong to anyone and

I especially have no feelings for him... not in that way!

Martin let Mary compose herself and then asked, "So... what will you do now?"

Mary dabbed her eyes with her handkerchief, "Well, I don't feel things are really resolved. I told John I was going to leave...not knowing where I would go. We talked some more and we agreed I would stay. I am uncomfortable about it but I need to be there; I need to be near him. It's a strange arrangement. But I need to be here in town for about three more weeks. So... I'll put up with it for the time being."

Martin thought he would seize on the opportunity, despite its awkwardness, to ask a little about Mary's background and what brought her to Tombstone. "Three more weeks?" he inquired.

"Yes, three more weeks, give or take a day or so" came the reply, short and succinct, the stern look on her face said that that line of questioning would not continue, that Martin was heading for an area not to be entered.

Again, Mary was being evasive about herself. But Martin took her cue, and changed the subject. "It's such a nice day, Mary. Why don't we go for a picnic this afternoon?"

Mary's face suddenly brightened, "A splendid idea!"

Martin showed equal enthusiasm, "I'll secure a horse and buggy at the OK Corral and meet you at your house about noon?"

"I'll be waiting!" came the eager reply.

Thursday June 22, 1882 11:50AM

Martin secured a horse and spring wagon at the OK Corral. Despite his claim that he "drove" a freight wagon, his only "lessons" on driving a horse-drawn wagon came from watching western TV shows and movies. But somehow he managed to maneuver the "1882 truck" the few blocks to Mary's house, pulling up at 11:50AM.

Martin had not yet had a chance to secure the reins when Mary came bounding out the front door. Martin and Mary exchanged smiles as she approached the wagon, but Martin's smile suddenly turned sour as, from the corner of his eye, he caught a man peering at them from inside the house, trying to conceal his presence with the lace curtains. The man caught Martin's look, and drew back out of sight.

Martin stepped from the green, rather battered wagon, greeted Mary with a light kiss, and helped her step up to the tall seat. Pulling himself up onto the seat, Martin prepared to leave. Just prior to snapping the reins, Martin again looked at the window where the man had been. The same eyes were again peering through the window – cold black eyes, unblinking – almost as if the person behind them were dead. Dead....

Mary seemed oblivious that the two men had exchanged a fleeting glance. The wagon pulled away and headed east as Martin began the conversation, "Your err... friend – did you say his name was John?"

Mary heard Martin...but decided she was not willing to follow the conversation and it irritated her that he was again trying to pry into her business. Yet, she was still drawn to him – both romantically, and in a way she could not describe! She replied with, "It should be a splendid day for a picnic!"

*****

The days passed, and Martin began to get used to, and even enjoyed living in his new environment. Martin and Mary continued to see each other, enjoying many meals and picnics together. Their conversations ranged from local and national politics to conditions at the local mines, to world events. Martin was impressed with Mary's range of knowledge. Mary was impressed with Martin's familiarity with Tombstone. But neither let on to the other that they were impressed as both knew that it would lead to a question about how each came to be so knowledgeable... and subsequently, questions about Mary's background. And that was a place Mary was not willing to go – yet. Moreover, Martin had his own secrets to keep.

But Martin could not help wondering about her, and what she may, or may not have to hide. What bothered him the most was the man at her house, and how he always seemed to be there, peeking at them through the curtain lace. Apparently, Mary and the man had come to some agreement about their relationship as she had not again greeted Martin with tears in her eyes. Yet Martin could not help thinking what an odd relationship it was. It would have been odd in 2008, and was beyond strange for 1882.

Mary's secretive and evasive demeanor was wearing on Martin. Yet, he was attracted to her, and couldn't help but feel that she somehow was part of what he was supposed to discover.

Martin spent countless hours wandering around the city, trying to keep a low profile. His plan, such as it was, was to locate Johnny Ringo, and tail him to discover his killer – or ascertain that his demise was of his own hand. "Not much of a plan", he thought. But he couldn't think of any alternative. And Ezra was no help. Every time Martin asked him about how to proceed, Ezra simply smiled and told Martin he had to figure it out for himself.

Martin spoke to few people outside of Ezra and Mary. During the day, he would listen-in on other people's conversations in the street, in stores, and any place he found people engaged in conversation, looking for any clues about Johnny's whereabouts. At night, he would frequent the various saloons, hoping to find his prey – but with no luck.

Friday June 30, 1882 4:00PM

Martin stepped out of his room at the San Jose House to once again, stroll down Allen Street to see if he could pick up any clues as to Johnny Ringo's whereabouts. As he glanced across the street, he noticed Mary Parkhurst at Hoefler's General Store and approached the store to say hello to her.

As Martin approached, Mary was facing away from him, conducting business with the store clerk, in the process of purchasing some fruit, and did not see Martin approach. However, he came within ear-shot of Mary's parting remarks.

"Will there be anything else, Miss Parkhurst?" asked the clerk.

"No, thank you." came the reply. "Just the fruit today."

"And should we put this on Mr. Thornton's account today?" asked the clerk.

"Of course..." replied Mary. "Don't we always?"

Martin had been charging everything to Ezra since he arrived in Tombstone since the money he had could not be used, having been minted after 1882. Any passage of that money would have given him away... not to mention that the money looked decidedly different.

Whenever Mary and Martin would have a meal together, Martin would always, and very discretely, take the waiter or restaurant-owner aside and ask them to charge the meals to Ezra. And always, and with equal discretion, they were glad to comply.

But why Mary would charge something to Ezra was a mystery to Martin. He stepped inside the store; "Good afternoon, Mary!"

Mary quickly turned; and seeing Martin, turned beet-red, not sure if he had heard her or not. Martin saw this, but maintained his composure. He could tell from the look on her face that she was somehow tied to Ezra, but he was not sure how. What he was fairly certain of however, was that she wanted to be as secretive about that relationship as she was about the relationship with her room mate.

The two exchanged pleasantries, and agreed to join each other for dinner later that evening.

Martin headed south on Fifth Street, arriving at the corner of Fifth and Allen, entering the Crystal Palace Saloon. He needed some time to think about his situation, and what Mary might be up to charging things to Ezra. Martin took a table near the door, ordered a beer, and sat down to think.

A few moments later, Martin was downing his last sip of beer when a well-dressed, slightly-built man approached Martin. The man extended his hand. "Hello. My name is George Parsons. I don't know your name but I've seen you around town... and I know you are looking for Johnny Ringo. May I join you?"

Martin thought this might be the break he needed. He knew, historically, that Ringo was due to show himself in Tombstone on July 2nd, although he had hoped to run into him sooner. Martin stood and shook hands with Parsons, "Of course Mr. Parsons. My name is Martin Hickman. Can I buy you a beer?"

"That would be wonderful... on a hot afternoon..." answered Parsons.

A waiter brought two beers to the table; and then Parsons began, "I don't think you're going to find Johnny Ringo, Mr. Hickman. I think he has left the country... for parts unknown! I know you have been here for many days looking for him and I hate to see you waste your time."

Martin took his first sip of beer. "How do you mean, Mr. Parsons?"

Parsons took on a serious countenance, "If Wyatt Earp was chasing you, where would you go? If I were Ringo, I would put as much distance between myself and Earp as possible... possibly head back to the States. Maybe I'd hole-up in some place like New York... some place where I could blend into the crowd and become anonymous."

Martin set his beer on the table, and listened more intently.

Parsons went on, "Wyatt holds Ringo, and others, responsible for the death of his brother, Morgan, and the attempted assassination of his brother, Virgil. The last anyone knew, the Earp party, along with Doc Holliday was in Colorado. That's a long way off. But vengeance, Mr. Hickman, knows no geographical boundaries. I'm sure Ringo knows that, and knows Wyatt and his party will stop at nothing to take revenge. I don't think you're going to find Ringo, Mr. Hickman. I don't know what you want with him... and it's none of my business. But my advice is, get on with your life, and forget about Ringo. You're not going to find him!"

The two men chatted briefly; Parsons finished his beer, and left Martin to his thoughts. Martin began to think that maybe he really wouldn't find Ringo, even knowing that, historically; he was due to appear in Tombstone on July 2nd. All Martin could do was wait.

The Death of Johnny Ringo

Saturday July 1, 1882 12:25PM

Martin hurried along Fifth Street turning onto Allen on his way to a pre-arranged lunch at 12:30 with Mary. He walked into the Can-Can restaurant and looked about for Mary but didn't find her. He took a table, ordered a drink, and waited.

Time passed. It wasn't like Mary to be late for a date. In fact, she was usually early for their lunches and dinners. Finally, at 12:45 Mary appeared, and it was apparent that she had been crying. Martin stood saying nothing, escorted Mary to her chair, and waited for her to compose herself.

After several minutes, Mary found her voice. Speaking very low to prevent others from hearing, Mary started, "John and I had a terrible falling out! We had some words. He's extremely jealous!"

"Jealous?" Martin retorted. "Of what?"

"Of you!" came the reply.

"Me? Why me? Does he think you and I are more than... just friends?" Martin exclaimed.

"John thinks we're... well...lovers. He's unbelievably jealous. But I swear, John and I have no romantic ties at all. He's delusional! He left the house a few minutes ago. I don't know where he's headed. I do hope he's not after you! He can get really nasty – really nasty!"

Martin stopped to think for just a moment. Horrible thoughts ran through his mind as a strange reality set in. "This is Tombstone – Tombstone! This is the town that purportedly has a man for breakfast every morning. Will I be on tomorrow morning's breakfast menu? I don't own a gun. Will I be able to defend myself if this guy comes after me?"

Mary continued, "Maybe he'll just do what he usually does – get rip-roaring drunk and pass out! At any rate, I don't feel I can stay there any more. After lunch, I'm going to get a room at the Grand Hotel, if there are any rooms available."

Martin thought for a moment about the situation and then asked, "Can you afford a room there? I mean..."

"Yes" Mary replied. "I'll be fine."

Sunday July 2, 1882 12:15PM E.T. Thornton Mercantile

Martin stopped by to see Ezra, although he wasn't sure why; a strategy meeting, perhaps? What would he do when he finally found Ringo? How and where would he find Ringo? Martin hated the uncertainty. And now he had Mary's enraged pseudo-boyfriend to worry about. He wondered if it was all worth the trouble... but what choice did he have?

271

Martin entered the store, and without even saying hello to Ezra who was standing behind the counter, he started in, "Ezra... it's July 2nd. Ringo is due in town today!"

"Indeed he is, Mr. Hickman!" came the reply.

"How will I know him? I mean... I've only seen that one picture of him... the one published in all the history books. Will he be difficult to find?" asked Martin.

"Don't worry" smiled Ezra. "You'll have no problem finding him!"

"Well... I dunno" said Martin. "I've been here for days and haven't seen him. Who knows, maybe I've walked right into him and didn't even know it. I feel like I've wasted the last couple of weeks!"

"Not wasted, Mr. Hickman..." said Ezra. "You've met Miss Parkhurst... and I know you two are fast friends!"

"Ahh yes... Miss Parkhurst..." said Martin. "We have a lunch date. I gotta go!"

Martin exited the store, and headed west down Allen Street, along the covered boardwalk. As he approached the corner of Fifth and Allen, up ahead he saw Mary exiting the Grand Hotel. Mary walked toward Martin to meet him halfway. As the two approached the halfway point, the doorway of the Crystal Palace Saloon, the door flew open and a scruffy, unkempt man, tumbled out into the street, face-down, creating a small dust cloud where he landed. The man who ejected him stood in the doorway bellowing, "You'll not create any more trouble in my saloon, Johnny Ringo! Don't come back until you sober up!"

Martin stopped dead in his tracks. Ezra was right; Ringo was not hard to find!

Ringo rolled over on his back, obviously very drunk. He had the look on his face of a man-defeated. As Mary approached, Martin saw Ringo look at Mary, raising his hand to cover his eyes from the bright Arizona sun. Their eyes met, and Martin could tell there was a connection between the man lying on the ground, and refined woman he had come to know as Miss Mary Parkhurst, but with the look passed between the two, he felt that she had even more reason now to be evasive.

Ringo raised himself on one elbow and called out, "Mary..?"

A strained look on her face, Mary replied, "John – you need to get yourself together. We both know no good can come from this type of behavior!"

Suddenly Martin made the connection! Mary's "John" was in fact... Johnny Ringo! Ringo looked over at Martin, their eyes met, and a cold chill went up Martin's spine! He had visions of actor

Michael Biehn as Johnny Ringo from the movie *Tombstone* – spinning his pistols – and sticking them in his face. But the Johnny Ringo lying in the dust at his feet did not exactly meet the macho movie image he had come to know.

Saying nothing more, Mary turned and headed for the Can-Can restaurant. Martin looked one more time at Ringo who now was watching Mary walk down the street. Martin quickly stepped around Ringo and followed Mary.

Martin and Mary settled into their usual table at the Can-Can. In a hushed tone, Martin started the conversation with, "Johnny Ringo? Your John is Johnny Ringo? All this time, you've been hiding Johnny Ringo? Of all people... Johnny Ringo?"

Mary took on a serious tone, "I have my reasons, Martin. Besides, since the Earp party left Tombstone, Johnny has been deathly afraid that Wyatt would catch up with him – maybe kill him in his sleep! He read about what happened to Frank Stillwell at the Tucson train yard, filled full of holes at the hands of Wyatt Earp. He read about Curly Bill, nearly cut in half and killed from a shotgun blast from Wyatt Earp. Despite what some people may think of him, despite a tough-guy image, Johnny is really scared – and depressed about having to hide for months – and even more depressed since you showed up and we started seeing each other."

Martin simply sat looking at Mary, trying to understand the total gravity of the situation. He also thought about another strange choice of words she just used. He wasn't sure when the term "tough-guy" was coined, but it seemed that it did not belong to the lexicon of 1882.

A vision of Michael Biehn as Johnny Ringo flashed through Martin's mind again. Despite seeing the real Johnny Ringo, a pathetic shell of a man lying on a dusty street, he could not help but feel that he may be in danger – grave danger – from a psychotic mad-man who killed for sport. Martin finally found his voice, "So...if you have been living with Johnny Ringo for a while, how well do you know him? That is to say, am I in danger?"

Mary thought for a moment, then answered with a poignant question, "Do you own a gun?"

Another chill went up Martin's spine as he delivered a terse reply, "No."

Both of them came up with the same idea at the same time. Mary started, "So after lunch, shall we make a stop at.."

Martin finished her sentence with, "...Spangenberg's Gun Store? Yes, by all means!"

Martin felt better knowing he was "heeled" and had a fighting chance in the event Ringo wanted to "make a fight" with him. The law about not carrying guns in town was still in effect so Martin secured a shoulder holster, altering it so the chest strap was not needed, thereby fully concealing his .45 Colt under his ever-present sack-coat.

Over the next five days, Martin played a cat and mouse game with Johnny Ringo, trying to stay out of his way, but at the same time, trying to "tail" him and learn what he could about who might be his killer.

Ringo was never hard to find. Find some commotion, and Ringo was usually in the middle of it. He sullenly wandered from saloon to saloon, keeping his tongue "well lubricated" with whatever he could afford if he had a good hand at cards, or whatever his few friends would buy him.

Ringo's drunken behavior was manic, and grossly detestable to Martin. Ringo went from quiet and sullen, like a sleeping volcano, to a wild maniac, defiling the Earps, and most everyone else he didn't like – which was most people in Tombstone. One moment Ringo would be in a stupor and the next moment, throwing vile language about the room with no regard for women or children who might be within ear-shot.

Fortunately, Ringo went un-heeled, knowing that if he was armed, and being that obnoxiously drunk, he would certainly land behind bars. Just the same, Martin secreted his own Colt under his coat.

The more obnoxious and vile Ringo became, the more it bothered Martin... not because of the vileness in and of itself, but the more people he aggravated, the more people had a reason to, if not shoot him, at least cause him some severe harm. It seemed to Martin that his quest to find Johnny's killer was quickly becoming more complicated. It seemed that most everyone in town hated him and would not mourn at his demise.

Saturday, July 8, 1882 8:20AM

Martin had spent the prior evening trailing Ringo from saloon to saloon as he drank himself into a haze, finally finding his way back to his little white house on Safford Street and passing out. With that in mind, Martin calculated that he could walk the streets without fear, at least for a short time while Ringo slept-off his most recent drunken escapade. Martin took the opportunity to meet Mary at the Grand Hotel, and stroll down Allen Street, enjoying the early morning air and fresh feel of a new day.

In fact, Martin was so sure Ringo would be sleeping-in, and then nursing a roaring hang-over until at least noon, he didn't bother wearing his Colt. Moments later, he wished he had.

As Martin and Mary approached the Allen Street entrance to the OK Corral, they saw the last thing they expected – Johnny Ringo – astride a horse, and fully armed with twin gun belts and twin Colts. Mary grabbed Martin's arm.

Ringo looked down at the pair from his large grey stallion, steely-eyed, and intense. Martin's blood ran cold. Only seconds elapsed, but it seemed like an eternity when Ringo broke the intensity of the moment, and looked directly at Mary, "I'm leaving, and don't expect to be back."

Ringo gave only a passing, yet intense glance at Martin, then spurred his mount, and headed out of Tombstone.

Martin and Mary looked at each other, and gave a collective sigh of relief.

Wednesday July 12, 1882 8:45AM

Martin pulled-up his rented spring wagon in front of Ezra's mercantile and went in for a few supplies to sustain himself for a few days in the wild. Out for a morning walk, Mary saw Martin loading items into the wagon and hurried down the boardwalk to see what was going on, fearful that her new-found friend was departing the area.

Mary entered the store and Martin and Ezra turned to greet her. "Martin... you're not leaving us are you?"

Ezra and Martin both smiled at her. Martin said, "Only for a few days. There's something I have to do. I'll be back... I promise!"

Noticing Martin's pistol in his shoulder holster, Mary commented, "It must be a dangerous mission. I haven't seen you wearing your pistol since Johnny left town."

Martin just looked at Mary trying to digest her statement. It wasn't what she said, but how she said it. Women, especially women of 1882 didn't often use phrases like "dangerous mission." Again, her language seemed inconsistent with 1882 conventions.

Martin answered, "I'll be out... err... camping for a short time in an area called... er... Turkey Creek Canyon. You never know what you'll run into in the wild. Coyotes... Indians... bandits... You just never know. Rather to be safe than sorry! You'll be the first person I see what I get back!"

Mary inquired further, "When do you expect to be back?"

Martin answered, "A couple days... no more. I expect to be back by the end of the day on Friday."

Mary walked over and gave Martin a little kiss on his cheek. "Alright... I'll see you then! Good-bye Martin."

Then looking at Ezra, Mary said, "Good-bye Ezra!"

Martin could tell when Mary said good-bye to Ezra that she knew him in more than a passing manner... more than just a slightly eccentric man who operated a mercantile store in Tombstone... but he still could not figure out what the connection might be.

As Mary exited the store, Martin turned to Ezra. "Alright, I need some help with directions. I have enough supplies to stay out for a few days but I'm not quite sure where to go. Now, the coroner's report from July 14, 1882 stated that Ringo was found in a clump of oak trees, 20 yards north of the road leading to Morse's Mill, a quarter mile west of B.F. Smith's house in an area called Turkey Creek Canyon. A fairly good description I guess... but how do I get there?"

Ezra drew a map for Martin and explained how to get to the spot where Ringo would be later be found... dead. Handing the map to Martin, Ezra smiled, "You're very close to finding Ringo's killer. You will unravel a mystery that people have been debating for, well... as you know... over 100 years. You must be excited. It will be quite a feather in your hat as a writer... and historian!"

Martin grabbed the rest of his supplies off the counter and turned to leave saying, "Indeed it will, Ezra. Indeed it will. See you in a few days!"

Wednesday July 12, 1882 1:15PM

Martin arrived at the area described by Ezra... and the coroner's report. He parked his wagon a short distance away, and hobbled his horse. Taking only a canteen of water, Martin made his way to the clump of oak trees... and waited.

Settling into a clump of bushes, trying his best to secrete himself, Martin's mind began to race. Was this really 1882? Would he really, finally, discover Ringo's murderer? Or would he witness a drunken and depressed Ringo turn a gun on himself? Who would show up first, Ringo or his murderer... or murderers? Martin muttered to himself, "I would give anything for a digital camera right now!"

He then considered that things could go a very different way. What if Ringo showed up first? How long would he have to wait? What if the murderers discovered him hiding in the bushes after they shot Ringo? Would they shoot him to ensure that there would be no witnesses? Again Martin muttered to himself, "If this is a dream, it sure seems real!"

Martin calculated that the temperature had to be over 100 degrees as a trickle of sweat ran down his nose. Just as he was thinking about how to deal with the heat, he heard someone approach the clump of trees. A moment later, Johnny Ringo arrived, just as he had been described; light colored hat, blue shirt, vest, and pants.

Obviously, Ringo was very drunk, and very overheated. Needing to shed some weight, he dropped one gun belt on the ground, and then sat in the crook of a large oak tree. Martin thought to himself, "This is the way he was found. Maybe he'll just pull the trigger and save me some wait-time. But what about that gun belt? His gun belt was on upside down when he was found."

Martin didn't have much time for rumination. A loud sneeze caught him totally by surprise and alerted Ringo that he was not alone. Immediately Ringo was on his feet, gun at the ready, and looking wildly about.

Martin froze, his heart pounding so hard he thought it would leap out of his chest, his eyes peering through the bushes, fixated on Ringo. Despite his drunken haze, Ringo found the pair of eyes in the bushes, and pointed his gun directly at Martin. "Come out!" Ringo commanded.

Martin stood up. Their eyes met and Ringo began to speak, "Well, Mr. Hickman. You are the last person I would have expected to see again. You steal my lady friend and now what do want? Did you want to kill me... Mr. Hickman? Make sure I really didn't come back?"

Again Martin's mind was racing. How could he tell Ringo what had brought him to that time and place?

Ringo continued, "I couldn't shoot you while we were in Tombstone. That would have been too obvious! And quite frankly, you are not worth going to prison over. But this is a most fortuitous opportunity!"

Ringo raised his pistol to shoot. Martin thought to himself, "This is not supposed to happen! Could I have changed history this much? Am I going to die here in 1882... years before I am born?"

At precisely the moment he thought he had breathed his last, a noise to Ringo's left, possibly an approaching person caught Ringo's attention. Evidently, Ringo thought the approaching person posed a bigger threat, and turned his head in the direction of the rustling. Martin took advantage of the diversion, pulled his pistol, pointed it in the general direction of Johnny Ringo, cocked the hammer, and pulled the trigger; sending a .45 caliber slug through Ringo's right temple, killing him instantly.

Martin stood motionless, for what seemed like an eternity, his pistol still smoking, as he tried to grasp what had just happened.

Seconds later, a man, dressed all in black except for a white shirt and red cravat-style tie, with a long, ash-blonde regal moustache emerged from some brush. Martin turned in the man's direction, absent-mindedly, still holding his pistol in a firing position. A deep, booming voice called out, "I'm a friend! Don't fire!"

As the man approached, Martin could tell from his demeanor that this man did not mean him any harm. Martin holstered his pistol.

As they came face to face, the man in black spoke, "I've been tracking Ringo since yesterday... from Galeyville. On one hand, I was hoping he would drink himself to death and save me a bullet. On the other hand, I wanted him to know that it was me that was sending him to his maker; a reckoning for the death of one brother, and the attempted assassination of another. I guess you did me a favor!"

Martin thought for a moment... "the death of one brother and the attempted assassination of another...". In astonishment he blurted out, Why you're..."

The man finished Martin's sentence, "...Wyatt Earp. Yes indeed."

The two men looked at each other for a moment, each man thinking about what should happen next. Then Wyatt asked Martin for his pistol, trading it with the pistol that Ringo had just held on him. "Here" said Wyatt. "Consider this a prize!"

Wyatt continued, "I don't know if anyone saw you head out this way. If they did, Ringo's shooting could be traced to you and you could be charged with murder. Or perhaps it was self defense. Either way, it could be messy legally speaking. But listen friend, ridding the country of a miscreant like Johnny Ringo is not something anyone should hang for! Go back to Tombstone. Act like nothing has happened. I'll fix things up here. Don't worry about it."

Overwhelmed with the events of the past 5 minutes, worried that he could be charged with a murder, but trusting that Wyatt would be a friend, Martin simply turned and made his way back to Tombstone.

Wednesday July 12, 1882 5:45PM

Arriving in Tombstone, Martin checked his wagon and horse at the OK Corral, then headed straight for the Grand Hotel, and Mary's room. He wasn't sure what he was going to tell her, or how he was going to tell her. Would she believe him? He could hardly believe the day's events... and he was part of it all.

Martin knocked politely on the door to Mary's room. Mary opened the door smiling as always. But her smile quickly turned sour as she saw the angst on Martin's face. She invited him in saying "You're back early!"

Trying to find the words he would use, Martin paced back and forth across the room a few times, then placed both hands on a wash stand to support himself and stared downward. The washstand contained a pitcher of water, a bowl, some loose coins and a few personal items of Mary's. Looking down at the wash bowl Martin finally blurted out, "You're not going to believe what happened today! I shot a man... murdered him!"

As he tried to refocus himself after blurting out his news, it occurred to him that the coins he was staring at seemed out of context with 1882. One would expect to see $5 gold pieces. What he saw were pennies, nickels and dimes, and quarters – more modern coins. He picked up a quarter that looked particularly shiny and new and looked at the date – 1945. Now he was more confused than ever.

As he turned to face Mary, she replied to his statement, "If I were to guess who that man was, I would say it was Johnny!"

Martin turned white as a boiled bed sheet and his jaw dropped. "But... how... how did you know.... I mean I...?"

Before Mary could conjure-up the words to explain herself to Martin, he turned and retrieved the shiny 1945 quarter from the wash stand. Holding it between is thumb and forefinger, he held it up for Mary to see saying, "And what about this, Mary? This coin says 1945 – 1945! That's 63 years into the future!"

Mary smiled a wryly, "Martin Hickman, I'm sure you know a lot about the future... in fact... I bet you know a whole lot more than I do!"

Martin wasn't sure what Mary might know, or not know about him and his situation and so decided to simply remain quiet and just let Mary do some more talking.

She continued, "My grandfather, John P. Clum, lived in Tombstone from early 1880 to the late fall of 1882. Before he died in 1932, he used to tell me stories of Tombstone, the people, the events, the gunfights and the gunfighters. He also told me about a man who seemed to know everything and everybody surrounding Tombstone – a man who had a way of 'making things happen' was how my grandfather described it. That man was Ezra T. Thornton. He said if I ever wanted to know anything about Tombstone or its people, to look-up Ezra. Well, probably because of my grandfather and his stories, I developed a real love of the old west and decided to write about the character that intrigued me the most."

Martin butted in, "That had to be Johnny Ringo!"

Mary replied, "Exactly. I was intrigued by the mystery of his death, but more than that, I really wanted to know what he was like as a man. From reading the many stories that have circulated throughout the years about Tombstone's characters, Johnny's seemed to be the most maligned. So I thought, I would find the truth about Johnny, and write about it. You see Martin, like I told you, I truly am a writer. Or to be more precise, I am, or was, a war correspondent for the *Washington Star*. Once the war, WWII was over, and I had some free time, and with travel restrictions lifted and fuel more plentiful, I thought I would come to Tombstone to start my research. I stopped in at Ezra's store, not really expecting him to be there after all this time, but there he was!"

Martin could not believe his ears. "So... let me see if I understand this. You are here from 1945?"

Mary threw up her arms indicating a frustration, "Exactly! Strange as it may seem! I can't understand it either. Anyway, I told Ezra what I wanted to do. He told me if I really wanted to get to know Johnny, I should have a more intimate relationship with him... be his girlfriend. I laughed at that ridiculous remark. Ezra smiled, handed me a cold bottle of sarsaparilla, and we talked about it a little more. Then he invited me to walk out the back door of his store... and when I did... it was 1882. He walked me over to Johnny's house, introduced me, and before I knew it... I was renting a room from Johnny Ringo!"

Martin slumped into a chair trying to fathom what Mary was telling him.

Mary continued, "I knew the date Johnny was found dead. I just wasn't sure precisely when, during that day, that he died. When you told me you were headed out to Turkey Creek Canyon, the place where Johnny was found, I then knew precisely how he was to die... and that you would be his killer!"

Martin's stomach knotted-up.

"But don't worry, Martin" replied Mary. "Pretty soon, as you know, a nice man by the name of John Yoast will come through Tombstone and tell everyone how he found Johnny in that clump of trees... and that will be story we will all live with!"

"But what about the other oddities about Johnny's death?" asked Martin? "What about the fact the one gun belt was on upside down... his boots were off...and strips of his undershirt were wrapped around his feet! What about that?"

Mary shrugged, "My guess is those were all what you might call 'red herrings', diversions concocted by Wyatt Earp to purposely throw people off."

Now wide-eyed at the mention of Wyatt Earp, Martin said, "You know Wyatt was there too?"

Mary looked down for a moment, calculating her words, and then replied, "After you left for Turkey Creek, I went back to Ezra's store to ask him if you were to be Johnny's killer. He replied that both you and Wyatt were headed for a meeting with Johnny – a meeting with destiny - and that ultimately, one of you would be Johnny's killer. He just wasn't sure which one of you it would be. He also explained that you too are a writer from the future... from 2008... also looking for a truth to write about – the truth about Johnny Ringo's death! But don't worry, your secret is safe with me. Who in the 1940's would believe I have been keeping company with somebody from 2008... in 1882!"

Martin finally smiled, "Well... I guess we both got what we came for. But what do we do now? What brought us to this time and place and circumstance no longer exists. With Johnny gone... what will happen next?"

Looking at each other, Mary and Martin proclaimed in unison, "Ezra Thornton!"

Martin and Mary hurried out onto Allen Street, headed for Ezra's store. What they found when they exited the front door of the hotel amazed them both. The dirt in the street had been replaced with pavement. The horses and carriages had been replaced with 1930's-era cars. The clothing on the people in the streets, including Mary's new wardrobe said "mid-1940's!"

But Martin's clothing had not changed – he was still dressed in his 1880's-era business suit, white shirt, derby hat, and cravat tie. They both stopped for one incredulous moment to observe each other. Mary commented, "Everyone probably thinks you are a reenactor!"

Looking out on Allen Street and seeing a few people strolling up and down the street in 1880's wear, Martin didn't feel so out of place and the two hurried down Allen Street to Ezra's store. As they reached the intersection of Fifth and Allen Streets they noticed two reenactors coming towards them, one dressed in a 1880's style business suit similar to Martin's, and the other dressed all in black with a regal moustache and searing blue eyes. As they approached, another reenactor called out to the two, "Hello Mayor Clum! Hello Wyatt!" As Mary and Martin passed the two men, they simultaneously winked at the couple. Mary looked at Martin and without saying a word, the same thought passed between them, "Were those men reenactors.. or...?"

Moments later, they arrived at Ezra's front door, and Mary walked a few extra steps to look around the corner onto Sixth Street. Sure enough – her Ford was still there on Sixth Street – right where she left it parked. She stepped back to the front door where Martin was waiting. Just then, Ezra appeared at the door.

"Well" he started. "It would appear that you both got what you came for!"

"And more!" Mary replied looking at Martin.

Ezra smiled broadly at Mary. "You're car and typewriter awaits you! Have a safe trip back to Washington, D.C.!"

Mary planted a little kiss on Martin's cheek, and without a further word she turned, and was gone.

Ezra then turned his attention to Martin. "Enjoy your evening here in 1946, Mr. Hickman. Your room is still your room at the San Jose House. Sleep well... you have a busy day tomorrow!"

Martin exclaimed, "A busy day? Doing what?"

Ezra laughed, "Why have you forgotten? You have a book signing tomorrow at the Tombstone Territorial Book Store!"

Saturday, June 21, 2008 12:05PM Tombstone AZ

Business was brisk at the Tombstone Territorial Book Store... as it was most Saturdays' during the summer tourist season. Author Martin Hickman, dressed in his finest 1880's wear was smiling and signing books, and enjoying himself talking to the patrons.

Ezra Thornton stepped into the store, greeted store-owner Lilly Putnam, gave her a wink, then stepped over to the table where Martin sat. Picking up one of the books from the table in front of Martin, Ezra adjusted his glasses on his nose and read the book's title aloud, "*The Death of Johnny Ringo!*"

Ezra then looked about, and noticed a small crowd starting to gather. Seeing the growing audience, Ezra addressed Martin, "The death of Johnny Ringo is quite a controversy, Mr. Hickman – and has been since he died in 1882. Does your book dispel any of the rumors or controversy surrounding that unfortunate incident? Have you finally discovered who, in fact, killed Johnny Ringo? Or was it suicide? Do you reveal how that poor young man died?"

Martin smiled proudly; "Well Mr. Thornton, there are many different theories as to how Ringo died. Are you familiar with them?"

The Real Story Behind "The Death of Johnny Ringo"

In the annals of the old west, perhaps no other death was more contested at the time, and continues to be controversial today, than that of John Peters Ringo.

Johnny Ringo was born May 3, 1850 in the town of Washington,

Indiana, the son of Martin and Mary Peters Ringo. Four years later, Johnny would welcome his only brother, Martin, into the world, and later, three sisters.

The family would move to Missouri and later to San Jose, California. Violence would visit the Ringo family on their way out west when the younger Martin shot himself with his own shotgun in a horrible accident.

Johnny Ringo stayed in San Jose, working as a farmer (hardly the image we have today) until around 1870 or 1871. Eventually he found his way to Texas where, on Christmas day, 1874, he was arrested for firing his gun into the air. On April 14, 1875, he was arrested for the infraction, and then released on bond.

Ringo left Texas, and headed, with many others, to Arizona Territory and the new, rich, silver strike at Tombstone. There he blended-in with the rowdier bunch and on December 9, 1879 got into an argument with Louis Hancock over whether Louis would drink whisky or beer. Ringo liked whisky; Hancock liked beer. Apparently, Ringo was buying, took offense at Hancock's lack of bar-room decorum, and shot him, resulting in an arrest. Ringo made bond and was released.

Johnny Ringo pops up in various other places during this period including a land purchase along with Ike Clanton in Silver City, New Mexico. He also served as an election judge in San Simon, AZ.

In the early summer of 1881, Ringo traveled to Texas where he was arrested for disturbing the peace by Marshal Ben Thompson, and was fined $25 plus costs. By August, Ringo was back in Arizona Territory, losing big at a card game in Galeyville. Unable to borrow funds to continue his game, Ringo found a compatriot and the two men held-up the game, absconding with $500. In November, Deputy Cochise County Sheriff Billy Breakenridge went to Galeyville to retrieve Ringo, and make him answer to charges.

On December 1, 1881 he was brought before Judge Stillwell and pleaded not guilty. Since no witnesses showed up to testify against him, the case was continued.

It was during this time that rumors began to spread that Ringo was involved in a stage hold-up and Ringo held Wyatt Earp and Doc Holliday responsible. An argument ensued nearly resulting in a shooting. All three were arrested. Wyatt's charges were dismissed as he was a US Marshal at the time and was able to legally carry firearms. Ringo and Holliday were fined $30 each in Judge Wallace's court, thereby ending the legal affray, but not the growing hatred Ringo had for the so-called "Earp faction" in Tombstone.

January, 1882 found Ringo in jail again, when his bond was revoked for the Galeyville holdup. While in jail, he heard that the

Earp posse planned to ride to Charleston to arrest Ike Clanton. In an effort to help his compatriot, Ringo asked his lawyer, Briggs Goodrich to arrange bond to get him out of jail to go help Ike Clanton. Goodrich told Sheriff Johnny Behan that bail had been arranged. Before confirming the transaction, Behan let Ringo out of jail. Ringo was now officially an escaped prisoner and Earp brother James quickly wrote out an affidavit for him calling for his re-incarceration. Another posse was quickly formed and headed towards Charleston looking for Ringo... with Ringo's lawyer in close pursuit. Ringo was herded back to Tombstone and was again arraigned for the Galeyville incident. On January 31st, he pled not guilty and was released on $3,000 bond. At a February 2nd hearing, witnesses again failed to show.

A few weeks later in mid-March, Morgan Earp was assassinated as he played pool in Campbell and Hatch's Saloon. Many considered Ringo a principal in the shooting. However, a statement from Ringo's lawyer noted specifically that Ringo no longer wanted any part of the Earp/Clanton feud and that he was "going to look after himself, and anybody else can do the same..." Despite those words, Ringo rode for several days with the Behan posse out looking for the Earps, wanted for the killing of Frank Stillwell in Tucson in retaliation for Morgan's murder.

Ringo returned to Tombstone to again answer to charges in the Galeyville incident. Again, no witnesses could be found to testify against him. Eventually, the charges were dropped and his bond returned... and Johnny Ringo left Tombstone towards the end of May, ironically, with no legal clouds over his head!

What happened to Johnny Ringo between the end of May and beginning of July is unknown. However, he returned to Tombstone on July 2, 1882 in a sullen state, and began drinking heavily. On July 8th he left Tombstone for the last time.

The next evening, Ringo was spotted in Galeyville, still hitting the liquor quite hard... and feeling very depressed. On July 11th, he left town and on July 14th teamster John Yoast found Ringo in a sitting position in the crook of a large tree, dead of a single gunshot wound to the head. Yoast recognized Ringo from his days in Texas and called several men to the scene.

In Ringo's right hand was a .45 Colt. A bullet had passed through his right temple and exited out the top of his head. One must wonder how a person could fire a large caliber pistol into their head, and continue to clench the weapon in their hand in death.

But that was not the only strange thing about Ringo's death.

He was found with his boots off and torn bits of his shirt wrapped around his feet. Apparently, he had walked a short distance in that fashion. Also, one of his cartridge belts was on upside down. There was also a small cut on his scalp with a small piece of his hair gone. His horse was not at the scene but found later, still saddled.

This all added up to a number of controversies.

The coroner's jury noted that Ringo's pistol, a 6-shooter, held 5 cartridges. During that time (and even today) it was common to carry five cartridges in a single-action revolver allowing the hammer to rest on the empty chamber, thereby preventing an accidental discharge should the hammer be jolted or the gun dropped. But, it was also common to carry a full charge of ammo if the gun's owner suspected trouble and thus the need for the extra firepower. However, it would appear that Ringo had been carrying six, and had one spent shell. Otherwise, the coroner's jury would not have even considered suicide.

There is also speculation that Ringo's death could have been something other than suicide since there was no mention of gunpowder burns on his face. However, any powder burns may have been disguised as the body may have turned black in the July heat. It is estimated that Ringo's lifeless body sat in the broiling sun of an Arizona summer for almost 24 hours before he was found.

And then, despite what the coroner's jury found, there is still the controversy of suicide or murder. In the old west, many men carried guns, and weren't afraid to use them to settle a score – once and for all.

One theory says Buckskin Frank Leslie shot Ringo. It was rumored that Leslie had been seen looking for Ringo the day before. Leslie supposedly told a guard at the Yuma Territorial prison (where he was serving time for killing his wife) that he had killed Ringo. One theory says that's true, but it is more likely that he claimed the killing for whatever notoriety it may have brought.

Some think Wyatt Earp shot Ringo. This may have been perpetrated by Arizona Historian Frank Lockwood when he noted that Wyatt had told him that he shot Ringo although this is widely disputed. This theory was furthered by Earp historian John Gilchriese who noted that Wyatt "could have" shot Ringo by making a quick trip to Arizona over the course of about 6 days. This theory was echoed by another Earp researcher, Glenn Boyer who claimed to have heard it directly from Wyatt's wife Josephine Marcus Earp. However, much of Boyer's work has been discredited as at least partly if not largely fictional.

Some think an Earp confidant named Lou Cooley could have shot Ringo when he rode with an Earp posse, hunting down cow-boy members in the wake of Morgan's assassination.

An even more bizarre idea has infamous gambler Michael O'Rourke aka Johnny-Behind-The-Deuce shooting Ringo although a motive is sorely lacking.

One theory widely promoted by the movie *Tombstone* is that Doc Holliday killed Ringo. It made a terrific movie scene, but Holliday was in Colorado at the time and could not possibly have traveled that far in the short amount of time he had to do the deed.

It is the general consensus among contemporary historians that John Peters Ringo was despondent over something, although no one knows what, and simply killed himself.

What is your theory?

As for locations and people used in the story...

Ezra' mercantile store was once the site of McKean and Knight general store. It is presently (in 2010) the Silver Nugget Bed and Breakfast.

The San Jose House still exists on Fremont Street, and is one of the oldest hotels in Tombstone.

Hoefler's General Store was located across Fifth Street from the San Jose House around 1882.

In 2010, a large, dirt parking lot existed at the corner of Fifth and Fremont for the Adobe Lodge Hotel. In 1882, this area was occupied by several low, wood-frame buildings housing several stores and small shops. On the west side of Fifth Street between Fremont and Allen Streets was a grocery store, assay office, jeweler, barber, and the Lenoire Funiture Store.

On the east side of Fifth Street between Fremont and Allen was the Tombstone Post Office and Spangenberg's Gun Store. At some point Spangenberg's Gun Store moved to Fourth Street and survived as Spangenberg's until 2008.

George Parsons indeed lived in Tombstone. He is best known today as an inveterate diarist whose long-kept record of every-day life in Tombstone has for years served as a valuable source of information for historians and authors.

Marjorie "Midge" Clum Parker was a granddaughter to former Tombstone Mayor John P. Clum. She worked for the *Washington Star* as a reporter during WWII. John Clum's son, Woodworth (Marjorie's father) was, at one time, the City Editor for the *Star*.

Chapter 13: TOO TOUGH TO DIE

"What I need from everyone here, and as many people as you can muster together, is the most important thing of all – the strong belief that Tombstone is truly the town too tough to die. If you believe in that mantra, we can make this happen. Together we can save Tombstone!"

Ezra T. Thornton October 27, 2029

Saturday June 1, 2028, 4:15PM

"Headed over to the committee meeting, Ezra?"

Ezra Thornton was just locking the door to secure his mercantile store for the day. Dressed, as always in his finest frock coat, red brocade vest and top-hat, Ezra looked as elegant and regal as ever – a stark contrast to the growing dinginess and decay of Tombstone. The Arizona sun was still shining bright, warm and inviting along Tombstone's Allen Street - but not inviting enough to draw the tourists of past years.

Several shop owners stood in the doorway of their stores looking forlornly at the almost empty street. A few reenactors stood on street corners, has they had for years, hawking local restaurants but their "barking" simply drifted off with the summer breeze down Allen Street and into the desert.

Ezra turned around to see Mayor Fuller standing right behind him. Tim Fuller, a middle-aged man of slight build and broad smile had lived in Tombstone the better part of his life – and loved it. He had written a several best-selling books about Tombstone and was now known, not only as the town's mayor, but as the resident historian. Despite recent developments in the town, Tim always wore a smile, and was the town's biggest promoter – not unlike the town's first elected mayor, John Clum. As a town promoter, Mayor, and local merchant; operating the local bookstore for several years, Tim usually went about his daily routine dressed in 1880's-style clothing.

287

This day found Tim in a 1880's-style black suit and black brocade vest, black cravat tie, and a tall derby.

Ezra finished locking the door, then turned about and seeing the grinning mayor, matched him smile for smile. "Why yes – that is exactly where I'm headed. I haven't had a customer in the past two hours anyhow!"

The two men turned and walked west on Allen Street one block to Fifth Street and entered the Crystal Palace Saloon.

Fewer patrons over the past few years had forced Crystal Palace management to replace many of the tables with video games which now stood along the east-facing wall – a space once occupied by faro games and roulette wheels. As their eyes adjusted from the bright sunlight of Allen Street to the dim light of the saloon, Ezra and Tim could make out two locals nursing beers at the bar, and several men seated at a table at the far-end of the room. Other than that, the saloon was empty.

One of the men at the table motioned to them. "Tim! Ezra! You're just in time!"

Tim and Ezra joined the three other men at the table. One, Ben Turnbull was the head of the local historical society, another, Pat Kelton was the president of the Chamber of Commerce and the third man, Roger Patterson was a local realtor. As Tim and Ezra seated themselves Pat pronounced, "The 99th annual Helldorado committee will now come to order!" To make the announcement official, he pounded his empty beer mug on the table, as if it were a gavel.

Roger, the real estate man opened the conversation, "Are we sure we really want to do this? Will anyone even come to Helldorado this year? Is it really worth all the effort? As you gentlemen know only too well, the last few years have been less than stellar!"

Ezra chimed in, "But gentlemen, gentlemen... this is Tombstone and October is coming. We have to have a Helldorado celebration. Tradition dictates it and history commands it. Where would we be without a Helldorado celebration in October?"

The men stopped for a moment and just looked at each other. Then, Ben Turnbull broke the ice with, "Ezra's got a point. It was the Helldorado celebration that revived the town way back in 1929. The same celebration can revive it again!"

Roger retorted, "Ben... that was a different time and different circumstances. Back then, everybody threw-in together. The whole town pitched in – merchants, residents, reenactor groups – everyone. Today, many of the businesses are boarded up thanks to Clark-Gray and Company. And the ones that are open are as dingy and pathetic as can be – many of them simply selling tee shirts, mugs and the like. Hell, we don't even have a decent restaurant any more. Where will people eat? I tell you this place is in worse shape than in 1929!"

Pat finally spoke up, "Roger is right... much as I hate to admit it seeing that I am the president of the Chamber of Commerce. Clark-Gray and Company has been buying up all these old places and boarding them up. Why? I don't know. They are not talking. And the merchants have been arguing for the last 50 years about whether the town should return to its roots and be more historically correct, or become more commercial. Well... today, thanks to Clark-Gray and Company, it's neither... and it looks like everyone lost."

Pat's face went from animated to sullen as he turned to Mayor Fuller and almost whispered, "Tell them Mr. Mayor."

All eyes turned to the Mayor, his eyes fairly twinkling a moment ago turned suddenly dark. "Yesterday I received word that Tombstone lost its historical status. It seems Tombstone has developed into two extremes, neither one qualifying it for historical status. Either the building is dilapidated and falling down with windows and doors boarded up, or the owner has modernized the store front to attract people. Between the modernization and the dilapidation, the National Historical Preservation Commission has taken us off their list. Gentlemen, Tombstone has become just another collection of tee-shirt shops to which few people come."

Roger took a sip of his beer and added, "Not that I want to make matters any worse, but it looks like the sale of the Bird Cage will go through any day now. Before long, Clark-Gray will own one of the most recognizable icons in Tombstone – and probably board it up like they have everything else they have bought!"

The men stopped and looked at each other again in a long pause, each taking a sip of their beer – as if the sudsy brew enhanced their capacity to find a silver lining in the otherwise dismal future of Tombstone.

Ezra stood up and became very animated, "So the score is historians zero, merchants, soon to be zero – unless we can find a way to revive the glory that was once Tombstone, perhaps bring some of those reenactor groups back here - maybe even revive a group of locals for re-enactments. This calls for some drastic action. I say we give it all we've got. Invite the world, put on a show! Tombstone is too tough to die! Let it not be known that the greatest old-west town in history went out with a whimper – at least, not on our watch! And Tim... not on your watch!"

Based on Ezra's rousing words, Tim took the liberty to stand and raise his half-empty mug in a toast, "Then let's give it a shot. Let's throw a celebration! Let's do what we can with what we've got. We'll promote the event starting today. People will come, you'll see. It'll be great once again!"

The other men raised their mugs in unison and all smiled, all the while wondering in the back of their minds how they were going to make it happen. With half the town's buildings boarded up, the existing shops and stores just barely holding on, and the city in general disrepair, nobody wanted to come any more.

Those people looking for the history of the town could only see dinginess and despair. Those that came for the commercialism saw few shops and dirty, unkempt streets where seldom did anyone smile. Few tourists showed up and most of the reenactor groups had turned their attention to other venues.

Even the afternoon gunfight re-enactments, an entertainment staple for almost 100 years had been reduced to one show a day – if the locals could muster enough reenactors and throw a skit together.

Despite all odds, the Committee threw a party in October – the 99th annual Helldorado celebration - but few people attended. Despite newspaper and television ads, internet advertising, and a rigorous grass-roots effort among fellow historians, the event was a monumental flop. All agreed it looked like the end of the trail for Helldorado, and more importantly for the town. It looked like apathy, town politics and an insidious outside force, namely the Clark-Gray Holding Company, had finally killed what the loss of silver could not. From all appearances, Tombstone was lying in its deathbed, waiting for just a few more merchants to close... or their buildings to be purchased by Clark-Gray to allow the holding company to pull the final sheet over Tombstone's head.

One year later... Saturday June 2, 2029, 4:30PM

"Headed over to the Helldorado committee meeting, Ezra?"

Ezra Thornton was just locking the door to secure his mercantile store for the day. Turning, he saw former Mayor Tim Fuller, smiling as usual in his 1880's-style clothing – despite the broiling Arizona sun. Joining Fuller was the current mayor; Arthur Rawlins dressed in a casual golf-style shirt, khaki pants, and tennis shoes.

Ezra looked directly at Fuller and smiled, "I'm having a deja-vu, Tim. It seems we've done this before!'

Tim returned the smile, "Indeed we have... and with disastrous results I might add – despite all our efforts! Last year's Helldorado was a real bust if ever there was one!"

Mayor Rawlins shook hands with Ezra, "Good to see you Ezra. And with your help, and the help of the Helldorado Committee and the merchants and residents, this year will be different, gentlemen. This is the 100th anniversary of the Helldorado event, and the 150th anniversary of the founding of Tombstone. This is going to be big -

really big! We'll have people here from all over the world coming to Tombstone. You'll see!"

Ezra looked out across Allen Street to the Bird Cage Theater, an icon that had represented Tombstone since December, 1881, now decaying and boarded up as it had been for many years around the turn of the twentieth century.

Looking further down the block, few stores remained, most of the buildings being vacant, some boarded up, some simply abandoned – a few had broken windows with sharp shards of glass remaining in the frame. The dirt covering Allen Street's asphalt spread 20 years prior had lost whatever properties it might have had to retard the propagation of dust, and small "dust twisters" moved about Allen Street. "Not unlike 150 years ago" thought Ezra.

Ezra looked at the mayor, "What are they going to come to Mr. Mayor? And even if they do come, how will we take care of them? The only gas station we had closed a few months ago, we are down to one restaurant and it's only really a coffee shop at that. We are down to one real motel and a couple of bed and breakfast places. I sure hope you have a plan!"

"I do indeed sir!' beamed the Mayor.

Ezra looked at Tim Fuller quizzically saying, "Do you know what the heck he's talking about? All I see here is desolation and a town few people would want to visit. The history is gone, the commercialism is gone... and we should all be gone!"

Ezra and Tim looked at the Mayor again, their countenances seeking an answer. But Mayor Rawlins could only smile wider and reply, "Gentlemen, the 100th annual Helldorado Committee meeting awaits us!"

The three men walked down Allen Street, hot, dusty, and almost devoid of tourists. Two or three reenactors walking aimlessly about, properly dressed and "heeled" but seemingly out of place and forlorn.

Walking past the now-shuttered Crystal Palace Saloon, the site of so many Helldorado Committee meetings of years past, the three entered the Grand Saloon, formerly the Grand Hotel during Tombstone's hey-days, and for the past 50 years, a favorite "watering hole" for locals and visitors.

The three joined other committee members already seated at a table just inside the door, and sipping on cold beers. Mayor Rawlins stood while waiting for Ezra and Tim to seat themselves. Once seated, Rawlins began to speak, "Gentlemen, as the head of the 2029 Helldorado Committee, I want to start by saying that this will be the biggest, flashiest, most momentous Helldorado celebration ever! No expense will be spared! I have already arranged to have a catering company set up two large tents, one on each end of Allen Street so people will have a place to eat. I have arranged special deals in area motels and hotels in Benson, Sierra Vista and Bisbee for both tourists and reenactors so everyone who wants to stay for a few days will be able to. The Grand Saloon will have a beer garden on the vacant lot next to Schieffelin Hall. The Crystal Palace and Bird Cage will again be opened! The Epitaph office will again be open and I've arranged for a printer in Bisbee to create a paper each day of the event that looks like the 1880 original.

The committee looked incredulously at Mayor Rawlins; amazed not only at what he was saying, but that apparently, he had been doing some work of his own without the committee.

Ezra spoke first and looking directly at the standing Mayor asked, "And just whose money are you not going to spare? As I recall, we are still in debt from last year's event!"

"And how are you going to get the Clark-Gray Company to open the Bird Cage and Crystal Palace? Both have been boarded and closed since Clark-Gray took them over several months ago!" said Tim.

Mayor Rawlins smiled and held up his hands to calm the group. "Gentlemen, I have been working with the Clark-Gray Company for weeks now and they have agreed to pay all expenses for this year's event. And... they will re-open the Bird Cage and the Crystal Palace. They will take care of all the advertising, will secure the entertainment; and take care of all planning and logistics. All we need to do is direct them."

After a long pause, Ezra again spoke; "And why the change of heart from Clark-Gray? They have effectively been killing Tombstone for several years now. Why, in another year or two they will own everything, and then they can do what they want with it – as a single entity! Just think of the ramifications of owning a whole city – and we let them do it! What are they planning, Rawlins? Nobody goes to this much trouble of buying all the property in the city, essentially shutting the city down, and then throw a party for it. I just don't get it!"

Rawlins again put up both hands to calm the growing tension at the table saying, "Gentlemen, I cannot divulge all yet, but come October, we will see the rebirth of Tombstone. Trust me on this. That's all I can say for now. So let's get started organizing the committees shall we?"

The committee set to work organizing what would be the biggest Helldorado celebration the city had ever seen. Mayor Rawlins presented the committee with a checkbook, the balance of which was more money than they had spent on Helldorado in the past 5 years combined. And the first check was gone, Mayor Rawlins having paid the prior year's debts in a show of good faith that Clark-Gray had turned about 180 degrees and was now ready to work with Tombstone, rather than try to crush it out.

The committee agreed it was refreshing to work with a sizeable budget; but were leery of Rawlins' association with the monolithic real estate holding company who had been methodically killing the town.

Saturday October 26, 2029   10:00AM

After months of work, Mayor Rawlins' dream had become a reality. Despite many stores and buildings remaining shuttered, those that were open sported red, white and blue bunting across the front of their store as if it were the Fourth of July! American flags and Arizona state flags were everywhere. As in the days during the early 1990's when reenactor groups flourished on the heels of the movie *Tombstone*, groups from California, New Mexico and Nevada assembled on Allen Street.

The massive ad budget bequeathed by Clark-Gray secmingly did the trick! Throngs of tourists lined Allen Street for the start of the grand parade marking the beginning of the day's festivities. As promised, two large, white tents marked either end of Allen Street doling out breakfast, lunch and dinner to visitors and locals.

The air was cool but the bright Arizona sun would soon make things quite temperate and comfortable. Parents holding toddlers with balloons milled about. Mounted Tombstone police moved slowly down Allen Street keeping an eye on everything.

On the corner of Fourth and Allen Streets, the very nerve center of the town, a raised platform had been erected. A podium, draped in red-white and blue bunting had been placed upon it.

Ezra had been nominated to approach the podium first and introduce the mayor who would then introduce a representative from the Clark-Gray Company. Ezra anticipated introducing the Mayor who would say a few words, then introduce Michael Gray who would have an equally short speech and then the signal would be given for the parade to start from the east end of Allen Street. Little did he know that the next few moments would take his breath away.

Ezra sat in a folding chair on the platform along with the Helldorado Committee, representatives of the Chamber of Commerce, members of the City Council, and several other dignitaries. Sensing that this would be a momentous occasion, tourists, locals and especially those who were "history conscious" approached the platform to hear the speeches, amplification being secured through only two loud speakers.

At precisely 10AM, Ezra approached the podium, greeted the assemblage, and introduced several key people on the platform. He then introduced Mayor Rawlins who stepped to the podium, and began to speak:

City Council members, Helldorado Committee members, distinguished guests, residents, visitors and friends. Today, is a red-letter day in the annals of Tombstone, Arizona. Not only does today mark the 100th anniversary of this most venerable celebration we call Helldorado, and the 150th anniversary of the founding of our great city. Today will go down in history as the day Tombstone was reborn – the day Tombstone rose from the ashes and became revitalized with new businesses, new residents, and a new way of doing business. It will be cleaner, safer and bigger. It will have an economy where everyone can prosper. It will become a city that people will want to move to – not away from.

The crowd was stunned! From the people on the elevated platform to the tourist at the farthest reaches of the crowd, everyone stood spell-bound. All felt as if this was the moment just before a falling bomb makes contact with terra-firma.

Mayor Rawlins continued:

As all locals know, for several years now the Clark-Gray Company has been purchasing land and buildings in and around Tombstone. Some of you have cursed them for destroying our town. But you will see in a moment the benevolence of the Clark-Gray Company. For the past few months, I have been working with the Clark-Gray Company to help facilitate the plan Mr. Michael Gray will now reveal. Ladies and gentlemen, it gives me great pleasure to introduce the man who will come to be known as Tombstone's biggest benefactor, Mr. Michael Gray!

Everyone applauded as Michael Gray took the podium and adjusted the microphone.

Ezra looked out over the crowd and it was easy to tell who was who. The visitors and tourists applauded and smiled politely, having a sense that they were about to be part of something important, but not sure of the ramifications of what Mr. Gray was about to announce.

The locals stood applauding, but with a most concerned look on their faces. They knew that Tombstone had been sliding downhill for a long time, and knew only too well that the town needed a shot in the arm, but was not sure if the shot would be painful or not.

The historians and reenactors stood applauding but had a slightly different look on their faces. They wondered if Tombstone would remain – Tombstone. Would the city still have historical significance, despite the fact that the town had long since been removed from the Historical Registry?

Dressed in a conservative business suit, his neatly combed hair slightly rustling in the morning breeze, Mr. Michael Gray of the Clark -Gray Company cleared his throat, adjusted the microphone one more time, and began to speak as visitors and reporters alike raised their cameras to catch his image:

Mayor Rawlins, City Council members, Helldorado Committee members, distinguished guests, residents, visitors and friends. Today, is indeed a red-letter day in the annals of Tombstone, Arizona. Today will mark the rebirth of Tombstone! For so many years, Tombstone's economy has been faltering. First, the silver ran out, then the tourist trade ran out, and lately the residents have been running out. Today's full-time residents only number about 500! Much of the city's buildings were erected 150 years ago. Wood and adobe construction can only last so long before it becomes unsafe and a hazard. With a faltering economy and decaying buildings, jobs are scarce and do not pay well. Given the current situation, there is no reason to come to Tombstone or live in Tombstone. There are those that say the 'Town Too Tough To Die' is gasping it's last breath and will soon take it's place along with it's former residents on Boot Hill. I see things differently! I see commerce, new jobs, new industries and revitalization not only of Tombstone, but of the entire southeastern corner of Cochise County. Within the next few months the entire historic district will be leveled including both sides of Allen Street, Toughnut Street, and Fremont Street from First Street to Sixth!

Ezra leapt to his feet! What Gray was proposing was to level the entire historical district of the town, including his store – which he still owned and would never sell! How did Gray propose to level a building he didn't own?

A distinct buzzing could be heard coming from the crowd. Some people looked happy, some looked saddened, some, like Ezra, were quite angry.

Gray waited a moment for what he had just said to sink-in and the buzzing to subside. Then he continued.

Allen Street will be completely rebuilt with safe, modern construction. Stores, shops and restaurants, fresh and new will line the street. These businesses will serve a new community of retirees who will live in three-story condominiums, which will line Toughnut and Fremont Streets. Eventually, Tombstone will have 10 to 15 thousand new residents. But the new residents will need more than a few shops and stores. Within a year of the start of construction, retail giant Pick-N-Pay will have a presence in Tombstone followed by grocery retailer Champaign's Super Mart. Of course, with retirees, medical care will be required. A new, state-of-the art hospital will be erected as well as doctor's offices, an emergency clinic and a convalescent home. Everything a retiree needs will be close by. And... to entice people to come here, and seeing they are already aged, and may be repelled by the name Tombstone, we have already applied to the state to change the name of the town to Schieffelinville, after Tombstone's founder. Jobs, commerce, prosperity... it will all be here... in Schieffelinville!

At this point Michael Gray paused, expecting a rousing ovation. A few applauded. Ezra scowled. And a few angry people began to shout. After a few seconds, the angry shouting became the predominant sound coming from the crowd. "What about Tombstone's history? What about the Bird Cage? What will become of these historic icons? You can't destroy them!"

Gray was stunned. He was expecting questions about the historical sites, which he had not yet addressed; but was not expecting the virulent manner in which many reacted. The din grew louder. Shouts of "Hang him! Hang him" began to resound from across the street.

Ezra stepped to the podium and raised his hands to try and calm the crowd. Grabbing the microphone, Ezra exercised his best chivalry, "Ladies and gentlemen... please calm down. Listen to what Mr. Gray has to say. I'm sure he has made some sort of provision for Tombstone's history...". Ezra turned back to the harried speaker who had taken a few steps back, "... haven't you Mr. Gray?"

Gray again took the microphone as the crowd started to calm down somewhat.

Too Tough to Die

Indeed, Mr. Thornton, we have made provision to preserve Tombstone's history in a very unique way. As we build Schieffelinville, we will build Tombstone Territory, a recreation of the original town, made to look like it was in 1879, erected just outside the present city limits on the road to Bisbee. Each of the main historical sites will be painstakingly recreated for future generations to enjoy, built with modern materials so they will be safe and secure for years to come. To be included will be the Bird Cage Theatre, the Crystal Palace Saloon, the OK Corral, The Tombstone Epitaph office and more. We expect movie production companies to use Tombstone Territory as a stage set for western movies. This will attract tourists and the tourist trade in Cochise County will be revived. This will bring more people to Tombstone Territory and Schieffelinville creating even more jobs. To accommodate what I expect to be a large influx of tourists and movie people and movie stars, we are presently talking with two major hotel chains to build hotels here. We anticipate at least two hotels with 500 rooms each, one with a gambling casino. Yes friends... this is the prosperity you have been waiting for. And Clark-Gray and Company are just the ones to bring it to you. Are you behind me on this?

Again, Gray was expecting rousing applause. The tourists applauded; the locals just stood in awe. A voice from the back of the crowd belonging to a well-heeled reenactor could be heard, "Sure we're behind you Gray... with a loaded shotgun!"

Michael Gray concluded his remarks, a reenactor fired off a blank shot-gun blast marking the signal for the parade to start and the marchers stepped off.

The next day, Tucson's *Citizen* newspaper carried the headline; "The Day The Town Too Tough To Die, Died". A subtext read, "Mayor Rawlins' Popularity Plummets".

Not unlike the political climate that existed in Tombstone in the 1880's, where people sided with the Earp or cow-boy factions, residents became polarized for or against Gray's proposal. Some people were angry, some despondent, writers and historians visiting the city were disgusted, some of the reenactors wept, knowing that Tombstone as they knew it, and they way it had been known for 150 years would soon pass into memory. "Tombstone Territory" – a purely commercial venture would not be the same.

Following the parade, Michael Gray met with local business people at Schieffelin Hall to outline his plan. As soon as the Helldorado festivities had concluded, Gray was ready to begin the demolition of the stores and businesses he already owned. Heavy

297

construction equipment had been poised in Sierra Vista and could be in Tombstone in a matter of hours. He only had two problems, neither of which he thought was insurmountable. One was buying the property from the few hold-outs, like Ezra. And two, what to do with the rubble created by tearing down the entire town.

As soon as the rubble could be cleared, builders were ready to begin erecting the first new buildings Allen Street had seen since 1882. Work would also begin immediately on the Schieffelinville Hospital and the Tombstone Territory park.

To the business owners that remained, Gray was prepared to offer substantial sums to acquire their property. Some business owners smiled, thinking they would press the Company for an outrageous sum of money for their properties. Ezra with his mercantile store, and former-mayor Tim Fuller with his book store vowed not to sell – at any price. It was the principle of the matter. Even if they did not have the most historically important pieces of property, both had been here since the town's founding.

About the only buildings the Clark-Gray Company couldn't buy was the old Cochise County Courthouse which remained a State Historic Park, and Tombstone's ancient city hall, built in 1882 which was still in use. The Company offered to remove the Courthouse to the Tombstone Territory site, and replace the city hall with a modern structure.

Sunday October 27, 2029   9:00AM

At 9AM, Ezra Thornton arrived at his store to get ready for what he thought might be some of his last days in the mercantile business, still not sure how the Clark-Gray Company would acquire his property or what would happen to it. As he rounded the corner of Sixth and Allen and stepped onto the boardwalk he was surprised to see former mayor Tim Fuller "holding court" from the park bench in front of his store addressing a cadre of local residents, angry business owners, reenactors both local and visiting, as well as other concerned citizens; about 30 people in all.

Ezra stopped in his tracks upon seeing the congregation. "What's this?" Ezra inquired. "Judging from the state of affairs around here, if this was 150 years ago, I'd say you folks were forming a 'necktie party' for Mr. Michael Gray!"

"Nasty Ned", one of the local reenactors spoke the group's conscience with, "Not a bad idea. I'll volunteer to make the noose!" Everyone sort of half smiled at the remark, knowing that it was said only partly in jest.

Tim rose from the bench and looked straight at Ezra. "I'm not sure where to turn Ezra. And neither are these folks. Many have spent their lives here, own businesses here, and want to see Tombstone prosper again, but not this way. It has been suggested that we get legal representation, get an injunction against Clark-Gray and Company. We may be able to stop them before they do too much damage. But this thing could be tied up in the courts for years! I don't want to wait years for a resolution, but I know this is a very thorny issue – and I'm sure Clark-Gray has plenty of lawyers on hand and probably anticipated this anyways and has a back-up plan. I just don't know...".

A voice from the back of the small crowd asked to no one in particular, "A similar problem happened here back at the founding of the city. What did Tombstoners do back then?"

Local historian Ben Turnbull answered, "Lawyers were involved back then too – and judges – and a lot of violence. An injunction was issued against those who would defraud the public and the common good. But, you are right, the cases dragged on for years. Many cases were never resolved. Even today, many properties here in town have shaded titles. The only thing that stopped the shenanigans back in the 1880's was the eventual deaths of the principal players and the unwillingness of their heirs to pursue the issue, knowing that it was wrong in the first place."

Again a voice from the back of the crowd could be heard, "Lawyers cost money, and lots of it. Is there anyone present who could fund such a venture?"

Everyone looked at Ezra, knowing that he had been a successful businessman in Tombstone for many years and probably had a large cache of money, perhaps some silver bars buried under his store. For just a moment all went quiet while everyone waited for Ezra to respond, each person hoping that Ezra would step up to the challenge, but each knowing that it was not the responsibility of one person to save the entire town. For that moment, Ezra's face was blank, as if in deep thought.

After what seemed like an eternity, Ezra's face suddenly lit up. Everyone seemed relieved, yet still pensive not knowing what trick Ezra might have up his sleeve. "I have the answer!" Ezra proclaimed. "Everyone follow me!"

Ezra turned and unlocked the door to his store and entered. Everyone followed. Coming upon the huge wooden barrel in the middle of his store, Ezra reached in retrieving a bottle of cold sarsaparilla; one for each of his following; and began to hand them out as everyone gathered around.

Tim Fuller chuckled, "The answer to our problem is sarsaparilla?"

Ezra grinned directly at Tim. Then turned has attention to the small gathering and replied, "I knew that this day would come.

Sooner or later, this day would certainly come. And here we are – at one of history's crossroads." Ezra shoved his hands into his vest pockets. "If you want to make it my job to pick the correct path, I am at your disposal!"

Tim Fuller spoke up, "Sure Ezra... we want to take the correct path and save Tombstone. But no one is expecting you to single-handedly come up with a pile of your own money for lawyers!"

Ezra smiled again, "Mr. Fuller, to use a phrase from the past... we won't be needing any stinking lawyers, or stinking judges or a lot of money. What we need is about 20 acres of land, which I happen to own just north of the city, on State Road 80, secured years ago in anticipation of this day."

Everyone looked puzzled as Ezra continued, "We also need a little ingenuity, which I will be happy to provide, as well as a small dose of persuasiveness, which I will also be more than glad to provide."

Tim Fuller again spoke up, "It sounds like you are doing all the work Ezra – such as it is – if we only knew what you were up to. How can we help? And what precisely do you plan to do?"

Ezra took a long pause and looked at everyone in the crowd, studying their faces and the intense interest they were taking in Tombstone's future. "What I need from everyone here, and as many people as you can muster together, is the most important thing of all – the strong belief that Tombstone is truly the town too tough to die. If you believe in that mantra, we can make this happen. Together we can save Tombstone!"

Everyone looked at each other in disbelief. It seemed like a Pollyanna-ish plan with a lot of feeling and no substance. No one still understood what Ezra had in mind.

Ezra smiled once more, "And now ladies and gentlemen, if you will excuse me, I need to meet with Mr. Gray!"

Sunday October 27, 2029   1:00 PM   Corner of Allen and Third Streets

Michael Gray sat at a booth at a local coffee shop on the corner of Third and Allen Street, staring out the window, trying not to notice the icy stares he received from the many patrons. Expecting to be venerated by the locals, Mr. Gray, in one short speech, became one of the most reviled people in town. Few looked forward to payment from the Clark-Gray Company for their businesses, and almost nobody wanted to see the true history of Tombstone lost to commercialism.

"Thank you for seeing me, Mr. Gray!" Ezra's cheery voice broke Gray's concentration as he stood at the table removing his hat and frock coat. Gray managed a smile despite his consternation.

"Sit down Mr. Thornton. What's on your mind?"

Ezra sat down, ordered lunch for the two of them and then began. 'I understand you need to find a place to put the rubble from the demolished buildings?"

"That's correct" was the reply. "We have a few options, none of them very good and all expensive. But I have our lawyers and contractors working on it. I'm sure they will come up with something soon. In the last few years with all these laws regarding waste disposal and the environmental impact is murder for land developers."

Ezra leaned forward and lowered his voice. "What if I could provide you with a place to dump the rubble? You wouldn't need any EPA approvals or any kind of local permits. There would be no cost except what it would cost you to haul it about five miles north of the city – to a piece of property I own. It will be dumped about 500 yards off the main road – out in the desert."

Gray leaned forward and replied in an even lower voice, "What's the catch? There has to be a catch. What's your angle, Thornton?"

Ezra leaned forward even further and said almost in whisper, "The only catch is the rubble from one building cannot be mixed with the rubble from another. And when you deposit each truckload of rubble on my property, it must be dumped precisely where I tell the driver to dump it. Precisely... where I want it... no exceptions!"

Gray looked puzzled. "Are you sure you want to do this? That's going to make one heck of an unsightly mess out there. And what about the EPA? Once they see it we'll both be in hot water! I don't know about this...?"

Ezra smiled, "I'll take care of everything. Don't worry! The EPA will never see it. Trust me on this!"

Gray smiled, still uncertain about the affair, but still needing a place to dispose of the rubble... and wanting to save some money doing it.

"Oh.. one more thing." Ezra added.

"Yes?"

"Do what you will; strike whatever deal you can with the remaining businesses. But I will not sell my mercantile store – however I will make sure it is moved. And for the Bird Cage, I will pay you a fair price for it, and make sure that it gets moved as well – my own way. I cannot allow either my mercantile store or the Bird Cage to be demolished. However I will make sure both get moved. Once moved, you can do what you want with the dirt under them.

That is my only condition. If you agree, we have a deal!"

Both men sat back as the waiter set their plates down before them. Lunch was served.

Gray smiled across his sandwich, "Done! I'll have my lawyer draw up the paperwork!"

Ezra extended his hand across the table, "No paperwork required. I do things on a smile and a handshake."

The two men shook hands. To the many patrons who had been watching the men the whole time, it almost looked as if Ezra was "selling out" to commercialism, making a deal with the devil as it were. But those who knew Ezra knew he had Tombstone's best interest at heart – even if they didn't know or understand what he was doing.

The men continued to talk, working out the details of their arrangement over lunch. Ezra then walked back to his store, stopping along the way to talk briefly with reenactors and other business owners, asking them to meet him at his store at 6PM.

Sunday October 27, 2029 6:00PM

A crowd of almost 100 people gathered in the street in front of Ezra's store – among them many reenactors, a few local business people, media people, and the just plain curious. Some talked about how they had seen Ezra in the café making a treasonous "deal" with Gray – a seeming deal with the devil himself. Some began to doubt Ezra's benevolence although everyone knew he had lived in Tombstone for a very long time and loved the city and its history.

At precisely 6PM, the front door to the mercantile store opened and Ezra T. Thornton stepped out, regally dressed as always. Despite the many tourists across the street at the Bird Cage and walking about the area, everything seemed to quiet down as soon as Ezra walked out and began to speak:

Ladies and gentlemen, as many of you know, I have always been a proponent of Tombstone, and the history and legend of this city. It is an important part of American history. Many buildings here including the Bird Cage, Crystal Palace, Epitaph office and others are icons and are irreplaceable. The OK Corral is hallowed ground inasmuch as the old west is concerned. I have tried my best to preserve the city and its history. But it seems that the Clark-Gray Company have some solid claims on the properties they have purchased. They own them fair and square and there is nothing we can do about it now. The buildings will be demolished and the Clark-Gray Company will build new stores and restaurants along Allen Street and new housing and a new hospital.

A voice rose from the back of the crowd, "So why did you call us out here, Ezra. We figured you might have talked them out of it! Or at least found some legal way around it?"

Ezra continued:

Tombstone will be preserved despite Mr. Gray's plans going forward. He will have his stores and shops and housing built, and Tombstone will continue to be Tombstone – only better! I cannot fully explain it, but it will be done. Now then; by this time next year, Mr. Gray expects to have the entire city demolished, new housing started and Tombstone Territory started. He plans to have the 101st Helldorado celebration although I'm not sure how he will pull that off with a demolished town and half-built theme park. At any rate, I would ask all who want to preserve Tombstone to meet me at the corner of 4th and Allen Streets at noon on Saturday of the Helldorado weekend next year. For the reenactors, historians and writers, please tell your friends. Spread the word. Tombstone will be saved. And remember, no matter what the town may look like when you arrive here next year... you must have faith! Remember – Tombstone is the town too tough to die!

One year later... Friday October 24, 2030 3:00PM

Greg and Belle Dumas turned off the Interstate 10 freeway onto Arizona State Road 80 and headed south to Tombstone. They were part of a reenactor group from California who had been performing for years in the Riverside, California area where they lived. Greg always played the part of one of the Earp brothers in the re-enactments; sometimes Wyatt, sometimes Virgil or Morgan, but always an Earp to honor his father, Bobby who had been killed years before in a horrific accident during a reenactment.

Greg turned to his wife sitting in the passenger seat of their pickup truck, "Read that invitation again, honey if you please."

Belle reached into her handbag on the floor of the truck and pulled from it a neat, formal invitation card and began to read:

Dear Mr. and Mrs. Dumas,

You are cordially invited to participate as reenactors in a recreation of the OK Corral gunfight to be held Sunday, October 26, 2030 at 2:30PM as part of the 101st annual Helldorado celebration. Please meet your fellow reenactors at the corner of 4th and Allen Streets in Tombstone at precisely noon on Saturday, October 25th for further instructions.

A room has been reserved for you in your name at the all-new Cochise Marriott Hotel at the corner of Fifth and Fremont Streets. All expenses have been taken care of.

Sincerely,

Mr. Ezra T. Thornton

Greg and Belle looked at each other for just a moment, then Belle spoke up, "Are you sure you want to do this? This just seems weird! I mean, we have never been to Tombstone, and now after we hear about the place being torn down, we decide to go, and at the behest of a person we have never met!"

"Well, that's true; we've never met him" Greg replied. "But I heard my dad talk about him a few times. My dad met a Mr. Ezra T. Thornton in Tombstone back in the 1960's. But it can't possibly be the same Ezra Thornton. I mean, my dad mentioned that he looked to be 60 years old back in the 1960's. That would mean that he would have to be... uh... about 130 years old now! This must be Ezra's kid that sent this to me!"

Belle chimed in, "And why was it sent just to us and not the rest of our reenactment group?"

"Yes" replied Greg. "It is strange. And that's exactly why I wanted to go. I mean, think about it – my father died doing a recreation of the OK Corral gunfight. And now, here we are, being invited to Tombstone to participate in the same reenactment! It's creepy!"

The couple drove along the two-lane road in silence for several more minutes. Then, about five miles just outside of Tombstone, in an otherwise desolate area of desert; Greg spotted a horse-drawn wagon a few hundred yards off the highway. It was fully-enclosed, and bright red, not unlike a circus wagon of over 160 years prior. Surrounding the wagon were large piles of debris – crumbled adobe, splintered wooden beams, and twisted, corrugated metal roofing. Greg could see there was lettering on the side of the wagon but could not make out what it read.

Greg and Belle looked at each other in disbelief. It seemed surreal. But not sure of what to make of it, and wanting to check into their hotel room, the couple continued on.

A few moments later the Dumas' truck pulled into Tombstone. As they slowly drove down Allen Street the couple was devastated by what they saw. Buildings had been leveled on both sides of the street – some which had stood since 1879! In their place, new, modern buildings were being erected. Looking across the vacant lots to Toughnut Street, more buildings were being erected. A sign in front of one stated that in a few months, the building would be known as Rawlins Arms, a retirement center named after the current Mayor. Looking through the vacant lots on the north side of Allen Street were more buildings in various stages of development, one that was actually completed was the hotel where Greg and Belle were slated to stay.

Many reenactors, dressed in the 1880's clothes milled about the streets looking distraught or angry. As Greg and Belle reached the corner of Sixth and Allen Streets they couldn't help notice that the building on the north east corner had not fallen victim to the wrecking crews. In fact, it looked like it was brand new, but built to 1879 standards. Was it brand new or perfectly preserved she thought. "Look at the sign over this building" Greg remarked, "E.T. Thornton – Mercantile. I wonder if...nah... it can't be! It's gotta be the father's store run by the son... or grandson. But why does it look so new?"

Not to be outdone by its neighboring building, the Bird Cage Theatre across the street also looked fairly new, obviously not coming under the same jurisdiction as the other buildings on Allen Street.

Turning left on Sixth Street and arriving a few seconds later at the corner of Sixth and Fremont, Greg intended to take a left and go to their hotel. But at the corner, he noticed a sign which read, Visit Tombstone Territory – A Re-Creation of the Town Too Tough To Die – 2 Miles Ahead". Greg looked at Belle, then swung the truck right and headed east. Two miles later, Greg and Belle pulled up in front of Tombstone Territory, still under construction – or so they thought.

Rather than truly recreate Tombstone, the builders had erected many movie-style buildings with a front only or some with three walls and an open back - more a cheesy movie set than a recreation of the town. A few buildings had four walls but most had a front only, and many were two-dimensional but painted to look three dimensional. Some of the fronts were marked "Crystal Palace Saloon" or "Tombstone Epitaph" but none looked like the buildings Greg and

Belle had seen in pictures. The place looked more like a "B" movie set of the early 1930's.

"This is such a sham!" Belle cried.

Greg replied, "Let's hope this Ezra Thornton character has some good news tomorrow at noon!"

Saturday October 25, 2030 12:01AM

With few buildings standing, a cold wind howled down Allen Street. What few street lights had existed before had been torn down by the builders in anticipation of replacing them with modern, high-intensity lamps. But with the new lamps yet to be installed the street was unusually dark.

Ezra walked down Sixth Street from his home, and turned onto Allen, crossed the street, and went to the side door of the Bird Cage which brought him backstage just behind the curtain.

As soon as he entered he could tell the frivolity had already started. A warm glow of light emanated from the front side of the heavy, red satin curtain. The tinkling of beer mugs and wine glasses could be heard, mixed with the laughter of both men and women. Over this din could be heard a small orchestra, tuning-up, and getting ready to accompany the night's entertainment. The strong smell of cigar smoke mixed with lady's perfume for a very unique olfactory sensation.

Ezra walked across the darkened stage, to center stage and parting the curtains stepped into the light. There before him, just as he had shown author Rod Livingston, were all the luminaries of Tombstone; the Earp bothers, various members of the cow-boy gang, Johnny Behan, Billy Breakenridge, Milt Joyce, John Clum – everyone.

Ezra moved down a short flight of stairs off the stage to the main floor and in a moment found Mayor John Clum. The two men shook hands.

"I understand you are just about ready, Ezra?" said the Mayor, smiling warmly.

Ezra returned the smile, "Indeed I am Mr. Mayor. Tomorrow night at this time, it will be a whole new life for everyone here. We can leave Schieffelinville and Tombstone Territory behind!"

At that moment Ed Schieffelin happened by. Feigning a concerned look, Ed turned to Ezra, "Hey; I kind of like that name – Schieffelinville. It has a nice ring to it!"

Ezra and Clum laughed and Ezra replied, "Well Ed, you can come to town any time you want, but once you see what I have in store for you, you won't ever want to come here again!"

Turning to Mayor Clum, Ezra took on a darker tone saying, "Spread the word; this is your last night here. Oh... and tell Wyatt I have someone special for him to meet!"

The two men nodded. Ezra turned and headed back out to the cold breeze of Allen Street. All was ready.

Saturday October 25, 2030 12:01PM Corner of Fourth and Allen Streets

Ezra walked the two blocks down Allen Street from his store to the corner of Fourth and Allen. It was a cool and overcast day – most uninviting - not unlike the weather on the same day in 1881. As Ezra walked passing many vacant lots where stores and shops had stood for 150 years he could not help but feel saddened. All evidence of the former buildings had been removed, every adobe brick, every piece of concrete, every stick of wood – gone.

Only a year ago, throngs of people had stood waiting for the 100th anniversary parade. Today, a few people milled about looking at the devastation, and looking in disgust at the new buildings going up. The festivities for this year were being held in the new Tombstone Territory park outside the city proper – which left few people on Allen Street. That is – except the small crowd gathered at the corner of Fourth and Allen.

Ezra approached the crowd, and lacking the podium that he had had the year before, Ezra jumped up onto a shipping crate that builders had left. Ezra looked over the crowd – mostly reenactors dressed in 1880's wear, former mayor Tim Fuller, historian Ben Turnbull, historians of both the armchair and serious nature were joined by a few local business people and some long-time residents. Also among the crowd were Greg and Belle Dumas.

In his loud, booming voice, Ezra began to speak:

Ladies and gentlemen, thank you for coming. The fact that you are here, standing at the corner of what used to be the center of town, and not out at the Helldorado celebration at the Tombstone Territory park tells me that you all are believers – you believe that Tombstone is the Town Too Tough To Die. Although looking around you now, you may think that Tombstone is dead. But have heart! Today... together... we are going to save Tombstone! We are going to see a rebirth of the old west. Ladies and gentlemen, prepare yourselves for 1881! Four busses will arrive here momentarily. If you believe that Tombstone is too tough to die, get on the busses and follow me. Our destination is only a few minutes away!

As Ezra finished speaking, four large tour busses began lumbering down Allen Street, having been concealed behind Ezra's store and the Bird Cage Theatre. The busses stopped in front of the crowd and Ezra directed everyone to get on. Once loaded, the busses headed north out of town on State Route 80. Within a few minutes, and about five miles north of town, the busses veered off the pavement onto a dirt road. Everyone looked incredulous and could not imagine where they were headed.

After a short drive across the desert floor the busses slowed to a crawl. It seemed like they were driving down a street, a street that was determined by how piles and piles of rubble were arranged. The piles were everywhere. Orange traffic cones and white chalk lines, similar to the chalk lines used to define a baseball diamond, seemed to outline fairly wide walkways or possibly streets around the piles of rubble. Everything seemed to be spread out over a 20 or so acre area. As they drove slowly along, they could see the detail of the piles of debris, crumbled concrete, a few bricks, lots of half broken and crumbling adobe bricks and lot of splintered wood.

In a moment, the busses stopped and everyone got out. Oddly, they stopped right in front of two lots which were completely devoid of rubble, the only two lots. Once everyone was out, the busses moved off and Ezra was left standing in what looked like a dump, on the desert floor, with about 225 people, some of whom started to grumble about how they were being somehow "taken" but not sure how or why.

In his inimitable style, once again, Ezra addressed the crowd;

"Ladies and gentlemen, if you believe – if you REALLY believe that Tombstone is the Town Too Tough To Die, then close your eyes and picture the Bird Cage Theatre as it was on opening night in December, 1881. Keep your eyes closed and I will count to three. When I say open, you will open your eyes and see the all new Bird Cage Theatre."

The crowd was doubtful, but lacking any options, they all decided to play along. Ezra continued; "One... two... three. Open your eyes."

Everyone opened their eyes and there before them stood the Bird Cage Theatre, just as it had been in 1881. While everyone stood in amazement staring in disbelief at the old bawdy house, Tim Fuller had the forethought to turn around and upon doing so exclaimed, "Look, it's Ezra's store!"

Indeed, Ezra's store now occupied what had been the only other "clean" lot in the area. To better address his now incredulous followers, Ezra leapt up to the wooden boardwalk in front of his store and proclaimed, "Mr. Fuller, will you please help me in handing out a bottle of sarsaparilla for everyone!"

Ezra and Tim went into Ezra's store and the ever-present barrel of sarsaparilla bottles. Once everyone had a cold bottle of refreshment, Ezra led his group on a short walk to what looked like an intersection, clear space around which heaping piles of rubble stood. Addressing the crowd he said, "I will ask you all to indulge me one more time. If you believe... if you REALLY believe that Tombstone is the Town Too Tough To Die, then close your eyes one more time. Close your eyes and picture the town. It is 1881, the mines are booming, the saloons are rolling, and Tombstone is a wide-open mining camp on the new frontier. We are standing on the corner of Fifth and Allen Streets. I will count to three, and when I ask you to open your eyes, you will open them and behold, the Crystal Palace Saloon. One... two... three.. open your eyes."

When everyone opened their eyes, it was not as Ezra had predicted – it was better. The entire city of Tombstone had been recreated – every store, every shop, every home, and every shack and tent. In the blink of an eye, it was again 1881. The piles of rubble had somehow been magically re-assembled into the original buildings. It was all here.

In appreciation, everyone applauded. Ezra held up his hands, "For those of you who do not have period clothes, I will see you at my store momentarily to make sure you are properly outfitted. Feel free to walk about the town. Familiarize yourself with it. If you are hungry, the Russ House is open and staffed at the corner of Fifth and Toughnut Streets. If you are thirsty, the Crystal Palace and Oriental are open and staffed – serving the finest liquors and cigars – and all on the house. My treat! As you venture across Fremont Street you will notice a number of houses. Find a house with your name on it. This is where you will stay tonight! You may want to rest up a bit because you are all invited to a very special show tonight at the Bird Cage beginning at mid-night. Don't be late! I'll see you in front of the Bird Cage at precisely midnight. Enjoy your day!"

Greg and Belle Dumas wandered into the Crystal Palace – it was like stepping back in time. A long, mahogany bar ran down the left side of the building, the back-bar being huge, standing perhaps 12 feet tall. The back-bar was fully stocked with wines, whiskeys and various other liquors neither Greg nor Belle had heard of before, no doubt, of 1880's vintage. Just then, Ezra strolled through the door and proclaimed; "A don't forget... its open bar. Please help yourselves!"

Greg approached Ezra. "Ezra, my invitation said I was supposed to take part in a recreation of the OK Corral gunfight. Well, in view of what's going on here – is that invitation still valid?"

Ezra smiled, "It is indeed still good. Tomorrow, you will play Virgil's part. You know the lines I'm sure!"

Greg took on an air of concern, "Yes... I've played all the parts at one time or another, even the cowboy parts. But what re-enactment group will I be working with? I mean... shouldn't we rehearse? I know I've done this OK Corral shootout thing so many times I could do it in my sleep, but these other guys. I..."

Ezra smiled and reassured Greg, "These men are professionals. They've done it plenty of times too. Don't worry! You'll be fine!"

Saturday October 25, 2030 11:50PM Corner of Sixth and Allen Streets

The night air was cool but the 225 believers didn't feel it, being so excited in anticipation for whatever Ezra would come up with next. Each person or couple had found the house with their name on it, rested, eaten a good meal at the Russ House, and were now ready for almost anything as Ezra seemed to able *to do* most anything.

Gas street lights gave a soft glow to Allen Street, the other streets being quite dark, illuminated by only the lights that were left burning in the houses. Ezra's store was lit quite brightly, the glow falling across Allen Street to the Bird Cage Theatre which was still dark, the front doors closed tightly.

Ezra stepped off the street onto the wooden boardwalk to once again address his followers; "At precisely midnight these doors will swing open. The admission is free, the drinks are complimentary and tonight's show, a compendium of dancers, jugglers and more... direct from San Francisco should be stunning. And you might meet a few people you know. Enjoy yourselves!"

Greg and Belle looked at each other in amazement. Greg noted, "Who would we know out here in the desert?"

Belle replied, "Yes... in the middle of this seeming fantasy land?"

At precisely midnight the three double front doors of the Bird Cage swung open simultaneously, gas lamps were lit, and the place was already crowded with people – although none of Ezra's followers saw anyone enter! Cigar smoke wafted across the lobby. A small bar on the left side of the lobby was already five-deep with patrons waiting for a drink. On the other side of the lobby, a roulette wheel, eternally clicking, satisfied the appetites of the gambling crowd.

Ezra's band of believers moved in not quite knowing what to think, each in turn being recognized by the ticket taker allowing them into the main room. Greg and Belle found two seats near the back of the room and sat down, furtively looking about for people they were *supposed* to recognize. Greg thought he recognized a few people from pictures he had seen – Tombstone residents from 1881 – but it couldn't be! It just couldn't be!

A moment later Ezra, who had been buzzing around the main floor talking to seemingly everyone finally got to the Dumas's in the back row. With Ezra was a seemingly frail man with a blond moustache, dressed all in gray. "Greg and Belle, may I present Doctor John Henry Holliday!"

Greg and Belle looked at each other in disbelief. Greg looked "Doc" square in the eye, "Doctor John Henry Holliday – Doc Holliday?"

Doc smiled, "Indeed sir! Of the Georgia Hollidays to be precise!"

At that moment a very dapper man approached Ezra. The man was of medium height and build, and looked to be about 30 years old yet was prematurely bald. He addressed Ezra, "Ezra, won't you introduce me to your friends?"

"But of course" came the reply. "Belle and Greg, please meet Mayor John P. Clum. Mr. Clum also operates *The Tombstone Epitaph* newspaper here in town as well!"

Before the night was over, Ezra's small troupe had met everyone they had ever read about in Tombstone. They were all there - everyone except Wyatt and Virgil Earp... who were conspicuously absent. But Ezra assured everyone they would get to meet Wyatt and Virgil tomorrow afternoon... at 2:30PM... at the OK Corral. It was truly 1881 all over again.

At 4AM as the sun began to peek over the mountains, Ezra took the stage to make an announcement, "This concludes this evening's festivities. This afternoon we will have a re-enactment of the OK Corral shootout. Please be in the viewing stands no later than 2:15PM. The fight will commence, exactly as it did almost 149 years ago, at 2:30PM. And, Mr. Dumas... please be at Hafford's Corner at 2PM to meet your brothers. You will walk down to the OK Corral exactly as it was done in 1881. At the conclusion of the fight, I will make a very important announcement you won't want to miss! See you all then!"

Sunday October 26, 2030 1:30PM

Greg and Belle rose to find a closet full of clothing, all period-correct – and in all the correct sizes. Since he was going to play the part of Virgil Earp, Greg dressed in the best black vest, pants and frock coat he could find in the closet. He topped it off with a black tie and stove-pipe boots. Belle dressed in a polonaise dress and looked every bit the part of a "society lady."

The two left their house and headed toward Allen Street. The streets were full of people – not just the people that had joined them on the busses – but other people, and lots of them. Well-dressed businessman rubbed elbows with dirty miners, dusty bullwhackers, tattered soiled doves and finely dressed women. A Well-Fargo stage kicked up a trail of dust as it pulled into Tombstone with more arriving passengers.

Greg sent Belle along to the OK Corral to secure a place in the stands for herself and he moved on to Hafford's Saloon. As Greg approached he could see two other men dressed all in black and another man dressed in gray standing in the street.

One of the men Greg recognized as Morgan Earp motioned to him, "Come on Virgil. We've been waiting for you!"

As Greg approached the men he reached out his hand to whoever would grab it, "Hello, my name is Greg Du..."

Before he could spit out his name, one of the men in black interrupted him, "Yes, I know. You're Greg Dumas."

Greg looked at the man, and then looked quizzically at Morgan and Doc. He thought, "If I know this is Morgan and Doc, and I'm playing the part of Virgil this must be... Wyatt Earp?"

Greg looked for a moment at the man shaking his hand and smiling. His hair was blonde, just like Wyatt's. He had a 'regal moustache' as Wyatt had had. He had piercing blue eyes – as had been described about Wyatt. But there was something about the man that caused Greg to pause – something familiar that he could not place.

After what seemed like an eternity, Wyatt' spoke, "Greg Dumas... of Riverside California. Hello son. I was wondering if I would ever see you again!"

Greg's face lit up! He thought, "If Ezra could recreate Tombstone out in the middle of the desert, then why not bring back his slain father!"

The two men embraced. Wiping a tear from his eye, Wyatt turned to Doc and Morgan and said, "I don't remember reading about any tearful reunion prior to the fight. Let's get this right. Johnny Behan is just about to start down Fremont Street to tell us he has disarmed the cow-boys. Come on. We've got some shooting to do!"

The four men walked up Fourth Street to Fremont then turning left walked the block to the OK Corral. Turning into the vacant lot between Harwood's Boarding House and Fly's Photography Studio, Greg delivered his line, "Throw up your hands. We're here to disarm you!"

A moment later the shooting commenced, just as it had in 1881. Greg looked nervously at Wyatt, somehow half expecting something to go terribly wrong again. But when the gun smoke cleared, Wyatt stood tall and the three cow-boys lay dead. A moment later, a call of "clear", the reenactor's signal that the action had ceased, brought the cowboys back to life. In this version of the OK Corral shootout, nobody really died.

As the "actors" brushed themselves off, Ezra took center stage in front of the bleacher seats to address the crowd. "For those people who came here with me on the busses, you now have a choice to make! Your lives, as you have known them, are waiting for you in the year 2030. If you want to return to them, the busses are waiting just outside of town to bring you back to... uh...Schieffelinville. When you arrive in Schieffelinville, all knowledge of your weekend here will be erased from your memory. It will be as if this never happened. If you wish to stay... if you want to be a part of the Town Too Tough Too Die, you each have a home here and can stay as long as you like. You can build your lives, contribute to Tombstone's economy, and it will forever be 1881. The choice is yours. Do whatever you like, but the choice must be made now. The busses are waiting at the far east end of Allen Street."

Monday October 27, 2030

The *Tucson Chronicle* carried two main stories on its front page. One described the dismal showing of the 101st Helldorado celebration held at the new Tombstone Territory park and hosted by the Clark-Gray Company. It described virtually no reenactors showing up for the event and the few tourists that came turned and left in disgust.

The other major headline read: "Four Busses Found Abandoned On State Road 80"

The story read:

Four charter busses, believed to have been chartered from a Tucson bus company by long-time Tombstone resident Ezra T. Thornton were found by Arizona State Police yesterday afternoon, abandoned 500 hundred yards off State Road 80. Police state that witnesses saw approximately 200 people boarding the busses around mid-day in downtown Schieffelinville, Thornton among them. Arizona State Police spokesperson Larry Norton noted that foul play was not ruled out but could not be discounted. "There was nothing amiss on the busses, no signs of a struggle. It looked like everyone just got out into the desert and walked off the busses - but strangely, didn't leave any footprints." Norton said. Tire tracks lead out to the desert a few hundred yards and then stopped. There were no footprints found near the buses to indicate a direction of travel by the occupants. In a seemingly related incident, local police are investigating the apparent disappearance of scores of people who had been staying at the Cochise Marriott Hotel. The exact number is not certain at this time. Hotel general manager and local real estate developer Michael Gray noted, "It's so bizarre. People have apparently abandoned their rooms and all their personal belongings and their cars. I can't imagine where all these people went."

The Real Story Behind "Too Tough To Die"

In its earliest days, not everyone in Tombstone counted on pulling rock out of the ground for their source of wealth. In a mining camp there were numerous ways to make money.

During the early 1880's, under federal law, upon the incorporation of a city, rights to the land within the city were given to the Mayor to hold in trust, and hold for sale by the city entity to raise money for the operation of the city.

On May 22, 1880, Tombstone Mayor Alder Randall, who had been holding the rights under the new city charter sold nearly the entire surface of the city of Tombstone to speculators for $5.80. The speculators would become known as the Tombstone Townsite Company, the principals being James Clark and Michael Gray. The term "Clark Gray and Company" became widely used in Tombstone, interchangeable with the Tombstone Townsite Company.

The then-future mayor and publisher of *The Tombstone Epitaph*, John P. Clum wrote, "...our citizens are to be ousted from their homes or mercilessly 'bled' by the projectors of said scheme, while our city treasury is to be defrauded of revenue resulting from the sale of lots which must represent the aggregate of $200,000, a sum which the city can ill-afford to illegally and unjustly transfer from its exchequer to the pockets of a scheming few."

The Townsite Company claimed title to all lots. A large part of the area was covered with mining locations, the owners of which, a second party in the controversy, claimed all surface rights for mining operations. A third party, the actual bona-fide citizen who claimed title to his lot by reason of occupancy added another dimension to the heated debate.

The Epitaph supported the lot-occupants as the rightful owners of the properties. The controversy raged with varying degrees of bitterness' on all sides. People met in the street at night, orators for each side stood on soap boxes promoting their side of the affair and decrying their opponents. Clum described the situation as, "... tense, and on several occasions we had difficulty in restraining riotous demonstrations."

Clum considered it his duty to wage war against what he felt was a great injustice and began to issue daily rebukes against the Townsite Company's attempt to convey 2,300 of the town's 2,385 town lots to non-resident partners in New Orleans and California.

On August 3, 1880, *The Epitaph* reported that a petition was circulating throughout the town condemning everything the Tombstone Townsite Company was doing. The completed petition was forwarded a few days later to US land Office Commissioner James A. Williamson along with a cover letter from Judge Wells Spicer asking that the patent for a townsite be withheld until after the next election when they expected to have voted Mayor Randall out of office.

In a letter to the San Diego Daily Union dated August 3, 1880, Clara Spaulding Brown, a Tombstone resident and special correspondent to the San Diego paper wrote of the Townsite Scandal:

Gray claims to own the town-site, having been one of the first upon the field, and hopes to realize a goodly fortune by the sale of lots for which he never paid a mil. But this is mineral land, and un-surveyed, and he cannot lay claim to 160 acres of land with impunity. The matter will probably occasion a protracted law suit and must be settled in a competent court of justice.

On the evening of August 7, 1880, a meeting was held in Ritchie's Dance Hall on Fifth Street between Fremont and Allen Streets, to discuss the townsite problems.

On September 25th, both *The Epitaph* and the *Nugget* reported that the Tombstone townsite patent had been issued. *The Epitaph* noted, "Alder Randall is but human, at most, and has intellect enough to know that he has attempted a great wrong and fraud upon the entire mass of people of this town. The people who are sought to be defrauded and robbed are but human also, and if they rise in their might to assert their rights the one man cannot then stand before the many."

Everyone was up in arms over the affair. In his book, *Wyatt Earp – The Biography*, author Timothy Fattig wrote, "Whatever the financial, cultural, and political divisions existing in the city, no one could be found who would uphold the actions of the Townsite Company."

In one instance, a man chasing his horse ran across a mining claim and was met with the muzzle of a shotgun by another man paid to defend the land for its owner. The guard claimed he would have shot the horse-chaser had he not stopped upon command as that was what he was instructed to do. This type of anarchy did not make things any easier for law enforcement officers Sheriff Shibell and Deputy Sheriff Virgil Earp.

The patent was then recalled and went back and forth between Washington and Florence, Arizona and finally arrived in Tombstone on November 6th. That very afternoon, Clum led other prominent Tombstone citizens on a march into Alder Randall's office but he would not be intimidated and informed the fuming businessmen that the patent had already been forwarded to Tucson for recording and that as soon as that was done, he would convey the entire town to Clark, Gray and the others.

The transfer of the townsite patent took place on November 8th. Clum noted. "The so-called mayor of Tombstone should be presented with a collar inscribed, Clark, Gray & Co. – their dog."

The atmosphere intensified. More torchlight processions were seen wending their way through the streets at night. Threats of mayhem and death were leveled from both sides, the citizens having little faith in the courts to sort out matters and lesser faith in the veracity of the Townsite Company.

Claim jumping became an everyday occurrence, quite often being settled at the business end of a shotgun.

Mayor Alder Randall felt the pressure – from the constant discontent in the streets to the constant diatribe from Clum's newspaper. By November 19, the situation was too hot for Mayor Randall who left suddenly for parts unknown.

On December 1st, the Citizen's League filed suit against the Townsite Company and Alder Randall which resulted in the issuance of an injunction by District Court Judge Charles French thereby preventing the company from conducting any further business.

Cobbled legally, the Townsite Company turned to more drastic measures, Clark and Gray hiring a team of men to actually move houses off lots. (Houses in those days were small and not secured to foundations.) They succeeded in moving one house belonging to a judge who was loudly outspoken against the Townsite Company. Held at gunpoint, the men stopped moving the house, but not before they had conveyed it to the middle of the street. Concerned townspeople banded together and moved the house back onto the lot.

Despite the absence of Mayor Randall, and not knowing that Randall would never return, Clum could not help but inflict one more jab at him. *The Epitaph* article of December 5, 1880 entitled, "FOILED – Clark, Gray & Co. Find Yesterday Not A Good Day For Moving" concluded with, "One feature that came to light yesterday, which may cause surprise, is that the gang have a permit from the Mayor to carry concealed weapons. Take notice, and govern yourself accordingly."

On June 22, 1881, a large portion of Tombstone burned to the ground, the result of a cigar touching off vapors from a whisky barrel. Marshal Earp appointed twenty-seven special deputies to guard the charred remains of the town against looting and lot-jumpers. That evening, under cover of darkness, Clark-Gray and Company descended on the town. Still bound by Judge French's injunction, the Townsite men turned to violence to try to force some people off their charred ruins. However, backed by Mayor Clum, Marshall Earp and his men were swift and able to fend-off the Townsite Company thugs.

The Townsite scandal was dragged through the courts for several years. By 1889, given to the sheer virtue of time, a changing political and business climate in Tombstone, the decline of the silver market, and the ultimate death of the last principal, James Clark, the Townsite scandal was effectively a thing of the past.

However, even today, when looking back through various land deeds, there exists a degree of uncertainty trying to find who owned what in the early 1880's.

As for the term, "The Town Too Tough To Die"; by the 1920's, Tombstone was in a steep decline.

Little mining was being done and was not commercially viable. Some tried to market the town as a place to come for a vacation to enjoy the warm, dry climate – especially for asthmatics and others with respiratory problems. But the town's name simply did not lend itself to a feeling of health and rejuvenation.

Writers like Frederick Bechdolt, Stuart Lake and Walter Noble Burns were creating the legend we know today as Tombstone, making household names of Wyatt Earp, Doc Holliday, and others.

In 1929 the city held its first annual event to promote Tombstone's history, and cash in on the growing popularity of Wyatt Earp and other Tombstone luminaries. They called it "Helldorado."

In 1930, Walter and Edith Cole assumed the assets of *The Tombstone Epitaph* newspaper. To express the general demeanor of the town at the time, the Coles placed on their masthead, "The Spirit Of Tombstone Is To Never Say Die." The saying was later embellished to say, "The Town Too Tough To Die."

Tombstone's well-deserved sobriquet is still widely used today; and Helldorado continues to be the city's most popular event drawing people from all over the world for the festivities, held annually the third weekend in October.

Epilogue

The mercantile store of Ezra T. Thornton is, of course, only fictional. However, situated at the northwest corner of Allen and Sixth Streets in Tombstone, directly across Allen Street from the Bird Cage Theatre, it is based on a real spot of real-estate that has seen a number of businesses over the years.

Today (2010) the northwest corner of Allen and Sixth Streets is occupied by the Silver Nugget Bed and Breakfast featuring the only lodging on Allen Street with a balcony overlooking Tombstone's most famous thoroughfare. The first floor features a gift shop, an old-time ice cream parlor, and a dining room featuring karaoke singing on Saturday nights.

But it didn't start out that way.

In September 1879 the business of McKean and Knight Grocery and Mercantile opened for business and occupied the space. They carried a very eclectic fare of goods from groceries to farm products to fruits, clothing, boots and miner's supplies. James McKean and Isaac Knight did a roaring business until they were wiped out by Tombstone's first big fire on June 22, 1881.

Backed by creditors from San Francisco, they quickly rebuilt, this time out of brick, not wood, and restocked their shelves. But the town went into a decline and the store went out of business in March 1882

A second person tried to make a go of it as a mercantile store but soon failed.

The place then became the tin shop of Tom Aitcheson who sold stoves. It is unknown how long Mr. Aitchison sold stoves at the location but by 1891 it was a grocery storage facility for one George Fitts. It is unknown when Mr. Fitts moved out, but the building was vacant for a long time afterward.

Then, with the advent of the automobile, and the auto's need for gasoline, and with more tourists heading for Tombstone, the corner became a gas station. In 1935 Bedford Moody of Benson leased the property from Margaret Cummings, and began tearing out the front and side of the building on both the Allen Street and Sixth Street sides creating a "drive-thru" where people could purchase gasoline. It became the American Automobile Service Station. By 1937 it was known as Criswell's Garage – Clarence Criswell, proprietor.

By 1969, the gas station was gone, the building enclosed again, and it became the Silver Nugget Museum owned by Theda and Sam Medigovich. The museum's grand opening was held August 23, 1969 featuring Cochise County artifacts the couple had amassed over 30 years.

Sometime in the 1980's, the museum was closed and all the artifacts auctioned off.

Acknowledgements

The "real story" behind *Tombstone Tales* is gathered from many different sources over many years of reading and studying Tombstone's history. Where applicable, I have noted specific sources here for each story.

Chapter 1: The Prospector
Miscellaneous sources

Chapter 2: The Gunfighter
Miscellaneous sources

Chapter 3: The Man Who Saved Wyatt Earp
H.F. Sills, Mystery Man of the O.K. Corral Shoot Out by Jane Matson Lee and Mark Dworkin as seen in the WOLA Journal Spring 2004

Chapter 4: The Stage Driver
Miscellaneous sources

Chapter 5: The Writer
Desert HonkyTonk by Roger Bruns Fulcrom Publishing copyright 2000

Chapter 6: The Immortals
Special thanks to Official Arizona State Historian and friend, Marshall Trimble

Chapter 7: Brunckow
• *Nantan: The Life and Times of John P. Clum Volume 1* by Gary Ledoux Trafford Publishing copyright 2007
• *Apache Agent* by Woodworth Clum copyright 1936
Cochise County Stalwarts by Lynn Bailey and Don Chaput Westernlore Press copyright 2000

Chapter 8: Justice and Redemption
• *Tombstone's Epitaph* by Douglas Martin University of New Mexico

Press copyright 1951

- True West magazine March 2005 from an article entitled *Johnny-Behind-The-Deuce VS Phillip Schneider* by Bob Boze Bell based on research by Neil Carmony
- *Wyatt Earp The Biography* by Tim Fattig   Talei Publishing copyright 2002
- *A Tenderfoot In Tombstone The Private Journal of George Whitwell Parsons: The Turbulent Years: 1880-82* by Lynn Bailey Westernlore Press copyright 1996

Chapter 9: Nantan
Nantan: The Life and Times of John P. Clum Volume 1 by Gary Ledoux copyright 2007

Chapter 10: Return to Tombstone
Story entitled, *Bronco Bill Came C.O.D.* by Tombstone's official historian and my friend, Ben Traywick published November, 2004 in *The Tombstone Epitaph*

Chapter 11: The Bad Man
Special thanks to author Harry McNeer for the photo of Russian Bill's grave site.

Chapter 12: Who Killed Johnny Ringo
Special thanks to fellow authors and friends, Steve Gatto and Sherry Monahan

Chapter 13: Too Tough To Die
Miscellaneous sources

Epilogue:
Story entitled *Groceries, Cars and Karaoke* by author and friend Rita Ackerman as seen in the *Tombstone Times* September 2009

About the Author

A native of New Hampshire, author Gary Ledoux has had a long-time love of the old-west in general, and Tombstone and its characters in particular.

His articles have appeared in various magazines including *True West*, the *Tombstone Epitaph* and the *Tombstone Times*. His "Yesterwest" column appears monthly in the *Tombstone Epitaph* and *Tombstone Times*.

His first book, *Tombstone: A Chronicle In Perspective* was published in October 2002. That was followed by *Nantan: The Life and Times of John P. Clum Volume 1* in October 2007 and *Nantan: The Life and Times of John P. Clum Volume 2* in September 2008.

He has been a featured writer at the Warren Earp Days Book Festival in Willcox, AZ in 2003, and a featured writer for the Tombstone Book and Film Festival held in Tombstone in 2004. He was a featured writer and speaker for a similar event held in Tucson in 2005, and again in Tombstone in 2006, 2007, and 2008.

He was a contributor to the October, 2006 OK Corral 125th anniversary event in Tombstone conducting a panel discussion entitled, "Tombstone in the Movies and Television" and gave a speech on Tombstone's Allen Street in character as Mayor John P. Clum.

He is a member of the *Wild West History Association* and has served as the Marketing Manager for *The Tombstone Epitaph* since September 2009.

Gary and his wife Rachel presently live in Whitewater, California.

To find out more about the author, or one of his favorite subjects, Mayor John P. Clum, go to www.YesterWest.com